Egyptian chariots carry shotgunners and haul heavy cannon into battle, Roman centurions fight at the whims of bug-eyed monsters, vigilant National Guardsmen hold the line against cannibalistic illegal aliens, and American soldiers wander savage lands, leading a massive AI-controlled BOLO tank, as they struggle to return home to a United States that no longer exists.

Featuring themes of duty, honor, and fortitude under fire, *New York Times* best-selling author S. M. Stirling presents thirteen stories of military men and women pushed to the point where myth and technology collide. These thrilling tales of alternate histories, apocalyptic futures, and hard-driving military science fiction demonstrate why Stirling has long been a fan favorite.

ICE, IRON AND GOLD

OTHER BOOKS BY S. M. STIRLING:

THE EMBERVERSE
   Dies the Fire
   The Protector's War
   A Meeting at Corvallis
   The Sunrise Lands
ISLAND IN THE SEA OF TIME
   Island in the Sea of Time
   Against the Tide of Years
   On the Oceans of Eternity
THE LORDS OF CREATION
   The Sky People
   In the Courts of the Crimson Kings
THE DRAKA
   Marching Through Georgia
   Under the Yoke
   The Stone Dogs
   The Domination (Omnibus of Vols. 1-3)
   Drakon
THE GENERAL (With David Drake)
   The Forge
   The Hammer
   The Warlord (Omnibus of Vols. 1 & 2)
   The Anvil
   The Steel
   The Sword
   The Conqueror (Omnibus of vols. 3-5)
   The Chosen
   The Reformer
The Peshawar Lancers
Conquistador

S. M. STIRLING

ICE, IRON AND GOLD

NIGHT SHADE BOOKS
SAN FRANCISCO

"Riding Shotgun to Armageddon" ©1998 by S. M. Stirling. Originally appeared in *Armageddon*.

"Three Walls-32nd Campaign" ©2001 by S. M. Stirling. Originally appeared in *Foreign Legions*.

"Cops and Robbers" ©1986 by S. M. Stirling. Originally appeared in *Far Frontiers Vol. IV*.

"Roachstompers" ©1989 by S. M. Stirling. Originally appeared in *New Destinies Vol. VIII*.

"Constant Never" ©1994 by S. M. Stirling. Originally appeared in *Dragon's Eye*.

"Taking Freedom" ©1999 by S. M. Stirling. Originally appeared in *Flights of Fantasy*.

"Lost Legion" ©1993 by S. M. Stirling. Originally appeared in *Bolos: Honor of the Regiment*.

"Ancestral Voices" ©1994 by S. M. Stirling. Originally appeared in *Bolos 2: The Unconquerable*.

"The Sixth Sun" ©1997 by S. M. Stirling. Originally appeared in *Bolos 4: Last Stand*.

"The Apotheosis of Martin Padway" ©2005 by S. M. Stirling. Originally appeared in *The Enchanter Completed*.

"Compadres" (with Richard Foss) ©2002 by S. M. Stirling and Richard Foss. Originally appeared in *Alternate Generals II*.

"The Charge of Lee's Brigade" ©1998 by S. M. Stirling. Originally appeared in *Alternate Generals*.

"Something for Yew" ©2007 by S. M. Stirling. This story is original to this collection.

ISBN 978-1-59780-116-4

Night Shade Books
Please visit us on the web at
http://www.nightshadebooks.com

CONTENTS

Riding Shotgun to Armageddon 1

Three Walls-32nd Campaign 25

Cops and Robbers 53

Roachstompers 63

Constant Never 96

Taking Freedom 118

Lost Legion 136

Ancestral Voices 170

The Sixth Sun 204

The Apotheosis of Martin Padway 290

Compadres (with Richard Foss) 325

The Charge of Lee's Brigade 339

Something for Yew 357

RIDING SHOTGUN
TO ARMAGEDDON

The cannon were keeping up well with the chariots; Pharaoh would be pleased.

Djehuty, Commander of the Brigade of Seth, was a little uncomfortable on horseback even after months of practice with the new saddle with stirrups. Still, there was no denying it was convenient. He turned his horse and rode back down along the track beside his units, with the standard-bearer, scribes, aides, and messengers behind him. The rutted track was deep in sand, like most of the coastal plain of Canaan... where it wasn't swamp mud or rocks. The infantry in their banded-linen corselets plodded along, their brown faces darker yet with dust and streaked with sweat under their striped headdresses of thick canvas. Big round-topped rectangular shields were slung over their shoulders, bronze spearblades glinted in the bright sun. After them came a company of Nubians, Medjay mercenaries from far up the Nile. Djehuty frowned; the black men were slouching along in their usual style, in no order at all... although anyone who'd seen one of their screaming charges could forgive them that. Then came one of the New Regiments, with their muskets over their shoulders and short iron swords at their sides. They wore only kilts and pleated loin-guards, but

1

there were leather bandoliers of papyrus cartridges at their right hips. Djehuty scowled slightly at the sight of them, despite the brave show they made with their feet moving in unison and the golden fan standard carried before them on a long pole.

Their weapons are good, he acknowledged. "But will they stand in battle?" he murmured to himself. They were peasants, not *iw'yt*, not real soldiers whose trade was fighting, raised from childhood in the barracks.

After them came the cannon themselves, wrought with endless difficulty and expense. Djehuty's thick-muscled chest swelled with pride under his iron-scale armor at the number Pharaoh had entrusted to him—a full dozen of the *twelve-pounders*, as they were called in the barbaric tongue of their inventors. Each was a bronze tube of a length equal to a very tall man's height, with little bronze cylinders cast on either side so that the guns could ride in their chariot-like mounts. Very much like a chariot, save that the pole rested on another two-wheeled cart, the *limber*, and that was hauled by six horses with the new collar harness that bore on their shoulders rather than their necks.

Better for the horses, he admitted grudgingly, passing on to the chariots. Those had changed in the last few years as well. Besides a compound bow and quiver on one side, there was a scabbard on the other for two double-barreled shotguns, and the crew was now three, like a Hittite war-cart—one being a loader for the warrior who captained the vehicle.

He reined in and took a swig from the goatskin water bottle at his saddle. It cut gratefully through the dust and thick phlegm in his mouth; he spat to the side and drank again, since there were good springs nearby and no need to conserve every drop. Years of work, to make the Brigade of Seth the finest in Pharaoh's service, and then to integrate the new weapons. Something his father had told him... yes: *To be good commanders, we must love our army and our soldiers. But to win victories, we must be ready to kill the thing we love. When you attack, strike like a hammer and hold nothing back.*

"Stationed in Damnationville with no supplies," he said, quoting a soldier's saying as old as the wars against the Hyksos.

"But sir, there are plenty of supplies," his son said.

Djehuty nodded. "There are now, boy," he said. "But imagine being stuck here on garrison duty for ten years."

The young man looked around. To their left was the sea, brighter somehow than that off the Delta. The road ran just inland of the coastal sand dunes; off to the right a line of hills made the horizon rise up in heights of blue and purple. Thickets of oak dotted the plain, and stretches of tall grass, dry now in midsummer. Dust smoked off a few patches of cultivation, here and there a vineyard or olive grove, but the land was thinly settled—had been since the long wars Pharaoh had waged early in his reign, nearly thirty Nile floods ago.

And those did not go well, he remembered uneasily—he'd been a stripling then, but nobody who'd been at Kadesh was going to believe it the great Egyptian victory that the temple walls proclaimed.

A village of dun-colored mud brick huts with flat roofs stood in the middle distance, dim through the greater dust plume of the Egyptian host passing north. The dwellers and their stock were long gone; sensible peasants ran when armies passed by.

By the standards of the vile Asiatics, of the hairy dwellers in Amurru, this was flat and fertile land. To an Egyptian, it was hard to tell the difference between this and the sterile red desert that lay east of the Nile.

"War and glory are only found in foreign lands," the younger man said stoutly.

"Well spoken, son," the commander said. He looked left; the Ark of Ra was sinking towards the waves. "Time to camp soon. And Pharaoh will summon the commanders to conference in the morning."

Pharaoh was a tall man, still lean and active in the thirty-sixth year of his reign despite the deep furrows in his hawklike face and the plentiful gray in his dark auburn hair. He stood as erect as a granite monolith, wearing the military kilt and the drum-shaped red crown of war with the golden cobra rearing at his brows, waiting as still as the statue of a god. The officers knelt and bowed their heads to the carpet before him in the shade of the great striped canvas pavilion. There was a silence broken only by the clank of armor scales and creak of leather. Then the eunuch herald's voice rang like silver in the cool air of dawn:

"He is The Horus, Strong Bull, Beloved of Ma'at; *He of the Two Goddesses, Protector of Khem who Subdues the Foreign Lands; The Golden Horus, Rich in Years, Great in Victories; He is King of Upper and Lower Egypt, Strong in Right; He is* User-Ma'at-Ra, *Son of Ra; Ramses, Beloved of Amun."*

The officers bowed again to the living god, and Pharaoh made a quick gesture with one hand. The officers bowed once more and rose.

Djehuty came to his feet with the rest. Servants pulled a cover off a long table. It was covered by a shallow-sided box, and within the box was a model made of sand mixed with Nubian gum, smelling like a temple on a festival day. Its maker stood waiting.

There is the outland dog, he thought. Mek-andrus the foreigner, the one who'd risen so high in Pharaoh's service. He wore Egyptian headdress and military kilt but foreign armor—a long tunic of linked iron rings. *Foreign dog. Disturber of custom.*

"The servants of Pharaoh will listen to this man, now Chief of Chariots," Ramses said. "So let it be written. So let it be done."

Djehuty bowed his head again. *If Pharaoh commands that I obey a baboon with a purple arse, I will obey,* he thought. Mek-andrus was obviously part Nubian, too, with skin the color of a barley loaf and a flat nose. *The will of Pharaoh is as the decrees of fate.*

The foreigner moved to the sand table and picked up a wooden pointer. "This is the ground on which we must fight," he said. His Egyptian was fluent, but it had a sharp nasal accent like nothing any of the Khemites had ever heard before. "As seen from far above."

All the officers had had the concept explained to them. Some were still looking blank-eyed; Djehuty nodded and looked down with comprehension. There was the straight north-south reach of the coast of Canaan, with the coastal plain narrowing to nothing where the inland hills ran almost to water's edge; a bay north of that, where a river ran into the sea. The river marked a long trough, between the hills and the mountains of Galilee to the north, and it was the easiest way from the sea inland to the big lake and the Jordan valley.

"The Hittites, the men of Kar-Duniash, the *Mariyannu* of the Asiatic cities, the Aramanaean tribes, and their allies are approaching from the northeast, thirty-five thousand strong not counting their auxiliaries and camp followers, according to the latest reports."

The pointer traced a line down through Damascus, over the heights, along the shores of the Sea of Galilee, then northwest from Bet Shean.

"Of those, at least five thousand are infantry equipped with fire weapons, with thirty cannon, and four thousand chariots."

None of the Egyptian commanders stirred; there was a low mutter of sound as the Sherdana mercenary commander translated for his monoglot subordinates, their odd-looking helmets with the circle of feathers all round bending together.

"Favored of the Son of Ra," Djehuty said. "If we are here"—he pointed to a place half a day's march before the point where the coastal plain pinched out—"can they reach the sea and hold the passes over Carmel against us?"

Mek-andrus nodded; he no longer smiled with such boorish frequency as he had when he first came to Egypt. "That is the question. They were here"—he tapped the place where the Jordan emerged from Galilee—"yesterday at sunset."

Another rustling. That was a longer distance than they had to travel, but it was over flat land with supplies to hand; in time of peace the harvest of the Jezreel went to Pharaoh's storehouses. The Egyptian force must cross mountains.

"Thutmose did it," Mek-andrus said. "If we take this pass"—his finger tapped—"as the Great One's predecessor did, we can be *here* and deployed to meet them before they expect us."

Thutmose . . . , Djehuty thought. Then: *Ah.* One of the great Pharaohs of the previous dynasty, the one that had petered out after the Accursed of Amun tried to throw down the worship of the gods. His eyes narrowed as he watched Mek-andrus. How did the outland dog know so much of Khem? Djehuty *knew* the barbarian didn't read the Egyptian script, so he couldn't have simply read the story off a temple wall the way a literate, civilized man might. The fire weapons themselves weren't sorcery, just a recipe, like cooking—plain saltpeter and sulfur and charcoal, whatever the peasants might think. But there was something not quite canny about Mek-andrus himself.

Yet the gods have sent him to us. Without Mek-andrus, the Hittites and Achaeans and other demon-begotten foreigners who knew not the Black Land or the Red would have had the new weapons all to their own. That would have been as bad as the time long ago when the Hyksos came with their chariots, before any Egyptian had seen a horse, and it had taken a long night of subjection and war to expel *them*.

"Who should take the vanguard?" Pharaoh asked.

Mek-andrus bowed. "Let Pharaoh choose the commander who has both wisdom and bravery… and many cannon, so that they can hold off the enemy host until the whole army of Pharaoh is deployed."

Remote as jackal-headed Anubis deciding the fate of a soul in the afterworld, Pharaoh's eyes scanned his generals.

Djehuty fell on his face as the flail pointed to him. "Djehuty of the Brigade of Seth. The vanguard shall be yours. Prepare to move as soon as you may. You shall cross the pass and hold the ground for the rest of our armies. So let it be written! So let it be done!"

It was a great honor… and possibly the death sentence for the Brigade of Seth.

Djehuty slid gracelessly down off the horse, keeping a tight grip on the reins as it whinnied and shied sideways. Its iron shoes struck sparks from the rocks beside the trail. The column was winding its way upwards, through rocky hills covered in resin-scented pine forest, towards the saddle between two peaks. He tossed the reins to a groom and walked back down the narrow twisting passage—it would be boastful to give it the name of road—as the sweating files of infantry and charioteers made their way upwards. The chariots were no problem; even the heavier new models could still be lifted easily by two strong men when the going became very rough. The cannon, though…

A wheel lurched over a rock and came down with a slamming *bang* that made him wince as if his testicles were being drawn back up into his gut. He let out a sigh of relief as the wheel stayed in one piece and the tough Nubian ebony of the axle *didn't* crack.

"Halt!" he called. "You, Senefer—get a company of infantry up here, a hundred men, and ropes." They could repeat the process with each gun from this point to the saddle of the pass, changing the infantry companies as needed.

He ran a hand along the sweating neck of the lead horse in the gun team, murmuring soothingly when it blew out its lips in weary protest.

"Peace, brother of the field of war," he said. "So, so, my pretty. Soon you may rest."

An officer must be thrifty with Pharaoh's goods. There was no sense in killing valuable horses with overwork when peasants were available.

"I do not like the thought of cowering in a hole," Djehuty said.

The valley stretched out before him, land flat and marshy in spots, in others fertile enough even by an Egyptian's standards. Stubble stood sere on that half of the plowland that made this year's harvested fields, blond-white and knee high; the fallow was densely grown with weeds. Olive trees grew thick on the hills that rose on either side of the southeastward trend of the lowlands; orchards of fig and pomegranate stood around hamlets of dark mud brick, and green leafy vineyards that would produce the famed Wine of the North. These lands were well-peopled, a personal estate of Pharaoh and on a route that carried much trade from the north in times of peace.

"All the courage in the world won't stop a bullet," Mekandrus said. "A man in a hole—a *rifle pit*—can load and fire more easily, and still be protected from the enemy's bullets. They must stand and walk forward to attack; and the Divine Son of Ra has ordered us to defend."

Djehuty made a gesture of respect at the Pharaoh's name. "So he has," he said. *You purple-arsed baboon,* he thought to himself. Pharaoh was a living god, but a commander in the field was not always bound by his sovereign's orders—it was the objective that counted. And occasionally Egyptians had committed deicide … *No.* He thrust the thought from him. That was a counsel of desperation, and Ramses had been a good Pharaoh, strong and just.

"How do you advise that we deploy, then?" Djehuty said.

He looked back. The land fell rapidly from the saddle, and most of the Brigade of Seth were out, forming up in solid blocks.

"Let us keep the pass to our backs," the foreigner said.

"So—half of a circle?" Djehuty said, making a curving gesture.

"No, not today. That would disperse the fire of our guns. Instead—"

Mek-andrus began to draw in the dirt with a bronze-tipped stick he carried. "Two *redoubts*, little square earth forts, on either end of a half circle whose side curves away from the enemy. That way they can give *enfilading fire.*"

"Please, O Favored of the Divine Horus, speak Egyptian; I plead my ignorance."

Mek-andrus looked up sharply. Djehuty gave him a bland smile; let him see how a civilized man controlled his emotions.

The foreigner nodded. He held both hands out, fingers splayed, then crossed those fingers to make a checkerboard. "*Enfilading fire* means that the paths of the balls or grapeshot from the cannon cross each other so," he said. "Instead of one path of destruction, they overlap and create a whole field where nothing can live."

The Egyptian's eyes went wide. He struggled within his head, imagining… and he had seen what cannon could do. *Those Nubians who tried to raid the fort,* he thought. A great wedge had been cut through their mass, as if sliced by the knife of a god. Within that triangle only shattered bone and spattered flesh had remained. Some of it still twitching and screaming. In his mind's eye he overlapped that broad path of death with thirty more, and put Hittite charioteers in place of naked blacks with horn-tipped spears. His hand went of itself to the outlander's shoulder.

"I see your word!" he exclaimed, smiling broadly. "Your word is a thing of beauty. And how shall we place the musketeers?"

Djehuty's son listened closely, waiting in silence until Mekandrus strode away. "Father and lord," he said hesitantly. "Is it possible that… some among us have been mistaken concerning the outlander."

His father shook his head. "He knows much," he said. "But it is still a violation of *ma'at*, of the order of things, that an outlander should stand so close to the Great One. And to be granted a Royal woman as his wife! Not even the Great King of the Hittites was given such honor, when we were allied with them and at peace. No," he went on, dropping his voice. "The day will come when the foreign dog who knows not the Red Land or the Black will have taught us all he knows. On that day …"

Father and son smiled, their expressions like a wolf peering into a mirror. Then Djehuty raised his voice: "Officers of Five Hundred, of a Hundred. Attend me!"

"They come," the Medjay scout wheezed, pointing behind himself with his spear. His body was naked save for a gourd penis sheath and his skin shone like polished onyx with sweat. His tongue lolled, his smell rose rank, compounded of seldom washing and the cow tallow mixed with ochre smeared on his hair. "Their scouts chased me, but I lost them in rough ground."

Djehuty nodded; the Nubian mercenaries in Pharaoh's host were recruited from desert nomads south of the great bend of the Nile—hunters, herders, and bandits. They could outrun horses, given time, loping along at their tireless long-legged trot. And they could track a ghost over naked rock, or hide in their own shadows. Djehuty knew it too well. His first command had been patrols along the southern frontier. You didn't forget waking up and finding a sentry with his throat cut and his genitals stuffed into his mouth, and nobody in camp any the wiser until the Ark of Ra lifted over the horizon. That was Medjay humor… but they were useful, no doubt of that, and true to their salt.

"Many?" he said.

"Many," the barbarian confirmed, opening and closing his hands rapidly. "As a Real Man runs"—that was their heathen name for themselves—"an hour's distance."

"Fetch my war harness," he said to his son. To a runner: "A message to the captains that the enemy approaches."

His chariot came up, the plumes on the team's heads nodding, and the Egyptian commander ducked into the leather shirt of iron scales. Sweat soaked the linen backing almost immediately; he lowered the helmet over his head and buckled the strap below his chin. The sunlight was painful on the bronze and gold that decked the light wicker and bentwood of the car, and the iron tires shrunk onto the wooden wheels. He climbed aboard, his son after him; the boy made a production of checking the priming on shotguns and pistols, but he was a good lad, conscientious. More eager than was sensible, but this would be his first real battle.

"Keep your head," his father warned, his voice gruff. "It's the cool-blooded man lives long on the threshing ground of battle."

"I'm not afraid, Father!" Sennedjem said. His voice started low but broke in a humiliating squeak halfway through. He flushed angrily; his mother had been Djehuty's first woman, a fair-skinned Libyan captive, and the boy's olive tan was a little lighter than most men of Lower Egypt.

"That's the problem, lad," Djehuty grinned. "You *should* be frightened." He turned his attention to the work of the day.

The signal fire on top of the bare-sloped hill to the southeast went out. "Soon now," Djehuty said.

Dust gave the chariots away. The Egyptian squinted; his

vision had grown better for distant things in the last few years, worse for close work. *Chariot screen,* he thought. Thrown forward to keep the Egyptians from getting a close look at their enemy's force before they deployed for battle. Whoever commanded the enemy host was no fool. Now he must do the same. Without a close description of his position, the enemy commander would be handicapped.

"Forward!" he barked.

Well-drilled, the squadrons fanned out before him. The driver clucked to his charges, touched their backs gently with the reins, and the willing beasts went forward. Walk, canter, trot; the dry, hard ground hammered at his feet below the wicker floor of the war-cart. He compensated with an instinctive flexing of knees and balance, learned since childhood. The enemy grew closer swiftly with the combined speed of both chariot fleets, and he could feel his lips draw back in a grin of carnivore anticipation.

Syrians, he thought, as details became plain—spiked bronze helmets, horsehair plumes, long coats of brass scales rippling like the skins of serpents, curled black beards and harsh beak-nosed faces. *Mariyannu* warriors of the northern cities, some rebellious vassals of Pharaoh, some from the Hittite domains or the ungoverned borderlands.

They came in straggling clumps and bands, by ones and twos, fighting as ever by town and by clan. He could see the drivers leaning forward, shouting to the horses in their uncouth gutturals, the fighters reaching for arrows to set to their bows.

"We'll show them our fire," he said.

A feather fan mounted on a yard-long handle stood in a holder at his side. He snatched it out and waved to left and right. The Egyptian formation curled smoothly forward on either hand. *Fast as ever,* he thought—the new harness let a team pull the heavier chariots without losing speed or agility. A drumming of hooves filled the air with thunder, a choking white dust curled up like the sandstorms of Sinai. The horses rocked into a gallop, nostrils flared and red, foam flecking their necks. The first arrows arched out, the bright sun winking off their points. Djehuty sneered: much too far for effective archery. Dust boiled up into the unmerciful sky, thick and acrid on his tongue. Soon …

"Amun! Amun! The Divine Horus!" the Egyptians roared. Savage war cries echoed back from the enemy.

"Gun!" he barked, holding out a hand. Check-patterned acacia wood slapped into it as Sennedjem put the weapon in his hand.

Thumping sounds smashed through the roar of hooves and thunder of wheels. Syrian chariots went over, and the high womanish screaming of wounded horses was added to the uproar. Djehuty crouched, raking back the hammers with his left palm and then levelling the weapon. Now. An enemy chariot dashing in out of the dust in a dangerously tight curve, one wheel off the ground. Close enough to see the wild-eyed glare of the *Mariyannu* poised with a javelin in one hand. Bring the wedge at the front of the paired barrels to the notch at the back. It wasn't so different from using a bow, the body adjusting like a machine of balanced springs; but easier, easier, no effort of holding the draw. Squeeze the trigger, nothing jerky about the motion…

Whump. The metal-shod butt of the shotgun punished his shoulder. Flame and sulfur-stinking smoke vomited from the barrels, along with thirty lead balls. Those were invisible—strange to think of something moving too fast to see—but he shouted in exultation as he saw them strike home. The horses reared and screamed and tripped as the lead raked them, the driver went over backward.

"Gun!" Djehuty roared, and Sennedjem snatched away the empty one and slapped the next into his father's grasp, then went to work biting open cartridges, hands swift on ramrod and priming horn. Djehuty fired again. "Gun!" Sennedjem put a charged weapon in his grip. "Gun!"

They plunged through the dust cloud and out into the open; the surviving Syrian chariots were in full retreat. Others lay broken, some with upturned wheels still spinning. One right at his own horse's feet, and the driver pulled their team around. A wounded *Mariyannu* stumbled forward with a long spear held in both hands; Djehuty shot him at ten paces distance, and the bearded face splashed away from its understructure of bone. Some of the shot carved grooves of brightness through the green-coated bronze of the man's helmet. Out of the corner of his eye he was conscious of Sennedjem reloading the spent shotgun, priming the pans and waiting poised.

"Pull up," Djehuty rasped. "Sound *rally*."

The driver brought the team to a halt. Sennedjem sheathed the shotgun and brought out a slender brass horn. Its call sounded shrill and urgent through the dull diminishing roar of the skirmish. Man after man heard it; the Captains of a Hundred brought their commands back into formation. Djehuty took the signal fan from its holder and waved it.

Meanwhile he looked to the northeast. More dust there, a low sullen cloud of it that caught the bright sunlight. He waited, and a rippling sparkle came from it, filling vision from side to side of the world ahead of them like stars on a night-bound sea.

"Father, what's *that*?" Sennedjem blurted; he was looking pale, but his eyes and mouth were steady. Djehuty clipped him across the side of the head for speaking without leave, but lightly.

"Light on spearpoints, lad," he said grimly. "Now it begins."

The redoubt was a five-sided figure of earth berms; there were notches cut in the walls for the muzzles of the cannon, and obstacles made of wooden bars set with sharp iron blades in the ditches before it. Djehuty waited atop the rampart for the enemy heralds; they carried a green branch for peace, and a white cloth on a pole as well—evidently the same thing, by somebody else's customs. And flags, one with white stars on a blue ground and red-and-white stripes. His eyes widened a little. He had heard of that flag. Another beside it had similar symbols, and cryptic glyphs, thus: U.S. COAST GUARD. He shivered a little, inwardly. What wizardry was woven into that cloth? A touch at his amulet stiffened him. Gilded eagles topped the staffs, not the double-headed version of the Hittites, but sculpted as if alive with their wings thrust behind them and their claws clutching arrows and olive branches.

So that is why the strangers from the far west are called the Eagle People, he thought. It must be their protector-god. He nodded; whatever else you could say about them, they must be wise in the ways of war.

"I am Djehuty, Commander of the Brigade of Seth in the army of Pharaoh, *User-Ma'at-Ra,* son of Ra, Ramses of the line of Ramses, the ruler of Upper and Lower Egypt," he barked. "Speak."

"Commodore Marian Alston," the figure in black-enameled steel armor said. It lifted off its helm. *No, she, by the Gods—the rumors speak truth. Odd, but we had a woman as Pharaoh once, and she led armies.* Djehuty's eyes went wider. The enemy commander was a Nubian; not part-blood like Mek-andrus, but black as polished ebony. His eyes flicked to the others sitting their horses beside her. One was a woman too, yellow-haired like some Achaeans; another was a man of no race he knew, with skin the color of amber and eyes slanted at the outer ends; the other two looked like Sherden from the north shore of the Middle Sea as far as their coloring went, although their hair was cropped close. A *Sudunu* stood uneasily by the foreign woman's stirrup; he stepped forward and bowed with one hand to his flowerpot hat to keep it from falling off.

"I shall interpret, noble Djehuty," he said uneasily; the Egyptian was fluent, but with the throaty accent of his people.

Djehuty glared for a second. Byblos, Sidon, and the other coastal cities of Canaan were vassals of Pharaoh; what was this treacherous dog doing aiding his enemies? Then he nodded curtly. *Sudunu* would do anything for wealth.

"Tell this woman that no foreigner goes armed in Pharaoh's dominions without his leave, on pain of death. If she and her rabble leave at once, I may be merciful."

The *Sudunu* began to speak in Akkadian, the Babylonian tongue. Djehuty could follow it a little; it was the tongue kings used to write to each other, and not impossibly different from the language of the western Semites, which he did speak after a fashion. The interpreter was shading the meaning. That often happened, since such a man was eager to avoid offending anyone.

"Tell her exactly, as I told you—don't drip honey on it," he broke in.

The swarthy, scrawny man in the embroidered robe swallowed and began again. The black woman gave a slight, bleak smile.

"Lord Djehuty," the interpreter began. "Commodore—that is a rank, lord—Alston says that she is empowered by her ... lord, the word means Ruler, I think—Ruler of an island across the River Ocean—and the Great King of the Hittites, and the Great King of Kar-Duniash, and their other allies, to demand the return *of George McAndrews*, a renegade of her people. If you will give us this man, the allied forces will return past the border of Pharaoh Ramses' dominions, and peace may return."

Djehuty puzzled over the words for a moment before he realized that the name was Mek-andrus, the outland favorite of Ramses. "Barbarians make no demands of Pharaoh," he snapped. *Although I would send him to you dragged by the ankles behind my chariot, if the choice were mine.* "They beg for his favor, or feel the flail of his wrath. Go, or die."

The coal-black face gave a slight nod. No, *not a Medjay,*

Djehuty thought with an inner chill. *Except in color and cast of feature.* They were like fierce children, their *ka* plain on their faces. This one had discipline; doubly remarkable in a woman. And she showed no sign of fear, under the muzzles of his guns. *She must know what they can do. Mek-andrus is of her people.*

If the stranger was a renegade from the service of his King, much was explained. He schooled his own face.

"Pharaoh commands; as it is written, so shall it be done," he replied. "This parley is over. Depart his soil, at once."

BAAAAMMMM.

The twelve-pounder leapt back, up the sloping ramp of dirt the gunners had shovelled behind it, then back down again into battery. Stripped to their loincloths, the crew threw themselves into action. One man shoved a pole with a wet sponge down the muzzle, twisting and withdrawing it, and the hot metal hissed. The powder came forward in a dusty-looking linen cylinder, to be rammed down with a wad of hemp and then the leather sack of lead balls. Stinking smoke drifted about them, and the confused roaring noise of battle, but the men labored on, wet with sweat, their faces blackened by powder fumes until their eyes stared out like white flecks in a black mask, burns on their limbs where they had brushed against the scorching bronze of the cannon.

These are men, Djehuty thought, slightly surprised. *More than that, they are men worthy to be called* iw'yt, *real soldiers.*

He wasn't sure about the warriors surging about his line, but whatever they were, they didn't discourage easily. He squinted through the thick smoke that stung his eyes, ignoring the dryness of his tongue—they were short of water, and he meant to make what he had last. This band of the foe looked a little like Hittites, stocky and hairy and big-nosed, but taller and fairer, and their gear was different. They didn't shave the front of their heads, either.

Here they came again, over ground covered with their dead. Swarms of them, sending a shower of javelins before them as they came closer.

BAAAAMMMM. BAAAAMMM. The guns were firing more slowly now, conserving their ammunition. Grapeshot cut bloody swathes through the attackers, but they kept on. Dead men dropped improvised ladders of logs and sticks; others picked them up and came forward. Their cries grew into a deep bellowing; the first ranks dropped into the ditch around the redoubt, where the spiked barricades were covered with bodies. Others climbed up, standing on their shoulders to scramble up the sloping dirt or setting up their scaling ladders. Some of them knew enough to cringe at the sound that came through shouts and cannonade. The sound of thumbs cocking back the hammers of their muskets.

"Now!" Djehuty shouted, swinging his fan downwards.

All along the parapet, hundreds of musketeers stood up from their crouch and leveled their pieces downward into the press of attackers.

"Fire!"

A noise that thudded into chest and gut, like one long shot that went on for a full second. A fresh fogbank of smoke drifted away, showing the ruin below—the muskets had been loaded with what Mek-andrus called *buck and ball*, a musket ball and several smaller projectiles. The ditch was filled with shapes that heaved and moaned and screamed, and the smell was like an opened tomb that had drained a sewer. Djehuty winced, very slightly; he was a hardy man and bred to war, but it was one thing to see men fall pierced with arrows, or gashed with the sword, but this… this was something else. Not even the actions in the south had prepared him for it; the barbarians there were too undisciplined to keep charging into certain death as these men had.

"They run away, Father!" Sennedjem said.

"Down!" Djehuty barked.

Everyone in the little earth fort took cover. Away in the gathering dusk, lights blinked like angry red eyes. A long whistling screech came from overhead, and then the first explosion. The enemy cannon were better than the ones Mek-andrus had made in Khem; instead of firing just solid roundshot or grape, they could throw shells that exploded themselves—and throw them further. He dug his fingers into the earth, conscious mainly of the humiliation of it. He, Commander of the Brigade of Seth, whose ancestors had been nobles since the years when the Theban Pharaohs expelled the Hyksos , cowering in the dirt like a peasant! But the fire-weapons were no respecters of rank or person. *And they will shred my Brigade of Seth like meat beneath the cook's cleaver.* So Pharaoh had ordered ... and it might be worth it, if it turned the course of the battle to come.

Earth shuddered under his belly and loins. He had a moment to think, and it froze him with his fingers crooked into the shifting clay. *Why only cannon?* he thought. From the reports and rumors, the newcomers had taught their allies to make muskets too, and better ones than the Egyptians had—something to do with twisting grooves inside the barrels. Yet all the infantry and chariots his Brigade had met here were armed with the old weapons; some of them fashioned of iron rather than bronze, but still spear, sword, bow, javelin.

The barrage let up. He turned his head, and felt his liver freeze with fear. Sennedjem was lying limp and pale, his back covered in blood. Djehuty scrambled to him, ran hands across the blood-wet skin. Breath of life and pulse of blood, faint but still there. He prayed to the gods of healing and clamped down; there, something within the wound. A spike of metal, still painfully hot to the touch. He took it between thumb and forefinger, heedless of the sharp pain in his own flesh, and pulled. His other hand pressed across the wound while he roared for healers, bandages, wine and resin to wash out the hurt. When they came he rose, forcing himself to look away and think as his son was borne to the rear.

"I don't like the smell of this," he muttered, and called for a runner. "Go to the commander of the northernmost brigade of Pharaoh's army," he said. "Find why they delay, and return quickly. Say that we are hard-pressed."

"Back!" Djehuty snarled.

He smashed the pommel of the sword into the fleeing spearman's face, feeling bone crunch. The witless howl of panic stopped as the man dropped boneless. Behind Djehuty, the men of his personal guard leveled their double-barreled shotguns, and the madness faded out of the faces of the soldiers who'd panicked. Those who still held their spears lowered them, and in the uncertain light of dawn he could see them shuffle their feet and drop their eyes.

"If you run from death, it follows you—and death runs fast," Djehuty said, his voice firm but not angry. "Remember that it is ruin to run from a fight, for you cannot fight and flee, but the pursuer can still strike at your naked back as he chases *you*. Return to your positions."

"Sir—" one said, desperate. "Lord, the thunderbolts strike us and we cannot strike back!"

"I know," Djehuty said. The bandage on one forearm reminded them that he ran the same dangers. "But they cannot take our position unless they send men forward to claim it, and those men you *can* strike." *Those of you still alive.* "Return to your companies! Strike the foe!"

He turned, stalking through rows of wounded men groaning on the rocky dirt, through shattered carts and dead horses—someone was skinning them for cooking, at least, and he must find who'd thought to organize parties to fill waterskins—and looked up the pass. Nobody, nobody but his reserves, and they were few enough.

If Pharaoh does not come, we will die here, he thought. Unless he withdrew now, leaving a rearguard ... No. *We have lost too many of our draught beasts. I cannot save the cannon or the chariots.* A grim satisfaction: *I have done my part, and my men as well. If the plan fails, it is not our doing.* Pharaoh's doing... he thrust the thought from him.

Then there *was* something in the pass: a messenger. A *mounted* messenger, plunging recklessly down the steep rocky way, leaning back with feet braced in the stirrups as his horse slid the final dozen yards almost in a sitting position. It hung its lathered head as the messenger drummed heels on its ribs and came over to him, wheezing as its flanks heaved like a bronzesmith's bellows.

The man looked nearly as done-in as his horse, his face a mask of dust. "Here," Djehuty said, passing over his water-skin.

The man sucked at it eagerly; the water was cut with one-fifth part of sour wine.

"Lord," he gasped after a moment. "From Pharaoh."

He offered a scroll of papyrus; Djehuty touched it to his forehead in the gesture of respect and broke the seal to read eagerly, his eyes skipping easily over the cursive demotic script, so different from the formal hieroglyphs of sculpture and temple.

Enemy ships with many guns at the Gateway of the North, he read, and grunted as if shot in the belly. That was the fortress of Gaza, the anchor of the Royal Road up the coast. Only if it was securely held could even a single man return to Khem across the deserts of Sinai. *Troops armed with fire-weapons are landing and investing the fortress. Pharaoh marches to meet them. Hold your position at all hazards; you are the rear guard.*

Djehuty grunted again, as a man might when he had just been condemned to death. That was where the cream of the enemy forces had gone, right enough.

"Sir!" Another messenger, one of his own men, and on foot. "Sir, the enemy attack!"

The steel *kopesh* was lead-heavy in Djehuty's hand as he re-treated another step; the ring of Egyptians grew smaller as they stood shoulder-to-shoulder around the standard. *For Khem,* he thought, and slashed backhand. The edge thudded into the rim of an Aramanaean's shield, and the leather-covered wicker squeezed shut on the blade. The nomad shrieked glee and wrenched, trying to tear the weapon from the Egyptian's hand. Djehuty's lips bared dry teeth as he smashed the boss of his own into the man's face, then braced a foot on his body to wrench the sickle-sword free. *For Sennedjem!* he thought, swinging it down. Distracted, he did not see the spearhead that punched into his side just below the short ribs. Bent over, wheezing, he saw the spearman staring incredulously at the way the bronze point had bent over double against the iron scales of his armor, then scream frustration and club the spear to use the shaft as a bludgeon. Exhaustion weighed down his limbs as he struggled to turn, to bring up shield and blade. Something struck him again, he couldn't tell where, and the world went gray. His last thought was that the earth tasted of salt with blood.

Bits of the formulae for addressing the Judge of the Dead flitted through Djehuty's head along with blinding pain as his eyelids fluttered open. But it was not jackal-headed Anubis who bent over him, but a foreigner with a cup of water. The Egyptian sucked it down gratefully before he thought to wonder at it.

Prisoner, he thought. *I must be a prisoner.* But he was not bound, and beneath him lay a folding cot with a canvas bead, not the hard ground. He turned his head carefully. He was under a great awning, amid rows of others. Sennedjem! His son lay not far away. Djehuty gasped relief to see his chest rising under a mummy's swath of bandages. But what was held in the clear glass bottle that was connected to his arm by a flexible tube?

Djehuty's eyes went wide when he realized that the same piece of sorcerer's apparatus drained into his *own* arm. Gradually the fear died, and the pain in his head became less. When the foreigner's black commander came, he was able to stare back with something approaching dignity as she sat on a folding stool beside his cot.

She spoke, and the *Sudunu* interpreter relayed the words: "You and your men fought very well."

Djehuty blinked, then nodded. Nevertheless, the scales had swung against him. "You deceived us very well. Ransom?" he went on without much hope.

She shook her head. "When the war is over, we will release all our prisoners."

Djehuty blinked again, this time in surprise, caught between relief and doubt. It would take a strong commander to deny victorious troops the plunder of victory, and the sale of prisoners was an important part of that. Even Pharaoh, the living God, might have difficulties. With an effort, he fought down bitterness against Ramses; what the Pharaoh decreed, must be done… even if it destroyed the Brigade of Seth at the word of the foreigner Mek-andrus.

"Your king must be a ruler of great power," he said.

"We have no king," she said, and smiled slightly at his bafflement. "We come from … very far away," she said. "In distance and years. You might call us exiles."

"Your whole nation?" he said in bafflement, as the explanation went on. *Powerful sorcery.*

"No," she went on. "Just one small island of us, and a ship. So we were stranded here and now."

"Ah," Djehuty said bitterly. "And with arts of war like none we know, you seek to carve out a great empire."

Long black fingers knotted into a fist on a trousered knee. "No. *Some* of us saw that they might become kings here, with what they knew. The rest of us… must fight to enforce our law upon them."

"No king…" Djehuty frowned. "I find that hard to believe. Only a powerful king can make a people strong in war."

She shook her head. "That is not so, Djehuty of the Brigade of Seth. We have arts that your people do not, is that not so?" He nodded, reluctantly. "Well," she went on, "not all those arts are arts of war. We have found that one man's wisdom is not enough to steer a great nation, and how to… to melt together the wisdom of many."

"I do not understand."

"Let me tell you," she said, "of a thing we call a *Constitution*, which is a government of laws and not of men…"

When she rose with a promise to return and speak more, his head was whirling as badly as it had when the spearshaft clubbed him. He heard words in the foreign commander's language:

"And that'll cause a lot more trouble than gunpowder, in the long run."

"Wait," he said. "One thing—what name will this battle be given? Surely it is a greater one than Kadesh, even." Let the chronicles remember it, and with it the name of Djehuty. Chronicles that did not lie, like the ones that called Kadesh a victory for Ramses.

She turned, smiling wryly. "We will name it from the hill that overlooks the battlefield," she said. "Har-Megiddo. Armagedon, in our tongue."

THREE WALLS-32ND CAMPAIGN

"**S**ir," Gnaeus Clodius Afer said. "Exactly which bunch of these *fucking* wogs are we supposed to be fighting, anyway?"

Gaius Vibulenus squeezed his hand on the mail-clad shoulder of the man who commanded the Tenth Cohort. Clodius Afer wore a red transverse crest across his helmet; he carried a staff of hard twisted wood rather than the two javelins the enlisted men bore, and his short stabbing sword was slung on the right from a baldric rather than the left side of his military belt: a centurion's gear. Gaius Vibulenus's Attic helmet had a white plume, and he wore a back-and-breast armor of cast bronze hinged at the shoulders. The Hellenic-style outfit marked him as an officer, a military tribune.

At least, it had when the legion sailed out of Brundisium to join Crassus's glorious conquest of Parthia. He'd been able to wear it because his family were wealthy landowners in Campania and politically well-connected; one more gentry sprig gaining a little military experience to help him with the *cursus honorum* to office, and hopefully a share of the plunder. Militarily he'd been a joke. The actual work of the unit was done by men like Clodius Afer. Since then, things had changed.

Hercules, but they've changed, Gaius Vibulenus thought, looking down the hillside where the Romans stood at ease and waited for the aliens who'd bought them from their Parthian captors to decide what they were going to do.

I'd like to know in more detail too. Usually they just march us out of the ship, we kick arse, and then we march back. He didn't like it when things got more complicated than that. The last time they'd gotten really complex... that had been the siege. The siege had been very bad....

To blank out the memory of ton-weights of stone grinding through his body Gaius Vibulenus looked over his shoulder, towards the group who would send the legion into action. The hulking presence of the Guild Commander was half a hundred paces away, surrounded by his monstrous toad-like guards mounted on their giant hyena-like mounts. The seven-foot spiked maces the guards bore glinted in the light of a sun paler than that the Roman had been born under, with a pinkish tinge to its yellow. The banded iron armor they wore creaked on its leather backing, and the scale-sewn blankets that protected their mounts rustled and clicked. The Commander—this Commander, there had been a dozen of as many different types—was himself as large as his hideous bodyguards, and dressed in the inevitable blue jumpsuit with the shimmer of a force-screen before his face. His hands dangled nearly to his back-acting knees, and when he was nervous claws like so many straight razors unfolded from the insides of his fingers. They were thin and translucent and looked sharp enough to cut the air.

Compared to him, the natives of this low-technology world were positively homelike, much more so than most the legion had fought in the service of the... creatures... who'd bought them. The group around the Commander were fairly typical. Almost homelike... if you ignored the fact that they had greenish feather fronds instead of hair, and huge eyes of a deep purple without whites, and thumbs on either side of their three-fingered hands. About half the delegation arguing with the Commander were females, their breasts left bare by the linen kilts that were their only garments—four breasts each.

One of the guard detail standing easy behind the tribute pursed his lips. "You know, some of them wog bitches, they're not bad looking," he murmured. "Wonder what they're shaped like under those kilts?" A couple of the naked attendants with collars around their necks, probably slaves, were male and equipped the same way as someone from Campania.

"Silence in the ranks!" Afer barked. In a conversational voice: "Sir?"

"It's a little more complex than usual, Centurion," Vibulenus said. "The... Guild—" he'd always wondered if that Latin word was precisely what the creatures who'd brought them *meant* "—is supporting the rulers of a kingdom southeast of here. *They're* in the process of conquering this area we're in, and they're facing a rebellion that they can't put down."

If the Guild used its *lasers* and flying boats, putting an end to the uprising would take about thirty minutes. For some reason Vibulenus had never even begun to understand, the Federation the trading guild served forbade the use of weapons more advanced than those of the locals of any given area. If the natives used hand-weapons of iron, the slave-mercenaries of the Guild had to do likewise. That was why they'd bought the Romans; the legion was very, very skilled with those tools, and had the discipline to slaughter many times their number of those who were less so.

"And *we're* supposed to pull it out of the pot for them, right?" Afer said. "Well, that's familiar enough." His eyes lifted over the ranks of the Roman legionaries, appraising the local help they'd be working with. "That'll be their lot, eh?"

Vibulenus nodded; the remark had been a conversational placeholder. The legion often had to work with local auxiliaries and it usually wasn't any pleasure... but it was as necessary here as it had been back in the lands around the Middle Sea, since Rome produced little in the way of cavalry or light missile-infantry. For instance, under Crassus they'd depended on Celtic auxiliary cavalry from Gaul to keep the Parthians away while they marched through the desert of Ctesiphon.

"And *that* didn't work all that well, the *gods* know," he murmured.

Afer nodded, understanding him without need for further words. They both remembered it more vividly than most things since: the dust and the thirst, the glitter of the mail and lances of the Parthian cataphracts whose presence forced them into tight formation... and the horse-archers darting in, loosing their clouds of shafts. Shafts thrown by their horse-and-sinew composite bows with enough force to slam the point right through the leather and plywood of a shield, forcing you back a pace with the whipcrack impact and leaving the triangular head of the arrow on the inside of your shield. If you were lucky; right through your mail-coat if you weren't, and your body lay with all its blood running out on the alkaline clay of Mesopotamia....

Vibulenus shrugged off the memory and looked at the locals. Many of them drove chariots, not much different from the ones immortal Homer had described, except that the pair of beasts which drew them had feathers rather than fur, and blunt omnivore fangs instead of a horse's grass-cropping equipment. They looked like big dogs or slim bears with the skins of pigeons, or at least that was as close as you could come to describing them in Latin. Each cart carried three of the beasts, a driver in a kilt, a spearman in a long coat of iron or bronze scales and carrying a big rectangular shield, and an archer. There were more feathery plumes on the helmets of all three. Their infantry...

Well, that's what we're here for, he thought. The infantry were a rabble, some of their spears only fire-hardened wood at the business end, none of them with much in the way of armor. The slingers and archers might be of some use.

"Gaius Vibulenus Caper," the Commander called.

Vibulenus sighed and adjusted his helmet. "Time to get the word," he said, and strode towards the toad-guards.

"Hasn't it ever occurred to these dickheads to *ride* the bloody things?" someone snarled.

Apparently not, Vibulenus thought.

The enemy were a huge shambling clot pouring out of the distant woods and across the lowlands. Their crest was cavalry—a line of chariots, not much different from the ones the Romans'—the trading guild's—allies used.

Gaudy, though, Vibulenus thought critically, looking at the enemy vehicles. Two of them collided as they swept in one-wheel-down circuits that were probably designed to show off the driver's skill. *And I've seen better coordination in a tavern brawl.*

The allied war-carts sweeping in from the flanks to meet the enemy were fairly uniform, and they moved in squadrons of four and larger units to horn and flag signals. Those of the enemy were decorated with feathers and paint, plumes and gilded bronze and silver, whatever their owners fancied or could afford—and the skulls of enemies past nailed to their railings. The skulls looked less human than the faces of the locals did alive.

Arrows flickered out. Vibulenus's eyebrows rose. A good two or three hundred yards, and they hit hard when they landed—that was almost as good as the Parthians. Chariots tumbled into splintered wreck, their passengers flying out like rag dolls with their limbs flapping until the bone-crunching impact. Others careened away driverless, or stopped as their beasts were injured—unlike horses, the local draft animals seemed inclined to fight when they were hurt, not run away. It was all as distant and safe as matched pairs in an arena in Capua; a few of the troops were even calling out *hoc habet* and making gestures with their thumbs.

"Looks like our wogs are thrashing their wogs, sir," Afer said after a moment. "Leastways with the chariots."

Vibulenus nodded. *But that isn't going to be what settles this fight,* he thought. The enemy infantry was still spilling out of the woods, and while the allied chariots were getting the better of the melee they still weren't free to range up and down shooting them to pieces. *Not many missile infantry,* he noted. Spearmen with seven-foot stabbing weapons and shields, and swordsmen with long leaf-shaped slashing weapons, the few slingers and archers were to the rear where they couldn't do much good. The local wogs were bigger than the Guild's allies, and their feathery head-tufts had a reddish or yellow tinge to the green. They painted their naked bodies in patterns as gaudy as the chariots of their lords; some of them wore strings of hands or disconcertingly humanlike genitalia around their necks, while others had torques of pure soft gold.

"Noisy buggers," Afer added after a minute.

Vibulenus nodded again. They were chanting in high-pitched squealing voices as they came, hammering their weapons on their shields and prancing with a high-stepping gait like trained horses. That changed to a flat-out run as they came within range of the chariot battle; it was a little like watching heavy surf rolling on a beach. The Roman tribune's brows went up as he watched. They might be savages, but they knew their business. Dozens of them swarmed around every allied war-cart, throwing clouds of short weighted darts, then dashing in to slash or stab at the chariot teams. Dozens of chariots went over in the first few minutes, or disappeared under mounds of hacking, heaving foemen. Then a trio of heads would go up on spearpoints, and the mob would move on to the next target with a loping movement like a pack of wolves. They ignored the auxiliary infantry as if they weren't there, despite a trickle of casualties from arrows and slung stones.

"They probably think everyone will run away when the

chariots pull out," the tribune said in a neutral tone. "Probably has gone that way for them, until now."

The allied chariots *were* disengaging, those still able to move—drivers lashing their beasts to reckless haste, high spoked wheels bouncing over irregularities at speeds that made even a heavy tuft of grass a menace to their stability. They had to get out, though, or go down like a beetle swarmed over by ants.

"Hercules. Must be twenty, twenty-five thousand of them," someone muttered.

"Yeah, we'll all have to throw both spears and then gut one each," his file-mate replied. "Don't any of 'em have armor, and this bunch aren't nine feet tall, either, for a fucking change."

The tribune's eyes went right and left along the long mail-gray line of the legion. Sure as shit, the auxiliary infantry posted on either flank *were* running; not as fast as the chariots, but there was a lot less chance of them rallying, too. Vibulenus sighed and reached up to settle his white-plumed helmet more securely on his head.

"*Limlairabu!*" the enemy soldier screamed.

Or something like that. Gaius Vibulenus swung his round bronze-faced officer's shield up and sideways with a mindless skill born of more years' experience than he cared to remember. His opponent was wielding his axe one-handed, with a small iron-rimmed buckler in the other hand. The axe handle was some springy hornlike substance, rather than wood—or maybe that was the way wood grew here—and the edge of the axe whickered through the air as it blurred towards him. The edge was good steel, and so was the spike on the other side. Either could give him a brain-deep head wound beyond even the Medic's ability to cure.

Crack. The axe took a gouge out of the rim of Vibulenus's shield, leaving creamy-white splinters and torn bronze facing in its wake. He stepped in, stamped a hobnailed foot down on the native's bare one, and stabbed underarm. The Spanish steel of his sword scarcely slowed as it went into the native's taut belly-muscles, but a sudden spasm locked flesh around the metal as he tried to withdraw it. With a wheezing curse he put a foot on the spasming body and wrenched it out, straightening up to look around. Oblong Roman shields closed around him as the first two ranks trotted past, into the unraveling enemy formation... .

Well, no, he thought, straining to catch his breath. *It never was a formation. More of a mob.*

Tubas snarled. *"Loose!"* he heard, and the massed javelins of the rear two ranks whistled overhead. They didn't have the densely packed shoulder-to-shoulder targets of the volley that had opened the battle, but there were still enough of the enemy crowded into the zone just behind the edge of combat that virtually every spear found a mark in a shield or in naked flesh. A frenzied mass scream went up; part of that was frustrated rage. Surviving warriors found they could neither pull the *pilum* points out of their shields nor use the javelins for a return throw if they did manage to wriggle them free, since the soft iron shanks of the weapons buckled on impact.

He was reminded of a wave breaking on a rock again, as he had been at the beginning of the battle, but this time it was the rock that advanced, crying out and stabbing. Vibulenus trotted forward, his head moving to keep the action in view as far as he could. So far it was pretty routine... routine for everyone except the luckless bastards the floating metal turtles were picking up. Particularly except for the ones the turtles *weren't* picking up. No matter how badly injured you were—no matter how *dead*, with a spear through the guts or your groin slashed up—if the turtles took you, you'd wake up. Weak, and crimson over most of your body, but that would pass and you'd be good as new, except for the memories. If the turtle rejected you, you were as dead as the men who'd taken a Parthian arrow under Crassus.

Sometimes he thought they'd been the lucky ones.

"Routine," he said. "But somehow I don't think so."

"Sir," Gaius Vibulenus said with desperate earnestness. "We don't *have* to storm the fortress."

The Commander had put his headquarters on a grassy knoll overlooking the valley. From here there was a clear view across a checkerboard of croplands and pasture toward the steep-sided plateau at the center of the basin. It didn't look like Campania here, but it looked a *lot* like say, Cisalpine Gaul; in a way that made it more disturbing than most of the howling wilderness the legion had been landed in. The trees that gave shade overhead weren't quite like oaks; the grain turning tawny-colored down below wasn't like wheat or barley—more like a set of kernels on a broomstick—and the grass had a subtle bluish tint beneath its green. Even the scents were *subtly* wrong, close enough to leaf mold and ordinary crushed grass that you started doubting if it really was different, or if your memories were fading. Vibulenus was aware that his perception of the environment wasn't typical, though; there had been a lot of comments on how homelike the place was. If it hadn't been for the example made of the last attempted deserters—the tribune suppressed a sudden white flash of rage at the memory of what the Guild lasers had done to those soldiers, those Romans, those *friends*—he'd have been apprehensive about men going over the hill. That object lesson had driven home two facts, though. You couldn't hide from the Guild sensors that could peer through solid rock, and you couldn't do anything about the lasers that could *burn* through solid rock.

The fort was disturbing in another way. Not that it was particularly sophisticated. He'd seen much better; that stone castle they'd besieged in the fifth campaign, for instance, the one built by the furry little wogs who looked like giant dormice. That had been like an artificial cliff. This was fifty or sixty feet of steep turf, and then a wall of huge squared logs; another log wall was built twenty feet within, tied in to the first with cross-timbers, and the intervening space filled with rubble and earth. The logs were big, forty feet to their sharpened tips, and they wouldn't burn easily—wood here didn't, for some reason, as if it had strands of glass inside it. That wasn't the problem. There were towers every fifty or sixty feet, too, full of archers and slingers and javelineers. But *that* wasn't the problem.

"Are you unable to take the fortress?" the Commander said, his voice the same neutral baritone that all the commanders had. That was more incongruous than the bestial snarling his mouth suggested would be more natural.

"Sir, no, we can take it," Vibulenus said. *The Commander is the problem.* "A week to build catapults, then we put in a ramp and some siege towers and go over the palisade. But there are better than ten thousand of them in there, and it'll turn into a ratfight—our discipline and armor are bigger advantages in the open field than in street-fighting. We'll lose a hundred, maybe two hundred men... and you've told us that the Guild can't replace our losses."

The Commander pursed his lips. "That is correct," he said.

Vibulenus's stomach knotted. The Guild could make the Romans immortal—unaging, at least—and it could repair anything but a spearpoint through the braincase. But it couldn't get more Romans. *Never more Romans. Never Rome again. Never home again—*

He cut off that train of thought with practiced ease. There were easier ways to die here than a spear or a sword; thinking about home too much was one of them. Even the Medic couldn't bring you back from a really determined attempt at suicide.

Attacking the Commander, for instance.

"That is correct," the Commander went on. "But it is essential that this rebellion be put down. If assets must be expended, then they must."

"Sir," Gaius Vibulenus went on, in a voice that must *not* shake with the anger that poured through him like boiling oil poured on a storming party. "There *are* ten thousand men in there. Each of them has to eat every day. You can see that they didn't have the time to get their harvest in, but it's nearly ripe—all their food-stocks must be low. If we invest the fortress, we can starve them out and solve the problem *economically*."

The Commander made a noncommittal sound, then blinked and looked at the fields and nodded. Vibulenus felt a slight chill. The Commander *looked* like something out of a nightmare… but in a way that response made him seem even more alien. He obviously hadn't thought of the harvest as something *important*.

"If you assets are encamped here, is there not a risk that the enemy will… I believe the term is *sally*? At night, for instance."

Vibulenus's head rose up. "Sir, we are *Romans*. I assure you that within a week, they'll no more be able to sally successfully than they could fly to Rome by flapping their arms."

"Now, *stay* there, ye bugger," the legionary grunted.

The pit he'd been digging was the depth of a man's arm, slanting forward at a forty-five degree angle. Inside it was a wooden stake only a little shorter, the upper point trimmed to a sharp point and fire-hardened. The soldier finished ramming the unhardened point into the soft earth at the base of the pit, flicked the stake to make sure that it was firmly seated, then moved on to the next pit, dragging his bundle of stakes with him.

The air smelled of freshly turned earth; from the rings of pits for the stakes, and from the square-section ditch ahead of them, twenty feet deep and neat as a knife-cut through cake. The ditch was an irregular oblong, intended to run all around the hill on which the enemy squatted; when the Romans began their siege works the ramparts had been black with watchers, but now only a normal number squatted or leaned on their spears atop the ramparts. Vibulenus cocked a critical eye at the massive excavation. The layout and initial digging had been done by the legion's soldiers, but much of the donkey-work was being handed off to local peasants rounded up by the auxiliaries. The main problem hadn't been resistance, but the simple blundering incompetence of backwoodsmen not accustomed to working in groups. Despite that the peasants were working hard—they'd been told that they could go back to their harvest when the circumvallation was complete. They even had a few tricks that the Romans hadn't run into before.

Their spades and picks were familiar enough, but instead of carrying dirt away in baskets they used a little box with a wheel in front and two handles behind—really extremely clever. *I wonder why we never thought of that?* Vibulenus wondered mildly, then turned.

Behind the rows of lilies were more rows of *stimulators*, short sticks with a pointed iron barb at one end, hammered into the dirt with the barb pointing inward towards the enemy. Behind *them* was a ditch ten feet deep, full of trees with sharpened branches making a forest of points; behind *that* was another ditch, this one to be flooded when they'd linked it to the river that ran through the valley. Behind that was the wall proper, an earthen rampart, then an upright palisade. From the base of the palisade bristling sharpened stakes pointed downward, into the space where the faces of attackers would be if they tried to scale it. Square-section towers of wooden framework reared along the growing wall, each a long javelin-cast apart. Building the rampart and towers was skilled work; the locals were just dragging up the necessary timber, and the legion's men were busy with adz and saw and hammer.

Vibulenus's mouth quirked. Nobody in the whole Roman world worked as fast and well as legionaries. Back home, work like this would be done by slaves. Not as well, and much more slowly.

Many of the legionaries were working on the fortifications; twenty-five hundred men stood to arms, in case…

A centurion named Pompilius Niger trotted up. He'd been a ranker when the legion left Campania for the east; a ranker, and a neighbor and friend of Vibulenus since childhood, since his father's farm adjoined the Vibulenii's estate.

"Found any honey yet?" Gaius Vibulenus asked, smiling slightly.

Niger shook his head. "No, they don't *have* any," he said in frustration. "The wogs, they crush a sort of thick reed and boil the juice. It's sweet, but it isn't honey, you know?" The junior centurion had been trying to find materials to make proper mead since they'd left Parthia. He was a round-faced young man… young in appearance, at least; his eyes had little youth left in them, although objectively they hadn't altered an iota since the Guild decided that their Roman *assets* were too valuable to be left to weaken with age.

"Anyways, sir," he went on, his voice growing more formal—business, then. "I wanted to ask you something. There's a *noise* over by the northern gates."

"Noise?" Vibulenus asked.

"Yeah. Sort of a *grinding* sound. Not really like troops mustering… more like *traffic*. Getting louder, though. So I sent a runner to Rusticanus—" Julius Rusticanus, the legion's senior centurion, the *primus pilus*, the "first spear" "—and I thought you'd like to know, anyway."

Vibulenus nodded; he'd been at loose ends. It was unlikely that men as experienced as Niger would miss anything obvious. He and the centurion began to walk over to the area covering the northern gate of the enemy fortress; there was a road running up to it, and it even had pavement. Not the smooth blocks Romans could have laid. It was rounded rocks from the riverbed, laid close together and pounded down into a lumpy surface that he supposed was better than the bottomless mud this alluvial soil would produce otherwise....

The tribune looked down at the rocks under his feet. The hobnails in his *caligulae* gritted and sparked on the flint-rich stones, and he remembered ...

"It's a breakout!" he snapped, picking up the pace to a trot. "Sound the alarm!"

"I had seen the reports, of course," the Commander said, in his neutral too-perfect voice, the voice of a hired teacher of rhetoric or a professional of the law-courts. *Nobody* spoke Latin like that every day. "But I admit that I am impressed."

He was fucking terrified, Vibulenus thought, carefully keeping his features blank, not shaped in the derisive grin that his mind felt. He didn't *think* that the Commander could read a Roman's facial expressions, any more than the tribune could make sense of what went on behind the Commander's faceshield. There was no sense in taking a chance, though.

"What was it that enabled you to anticipate the enemy's actions?" the Commander went on.

The sally had started with the abruptness of an axe dropping—a hinged section of wall that acted as a drawbridge had come down, and a wave of screaming spearmen had come tearing out behind a cloud of arrows and slung stones. *That* had been a diversion, though it might well have been a lethal one for a *sightseer* in a blue jumpsuit, if Roman cohorts hadn't already been falling in in front of him, and more grabbing up stacked shields and javelins along the wall, turning themselves from working parties into fighting men again with the smooth efficiency of a machine turning in a pivot.

From the way he'd reacted, the Commander had known it too. He'd screamed—the sound had come through as its natural guttural bellow, not being words—and crouched reflexively, the claws flashing out from his fingers like straight razors as his mouth gaped and showed rows of serrated teeth like a shark's.

The "ship" the Guild provided for its Roman assets could swallow waste, litter, and spare weapons through its skin. Vibulenus wondered if the Commander's blue jumpsuit could do the same with bodily wastes released in sudden panic. Not that the smell would stand out here; the windrow of bodies where the locals' berserk onrush had met the serried ranks of the legion was two deep in places. None were Romans; their wounded were being carried back by the floating turtle or limping along with the help of friends as they walked to the Medic. There weren't any who weren't... repairable. If they hadn't been warned, they'd still have *won*—Rusticanus had been taking precautions, on the theory that turning out for trouble never hurt—but the butcher's bill would have been heavier. An edge of the chill pride he felt was in his voice as he replied to the Guild's officer.

"Your Worship, it occurred to me that the wheels of the enemy chariots were iron-rimmed, and that the... the *grinding* sound reported would come from iron wheels moving over cobbles."

The infantry attack had been delivered with dreadful speed and intensity—the wogs might as well have been bloody *Gauls*, as Clodius Afer had commented—but it was only cover for the chariots behind. Those had made straight for the remaining gaps in the walls of the circumvallation. Some had gone into the ditches and pits; some had run into lilies or "stimulators." The Guild's local auxiliaries had taken a fair toll of the rest. Plenty of them had made it out into open country, though, and from the watchers' reports they were scattering in every direction. The auxiliaries tailing them were reporting that each group was making for its home tribal territory.

"Well," the Commander said. "Be that as it may. Yes, apparently your... engineering..." the cool mechanical voice had a tint of well-bred amusement "… has alarmed them to the point of demoralization. I think we may expect them to yield soon."

"Your Worship…" Vibulenus said. "No, I'm afraid that's not the purpose of this breakout."

The Commander didn't have eyebrows to arch, but somehow managed to convey the same silent doubt. The Roman tribune went on:

"Sir, I don't think they could have persuaded that many of their infantry to fight that hard just to cover a bugout by their overlords. And they're not just running, they're heading for their tribal homelands."

"So?"

"Your Worship, what they're doing… those ones in the chariots, they're the leaders, the landowners, the patricians—the men who'll be listened to. And what I think they're going to do is gather every wog in three hundred miles in every direction, every wog who can walk, and head straight here. As a relief force, to catch us and smash us against the anvil of the fortress."

He nodded to the great timber-and-earthwork fort looming above them. "While we fight the relief force, they'll sally against us, or vice versa. That's their objective."

Beside him, First Spear Rusticanus nodded and went on: "Sir… Your Worship … them wogs is pretty densely packed around here. There's going to be a *lot* of them coming at us."

The Commander went halfway into his defensive crouch again. The mechanism that turned his voice into too-perfect Latin wouldn't let squealing fright through into the tones. "Then you must storm the fortress *at once!* The Guild will not tolerate failure!"

Meaning your ass is in a sling if we lose, Vibulenus thought. Of course, the *legion's* ass was in the same unpleasant situation, and in a far more literal sense. He looked up the steep turf of the earthwork, at the great logs of the fort, at the locals prancing and yelling on the bulwarks.

"Your Worship!" he barked, in a tone that contained all he could put into it of servile enthusiasm. "Under your leadership, we *Romans* will now show you that the Guild's confidence in us is not misplaced!"

The Commander blinked, and let his rubbery pinkish lips cover the multiple-saw layers of his teeth. "You have a plan?"

"Sir, I do," Vibulenus said. He poured strength into his voice, as he might into a wavering rank. There was none of the concern he'd have felt for men in that situation, but he had to do it nonetheless—the blue-suited figure before him could order his men, *his* men, into a suicidal frontal attack. If he thought that would secure his position with the Guild, he'd do it in a moment. "My plan is—"

He went into details. The Commander raised a hand. "Surely there isn't time for all that?" he said.

Vibulenus exchanged a brief glance with the senior centurion, saw an imperceptible nod. "Your Worship, until now we've been assuming we had plenty of time. Now we'll show you what Romans can do in a *hurry*."

"Think they'll come, sir?" Clodius Afer said quietly. The ground in front of the outward-facing line of fortifications looked as if giant moles had been gnawing and chewing their way through it. There hadn't been time for neatness, and there wasn't a man in the legion or its impressed labor force that didn't have blisters even on hands calloused to the texture of rawhide. But the fortifications that fenced out the rebels' relief force were now complete, as complete as those that faced inward towards the native citadel. Light came from the towers that studded the Romans' walls, the light of something like pine burning in big metal baskets… and from three moons, two of them far too large. Vibulenus looked over his shoulder. The lights on the inner wall would show the bodies of the natives who'd tried to sally... and the skeletal forms of the civilians they'd driven out of their lines, to save their remaining food stores for the warriors. The Commander had ordered that any who approached the Roman works were to be killed.

Vibulenus grimaced slightly. He'd have forbidden taking any of them in, too; the Roman force and their auxiliaries had only about thirty days of supplies. But he'd have let them through and into the countryside, at least. None of them were fighting men. At least the stink of rotting meat wouldn't be quite as bad then.

"I think they're having trouble organizing their supply train," he said in a neutral tone, by way of replying to the other's question.

The enemy host sprawled out to the edge of sight was stunning, even in the dark. They'd built bonfires of their own, too. Painted figures in masks and bones capered and screamed around them, in religious rite or propitiation or sorcery or some unimaginable alternative. Other figures screamed and writhed in wicker cages on platforms built above the fires, sacrifices roasting slowly and then tumbling down as the supports under their containers burnt through. Between and behind the fires the enemy warriors seethed, like maggots spilled out of a putrid corpse. The firelight made the edges of their weapons a twinkling like stars on a broad lake, eddying and milling as far as sight could reach.

"Organize their supply train?" Clodius Afer asked. "Sir, them, they couldn't organize an orgy in a whorehouse. Three gets you one they're starving already, and it's less than a week since they showed up."

"So, yes, they'll come," Vibulenus said. "Soon, I think. Tonight. They can signal to the fortress, light reflected on mirrors."

The eddying and swirling was beginning to take on a

pattern, and drums were beating among the enemy. A minute later he decided that it was warriors pounding the butts of their spears or the backs of their axes against the rawhide inner surface of their shields. For a while it was discordant babble, and then more and more of them fell into a rhythm. Tens of thousands of impacts per second, not all together because the enemy force was simply too large, but it rippled across the Romans like thunder echoing in a mountain pass.

The noise was so stunning that Vibulenus missed the shouts and crashing noises coming from behind him for a moment. A runner came up, panting.

"Sir," he gasped. "Senior Centurion Rusticanus reports the enemy in the fort is making sorties—all three gates. They've got hurdles to fill the ditches, portable bridges, and grappling irons and ladders."

Vibulenus felt his mind go cold, into a distant place where everything moved like stones on a gaming-board. "My compliments to the First Spear, and carry on," he said.

"Hercules," Clodius Afer said. "Here they come."

The numbers of the barbarians charging forward towards the outer face of the Roman works were stunning. Not exactly frightening—not the way standing helpless under the Parthian arrow-storm had been frightening—but… impressive.

The light of the fire-baskets extended out as far as the initial deep trench. As the enemy reached it and bunched at the further edge, the catapults and onagers along the line of the siege works opened up. The torsion springs of the smaller devices threw six-foot javelins, or ten-pound rocks. Darts pinned three and four together at a time; rocks shattered torsos into loose bags of blood and splintered bone and exploded skulls with the finality of a hobnailed sandal coming down on a cockroach. The heavier throwing machines were usually used to batter down stone walls; here they threw man-heavy rocks into a target impossible to miss, sending the great rocks bounding and skipping through channels of pulped flesh.

The horde ignored it, dropping into the great ditch, handing down ladders, propping them against the inner wall and swarming upward.

A native trumpet shrilled, high and womanish. The towers along the Roman lines were crowded with the local auxiliaries, foot and chariot crews both. Arrows lifted in clouds, driven by the powerful horn-and-sinew bows, their three-bladed steel heads winking in the firelight. Lead bullets whistled out, hard to see in daylight and invisible now. Many of the auxiliaries were using staff slings, with the cord fastened to a yard-long hardwood handle. Lead shot from weapons like those could punch right through a heavy-infantry shield and kill the man behind it through his armor. There was plenty of ammunition.

"I think we underestimated our local allies, a bit," Vibulenus said, looking up. Another sleet of arrows crossed one of the moons—even now the size and reddish cloud-streaked color of it made his spine crawl slightly.

Clodius Afer grunted, shrugging his thick shoulders under the mail-coat. "Easy enough when they're sitting up in them towers, sir," he said.

Vibulenus nodded. The centurion had a point, but it was a bit of a parochial one. Bowmen couldn't slug it out like Roman legionary infantry, granted. But they could be extremely effective when used *properly;* Parthia, and campaigns since, ought to have taught them that.

"They needed something to keep those spearmen and axemen off them," he said musingly, wiping the palm of his right hand down the leather strips that made a skirt under his tribune's cast-bronze armor. "The way… the way those Parthians could ride away from us, shooting us up and we couldn't catch them, you see?"

Afer grunted again; by the sound of it, he *did* see. "They're killing a lot of the barbs," the squat man said. "But it ain't going to stop 'em."

Vibulenus picked up his shield. It was lighter than the oval *scutum* of the legionaries, although it didn't give the same degree of protection to the left leg—the leg you advanced in combat. It also had a loop through which he slid his forearm, and a handhold near the rim, rather than the single central handgrip of the line infantry's shield. It was Greek in form, like the rest of his gear. Romans had beaten Greeks all the way from Epiros to Syria, talking less and hitting harder—but when Roman aristocrats went to war, they wore gear that wouldn't have been out of place in Alexander's army. There was an obscure irony to that, he thought.

"You're right," he went on aloud. "They're not stopping for shit."

They did pause on the nearer edge of the ditch, massing before they charged. Arrows and sling bullets were slapping into them in a ceaseless barrage; he could see laborers bringing more ammunition up the ladders that marked the rear faces of the towers, out of the corner of his eye. The screams seemed to be as much rage as pain out there, though.

Hmmm. They're waiting for the ladders to be handed up out of the ditch… no, they brought enough to leave those. They're handing fresh ones forward, and bundles of brushwood.

Even dumb barbs learned, eventually. That was one reason his father had approved of Caesar, Crassus's political ally, and his conquest of the Gauls. You had to overrun them before they learned too *much*. Roman politics, more distant than those alien moons …

The enemy rushed forward again, the long rough-made ladders in the front ranks. Those dissolved in screaming panic as they ran full-tilt into the "stimulators," covered with hay and invisible in the night anyway. Thousands piled up before that jam, throwing the front ranks full-length into the barbed iron. More hands took up the fallen ladders, walking forward cautiously, or simply over the writhing bodies of their predecessors. The archers and slingers and the ballistae the

Romans had made switched their point of aim to the pileup behind the first ranks. Big figure-eight shields went up in an improvised roof, but most of the projectiles punched right through the light leather-and-wicker constructions.

"Still comin'," Afer said expressionlessly, the thick fingers of his right hand absently kneading the hilt of his sword.

"Not as many," Vibulenus said.

The legion's Tenth Cohort was drawn up behind them, a reaction force ready to rush to any part of the fortifications where the enemy made a lodgment. As they would, as they would...

"Holding them up like that in a killing ground, it's really softening them up for us," Vibulenus said. "Wouldn't care to meet all of them in an open field."

Afer grunted again, too proud to say aloud what they both knew; that horde would have overrun a single legion in a single shrieking rush. It could be done—the Cimbri had done it to three consular armies, before Marius caught them and smashed them. You needed a really good commander and enough numbers to keep from being flanked. Then, yes you could kill naked barbs like this all day until your arm got tired from gutting them.

As we're doing right now, Vibulenus thought coldly. The enemy were through the "stimulators" and into the lilies; those stakes were as long as a man's thigh, and they could kill rather than just cripple, but there were fewer of them. Now to the flooded ditch...

"Ready!" he said to the signalers.

The bridges that the enemy were manhandling forward were fifteen feet broad and twenty long, platforms of thick plank nailed onto beams to make a floor. They looked like staggering centipedes as they lurched forward towards the flooded ditch, supported on the hands and shoulders of scores of men... or at least of creatures very much like men. Very much, when you'd had a *really* broad experience of the possible alternatives. Squads with shields surrounded them on all sides, taking most of the arrows directed at the assault squads carrying the bridges; more crowded forward to take their places as they fell.

"Ready," Vibulenus said again, his eyes wide as memories passed somewhere deep in his mind, far below the level of the consciousness that moved and spoke.

On a distant... *planet* was the word the Guild employees used, but that made no sense; how could you walk on a "wandering star"? In a distant land, the legion had fought little furry wogs who had a number of valuable tricks. One of them was a compound of rock-oil, saltpeter, naphtha, pine-pitch, and quicklime. Not all the ingredients had been easy to find here, but something close enough could be cobbled together; vegetable oil would do nearly as well as the black stuff from the ground—

The bridges rose, paused as hands and poles thrust at them from behind—they looked as bristly as a wild hog's skin, with the arrows that thumped into them—and then toppled forward to fall across the water-filled ditch. Even before the massive timber weights stopped flexing and jumping, the first rank of shield-bearing warriors was charging across them, screaming.

"Flame!" the Roman tribune shouted.

The onagers thumped. They had a single thick cable of twisted sinew across the front of their frames, and a vertical throwing-arm fastened in the middle of the cable. Winches hauled it back, a missile was put into the cup at the end of the arm, and the release was slipped. The throwing arm slashed forward until it hit a massive braced and padded bar, supported on timber triangles pegged and mortised into the ground frame of the weapon. This time the cups had been loaded with large clay jugs, wrapped in oil-soaked cloth. Torches were touched to the wrapping, and it took fire with an angry crackling roar.

"Shoot!"

The onagers released, their rear edges kicking up as the throwing arms halted—that gave them their military nickname, "wild donkey." Like meteors, the jugs arched across the night. They wobbled, because the fluid inside them shifted as they flew. The onagers were inaccurate at the best of times, and they hadn't been able to sight them carefully, because there was no telling where the enemy would try to cross the ditch.

They still landed close enough, at least the ones Vibulenus could see. Flame splashed across the massed crowds waiting their turn to storm across the bridge nearest his position. Warriors leapt shrieking into the flooded ditch, but that didn't save them, because the quicklime only burned the fiercer in contact with water. It also burned *on* the water, floating with a redder, milder flame than he remembered from the distant land that had given him the idea. But it was fatal enough. The water was thick with heads, where enemy troops were swimming the ditch with the bundled sticks—fascines—they'd brought to fill the dry ditch beyond. Many of them ducked under the surface as they saw the waves of fire billowing towards them, but the only way for a naked man to keep his body down was to fill his lungs....

"Eat *this*," a legionary behind Gaius Vibulenus screamed as he cast his javelin, pivoting on his left foot and bringing his *scutum* around to balance the throw.

The Tenth Cohort were charging in line abreast down the ramparts, perpendicular to the parapet on their right hands. Ahead of them was the enemy bridgehead, ladders rearing over the sharpened stakes, feather-skulled figures howling and shaking their weapons at the oncoming Romans. The howls turned to screams as dozens of the heavy *pila* slashed down out of the night.

"*Roma!*" Vibulenus shouted as he ducked under the thrust of a long spear.

His round shield hooked aside a tower-tall one shaped like a figure eight, and his sword of Spanish steel punched upward under a rib cage. There was a crisp popping feeling as things parted under the sharp point and edge. Behind him Clodius Afer punched a native in the face with the boss of his shield, slid nine inches of sword in under a raised arm. The scrimmage was over in seconds; Vibulenus's sword was still making small stabbing motions in the air as he pivoted and looked for another opponent. The forward ranks of the Tenth Cohort spread out to cover the section of wall the enemy had swarmed; cutting the leather cords attached to the grappling hooks sunk in the rampart, pushing ladders over, throwing *pila* down into the crowded mass in the ditch below. They followed that with showers of one-pound stones still piled ready for use, and iron-shod stakes the auxiliaries' smiths had run up.

"Determined bunch," Vibulenus wheezed, letting his shield-arm drop. His bronze corselet squeezed at his ribs, and his mouth was dry and gummy. Somewhere he'd picked up a shallow slash over his left knee that he hadn't noticed until now, and it hurt like Hades himself was retracing it with a red-hot knife.

"They're running!" someone shouted.

Vibulenus pushed himself to the rampart. They were—and the fire from the towers was taking them in the back, now.

"Well, that's that," he said dully. *Now we wait a day or two until the ones in the fort surrender, and then we get back on the ship, and in a few weeks we all go to sleep and wake up for another fucking campaign.*

Clodius Afer held out a helmet full of water. "Here, sir," he said, with a quirking smile.

"Thanks," Vibulenus said. *Hercules, how many campaigns ago was it that he gave me that drink, the first time, those eight-foot-tall bastards with the carts?*

They weren't *quite* in the same position as that poor bastard in the old story, the one condemned to roll a boulder up a slope for all eternity and have it slip right down again. He'd been alone. If you were going to be in hell, at least it helped to have some good friends along.

He took the helmet and drank, then upended it over his own head and almost groaned at the feeling of cold water trickling down under his armor into the sweat-sodden tunic and overheated flesh.

"Heads up," Afer said tonelessly.

The Commander was coming, walking along with his gi ant iron-armored toad-guards. It was a little cramped here for their huge hyena-mounts; of course, this was also a bit closer to the sharp end than commanders usually came. Tired Romans snapped erect and into their ranks, stepping back for the bubble of space that commanders always required... and the spiked maces of their guards enforced.

The blue-suited figure walked forward, over and among the piled enemy dead. "Congratulations, Gaius Vibulenus Caper," the too-perfect voice said. "Once again, you brave warriors have prevailed over great odds."

The triangular face of the Commander swung forward to peer over the parapet. "*Very* great odds. In fact—"

Clodius Afer was as rigid beside the tribune as a statue cast from bronze. Vibulenus knew why, because his mind was as rigid with the need to control a sudden vision of two swords meeting together in the middle of the inhuman body, scissoring back to leave the torso split nearly in half, whatever the Commander used for guts spilling out on the enemy dead and the soaked dirt.... No. Better to go for the skull; two steps forward and he could put the edge right through the thing's temple, right to the central ridge of the blade—

Which neither of them was going to do. Because the guards might well smash them down before their swords were well drawn; the toad-things were *fast*, not just inhumanly strong. Because unless they managed to get the brain or spine, the

Commander would be revived just as mostly dead legionaries were. Because although trading their own lives for that of the Commander might be, *would* be perfectly acceptable, the legion would still be there, exposed to the Guild's vengeance and without centurion and tribune.

But it was so *tempting*.

The dead were piled several layers deep against the inner face of the parapet—deeper in the angle than the natural slipperiness of blood-lubricated dead flesh would allow. Not all of that flesh was dead. Vibulenus had let himself relax from the knife-edge concentration of combat, let his muscles feel the trembling exhaustion and stiffen with fatigue poisons. His sword was still rasping from its sheath when the three natives lunged erect, daggers glittering in their hands as they threw themselves towards the Commander.

Clodius Afer's shield slammed one sideways, and the centurion's sword gutted the native while he fought for balance.

Cursing silently, Vibulenus threw himself forward, forcing speed out of abused muscles. He didn't think the Guild would be much concerned with abstract rights and wrongs if the Commander was knifed in the presence of the *assets* who were supposed to absorb the hurt.

Something warm and salty struck him in the face. His vision blurred, but not so much that he couldn't see the follow-through of the Commander's ape-long arm and the track the four razor claws had cut through the native daggerman's neck. The Commander was smiling—Vibulenus saw the expression and hoped it wasn't really a smile—as he dug the claws of both hands under the last assassin's ribs and dragged him forward. Then, with an almost casual motion, he bit off the top of the local's skull.

"Incompatible proteins," he said, after he spat the mouthful out and tossed aside the corpse. "Where was I? Ah, yes. The natives hostile to the interests of the Guild and galactic progress were probably aware that the Federation bans advanced weapons on planets such as this." He beamed coldly at the Romans. Shreds of matter and feathery not-hair dangled between the multiple rows of teeth. "But as always, they underestimated the organizational skills of the finest trading Guild in the galaxy!"

The Commander turned and swept away, followed by his armored guards. Vibulenus smiled wryly as he sheathed his sword. "Good thing we can both resist temptation, isn't it?" he said.

"Sir, yessir," Clodius Afer said, cleaning his weapon and doing likewise. He turned his head to look out over the piled dead that carpeted the ground, to the edge of sight in the dull gray light of predawn.

"Looks like 'e said. They underestimated the fuckin' opposition, all right," he said.

Gaius Vibulenus Caper, military tribune, member of the Equestrian Order and citizen of Rome, put his hand on his fellow-Roman's shoulder. "They underestimated *us*, by the gods of my hearth," he said.

They both looked after the Commander, to where the blue-suited figure had vanished behind the smaller turtles that brought water to the legionaries, and the greater one that picked up the repairable dead. Far and faint came wailing from the fortress on the hill, as the natives saw their hope receding with the fleeing barbarians.

"And someday—" Afer went on.

Vibulenus smiled, an expression no less sharkish than the Commander's serrated rows of teeth. *Someday, someone in a blue bodysuit is going to underestimate us.*

Everyone made mistakes. But *that* was going to be the last mistake some Commander of the Guild's Roman assets ever made.

COPS AND ROBBERS

"Huon II Rex et Imperator." Marylou Stavros turned the quarter-ounce gold coin over in long brown fingers and read the other side. "Imp. Mint Vic. of N. America." Whatever the hell *that* meant.

The Greyhound terminal had the usual early-morning bustle; students, enormous Chicano families with string-tied bundles, and a few of the inevitable Bay Area crazies. Marylou felt almost conspicuous in her three-piece slacksuit, but that was Bureau policy.

She grinned, and flipped the coin. Policy would have put this in a plastic baggy, she thought. It's half the evidence we have, that and the locker number.

It had been her idea to scrape the pink-and-gray goo off Carstairs' Apple personal and read the number on the flickering screen. Not as good as getting to him before someone put a soft-nosed slug into the back of his skull, but if anything was going to break this microchip smuggling ring, this was it. And that would look very good, indeed, on her record. Which would annoy her supervisor. She strongly suspected that, under his high-tech exterior, he was unhappy with the changes since Hoover's day, when the only blacks in the Bureau were glorified janitors and women were barely tolerated as stenos.

She sighed happily and settled into the molded plastic seat across from locker number 73625; there was backup available right outside, but she intended to make this bust herself and doctrine be damned. Counterespionage work was even more boring than her old beat on the interstate hot-car file, and she decided that she had earned a little self-indulgence.

It was an hour later when the suspect walked casually up to the locker. Female, Caucasian, five-eight, hundred and twenty pounds, green eyes, blonde ponytail; windbreaker, Adidas, jeans. Not unusual for the San Francisco area, and neither was the graceful springy movement that suggested dance training. Marylou estimated her age at about thirty.

She allowed the suspect to open and clean out the locker; the Bureau had been in before her, and the attaché case held nothing but junk. It was impossible to tell that without laboratory equipment, of course.

Marylou flipped open the leather foldout. "F.B.I.," she said quietly. "Come with me, please."

The other woman smiled, and suddenly the agent felt less happy about what had seemed a routine bust. "I'm afraid that won't be possible," the blonde woman said, in a British accent. "Frightfully sorry."

Marylou was searching for the .32 at the small of her back when the world faded out.

Waking was slow and undramatic. The room was bare concrete, windowless, lit by a single dangling bulb; it held one bed, a washstand, and a chair.

She felt carefully at her head. No dizziness, nausea, or other signs of concussion, and no odd taste in her mouth either, which most drugs would have left. Her clothes were draped over the chair, complete except for the empty holster.

Marylou dressed and sat on the bed, lost in thought. It was difficult to imagine how she had been brought out of a guarded building, with agents staked out at all the exits. Pointless to think about it, she decided: She was here. That might be anywhere from Oakland to the Lubianka in Moscow; that she was alive at all meant that her captors wanted something from her, probably information. It was not a comforting thought; she knew too much about modern interrogation methods, especially the ones the opposition used.

The iron door opened with a clang. Marylou forced herself to rise slowly, face expressionless. Two guards came in, a man and woman, both in baggy gray-green uniforms with archaic-looking high collars. The guns were strange, too: horizontal-drum machine pistols with wooden stocks—large-caliber weapons from the size of the muzzles. The faces behind were blankly impersonal.

"Up," the man said. "You walk ahead, not slow and not fast. Move." The voice had a neutral American accent, which was curious.

Marylou moved to the door, which opened onto a bare corridor. Similar metal portals with peepholes were spaced along it, the unmistakable layout of a maximum-security prison.

"Where are we?" she said.

Without a word, one of the guards hit her under the short ribs with the butt of her submachine-gun—not hard enough to injure, but it winded her. Then both waited with bored patience.

Marylou headed up the corridor. "I can take the hint," she wheezed. The walls were damp, and despite the sough of ventilators, the air smelled musty. She guessed that the prison was underground; the length of the trip when they reached the elevator and started up confirmed it.

The elevator itself was strange, plushly carpeted in red and walled with gilt-frame mirrors; the controls were manual rather than automatic, and she suspected that it rose more slowly than the ones to which she was accustomed. The long journey gave her a moment for regaining self-command, and the sight of her own familiar toffee-colored face was reassuring. Silent, she raised the hawked nose she had inherited from her Greek sponge-diver father and gathered herself.

Girl, she told herself, you are in *deep* shit.

The upper level was a shock. The elevator gave directly onto an office that must have covered most of the floor. One wall was floor-to-ceiling tinted glass; the others were covered with delicate pastel murals of reeds and waterfowl. There were loungers draped in polar-bear fur, a sleek mahogany bar, a Hitachi stereo set, marble tiles on the floor. The desk was huge, and included a modern-looking data terminal. Behind it lounged the woman she had seen in the Greyhound terminal, studying a file folder and sipping at a cup. To one side, an Oriental girl in lavishly embroidered silk pyjamas knelt beside a wheeled breakfast tray.

"*Good* morning," the woman behind the desk said cheerfully in the same dulcet, aristocratic accent. "Now, agent ah, Stavros, I imagine you think you are in the hands of, how would you put it, K.G.B. agents?"

"Or East German," Marylou replied. Whatever the purpose of this charade, she was not playing along with it.

"Permit self-introduction. My name is Braithwaite, Colonel Valentina Braithwaite, I.D.S." She paused for a moment. "As to the situation, let your own eyes convince." The colonel's voice shifted to a command snap. "Hayes, Wherstein, take her over to the window."

Dazed, Marylou walked to the glass. It took a full minute for what she was seeing to register. They were overlooking San Francisco, on top of Telegraph Hill and twenty stories up. The geography was unmistakable, but the city was... different. The great Bay bridges simply were not there; the street plan was completely alien, planned around the hills instead of against them. The buildings were lower, none taller than the one in which she stood, and mostly in an ornate neoclassical style; the built-up area was far less than in her own city. Out over the harbor floated a... blimp? Then it passed over a ship, and the portholes snapped it into perspective; a dirigible, and huge, a thousand feet long at least.

For the first and only time in her life, Marylou came near to fainting. Her stomach heaved, and the air turned black before her eyes. She was vaguely aware of strong hands roughly supporting her into a chair, and a cold wet towel lightly slapping her cheeks. Awareness returned.

The colonel was standing before her. Distractedly, Marylou noted that her uniform was of some fine tweedlike cloth.

"So, we *are* part of a secret service," she was saying. "The Imperial Directorate of Security, loyal servants of His Royal and Imperial Majesty, Huon II, King-Emperor of Greater Britain." She snapped her fingers. "Mei-ling, bring the tray." Turning to Marylou, she continued. "Now, perhaps you'd like an explanation."

"…ministry of Pitt the Elder, in the 1760s," she concluded. "Now, in your history he fell from power at the end of the Seven Years' War, just when things were going well. Frightening to think how much can depend on one man, isn't it? And his successors bungled everything—the Peace and the Colonial troubles both.

"Here… and now…" she waved a hand. "Things went *so* much more smoothly. It's the *Ten* Years' War, to us: Pitt drove Britain on to complete victory instead of a partial one. We took all the French possessions, and the Spanish and Dutch as well: South America, Mexico, the Cape, Ceylon, Indonesia—the lot. The American colonies never became seriously disaffected, after that.

"Since then, we've gone from strength to strength, don't you know. Enough independent revenue made the Crown free of Parliament, so even poor crack-brained Georgie III was able to bring off the coup and make the monarchy absolute again." She smiled wolfishly. "One of the finer things about being in the secret police is that you can say that sort of thing and not be shot for lèse majesté. Our only real setback was the Great War, with the Russians, two generations ago; both empires fought themselves into exhaustion. Although I shouldn't complain, it was the manpower shortages that changed the ridiculous attitudes toward women that were so common then.

"Then, about a decade ago, the boffins came up with the Translevel Gate." She shrugged expressively. "The physics are beyond me. I took Classics at Oxford. Something about the gravitational warp effects of degenerate matter." She smiled, an oddly charming expression, lopsided and faintly raffish. "One of the few forms of degeneracy that doesn't interest me. And since then, we've been exploring, secretly, trading here and there for things like gold and diamonds, high value in relation to energy transport-costs. Just lately, microelectronics from your world and some 'nearby' ones, better than anything we can make. That was where our contact man made his mistake, paying Carstairs in coin of the realm instead of ingots, as if your people were preindustrial savages. I was sent along to, ah, shall we say, see to Carstairs."

"Why didn't you 'see to' me as well?" Marylou asked bluntly. The situation had sunk in, but she sensed it was only at an intellectual level. Her emotions were unconvinced; they felt numb.

The colonel paused to light a cigarette, and offered the slim platinum case to Marylou. "Tobacco on the right, Sonoma cannabis on the left. No?" She lit her own.

"We thought you might be useful to us. Besides, it would have been just a trifle awkward, blowing your head off right there in front of your confreres, wouldn't it? Much better to have you escort me out." At Marylou's expressions she laughed merrily. "Narcohypnosis, my dear, the same technique we used to interrogate you. You've been here nearly forty-eight hours, you know."

"And what if I decline to be 'useful'?" Marylou snarled, enraged beyond caution.

The colonel sighed, and turned to the guards. "Hayes, Wherstein, tickle her a little. Mei-ling, more tea."

Before Marylou could move, stiffened fingers drove into the nerve cluster beside her neck. A hand gripped her by the shoulder and jerked her erect; a palm-edge struck her over the kidney. Paralyzed, her lungs could only make a shivering grunt.

The guards were artists, not sadists: they worked with the impersonal detachment of surgeons demonstrating an anatomical dummy, working to inflict the maximum in pain and emotional degradation without tearing flesh or rupturing organs. And all through the "tickling," she was conscious of the colonel leafing through a file, sipping at her tea, and glancing up from time to time in cool appraisal.

At the end, the guards dropped her into the chair and wiped the blood and sputum off her face. The colonel rose and walked closer, perching one hip on the desk. She spread her hands.

"I am," she purred, "a *reasonable* woman. I wouldn't ask you to betray your country; only to, shall we say, look the other way when activities of ours occur, and furnish us with information. It's harmless. We have enough elsewhere, without tangling with a civilization which is, to be frank, technologically superior in most respects."

Marylou raised eyes blank with hate. "Why don't you use your fucking drugs?" she said hoarsely.

Valentina shrugged. "Oh, well enough for field-hands, but rather obvious if done thoroughly." She jerked a thumb at the Oriental who was placidly brewing tea. "Who's going to mistake that walking lump of meat for a human being? All conditioned reflexes. To be sure…"

She drew the heavy automatic at her waist and handed it to Marylou. The walnut butt weighed in her hand; she pointed it at the colonel and pulled the trigger, bitterly expecting the click of a hammer on an empty cylinder—and found that her finger would not pull. It was eerie, not a dramatic sensation; simply a finger resting limply on the metal when all her will wanted it to close. She swung the weapon away from her captor and it bucked and roared in her hand.

"Careful!" Valentina snapped. "That vase is Ming!" She took back the weapon. "Now, what do you say?"

"Screw you," Marylou replied, conscious of the sweat trickling down her spine. It might be wiser to play along, but… no.

Valentina raised an eyebrow. "What a delightful suggestion; I'm sure it could be arranged. Well, we'll just have to try more persuasion. If you prove too, too stubborn you could always join that officer of ours who gave the coins to Carstairs." The baring of teeth that followed was not a smile. "He's now engaged in overseeing coolies in the New Guinea copper mines; they can always use new hands."

She waved a hand. "Take her away. Oh, and tell the alienist we'll be needing him, and the pharmacopia. And prepare the mechanicals, as well."

It was about a week later when they drove up into what Marylou had known as the Santa Clara Valley. She was not sure of the date or very much else. The car was quiet but slow, steam-powered, and she stared quietly out at a landscape of vineyards and orchards interspersed with manor houses and workers' quarters. The mansion they came to was much like the others, except for the guards and heavy power lines.

Inside, she had expected something sleek and NASA-futuristic. Instead, there were banks of ornate brass meters, scaffolds, blue-coated attendants dragging wheeled carts full of cabbage-sized vacuum tubes, power lines snaking over flagstones. All it needs, she thought, is Bela Lugosi. Or Gene Wilder. The thought was a first break of light through the gray clouds that seemed to have settled on her mind.

Of course, there *was* some modern equipment; she

recognized the company names: Sony, I.B.M., Texas Instruments …

The technician showed Marylou and the colonel to a chalked circle on the floor. Alertness returning, Marylou felt a strange professional note of admiration for the faultless cover of the other woman's dress-for-success business outfit, slightly worn attaché case, and copy of the *Financial Times*.

The colonel handed her the .32, the last part of her original clothing. The technician noted something on a clipboard.

"Right, then, ma'am," he said. "You know about the effect of displacement in transit? Cheerio, then, Colonel."

A crackling scent of ozone filled the air. Marylou stood looking at the weapon in her hand.

"I hope you're not considering shooting me with that," Valentina said with amusement.

"Oh, no," Marylou said calmly. "But you forgot one thing."

"Whatever could it be?"

"That guns can shoot something else besides people," Marylou answered.

Even as she spoke, the Imperial agent was turning, lashing out with a bladed palm. But Marylou had already raised the pistol and begun firing into the towering banks of equipment. A giant hand seized them, and the world rippled and twisted apart.

Not having been moving during transition, Marylou awoke first. She used the time well; the colonel awoke with her hands cuffed behind her.

"You stupid blackamoor bitch!" she said. "You imbe-cilic—"

Marylou interrupted her with a hearty kick to the stomach. "You should have conditioned me against hitting you, too," she said.

"That would have been too limiting, wouldn't it?" she

replied sardonically.

Marylou kicked her again, then restrained herself with an effort. Above them, above the canopy of the prune orchard they had found themselves awakened in, a jet went by high overhead.

"Nearer my line than yours," Marylou said. The colonel opened her mouth, hesitated, decided to concentrate on moving, which is not easy over uneven ground with hands linked behind the back.

"I'm sure the authorities will be interested in your story," she continued, prodding the other ahead of her toward the verge of the orchard.

They walked for half an hour before they came to the building. It was a schoolhouse, reassuringly ordinary in whitewashed cinderblock. There were children playing noisily in the yard, and a group surrounding a cluster of teachers at the flagpole. For a moment, Marylou closed her eyes in pure relief.

And then she heard Colonel Valentina laughing, vengeful and triumphant, and opened her eyes to see the tall blonde woman staggering against a tree and shouting with mirth, as the blue and white and crimson flag of the Confederate States fluttered gaily in the bright California sun.

ROACHSTOMPERS

ABILENE, TEXAS
October 1, 1998
POST #72, FEDERAL IMMIGRATION CONTROL

"*Scramble! Scramble!*"

"Oh, shit," the captain of the reaction company said with deep disgust. It was the first time Laura Hunter had gotten past level 17 on this game. "Save and logoff."

She snatched the helmet from the monitor and stamped to settle her boots, wheeled to her feet, and walked out of the one-time Phys-Ed teacher's office. One hand adjusted the helmet, flipping up the nightsight visor and plugging the commlink into the jack on her back-and-breast; the other snatched the H&K assault rifle from the improvised rack beside the door. Words murmured into her ears, telling the usual tale of disaster.

"All right," the senior sergeant bellowed into the echoing darkness of the disused auditorium they were using as a barracks. The amplified voice seemed to strike her like a club of air as she crossed the threshold. "Drop your cocks 'n grab your socks!"

It was traditional, but she still winced; inappropriate too, this was officially a police unit and thoroughly coed. "As you were, Kowalski," she said. The Rangers were tumbling out of their cots, scrambling cursing into uniforms and body-armor, checking their personal weapons. None of that Regular Army empty-rifle crap here. *Her* troopies were rolling out of their

63

blankets ready to rock and roll, and *fuck* safety; the occasional accident was cheap compared to getting caught half-hard when the cucuroaches came over the wire.

Fleetingly, she was aware of how the boards creaked beneath their feet, still taped with the outlines of vanished basketball games. The room smelled of ancient adolescent sweat overlaid with the heavier gun-oil and body odors of soldiers in the field. *No more dances and proms here,* she thought with a brief sadness. Then data-central began coming through her earphones. She cleared her throat:

"Listen up, people. A and B companies scramble for major illegal intro in the Valley; Heavy Support to follow and interdict. Officers to me. The rest of you on your birds; briefing in flight. Move it!"

The six lieutenants and the senior NCOs gathered round the display table under the basketball hoop. They were short two, B Company was missing its CO... no time for that.

"Jennings," she said. A slim good-looking black from Detroit, field-promoted, looked at her coolly; her cop's instinct said *danger.* "You're top hat for B while Sinclair's down. Here's the gridref and the grief from Intelligence; total illigs in the 20,000 range, seventy klicks from Presidio.

The schematic blinked with symbols, broad arrows thrusting across the sensor-fences and minefields along the Rio Grande. Light sparkled around strongpoints, energy-release monitored by the surveillance platforms circling at 200,000 feet. Not serious, just enough to keep the weekend-warrior Guard garrisons pinned down. The illigs were trying to make it through the cordon into the wild Big Bend country. The fighters to join the guerrilla bands, the others to scatter and find enough to feed their children, even if it meant selling themselves as indentured quasi-slaves to the plains 'nesters.

"Shitfire," Jennings murmured. "Ma'am. Who is it this time?"

"Santierist Sonoran Liberation Army," she said. "The

combatants, at least. We'll do a standard stomp-and-envelopment. Here's the landing-zone distribution. Fire-prep from the platforms, and this time be *careful*, McMurty. There are two thousand with small arms, mortars, automatic weapons, light AA, possible wire-guided antitank and ground-to-air heat-seekers."

"And their little dogs too," McMurty muttered, pushing limp blonde hair back from her sleep-crusted eyes. "Presidio's in Post 72's territory, what're they—" She looked over the captain's shoulder. "—sorry, sir."

Laura Hunter saluted smartly along with the rest; Major Forrest was ex-Marine and Annapolis. Not too happy about mandatory transfer to the paramilitary branch, still less happy about the mixed bag of National Guard and retread police officers that made up his subordinates.

"At ease, Captain, gentlemen. Ladies." Square pug face, traces of the Kentucky hills under the Academy diction, pale blue eyes. "And Post 72 is containing a major outbreak in El Paso. For which C and D companies are to stand by as reserve reinforcement."

"What about the RACs? Sir," Jennings added. Forrest nodded, letting the "Regular Army Clowns" pass: the black was more his type of soldier, and the corps had always shared that opinion anyway.

"This is classified," he said. "The 82nd is being pulled out of Dallas-Fort Worth."

"Where?" Hunter asked. Her hand stroked the long scar that put a kink in her nose and continued across one cheek. *That* was a souvenir of the days when she had been driving a patrol car in D.C.

No more 82nd... It was not that the twin cities were that bad; their own Guard units could probably keep the lid on... but the airborne division was the ultimate reserve for the whole Border as far west as Nogales.

The major made a considered pause. "They're staging

through Sicily, for starters." Which could mean only one thing; the Rapid Deployment Force was heading for the Gulf. Hunter felt a sudden hot weakness down near the pit of her stomach, different and worse than the usual pre-combat tension.

Somebody whistled. "The Russian thing?" Even on the Border they had had time to watch the satellite pictures of the Caliphist uprisings in Soviet Asia; they had been as bloody as anything in the Valley, and the retaliatory invasion worse.

"COMSOUTH has authorized… President Barusci has issued an ultimatum demanding withdrawal of the Soviet forces from northern Iran and a UN investigation into charges of genocide."

"Sweet Jesus," Jennings said. Hunter glanced over at him sharply; it sounded more like a prayer than profanity.

"Wait a minute, sir," Hunter said. "Look… that means the RDF divisions are moving out, right?" All three of them, and that was most of the strategic reserve in the continental U.S. "Mobilization"? He nodded. "But the army reserve and the first-line Guard units are going straight to Europe? With respect, sir, the cucuroache—the people to the south aren't fools and they have satellite links too. Who the *hell* is supposed to hold the Border?"

The commander's grin showed the skull beneath his face. "We are, Captain Hunter. We are."

The noise in the courtyard was already enough to make the audio pickups cut in, shouts and pounding feet and scores of PFH airjets powering up. Pole-mounted glare-lights banished the early-morning stars, cast black shadows around the bulky figures of the troopers in their olive-and-sand camouflage. The air smelt of scorched metal and dust. Hunter paused in the side-door of the Kestrel assault-transport, looking back over the other vehicles. All the latest, nothing too good for the Rangers—and they were small enough to re-equip totally on the first PFH-powered models out of the factories.

Mostly Kestrels, flattened ovals of Kevlar -composite and re-active-armor panel, with stub wings for the rocket pods and chin-turrets mounting chain guns. Bigger boxy transports for the follow-on squads; little one-trooper eggs for the Shrike airscouts; the bristling saucer-shapes of the heavy weapons platforms.

She swung up into the troop compartment of her Kestrel, giving a glance of automatic hatred to the black rectangles of the PFH units on either side of the ceiling. "Pons, Fleischmann, and Hagelstein," she muttered. "Our modern trinity." The bulkhead was a familiar pressure through the thick flexibility of her armor. "Status, transport."

"All green and go," the voice in her earphones said. "Units up, all within tolerances, cores fully saturated."

The headquarters squad were all in place. "Let's do it, then," she said. "Kestrel-1, lift."

The side ramps slid up with hydraulic smoothness, and the noise vanished with a soughing ching-*chunk*. Those were *thick* doors; aircraft did not need to be lightly built, not with fusion-powered boost. Light vanished as well, leaving only the dim glow of the riding lamps. There was a muted rising wail as air was drawn in through the intakes, rammed through the heaters and down through the swiveljets beneath the Rangers' feet. There were fifteen troopers back-to-back on the padded crash-bench in the Kestrel's troop-compartment. One of them reached up wonderingly to touch a power unit. It was a new-bie, Finali, the company commlink hacker. Clerk on the TOE, but carrying a rifle like the rest of them; the data-crunching was handled by the armored box on his back.

Hunter leaned forward, her thin olive-brown face framed by the helmet and the bill brow of the flipped-up visor. "*Don't—touch—that*," she said coldly as his fingers brushed the housing of the fusion unit.

"Yes, ma'am." Finali was nearly as naive as his freckle-faced teenage looks, but he had been with A Company long enough to listen to a few stories about the captain. "Ahh, ma'am, is it safe?"

"Well, son, they *say* it's safe." The boy was obviously sweating the trip to his first hot LZ, and needed distraction.

The transport sprang skyward on six columns of super-heated air, and the soldiers within braced themselves against the thrust, then shifted as the big vents at the rear opened. The Kestrel accelerated smoothly toward its Mach 1.5 cruising speed, no need for high-stress maneuvers. Hunter lit a cigarette, safe enough on aircraft with no volatiles aboard.

"And it probably is safe. Of course, it's one of the doped-titanium anode models, you know? Saves on palladium. They kick out more neutrons than I'm comfortable with, though. Hell, we're probably not going to live long enough to breed mutants, anyway."

She blew smoke at the PFH units, and a few of the troopers laughed sourly.

"Captain?" It was Finali again. "Ah, can I ask a question?"

"Ask away," she said. *I need distraction too.* The tac-update was not enough, no unexpected developments... and fiddling with deployments on the way in was a good way to screw it up.

"I know... well, the depression and Mexico and everything is because of the PFH, but... I mean, I didn't even *see* one of them until I enlisted. It's going to be *years* before people have them for cars and home heating. How can it... how can it mess things up so bad *now?*"

Kowalski laughed contemptuously, the Texas twang strong in his voice. "Peckerwood, how much yew goin' to pay for a horse ever'one knows is fixin' to die next month?"

Finali flushed, and Hunter gave him a wry smile and a slap on the shoulder. "Don't feel too bad, trooper; there were economists with twenty degrees who didn't do much better." She took another drag on the cigarette, and reminded herself to go in for another cancer antiviral. *If we make it. Shut up about that.*

"Sure, there aren't many PFHs around, but we know they're going to be common as dirt; the Taiwanese are starting to ship out 10-megawatt units like they did VCRs, in the old days. Shit, even the Mindanao pirates've managed to get hold of some. See, they're so simple… not much more difficult to make than a diesel engine, once Hagelstein figured out the theory. And you can do anything with them; heavy water in, heat or electricity or laser beams out. Build them any scale, right down to camp-stove size.

"Too fucking good, my lad. So all those people who've been sitting on pools of oil knew they'd be worthless in ten, fifteen years. So they pumped every barrel they could, to sell while it was still worth something. Which made it practically worthless right away, and they went bust. Likewise all the people with tankers, refineries, coal mines… all the people who *made* things for anybody in those businesses, or who sold things to the people, or who lent them money, or…"

She shrugged. The Texan with the improbable name laughed again. "Me'n my pappy were roustabouts from way back. But who needs a driller now?"

"Could be worse," the gunner in the forward compartment cut in. "You could be a cucuroach."

That was for certain-sure. Hunter flipped her visor down, and the compartment brightened to green-tinted clarity. Mexico had been desperate *before* the discoveries, when petroleum was still worth something; when oil dropped to fifty cents a barrel, two hundred billion dollars in debts had become wastepaper. And depression north of the Border meant collapse for the export industries that depended on those markets, no more tourists… breadlines in the U.S., raw starvation to the south. Anarchy, warlords, eighty million pairs of eyes turned north at the Colossus whose scientists had shattered their country like a man kicking in an egg carton.

Fuck it, she thought. *Uncle Sugar lets the chips fall where they*

*lie and gives us a munificent 20% bonus on the minimum wage
for sweeping the consequences back into the slaughterhouse.*

The northern cities were recovering, all but the lumpen-
proletariat of the cores; controlled fusion had leapfrogged the
technoaristocracy two generations in half a decade. Damn
few of the sleek middle classes *here*, down where the doody
plopped into the pot. Blue-collar kids, farm boys, blacks; not
many Chicanos either. D.C. had just enough sense not to send
them to shoot their cousins and the ACLU could scream any
way they wanted; the taxpayers had seen the Anglo bodies
dangling from the lampposts of Brownsville, seen it in their
very own living rooms…

*Without us, the cucuroaches would be all over their shiny
PFH-powered suburbs like a brown tide,* she thought, not for
the first time. Strange how she had come to identify so totally
with the troops.

"But as long as these stay scarce, we've got an edge," she
said, jerking the faceless curve of her helmet toward the PFH.
"Chivalric."

"Chivalric?" Finali frowned.

"Sure, son. Like a knight's armor and his castle; with that, we
protect the few against the many." She pressed a finger against
her temple. "Pilot, we are coming up on Austin?"

"Thirty seconds, Captain."

"Take her down to the dirt, cut speed to point five Mach and
evasive. Everybody sync." The cucuroach illigs could probably
patch into the commercial satellite network—might have
hackers good enough to tap the PFH-powered robot platforms
hovering in the stratosphere. Knowing the Rangers were coming and being able to do anything about it were two separate
things, though. As long as they were careful to avoid giving
the war-surplus Stingers and Blowpipes a handy target.

The transport swooped and fell, a sickening express-eleva-
tor feeling. Hunter brought her H&K up across her lap and
checked it again, a nervous tick. It too was the very latest,

Reunited German issue; the Regulars were still making do with M16s. Caseless ammunition and a 50-round cassette, the rifle just a featureless plastic box with a pistol-grip below and optical sight above. They were talking about PFH-powered personal weapons, lasers and slugthrowers. Not yet, thank God…

"Thirty minutes ETA to the LZ," the pilot announced. Hunter keyed the command circuit.

"Rangers, listen up. Remember what we're here for; take out their command-and-control right at the beginning. That's why we're dropping on their HQs. Without that and their heavy weapons they're just a mob; the support people can sweep them back. We're *not* here to fight them on even terms; this is a roach stomp, not a battle." A final, distasteful chore. Her voice went dry:

"And under the terms of the Emergency Regulations Act of 1995, I must remind you this is a police action. All hostiles are to be given warning and opportunity to surrender unless a clear and present danger exists."

"And I'm King Charles V of bloody England," someone muttered.

"Yeah, tell us another fairy story."

"Silence on the air!" Top sergeant's voice.

Her mind sketched in the cities below, ghostly and silent in the night, empty save for the National Guard patrols and the lurking predators and the ever-present rats. Paper rustling down deserted streets, past shattered Arby's and Chicken Delights… out past the fortress suburbs, out to the refugee camps where the guards kicked the rations through the wire for the illig detainees to scramble for.

There would be no prisoners.

Very softly, someone asked: "Tell us about the island, Cap?"

What am I, the CO or a den mother? she thought. Then, *What the hell, this isn't an Army unit.* Which was lucky for her; the

American military still kept women out of front-line service, at least in theory. The Rangers were a police unit under the Department of the Interior—also in theory. *And not many of the troopies ever had a chance at a vacation in Bali.*

Hunter turned and looked over the low bulkhead into the control cabin of the transport. Her mouth had a dry feeling, as if it had been wallpapered with Kleenex; they were right down on the deck and going *fast*. Kestrels had phased-array radar and AI designed for nape-of-the-earth fighters. Supposed to be reliable as all hell, but the sagebrush and hills outside were going past in a streaking blur. She brought her knees up and braced them against the seat, looking down at the central display screen. It was slaved to the swarm of tiny remote-piloted reconnaissance drones circling the LZ, segmented like an insect's eye to show the multiple viewpoints, with pulsing light-dots to mark the Ranger aircraft.

The Santierist guerrillas were using an abandoned ranch house as their CP. She could see their heavy weapons dug in around it, covered in camouflage netting. Useless, just patterned cloth, open as daylight to modern sensors… on the other hand, there weren't many of those in Mexico these days. Then she looked more closely. There were *mules* down there, with ammunition boxes on their backs. It was enough to make you expect Pancho Villa. A Santierist altar in the courtyard, with a few hacked and discarded bodies already thrown carelessly aside … *Voodoo-Marxist,* she thought. *Communal ownership of the spirit world. Time to tickle them.*

"Code Able-Zulu four," she said. Something in her helmet clicked as the AI rerouted her commlink. "Position?"

"Comin' up on line-of-sight," McMurty said. Weapons Section counted as a platoon, four of the heavy lifters with six troopers each.

There were lights scattered across the overgrown scrub of the abandoned fields beyond the ranch house, the numberless campfires of the refugees who had followed through the gap the Santierists had punched in the Border deathzone. Some of them might make it back, if they ran as soon as the firefight began. .

Hunter reached out to touch half a dozen spots on the screen before her; they glowed electric-blue against the silvery negative images. "Copy?"

"Copy, can-do."

"Execute."

Another voice cut in faintly, the battalion AI prompter. "ETA five minutes."

"Executing firemission," the platform said.

The gamma-ray lasers were invisible pathways of energy through the night, invisible except where a luckless owl vanished into a puff of carbon-vapor. Where they struck the soil the earth exploded into plasma for a meter down. It wasn't an explosion, technically. Just a lot of vaporized matter trying to disperse really, really fast. Fire gouted into the night across the cucuroach encampment, expanding outward in pulse-waves of shock and blast. She could hear the thunder of it with the ears of mind; on the ground it would be loud enough to stun and kill. The surviving AA weapons were hammering into the night, futile stabbing flickers of light, and…

"Hit, God, we're hit!" McMurty's voice, tightly controlled panic. The weapons platform was three miles away and six thousand feet up. Nothing should be able to touch it even if the cucuroaches had sensors that good. "Evasive—*Christ, it hit us again, loss of system integrity I'm trying to—*"

The voice blurred into a static blast. "Comm override, all Ranger units, *down*, out of line-of-sight, that was a zapper!"

The transport lurched and dove; points of green light on the screen scattered out of their orderly formation into a beeswarm of panic. Hunter gripped the crashbars and barked instructions at the machine until a fanpath of probable sites mapped out the possible locations of the zapper.

"Override, override," she said. "Jennings, drop the secondary targets and alternate with me on the main HQ. Weapons?"

"Yes ma'am." McMurty's second, voice firm.

"Keep it low, Sergeant; follow us in. Support with indirect-fire systems only." The weapons platforms had magneto-powered automatic bomb-throwers as well as their energy weapons.

"Override," she continued. "General circuit. Listen up, everyone. The cucuroaches have a zapper, at least one. I want Santierist prisoners; you can recognize them by the fingerbone necklaces. Jennings, detach your first platoon for a dustoff on McMurty."

"Ma'am—"

"That's a direct order, Lieutenant."

A grunt of confirmation. Her lips tightened; nobody could say Jennings didn't have the will to combat, and he led from the front. Fine for a platoon leader, but a company commander had to realize there were other factors in maintaining morale, such as the knowledge you wouldn't be abandoned just because everyone was in a hurry. Furthermore, Jennings just did not like her much. The feeling was mutual; he reminded her too strongly of the perps she had spent most of the early '90s busting off the D.C. streets and sending up for hard time.

"Coming up on the arroyo, Captain," the pilot said.

"Ready!" she replied.

The piloting screens in the forward compartment were directly linked to the vision-blocks in the Kestrel's nose; she could see the mesquite and rock of the West Texas countryside rushing up to meet them, colorless against the blinking blue and green of the control-panel's heads-up displays. The pilot was good, and there was nothing but the huge, soft hand of deceleration pressing them down on the benches as he swung the transport nearly perpendicular to the ground, killed forward velocity with a blast of the lift-off jets, and then swung them back level for a soft landing. The sides of the Kestrel clanged open, turning to ramps. Outside the night was full of hulking dark shapes and the soughing of PFH drives.

"Go!" Hunter shouted, slapping their shoulders as the headquarters team raced past. Getting troops out of armored vehicles is always a problem, but designing them so the sides fell out simplified it drastically. Cold high-desert air rushed in, probing with fingers that turned patches of sweat to ice, laden with dry spicy scents and the sharp aromatics of dry-land plants crushed beneath tons of metal and synthetic.

She trotted down the ramp herself and felt the dry, gravelly soil crunch beneath her feet. The squad was deployed in a star around her, commlink and display screen positioned for her use. The transports were lifting off, backing and shifting into position for their secondary gunship role as A Company fanned out into the bush to establish a temporary perimeter. Hunter knelt beside the screen, watching the pinpoints that represented her command fanning out along two sides of the low slope with the ranch house at its apex.

"Shit, Captain," Kowalski said, going down on one knee and leaning on his H&K. She could hear the low whisper, and there was no radio echo, he must have his comm off. "That zapper's one bad mother to face."

She nodded. Landing right on top of an opponent gave you a powerful advantage, and having the weapons platforms cruising overhead was an even bigger one. The zapper changed the rules; it was one of the more difficult applications of PFH technology, but it made line-of-sight approach in even the most heavily armored aircraft suicidal. Heavy zappers were supposed to be a monopoly of the Sovs and the U.S., having one fall into the hands of any sort of cucuroach was bad news. The Voodoo-Marxists… She shuddered.

Particularly if they had good guidance systems. Finali was trying to attract her attention, but she waved him to silence. "Too right, Tops. We'll just have to rush their perimeter before they can gather on the mountain."

SSNLF guerrillas were good at dispersing, which was essential in the face of superior heavy weapons. On the other hand, this time it kept them scattered....

"Command circuit," she said. There was a subaudible click as the unit AI put her on general push. "Up and at 'em, children. Watch it, they've had a few hours to lay surprises."

There was little noise as the Rangers spread out into the spare chest-high scrub, an occasional slither of boot on rock, a click or equipment. That would be enough, once they covered the first half-kilometer. Shapes flitted through the darkness made daybright by her visor, advancing by leapfrogging squad rushes. Almost like a dance, five helmeted heads appearing among the bushes as if they were dolphins broaching, dodging forward until they were lost among the rocks and brush. Throwing themselves down and the next squad rising on their heels...

"Weapons," she whispered. "Goose it."

"Seekers away," the calm voice answered her.

A loud multiple *whipping* sound came from behind them, the air-slap of the magnetic mortar launch. A long whistling arc above, and the sharp *crackcrackcrack* of explosions. Mostly out of sight over the lip of the ravine ahead of them, indirect flashes against the deep black of the western sky. Stars clustered thick above, strange and beautiful to eyes bred among the shielding city lights. Then a brief gout of flame rising over the near horizon, a secondary explosion. Teeth showed beneath her visor. The seeker-bombs were homing on infrared sources: moving humans, or machinery; too much to hope they'd take out the zapper.

Time to move. She rose and crouch-scrambled up the low slope ahead of her. The open rise beyond was brighter, and she felt suddenly exposed amid the huge rolling distances. It took an effort of the will to remember that this was night, and the cucuroaches were seeing nothing but moonless black. *Unless they got nightsight equipment from the same sources as the laser*—She pushed the thought away.

"Mines." The voice was hoarse with strain and pitched low, but she recognized 2nd platoon's leader, Vigerson.

"Punch it," she replied, pausing in her cautious skitter.

A picture appeared in the center of the display screen, the silvery glint of a wire stretched across the clear space between a boulder and a mesquite bush. Jiggling as the hand-held wire-eye followed the metal thread to the V-shaped Claymore concealed behind a screen of grass, waiting to spew its load of jagged steel pellets into the first trooper whose boot touched it. Wire and mine both glowed with a faint nimbus, the machine-vision's indication of excess heat. Very recently planted, then, after being kept close to a heat-source for hours.

"Flag and bypass." *Shit, I hate mines,* she thought. No escaping them. The gangers had started using them in D.C. before she transferred. Bad enough worrying about a decapitating piano-wire at neck height when you chased a perp into an alley—but toward the end you couldn't go on a bust without wondering whether the door had a grenade cinched to the latch. That was how her husband had—Another flight of magmortar shells went by overhead; the weapons platform was timing it nicely.

Think about the mines, not why she had transferred. Not about the chewed stump of—Think about mines. Half a klick with forty pounds on her back, not counting the armor. No matter how she tried to keep the individual loads down, more essentials crept in. Fusion-powered transports, and they *still* ended up humping the stuff up to the sharp end the way Caesar's knifemen had. A motion in the corner of her eye, and the H&K swept up; an act of will froze her finger as the cottontail zigzagged out of sight. *Shit, this can't last much longer,* she thought with tight control. They were close enough to catch the fireglow and billowing heat-columns from the refugee encampment beyond the guerrilla HQ, close enough to hear the huge murmur of their voices. Nobody was still asleep after what had already come down; they must be hopping-tight in there.

Four hundred yards. The point-men must be on their wire by now, if the Santierists had had time to dig in a perimeter at all. For total wackos they usually had pretty good sense about things like that and this time there had been *plenty* of—

"Down!" somebody shouted. One of hers, the radio caught it first. Fire stabbed out from the low rise ahead of them, green tracer; she heard the thudding detonation of a chemical mortar, and the guerrilla shell-burst behind her sent shrapnel and stone-splinters flying with a sound that had the malice of bees in it.

The Rangers hit the stony dirt with trained reflex, reflex that betrayed them. Three separate explosions fountained up as troopers landed on hidden detonators, and there was an instant's tooth-grating scream before the AI cut out a mutilated soldier's anguish.

"Medic, *medic*," someone called. Two troopers rushed by with the casualty in a fireman's carry, back down to where the medevac waited. Hunter bit down on a cold anger as she toiled up the slope along the trail of blood-drops, black against the white dust. The Santierists were worse than enemies, they were… cop-killers.

"Calibrate," she rasped, "that mortar."

"On the way." A stick of seekers keened by overhead; proximity fused, they burst somewhere ahead with a simultaneous *whump.* Glass-fiber shrapnel, and anything underneath it would be dogmeat. Fire flicked by, Kalashnikovs from the sound of it, then the deeper ripping sound of heavy machineguns. As always, she fought the impulse to bob and weave. Useless, and undignified to boot.

"Designators," she said over the unit push. "Get on to it."

This time all the magmortars cut loose at once, as selected troopers switched their sights to guidance. Normally the little red dot showed where the bullets would go, but it could be adjusted to bathe any target a Ranger could see; the silicon kamikaze brains of the magmortar bombs sought, selected, dove.

"Come *on!*" she shouted, as the Santierist firing line, hidden among the tumbled slabs of sandstone and thorn-bush ahead of them, erupted into precisely grouped flashes and smoke. "*Now,* goddamit!" Fainter, she could hear the lieutenants and NCOs echoing her command.

The rock sloped down from here, down toward the ranch house and the overgrown, once-irrigated fields beyond, down toward the river and the Border. She leapt a slit-trench where a half-dozen cucuroaches sprawled sightless about the undamaged shape of an ancient M60 machine-gun; glass fragments glittered on the wet red of their faces and the cool metal of the gun. Then she was through into the open area beyond and the ruins of a barn, everything moving with glacial slowness. Running figures that seemed to lean into an invisible wind, placing each foot in dark honey. Shadows from the burning ruins of the farmhouse, crushed vehicles around it, her visor flaring a hotspot on the ground ahead of her and she turned her run into a dancing sideways skip to avoid it.

The spot erupted when she was almost past, and something struck her a stunning blow in the stomach. Air whoofed out of her nose and mouth with a sound halfway between a belch and a scream, and she fell to her knees as her diaphragm locked. Paralyzed, she could see the Claymore pellet falling away from her belly-armor, the front burnished by the impact that had flattened it. Then earth erupted before her as the mine's operator surged to his feet and leveled an AK-47, and that *would* penetrate her vest at pointblank range. He was less than a dozen yards away, a thin dark-brown young man with a bushy mustache and a headband, scrawny torso naked to the waist and covered in sweat-streaked dirt.

Two dots of red light blossomed on his chest. Fractions of a second later two H&K rifles fired from behind her, at a cyclic rate of 2,000 rounds a minute. Muzzle blast slapped the back of her helmet, and the cucuroach's torso vanished in a haze as the prefragmented rounds shattered into so many miniature buzzsaws.

"Thanks," she wheezed, as Finali and Kowalski lifted her by the elbows. "Lucky. Just winded." There would be a bruise covering everything between ribs and pelvis, but she would have felt it if there was internal hemorrhaging. A wet trickle down her leg, but bladder control was not something to worry about under the circumstances. She grabbed for the display screen, keyed to bring the drones down. The green dots of her command were swarming over the little plateau, and the vast bulk of the illigs further downslope showed no purposeful movement. Only to be expected, the Santierists were using them as camouflage and cover. Which left only the problem of the—

Zap. Gamma-ray lasers could not be seen in clear air, but you could hear them well enough; the atmosphere absorbed enough energy for that. The Rangers threw themselves flat in a single unconscious movement; Hunter cursed the savage wave of pain from bruised muscle and then ignored it.

"Get a fix, get a fix on it!" she called. Then she saw it herself, a matte-black pillar rising out of the ground like the periscope of a buried submarine, two hundred yards away amid artful piles of rock. *Shit, no way is a magmortar going to take that out,* she thought. It was too well buried, and the molecular-flux mirrors inside the armored and stealthed shaft could focus the beam anywhere within line-of-sight.

Zap. Half a mile away a boulder exploded into sand and gas, and the crashing sound of the detonation rolled back in slapping echoes. "Mark." Her finger hit the display screens. "Kestrel and Shrike units, thumper attack, repeat, thumper attack." The transports and airscouts would come in with bunkerbuster rockets. And a lot of them would die; as a ground weapon that zapper was clumsy, but it did fine against air targets....

"Damn, damn, *damn!*" she muttered, pounding a fist against the dirt. Another *zap* and the stink of ozone, and this time the gout of flame was closer, only a hundred yards behind them. Rocks pattered down, mixed with ash and clinker; back there someone was shouting for a medic, and there was a taste like vomit at the back of her throat. She groped for a thermite grenade—

"Captain."

It was Finali, prone beside her and punching frantically at the flexboard built into the fabric of his jacket sleeve. "Captain, I got it, I got it!"

"Got *what*, privat—"

There was no word for the sound that followed. At first she thought she was blind, then she realized the antiflare of her visor had kicked in with a vengeance. Even with the rubber edges snugged tight against her cheeks glare leaked through, making her eyes water with reaction. The ground dropped away beneath her, then rose up again and slapped her like a board swung by a giant; she flipped into the air and landed on her back with her body flexing like a whip. Hot needles pushed in both ears, and she could feel blood running from them, as well as from her nose and mouth. Above her something was showing through the blackness of the visor: a sword of light thrusting for the stars.

Pain returned, shrilling into her ears; then sound, slow and muffled despite the protection the earphones of her helmet had given. The jet of flame weakened, fading from silver-white to red and beginning to disperse. Stars faded in around it, blurred by the watering of her eyes; anybody who had been looking in this direction unprotected was going to be blind for a *long* time. It was not a nuclear explosion, she knew, not technically. There were an infinity of ways to tweak the anode of a PFH unit, and a laser-boost powerpack needed to be more energetic than most. Overload the charging current and the fusion rate increased exponentially, lattice energy building within the crystalline structure until it tripped over into instant release. There was a pit six yards deep and four across where the zapper had been, lined with glass that crackled and throbbed as it cooled. The rest of the matter had gone in the line of least resistance, straight up as a plasma cloud of atoms stripped of their electron shells.

"Finali?" Her voice sounded muffled and distant, and her tongue was thick. She hawked, spat blood mixed with saliva, spoke again. "Trooper, what the *hell* was that?"

"Deseret electronuclear unit, Captain," he said, rising with a slight stagger. A cowlick of straw-colored hair tufted out from under one corner of his helmet; he pulled off the molded synthetic and ran his fingers through his curls, grinning shyly. "U of U design, access protocols just about like ours. I told it to voosh."

Kowalski fisted him on the shoulder. "Good work, trooper." There was a humming *shussh* of air as the first of the Kestrels slid over the edge of the plateau behind them. "You roasted their cucuroach *ass*, my boy!"

Hunter turned her eyes back to the display screen; motion was resuming. "There'll be survivors," she said crisply, looking up to the rest of the headquarters squad. "We'll—"

Crack. The flat snapping sound of the sniper's bullet brought heads up with a sharp feral motion. All except for Finali's; the teenager had rocked back on his heels, face liquid for a moment as hydrostatic shock rippled the soft tissues. His eyes bulged, and the black dot above the left turned slowly to glistening red. His body folded back bonelessly with a sodden sound, the backpack commlink holding his torso off the ground so that his head folded back to hide the slow drop of brain and blood from the huge exit wound on the back of his skull. There was a sudden hard stink as his sphincters relaxed.

Above them the Kestrel poised, turned. A flash winked from its rocket pods, and the sniper's blind turned to a gout of rock and fragments. Kowalski straightened from his instinctive half-crouch and stared down at the young man's body for an instant.

"Aw, shit, *no*," he said. "Not *now*."

"Come on, Tops," Hunter said, her voice soft and flat as the nonreflective surface of her visor. She spat again, to one side. "We've got a job of work to finish."

"In the name of the Mother of God, señora, have pity!" the man in the frayed white collar shouted thinly.

The cucuroach priest leading the illig delegation was scrawnier than his fellows, which meant starvation gaunt. They stood below the Ranger command, a hundred yards distant as the megaphone had commanded. Behind them the dark mass of the refugees waited, a thousand yards farther south. That was easy to see, even with her visor up; the weapons platforms were floating overhead, with their belly-lights flooding the landscape, brighter than day. The Kestrels and Shrikes circled lower, unlit, sleek black outlines wheeling in a circuit a mile across, sough of lift-jets and the hot dry stink of PFH air-units.

Hunter stood with her hands on her hips, knowing they saw her only as a black outline against the klieg glare of the platforms. When she spoke, her voice boomed amplified from the sky, echoing back from hill and rock in ripples that harshened the accent of her Spanish.

"Pity on Santierists, old man?" she said, and jerked a thumb toward the ground. The priest and his party shielded their faces and followed her hand, those whose eyes were not still bandaged from the afterimages of the fusion flare. Ten prisoners lay on their stomachs before the Ranger captain, thumbs lashed to toes behind their backs with a loop around their necks. Naked save for their tattoos, and the necklaces of human fingerbone. "Did they take pity on you, and share the meat of their sacrifices?"

The priest's face clenched: he could not be a humble man by nature, nor a weak one, to have survived in these years. When he spoke a desperate effort of will put gentleness into his voice; shouting across the distance doubled his task, as she had intended.

"These people, they are not Santierists, not diabolists, not soldiers or political people. They are starving, señora. Their children die; the warlords give them no peace. For your own mother's sake, let the mothers and little children through, at least. I will lead the others back to the border myself; or kill me, if you will, as punishment for the crossing of the border."

Hunter signaled for increased volume. When she spoke the words rolled louder than summer thunder.

"I GRANT YOU THE MERCY OF ONE HOUR TO BEGIN MOVING BACK TOWARD THE BORDER," the speakers roared. "THOSE WHO TURN SOUTH MAY LIVE. FOR THE OTHERS—"

She raised a hand. The lights above dimmed, fading like a theater as the curtains pulled back. *Appropriate,* she thought sourly. *If this isn't drama, what is?* A single spotlight remained, fixed on her.

"FOR THE OTHERS, THIS." Her fist stabbed down. Fire gouted up as the lasers struck into the cleared zone before the mob, a multiple flash and crack that walked from horizon to horizon like the striding of a giant whose feet burned the earth.

The priest dropped his hand, and the wrinkles of his face seemed to deepen. Wordless, he turned and hobbled back across the space where a line of red-glowing pits stitched the earth, as neat as a sewing machine's needle could have made. There was a vast shuffling sigh from the darkened mass of his followers, a sigh that went on and on, like the sorrow of the world. Then it dissolved into an endless ruffling as they bent to take up their bundles for the journey back into the wasted land.

Laura Hunter turned and pulled a cigarette from a pocket on the sleeve of her uniform. The others waited, Jennings grinning like... what had been that comedian's name? Mac-Donald? Murphy? McMurty bandaged and splinted but on her feet, Kowalski still dead around the eyes and with red-brown droplets of Finali's blood across the front of his armor.

"You know," the captain said meditatively, pulling on the cigarette and taking comfort from the harsh sting of the smoke, "sometimes this job sucks shit." She shook her head. "Right, let's—"

They all paused, with the slightly abstracted look that came from an override message on their helmet phones.

"Killed *Eisenhower?*" Jennings said. "You shittin' me, man? That dude been dead since before my pappy dipped his wick and ran."

Hunter coughed conclusively. "Not him, the *carrier*, you idiot, the ship." Her hand waved them all to silence.

"...*off Bandar Abbas,*" the voice in their ears continued. "*They*—" It vanished in a static squeal that made them all wince before the AI cut in. The captain had been facing north, so that she alone saw the lights that flickered along the horizon. Like heat lightning, once, twice, then again.

"What *was* that, Cap?" Jennings asked. Even Kowalski looked to be shaken out of his introspection.

"That?" Hunter said very softly, throwing down her cigarette and grinding it out. "That was the end of the world, I think. Let's go."

"No. Absolutely not, and that is the end of the matter." Major Forrest was haggard; all of them were, after these last three days. But he showed not one glimpse of weakness; Hunter remembered suddenly that the commander of Post 73 had had family in Washington... a wife, his younger children.

She kept her own face impassive as she nodded and looked round the table, noting which of the other officers would meet her eyes. It was one thing to agree in private, another to face the major down in the open.

The ex-classroom was quiet and dark. The windows had been hastily sealed shut with balks of cut styrofoam and duct tape. No more was needed, for now; four of the heavy transports were parked by the doors, with jury-rigged pipes keeping the building over pressure with filtered air that leached the chalk-sweat-urine aroma of school. Hunter could still feel the skin between her shoulder blades crawl as she remembered the readings from outside. The Dallas-Fort Worth fallout plume had come down squarely across Abilene, and she doubted there was anything living other than the rats within sixty miles.

She pulled on her cigarette, and it glowed like a tiny hearth in the dimness of the emergency lamp overhead. "With respect, sir, I think we should put it to a vote."

The blue eyes that fixed hers were bloodshot but calm; she remembered a certain grave of her own in D.C. whose bones would now be tumbled ash, and acknowledged Forrest's strength of will with a respect that conceded nothing.

"Captain," he said, "this is a council of war; accordingly, I'm allowing free speech. It is *not* a democracy, and I will not tolerate treason in my command. Is that clear?"

"Yes, sir," she said firmly. "Without discipline, now, we're a mob, and shortly a dead one. Under protest, I agree, and will comply with any orders you give."

The ex-Marine turned his eyes on the others, collecting their nods like so many oaths of fealty. A few mumbled, Jennings grinned broadly, with a decisive nod.

"Dam' straight, sir."

"Well. Gentlemen, ladies, shall we inform the me—the troops?"

"'Tent-*hut!*"

The roar of voices died in the auditorium, and the packed

ranks of the Rangers snapped to attention. A little raggedly, maybe, but promptly and silently. The officers filed in to take their places at the rear of the podium and Forrest strode briskly to the edge, paused to return the salute, clasped hands behind his back.

"Stand easy and down, Sergeant."

"Stand easy!" Kowalski barked. "Battalion will be seated for Major Forrest's address!"

The commander waited impassively through the shuffling of chairs, waiting for the silence to return. The great room was brightly lit and the more than four hundred troopers filled it to overflowing. But a cold tension hovered over them; they were huddled in a fortress in a land of death, and they knew it.

"Rangers," he began. "You know—"

Laura Hunter's head jerked up as she heard the scuffle from the front row of seats; one of the tech-sergeants was standing, rising despite the hissed warnings and grasping hands. She recognized him, from B Company. An ex-miner from East Tennessee, burly enough to shake off his neighbors. The heavy face was unshaven, and tears ran down through the stubble and the weathered grooves.

"You!" he shouted at the officer above him. "They're all dead, an' you did it! You generals, you big an' mighty ones. *You!*"

Hunter could feel Jennings tensing in the seat beside her, and her hand dropped to the sidearm at her belt. Then the hillbilly's hand dipped into the patch-pocket of his jacket, came out with something round. Shouts, screams, her fingers scrabbling at the smooth flap of the holster, the oval egg-shape floating through the air toward the dais where the commanders sat. Forrest turning and reaching for it as it passed, slow motion, she could see the striker fly off and pinwheel away and she was just reaching her feet. The major's hand struck it, but it slipped from his fingers and hit the hardwood floor of the dais with a hard drum-sound. She could read the cryptic print on it, and recognized it for what it was.

Offensive grenade, with a coil of notched steel wire inside the casing. Less than three yards away. There was just enough time too wonder at her own lack of fear, *maybe the hormones don't have time to reach my brain,* and then Forrest's back blocked her view as he threw himself onto the thing. The *thump* that followed was hideously muffled, and the man flopped up in a salt spray that spattered across her as high as her lips. Something else struck her, leaving a trail of white fire along one thigh. She clapped a hand to it, felt the blood dribble rather than spout; it could wait.

In seconds the hall had dissolved into chaos. She saw fights starting, the beginning of a surge toward the exits. It was cut-crystal clear; she could see the future fanning out ahead of her, paths like footprints carved in diamond for her to follow. She felt hard, like a thing of machined steel and bearings moving in oil, yet more alive than she could remember, more alive than she had since the day Eddie died. The salt taste of blood on her lips was a sacrament, the checked grip of the 9mm in her hand a caress. Hunter raised the pistol as she walked briskly to the edge of the podium and fired one round into the ceiling even as she keyed the microphone.

"*Silence.*" Not a shout; just loud, and flatly calm. Out of the corner of her eye she saw Jennings vault back onto the platform, leopard-graceful: later. "Sergeant, call to order."

Kowalski jerked, swallowed, looked at the man who had thrown the grenade as he hung immobile in the grip of a dozen troopers. "'Tent—" his voice cracked. "'Tent-*hut!*" he shouted.

The milling slowed, troopers looking at each other and remembering they were a unit. Shock aided the process, a groping for the familiar and the comforting. Hunter waited impassive until the last noise ceased.

"Major Forrest is dead. As senior officer, I am now in command in this unit. Any dispute?" She turned slightly; the officers behind her were sinking back into their chairs, hints of thought fighting up through the stunned bewilderment on their faces. All except Jennings. He gave her another of those cat-cool smiles, nodded.

"First order of business. You two; take that ground-sheet and wrap the major's body, take it in back and lay it out on the table. Move." The two soldiers scrambled to obey. "Bring the prisoner forward."

Willing hands shoved the tech-sergeant into the strip of clear floor before the podium.

"Stand back, you others. Sergeant Willies, you stand accused of attempted murder, murder, and mutiny in time of war. How do you plead?"

The man stood, and a slow trickle of tears ran down his face. He shook his head unspeaking, raised a shaking hand to his face, lowered it. Hunter raised her eyes to the crowd; there was an extra note to their silence now. She could feel it, like a thrumming along her bones, a taste like iron and rust. *Be formal, just a little. Then hit them hard.*

"As commanding officer I hereby pronounce Sergeant Willies guilty of the charges laid. Does anyone speak in this man's defense?" Now even the sound of breathing died; the clatter of the two troopers returning from laying out the dead man's body seemed thunderloud. The spell of leadership was young, frail, a word now could break it. There would be no word; the certainty lifted her like a surfboard on the best wave of the season. She turned to the row behind her. "Show of hands for a guilty verdict, if you please?" They rose in ragged unison.

"Sergeant Willies, you are found guilty of mutiny and the murder of your commanding officer. The sentence is death. Do you have anything to say in your own defense?" The man stood without raising his face, the tears rolling slow and fast across his cheeks. Hunter raised the pistol and fired once; the big Tennessean pitched backward, rattled his heels on the floor, and went limp. A trickle of blood soaked out from under his jacket and ran amid the legs of the folding chairs.

"Cover that," she said, pointing to the body. "We will now have a moment of silence in memory of Major Forrest, who gave his life for ours. Greater love has no man than this." Time to get them thinking, just a little. Time to make them feel their link to each other, part of something greater than their own fears. Give them something to lay the burden of the future on.

"Right." She holstered the pistol, rested her hands on her belt. "Major Forrest called you all together to give you the intelligence we've gathered and to outline our future course of action. There being no time to waste, we will now continue." Hunter kept her voice metronome-regular. "The United States has effectively ceased to exist."

A gasp; she moved on before the babble of questions could start. "The Soviets were on the verge of collapse a week ago, even before the Central Asian outbreak. They, or some of them, decided to take us with them. Their attack was launched for our cities and population centers, not military targets." *Which is probably why we're still here.* "The orbital zappers caught most of the ballistic missiles; they didn't get the hypersonic PFH-powered cruise missiles from the submarines just offshore, or the suitcase bombs, and we think they've hit us with biological weapons as well. If there'd been a few more years…" She shrugged. "There wasn't.

"Here are the facts. We estimate half the population is dead. Another half will die before spring; it's going to be a long, hard winter. The temperature is dropping right now. Next year when the snow melts most of the active fallout will be gone, but there won't be any fuel, transport, whatever, left. You all know how close this country was to the breaking point before this happened, though we were on the way back up, maybe. Now it's going to be like Mexico, only a thousand times worse."

She pointed over one shoulder, southwards. "And incidentally, they weren't hit at all. We Border Rangers have held the line; try imagining what it's going to be like *now*."

Hunter paused to let that sink in, saw stark fear on many of the faces below. What had happened to the world was beyond imagining, but these men and women could imagine the Border down and no backup without much trouble. That was a horror that was fully real to them, their subconscious minds had had a chance to assimilate it.

"Some of the deeper shelters have held on, a few units here and there. Two of the orbital platforms made it through. I don't think they're going to find anything but famine and bandits and cucuroaches when they come back. Europe is hit even worse than we are, and so's Japan." She lit a cigarette. "If it's any consolation, the Soviets no longer exist.

"Major Forrest," she continued, "wanted us to make contact with such other units as survived, and aid in reestablishing order." Hunter glanced down at the top of her cigarette. "It is my considered opinion, and that of your officers as a whole, that such a course of action would lead to the destruction of this unit. Hands, if you please." This time she did not look behind her. "Nevertheless, we were prepared to follow Major Forrest's orders. The situation is now changed."

She leaned forward and let her voice drop. "We... we've been given a *damn* good lesson in what it's like trying to sweep back the ocean with a broom. Now we've got a tidal wave and a whisk."

A trooper came to her feet. "You're saying we're dead meat whatever we do!" Her voice was shrill; Hunter stared at her impassively, until she shuffled her feet, glanced to either side, added: "Ma'am," and sat.

"No. If we break up, yes, we're dead. Dead of radiation sickness, of cold, of plague, shot dead fighting over a can of dogfood."

Hunter raised a finger. "But if we maintain ourselves, as a fighting unit, the 72nd, we have a fighting chance, a *good* fighting chance. As a unit we have assets I doubt anyone on

Earth can match. There are more than five hundred of us, with a broad range of skills. We have several dozen PFH-powered warcraft, fuel for decades, repair facilities, weapons that almost nobody outside the U.S. and the Soviet can match, computers. *Most of all, we have organization.*"

She waited again, scanning them. *They're interested. Good.* "I just got through telling you we couldn't make a difference, though, didn't I?" Her hand speared out, the first orator's gesture she had made. "We can't make a difference *here.* Or even survive, unless you count huddling in a cabin in Wyoming and eating bears as survival. And I don't like to ski."

Feeble as it was, that surprised a chuckle out of them. "But we do have those assets I listed; what we need is a place where we can apply them. Where we won't be swamped by numbers and the scale of things. Where we can stand off all comers, try to make a life for ourselves. It won't be easy; we'll have to work and fight for it." The hand stabbed down. *"So what else is new?"*

A cheer, from the row where her old platoon sat. For a moment a warmth invaded the icy certainty beneath her heart, and then she pushed it aside. "A fight we can *win,* for a change. Better work than wasting illig kids and wacko cucuroach cannibals; and we'll be doing it for *ourselves,* not a bunch of fat-assed *citizens* who hide behind our guns and then treat us like hyenas escaped from the zoo!"

That brought them all to their feet, cheering and stamping their feet. The Border Rangers had never been popular with the press; few Rangers wore their uniforms when they went on furlough. Spit, and bags of excrement, sometimes outright murder not being what they had in mind. People with strong family ties avoided the service, or left quickly. She raised her hands for silence and smiled, a slow, fierce grin.

"Right, listen up! This isn't going to be a democracy, or a union shop. A committee is the only known animal with more than four legs and no brain. You get just one choice; come along, subject to articles of war and discipline like nothing you've ever known, or get dropped off in a clear zone with a rifle and a week's rations. Which is it?"

Another wave of cheers, and this time there were hats thrown into the air, exultant clinches, a surf-roar of voices. *Hysteria,* she thought. *They'd been half-sure they were all going to die. Then they saw the murder. Now I've offered them a door—and they're charging for it like a herd of buffalo. But they'll remember.*

"I thought so," she said quietly, after the tumult. "We know each other, you and I." Nods and grins and clenched-fist salutes. "Here's what we're going to do, in brief. How many of you know about the Mindanao pirates?" Most of the hands went up. "For those who don't, they got PFH units, hooked them to some old subs and went a'rovin'. After the Philippines and Indonesia collapsed in '93, they pretty well had their own way. A bunch of them took over a medium-sized island, name of Bali." Good-natured groans. "Yes, I know, some've you have heard a fair bit." She drew on the cigarette.

"But it's perfect for what we want. Big enough to be worthwhile, small enough to hold, with fertile land and a good climate. Isolated, hard to get to except by PFH-powered boost. The people're nice, good farmers and craftsmen, pretty cultured; and they're Hindu, while everyone else in the area's Muslim, like the corsairs who've taken over the place and killed off half the population. And I've seen the Naval intelligence reports; we can take those pirates. We'll be liberators, and afterward they'll still need us. No more than a reasonable amount of butt-kicking needed to keep things going our way." She threw the stub to the floor while the laugh died and straightened.

"Those of you who want to stay and take your chances with the cold, the dark, and the looters report to First Sergeant Kowalski. For the rest, we've got work to do. First of all, getting out of here before we all start to glow in the dark. Next stop—a kingdom of our own! Platoon briefings at 1800. Dismiss."

"'Tent-*hut*," Kowalski barked. Hunter returned their salute crisply, turned and strode off; it was important to make a good exit. Reaction threatened to take her in the corridor beyond, but she forced the ice mantle back. It was not over yet, and the officers were crowding around her.

"See to your people, settle them down, and if you can do it without obvious pressure, push the waverers over to our side. We need *volunteers*, but we need as many as we can get. Staff meeting in two hours; we're getting out tonight, probably stop over at a place I know in Baja for a month or so, pick up some more equipment and recruits.... Let's move it."

Then it was her and Jennings. He leaned against the stained cinderblock of the wall with lazy arrogance, stroked a finger across his mustache and smiled that brilliant empty grin.

"Objections, Lieutenant?" Hunter asked.

He mimed applause. "Excellent, Great White Raja-ess to be; your faithful Man Friday here just pantin' to get at those palaces an' mango trees and dancers with the batik sarongs."

Hunter looked him up and down. "You know, Jennings, you have your good points. You're tough, you've got smarts, you're not squeamish, and you can even get troops to follow you." A pause. "Good reflexes, too; you got off that dais as if you could see the grenade coming."

Jennings froze. "Say what?" he asked with soft emphasis. Hunter felt her neck prickle; under the shuck-and-jive act this was a very dangerous man. "You lookin' to have another court-martial?"

She shook her head. "Jennings, you like to play the game. You like to win. Great; I'm just betting that you've got brains as well as smarts, enough to realize that if we start fighting each other it all goes to shit and nobody wins." She stepped closer, enough to smell the clean musk of the younger soldier's presence, see the slight tensing of the small muscles around his lips. Her finger reached out to prod gently into his chest.

"Forrest was tough and smart too; but he had one fatal handicap. He was Old Corps all the way, a man of honor." There was enjoyment in her smile, but no humor. "Maybe I would have gone along with his Custer's Last Stand plan… maybe not. Just remember this; while he was living in the Big Green Machine, *I* was a street cop. I've been busting scumbags ten times badder than you since about the time you sold your first nickel bag. Clear, Holmes?"

He reached down with one finger and slowly pushed hers away. "So I be a good darky, or you whup my nigger ass?"

"Anytime, Jennings. Anytime. Because we've got a job to do, and we can't get it done if we're playing head-games. And I *intend* to get it done."

The silence went on a long moment until the lieutenant fanned off a salute. "Like you say, Your Exaltedness. Better a piece of the pie than an empty plate. I'm yours."

She returned the salute. *For now*, went unspoken between them as the man turned away. Hunter watched him go, and for a moment the weight of the future crushed at her shoulders.

Then the Ranger laughed, remembering a beach, and the moon casting a silver road across the water. "You said I was fit to be a queen, Eddie," she whispered softly. "It's something to do, hey? And they say the first monarch was a lucky soldier. Why not me?"

The future started with tonight; a battalion lift was going to mean some careful juggling; there would be no indenting for stores at the other end. *But damned if I'll leave my Enya discs behind,* she thought, *or a signed first edition of* Prince of Sparta.

"Raja-ess," she murmured. "I'll have to work on that." She was humming as she strode toward her room. Sleet began to pound against the walls, like a roll of drums.

CONSTANT NEVER

"Give me ale, you dog, and food, and be quick about it."

The *Ritter* Karl von Obersberg scraped some of the horse dung off his feet as he entered the village inn. Not that it would make much difference—the common room looked no better than the stable where he'd put his horses. Certainly it smelled no better, and there was smoke enough from the hearth in the center to make his eyes sting, but it was warmer and drier than the drizzle outside. The firepit was surrounded by the pine log pillars that held up the roof, branches still standing out like stubs. The knight hung his cloak on one to dry; it was woven of raw wool and usually shed water like a duck's back, but the long day's ride and last night's sleep under an oak tree had soaked it through.

There were carvings on the tree trunks. Bearded faces...

The Old Ones, he thought. These Saxon dogs were half-heathen yet, despite all the emperor's wars and priests. The thought did not improve the knight's temper.

"*Ale, I said, peasant swine!*" he roared, sinking back onto the bench, kicking the scabbard of his cross-hilted sword out of the way with a lifetime's unconscious habit.

Shaggy faces turned away from him around the room. One

scurried over with bowl and mug, both wooden. The ale was thin and sour, but there was meat in the stew, and the round loaf of black bread was nearly fresh. He ate methodically, half-conscious of the hating peasant eyes on him. Saxon eyes. That was why he'd kept his mailshirt on. He didn't think they'd try anything, not really. And if they did, he'd killed enough Saxons in his day—Saxons, West Franks, Bretons, Italians, Avars, Basques, Saracens, lately some Danes—that a few more wouldn't do much hurt.

Nor would it be a curse if they slew me, he thought. It bubbled up from somewhere in his gut, to be pushed away hastily. There was no need to think of dying. He was no youth, he'd seen forty winters and that was older than most fighting men lived to be. But there were years yet, much to be done.

Meanwhile his belly was full, and the ache in his hands and the shoulder where the old heathen priest's hammer had broken the bone was a little less. It was time to sleep.

He pulled a copper penny from his pouch and flung it at the tavernkeeper. "Blankets," he said.

"There is a shut-bed here, lord," the man said; the Saxon accent was rough to a Frank's ears, but Karl had learned it well enough in the wars.

"I sleep by my horses," he grunted.

Just as warm, cleaner and much safer—there were silver pennies in his pouch with the face of his namesake, the emperor, on them. Not many, but enough to buy this dung pile of a village.

The rain had stopped outside, but it was getting on to full dark. Karl took a brand from the firepit and raised it overhead as he pushed the rough plank door open. The chill bit at him, and he hurried to the warm straw and the comforting smell of horse.

It was hot. Hotter than hell, where the pagan dogs would burn forever. Karl was surprised for a moment—surprised that it was high summer and the setting sun was hot, surprised that he was young, moving without pain. Swift and fluid like an otter, his blows struck with bear strength. The knowledge that he dreamed faded.

The Saxon shieldwall was buckling. Locked together, the battle lines lurched, then moved a long step backward, back toward the great wooden temple that burned behind the enemy host. Flame birds crowed from the thatch of the roof, casting yellow light on the writhing carved figures of beasts and gods and men that covered its upswung rafters and door pillars. The dry crackling smell covered the scents of blood and dung and sweat from the thousands of men fighting and dying below. The swelling roar blurred their war shouts and the screams of the wounded.

Karl smashed his shieldboss forward into a yelling flaxen-bearded face, felt bone crunch beneath the iron. His sword hacked down into the neck of another, a dull cleaving feeling as the edge cut through a steerhide jerkin and into meat and bone. The Saxon line buckled and Karl shoved through, knocked one man sprawling with his shield and then blocked the thrust of a spear with it. The foot-long head stuck in the tough leather and wood; he chopped overarm at the shaft, behind the yard of iron wire wound around it beneath the point. The wood cracked across.

His comrades and sworn men pushed through at his back, guarding him from the Saxon spears, turning to take men on either side in the flank. A champion and his thegns hurled themselves at the Frankish warriors, desperate to close the gap. Karl grinned beneath his high-peaked helm and set himself, knees bent and round shield up beneath his eyes. The Saxon wore a spangen-helm of riveted plates, with a guard of chain mail hanging like a Saracen woman's veil below his cold blue eyes; his leather jerkin was sewn with rings of iron and brass, and he bore a light axe in one hand, a small buckler in the other. It was painted with the device of a red snake, grasping its tail in its jaws.

Karl raised his sword until the hilt was above his head, the blade between his shoulders. "*Christ and the emperor!*" he shouted. "Come and be slain!"

"*Wodan, ho-la, Wodan!*" the Saxon replied.

Then there was no time for words. The axe darted for his leg. His shield moved, and the sharp pattern-welded steel head bit into leather and linden wood, hewing chips. Karl roared and cut downward with his long slashing sword; the Saxon moved swiftly, relaxing one knee to take him out of the way and bringing the buckler around and up. The iron banged off the slanted surface, and the buckler punched out at him. He blocked it with his shield, caught the haft of the axe on his swordblade. They skirled together, the iron bands on the axe-haft grinding over the steel of his sword.

For long moments the two men strained against each other, locked like rutting stags in the springtime, their feet churning dirt made muddy with the blood of the fallen. They were knee to knee, close enough to smell each other's sweat, close enough to see the hate and battle lust in each other's eyes.

Strong, Karl thought with surprise. Few men could stand against him so. They broke apart, heaving backward, and cut at each other. Metal rang on metal, banged on shields. *Fast*. The Saxon was as fast as the serpent painted on his shield. The men around them paused for an instant, panting, while the leaders fought. Then Karl's foot slipped on a patch of mud. Steel punched his side, driving the iron mail through the padding beneath and into his skin. Breath hissed out between clenched teeth, and the axe rose to kill. In desperation he thrust the point of his sword at his foeman's face. The move was utterly unexpected—swords were not spears—and the rounded tip of the weapon shot up beneath the hanging veil of chain.

The Saxon screamed, thick and bubbling. He fell backward; his thegns rushed in, some bearing him away despite his thrashings, others closing ranks to hold off the enemy and buy their lord's life with their own. Over their shoulders the Saxon leader shouted, his voice blurred by his wound and the guttural local dialect of German:

"We meet again! I eat your heart, Frank!"

Karl forced himself erect, sucked air into his lungs. His eyes scanned the ranks; the enemy were weakening everywhere. Banners moved forward, marked with the Cross.

"Jesu Kristos!" he bawled. "Forward!"

The Franks formed a wedge on either side of him, bristling with spears. They struck the Saxon rearguard and stabbed, cut, clubbed them to earth. The lines had given way to clumps and bands of men who fought or fled, the Saxon host ravelling away toward the trees. Frankish cavalry from either flank pursued, but Karl waved his men on towards the temple doors. Bronze covered that oak, bronze and iron and gold, but they swung open under spearbutts.

Within was a great hall, reaching upward to a maze of rafters. The floor was smooth planks, not the rushes of a nobleman's dwelling; every inch of the walls was a riot of carving and painted wood. Alone in the center of the halidom stood the great log pillar carved into the likeness of the Irminsul—son of Seax, son of Wodan, god of the mainland Saxons. Ruddy light from the burning thatch made it seem to bleed. So did the red gold all around it. The blood of the sacrifices hung from the rafters was no more crimson; they were of the three kinds, hawk and horse and man. The man wore the Romish vestments and tonsured head of a Christian priest; Karl felt his face swell with anger at the sight. From the groans and cries behind him, it was the wealth of gold that struck his followers' hearts—and there was no reason Christ's man should not grow rich. Especially when he was the most promising of the emperor's knights....

Three men stood between them and the pillar. Old men, gray and white in the beards that reached to their waists; they were richly dressed in the ancient style, caps of stiffened doghide on their heads. One bore a warhammer with a head of polished stone.

"Go," he said. "The god takes back his house in fire, and you tread on holy ground. The god honors brave men; touch nothing here and you may live."

"Apostate!" Karl said. The Saxons had surrendered to the emperor before, made peace and agreed to pay tribute and accept the true faith. They were rebels, not foe-men . "Your life is forfeit. Take them!"

His men hung back; despite the order, despite the gold, despite the increasing heat as the thatch fire spread to the dense old oak timbers above. The ruddy light swept across the halidom's interior in flame and shadow, and the carvings seemed to move, painted beasts turning their eyes on living men. It was not so very long since the Franks had followed the Old Ones. Many of his men were Thuringians and other easterners, from lands converted generations after Clovis. They feared.

Karl knew his duty; the cross about his neck was a charm more potent than any heathen idol.

"Your demon cannot stand against Christ," he said, striding near. "His priest will be avenged."

"His priest cursed our king," the guardian of the shrine said. "The blood of a magician makes a strong curse. Even now that curse comes upon him."

He smiled. Karl felt his battle fury break free once more. He roared and swung; the steel was blunted and notched, but it sank deep into the heathen priest's side. He staggered, a loop of pink gut showing through his tunic. The more surprise when he struck in his turn, the stone warhammer chopping down on Karl's undefended shoulder. Mail would turn an edge, but it was no protection from a crushing blow.

Pain, pain lancing down his arm. He dropped the sword and staggered, breast to breast with the old man. And the heathen still smiled, with blood a sheet down his side.

"I curse you," he said. "I curse your tomorrows, until the battle fought is ended twice and curse by curse is slain."

A woman screamed.

Karl combed straw out of his gray-streaked beard, shaking off the dream—the same dream as always, haunting him like a night hag. The woman was probably no business of his. Then she screamed again—words, this time, and in a Frankish accent. A man cried out in pain as well. He came up out of the straw, snatching at his round shield as he did. The stable door banged open onto a dawn that held sunlight, weak and watery with autumn, but sunlight none the less.

A gang of youths was grouped around the woman; they'd pulled her off her palfrey, which was snorting and backing. One of them was clutching a slashed arm, dancing about and howling threats; as he watched a staff knock the knife out of the woman's hand.

They'd also pulled down her bodice, and obviously had more in mind, grabbing at her legs beneath her skirts despite her blows and curses. The woman was young but no girl, with black hair and green eyes, well-favored but not a noblewoman; Karl thought she might be a house servant, from the silver collar about her neck.

"Halt, swine hounds," he grated in a voice like millstones, and drew his sword despite the twinge in his shoulder.

His bones felt stiff and sore this morning, and the weak fall sun was not enough to warm them. He lumbered. That simply made him look more dangerous, like an ill-tempered bear prodded out of his den untimely and turning to rend the hunters.

"Stand off, Frank; this is no affair of yours."

The young Saxon's words were bold, but the grip on his cudgel was white-knuckled, and he looked right and left for the reassurance of his pack. None of them bore a sword or spear, although most had the *seax*, the long single-edged knife of their tribe, thrust under their belts.

Karl grinned and kept walking; the others backed out of his way. The leader cursed as he passed, and lashed out with the club. *The old boar knows,* Karl thought; he'd twitched his shield into the way before the younger man even started to move. You lost speed as you aged, but experience could compensate, if you had the wits. He slammed the hilt of his sword into the young Saxon's mouth and he went down like an oxen in the shambles, crawling in the gray slick mud of the laneway and spitting blood and teeth. Behind Karl's back came a shrill bugling, and the sound of crashing wood. A tall Ardennes stallion came trotting out into the street between the rows of huts half-sunken into the ground. He was sixteen hands at the shoulder and shaggy-massive; his eye rolled as he came up behind his master, and he chopped eagerly at the mud, throwing up huge clods with his platter hooves.

The Frank still smiled, showing the gaps in his teeth, and let the heavy broadsword swing negligently back and forth. "I am the emperor's man," he said mildly.

Implying that the local count would send soldiers if he disappeared; no longer strictly accurate, but he'd said the same thing often enough over the years when it *was* the truth for the words to carry conviction. Two of the village louts took their friend under the armpits and helped him away; the rest scattered.

The knight turned back to the woman; she'd pulled and pinned her dress back together, which was a pity—a fine pair of breasts they'd been.

"Thank you, my lord," she said.

Frankish right enough, he thought—from the Rhine-lands , at a guess. Those from further west had a whistling accent, when they hadn't abandoned the old tongue altogether for Roman speech. Karl thought that foolish; old ways were best, and had made the Franks masters of lands broader than Rome had ever commanded. Although he himself could speak

Latin—the spoken tongue—well enough to be understood anywhere in Gaul and to give simple commands in Hispania or Italy. Writing and the pure ancient language of the Caesars were for priests, of course.

"What are you doing here unescorted, wench?" he asked. Her horse was good, and the saddle well-made; her clothes were fine-woven wool, dyed saffron and blue. She looked him boldly in the eye, which he liked, as she retrieved her knife and sheathed it.

"On my mistress' business, my lord," she said, "which could not wait."

Karl nodded. "Come. Best we go." Best not to give those young dogs time to think; think of a spear thrust from behind a bush on a forest road, for instance.

With that in mind he saddled his war-horse and put the pack frame on the ordinary mount he kept for travel; his helm went on his head, and the long lance with the crossbar below the point rested in his right hand with its butt on the stirrup iron. The war-horse snorted again and sidled as the woman came up at his side. Perhaps it was her moonblood time; that disturbed stallions. They cantered out of the village and through its fields, stubble hidden in the last of the morning mist. She produced bread and hard cheese from her saddlebags, and a skin of real wine; he drank with relish, belching and smacking his lips. Once he'd drunk good wine daily, at the table of the emperor, but that was long years ago.

"My name is Ermenagarde, lord," the woman said. "What brings so brave a warrior to these lands?"

It was a goodly while since a pretty, well-spoken young woman had looked at him so. "I am Karl von Obersberg, the emperor's knight," Karl replied. "The old emperor, Karl the Great. Most recently I fought the heathen Danes in the north, for the margrave of the North Mark. I travel to Franconia to take up my lands."

Her look was demure, but he knew she saw the shabbiness of

his harness—his weapons and armor were good, and well kept, but the rest of his gear was not. And he had no servants.... *And the fief in Franconia is barely more than three peasant farms,* Karl thought sourly. Once he'd have given as much to a huntsman who served him well. He shook his head. Where had the years gone? The years when he'd been the strongest of the emperor's paladins, the bravest, one whose voice was listened to in council. There was no time he could point to and say: *Here I failed.* It had crept up on him, like the gray hair and the pain in his bones. *Enough.*

"What of you, wench?" he said roughly.

"My mistress is taken prisoner, as she rode to her wedding," she said, not calmly, but with fear well kept. "Her dowry with her, a great treasure, and all her escort slain or fled. She is of high birth, and her father's only child. I ride to bring her kinsmen; for vengeance, or to pay ransom."

Karl grunted and looked around. They had ridden out of the ryefields, into deep oak forest. That thinned, oaks gave way to pines, pine to naked heath knee-tall on the horses; the damp floral scent filled his nostrils. This was good country for bandits, and the new emperor did not keep them down as his mighty father had. Landloupers in the woods, Dane raiders on the seas—things were not as they had been in the great days.

"These are evil times," he agreed; the bride's father would have to pay a second dowry to get her free, and the bridegroom wouldn't be getting a virgin. "The count's castle is near," he said. "Why didn't you ride there, if masterless men overfell you?"

Ermenagarde hesitated. A suspicion narrowed Karl's eyes; bandits would find a knight's gear very useful indeed. But if she were a decoy, what of the struggle at the village? That slash she gave one of the louts was real enough; it might kill the man if it mortified, and wounds often did.

"Lord," she said slowly, "I fear if I tell you, you will think me crazed or demon-ridden. Come first to the count's fortress, and then I will tell you—and then you will believe."

"We can't reach the castle today," Karl said. Not without pushing the horses to exhaustion, which he would not do. A man with winded horses was no better than a man on foot, if he had to fight or run.

"Then, lord, I promise that I will tell you at the count's fort, but not before. And my word will be true, as God is my witness."

He nodded shortly. They spoke little after that, stopping a few times to let the horses drink or graze or roll. They made camp beneath an ash tree, tall and great, still with most of its leaves. When they'd eaten, Ermenagarde came to his blankets with a smile and no false modesty; he was glad of that, although of course it was the due of his rank. It would be a short ride to the count's in the morning, and he could demand hospitality—demand men to hunt down these bandits, if it came to that. He was feeling kindly, inclined.

"Christ have mercy, God have mercy," Karl said, crossing himself again and again.

The count's castle was built in the familiar pattern the old emperor had built to stake down his conquests—a rectangle of great upright logs on an earthen mound, with a three-story tower on another mound in the center, also of logs, laid horizontally, notched and squared. On the inner side of the fortress wall would be quarters for soldiers and servants, a smithy, storehouses, a well—whatever was needful. This was an isolated outpost, and so there was little in the way of a village outside the fort.

Now there was much less of everything. The thatch and wattle buildings were knocked flat, scorchmarks and mud to mark their passing. The huge oak timbers of the fortress wall were scattered like twigs. Many lay tumbled, the thick rawhide bindings which had laced them together snapped like single hairs. Others were frayed into splinters, as if they had exploded; still others were scorched and charred, though that might have happened afterwards, when thatch fell on cookfires and braziers. Fires often started so, in a burg that had been stormed.

"Catapults might have done this," he murmured to himself, drawing his sword and dismounting.

It was more for reassurance than otherwise. The emperor had catapults at Aachen, from the Greeks, or the Saracen caliph at Baghdad, gifts like the elephant that had shivered through a few winters in the north. Nobody would be building Roman war engines here, in this desolation of backwardness. This stank of magic.

What was inside was worse. Men—and women—clawed and torn, as if by some great beast, and burned by a fire like that of the Greeks. The count himself lay by the ruined gate of the inner tower. His face was still intact, locked in a grimace of despair; the helm had rolled free, and his bare pate was wet and shiny. The rest of him was charred. Karl prodded with the point of his sword, and found the expensive mailshirt the man had worn was now soldered together into a rigid cage of welded iron rings. The sword by his hand was melted like a wax candle. The charred scraps of a nightshirt beneath the armor proclaimed that the attack had come in the dark and by surprise. The knight imagined it: peace, the sleepy rounds of the sentries on the walls. Then flame arching across blackness, screams and terror, the great scaled shape descending....

He shook himself and looked around. The bodies had been looted; no surprise, peasants would have done that in the week or so they'd lain, whoever did the slaying. There were fewer bodies than he'd have awaited, in a place like this. No livestock, and many of the humans were mere fragments, a limb or a head. That brought unpleasant thoughts.

"Who did this?" he turned to Ermenagarde fiercely. "The margrave, the duke, perhaps even the emperor himself—they should know of it."

Ermenagarde made a sign against evil, one he recognized. "They could do nothing. What can soldiers do against the Wurm?"

Karl signed himself, sheathed his sword, and sat on a timber; he ran his right hand through his beard, the hairs sticking and catching on the thick cracked calluses on his palm and fingers. Trolls and night hags, drows and wurms… all more often heard of than seen. Yet they did haunt more often here, where the Old Ones lingered, than in lands long Christian. He himself had seen the whirling dust demons that the Saracens had brought with them from their deserts to Spain when they overthrew the Goths. He moved about, searching, and found the tracks of great three-toed clawed feet in the dirt, one baked to brick by the flames. The span was broad as his paired hands, larger than the largest bear he'd ever seen. From the spacing, it took strides near the length of a tall man's body.

"The margrave could send priests to exorcise a thing of evil," he rumbled, deep in his chest.

Ermenagarde pointed silently to the ruins of a chapel. Not even the body of the priest remained. Perhaps a bishop with holy relics might prove more effective; perhaps not.

Karl went on: "Then what could your mistress' kinsmen do?"

"Pay, my lord," she said bluntly. "Remember the story of Sigurd Fafnirsbane. Ever did the breed of the great Wurms long for gold; and many of them are not just beasts, but creatures who speak and think as men do. This one—"

"You have seen it?"

"With my own eyes; may I be stricken blind if I lie. This one longs greatly for more gold, though it lies on a bed of treasure. Only gold, or some great champion, may free my mistress. And the Wurm hungers for the flesh of maidens also, so it had best be soon. Its fear for its hoard is what keeps it penned close to its lair. Otherwise all the lands about would have been ravaged long ago."

Temptation seized Karl von Obersberg between one breath and the next. *I was the emperor's champion.* Now he was just an old man with many scars, shamed by the niggard generosity of the old emperor's son. In Franconia he'd sit and wait to die, with only his sister's daughters left alive of his kin. Somehow the time to marry had never come, the right match never presented itself; so he had no sons as yet, and no inheritance to give them. No bard would make a song of Karl von Obersberg's deeds; after the Saxon wars he'd seen fighting in plenty, but never where the greatest glory fell. Good useful work, but out of the eye of the great—he'd even missed the disaster where the rearguard was caught by the Basques when the emperor came back from fighting the Saracens in Spain. The pass *he'd* been sent to secure *was* secured, and used... but it was the men who'd died at Roncesvalles who'd gotten the gift of undying fame.

Like Sigurd. Though he'd been only a heathen, men still knew Sigurd's name centuries later. And there was a horde of gold, too. With gold and the head of a great Wurm, his fame and might would run from Brittany to the Slav marches. Beyond, even into the lands of Danes and Greeks. Part of the wealth he could spend to buy the favor of the Franconian lords he knew, favor that would bring him a real fief. Noble fathers would fight to give him their daughters' hands; he had good seed in him yet to breed sons. He might even take this noblewoman whom the Wurm held captive—she'd still be virgin, having been hostage to a beast rather than men, and her father would be grateful.

You go to your death. Karl had fought and wandered for twenty years and more, and learned to calculate the odds. What of it? Better a chance at glory than the certainty of his last years crouching by a niggard hearth, biting the coals and dreaming of when he was a man.

"I'll free your mistress," he said abruptly, standing and

looking around once more. The dead should be given burial, or at lest dragged into shelter against beasts. He could hear a wolf pack now. They would be in among the ruins, when the Wurm's scent washed away. "It would be a knightly deed, to rescue a noblewoman from so foul a thing. And a Christian one."

She knelt, bowing her head. "Thank you, my lord!" Her voice was trembling. "I feared… I feared it would be too late when I came to my mistress' father's house. The beast is cunning, but it hungers for the flesh of maidens only less than it craves gold."

"Come," he said to Ermenagarde. She was watching him with awe; yet with a hint of calculation in her green eyes. No doubt thinking of her prospects if he did the thing; they would be no worse than now if he died. "Tell me of this Wurm."

The cave was in a low hillside, tunneled into sand and clay. Scorchmarks showed about it, the very earth fused into glass about the mouth. Outside was a broad flat area of dirt pounded to the consistency of rock where the Wurm wallowed and basked. Trees had been pushed aside or snapped off or burned for half a league about, except for a few huge oaks; the damage was long enough ago that saplings sprouted fifteen feet from some of the stumps. Karl von Obersberg frowned at them thoughtfully, noting the lay of the land, snuffing at the wind—from the cave area, thankfully. The songs didn't say if Wurms had a good nose for scent, but he was going to act as if they were as keen as slothounds until it was proved otherwise. He could smell *it*, a stale rank serpent's stink.

Beside the cavemouth was a thick pillar driven into the ground, ancient oak cracked and mossy. Karl's eyes were no longer keen at short distances, but as if to compensate for that loss they'd grown better at distance. Across half a league he could see the form of the woman chained to it, her hands high above her head. A young woman, he thought, richly dressed, with jewels sparkling at throat and belt. Her golden hair hung to her knees, hiding her face, but that was no matter. If she was beautiful, all the better; the bards would make her so, regardless, in their songs, once he'd slain the Wurm. From what Ermenagarde said, the family was rich, Saxon nobles who'd stood by the emperor in the wars, and been rewarded well for it.

"How will you slay the Wurm?" the serving woman asked. She sounded as if curiosity devoured her like wolves; all through the day while he patiently quartered the area, he'd said nothing.

Karl grinned tautly. "In knightly fashion, with the lance," he said. "It's the only weapon likely to harm so large a beast, in any case. Get you gone over there"— he pointed to a dense thicket—"and hide in safety. I will make ready."

Ermenagarde licked her lips, tasting the salt sweat of fear. This Karl was a mighty warrior, that was plain to see, and a wise one. Still…

What is he doing? He'd been gone long enough for the shadows to move a hand's breadth. Then he trotted out of the woods again, onto the open ground. His cloak clung to him, and the horse—the horse was sopping wet. Her lips moved silently. *Clever.* Very clever indeed, but he seemed to have left his lance behind. Instead he lifted the aurochs' horn from its sling by his side and sounded it, a ripping blat that echoed back from woods and hill. Again and again he sounded it, until the clearing rang. Between blasts he roared a challenge.

The Wurm came forth. Four times longer than a man, low slung on feet like an eagle's, with legs that jutted up beside its ridged backbone in high-elbowed tension. Its body was much like a crocodile's, but the neck was much longer and the head narrow. Red eyes peered out from beneath a shelf of bone; when the mouth gaped, teeth showed like daggers of yellow ivory.

Ermenagarde caught her lip between her teeth. The Wurm gathered itself to leap... and Karl von Obersberg turned tail and ran, as fast as his horse could gallop. That was quickly, since he rode his trail horse, not the heavy war steed.

The woman watched for a second, open-mouthed. *A coward? He is a coward?* There was not a strand of gray in her black hair, but she was no girl in her judgment of men, and she knew Karl better than *that*.

The Wurm pursued, in a hunching, bounding run. Sunlight shone on scales like enameled metal. Flame bloomed forth from the jaws, setting the scrub alight; when the bulk of the charging monster struck the trees, even the whippy saplings were crushed to splinters. Trees broke. Flame billowed up again amid a scream of rage vaster than hills.

Then there was another shriek, of pain this time, and a billow of fog. Ermenagarde's eyes widened; she ran for the cavemouth with her skirts hitched up in her hands and her knees flashing.

"Quickly, Lady Gudrun!" she gasped, fumbling with the other woman's manacles. Then she darted into the cave, came out with two hunting bows and quivers. "We have little time. Something is wrong."

They kirted their skirts through their belts and dashed out along the trail of the monster.

The cold wetness of the cloak and the sudden padding under his mail hauled at Karl as he rode out into the clearing; no colder than the knot of fear beneath his breastbone. Only a lad new to battle thought he could not die. Wrong then—he'd seen so many perish with their bright swords unblooded—and a greater error here, where he fought something not of this world. That was good; it was his revenge on the world itself. He raised the horn to his lips and sounded it, slitting his eyes until the drops caught in his eyelashes sparkled like jewels against the morning sun.

"Come forth!" he called, between blasts. "A Christian knight calls you forth to die, monster! Spawn of Sathanas, come forth!"

He'd thought himself prepared. When the Wurm came forth, he felt his bowls loosen and stopped them just in time. Five times the weight of a bear, he decided, and teeth the length of daggers, and a hide like an elf-lord's armor in a ballad, fitted jewels that shone in the sunlight. And it breathed fire.

I COME, CHRISTIAN. The voice rang between his ears without going through them, soundless. It was huge, and very weary.

Karl's horse tried to buck, turn, and flinch all at the same time. He controlled it with a brutal jerk of the reins and pulled its head about. Once the beast realized what he was trying to do, it stopped fighting him, put its head down, and ran. He doubled the reins in his fists, bracing his feet to keep some control, and steered the berserk animal down the path he'd selected.

Fire exploded at his back. The wet cloak sizzled, and he could smell singed wet horsehair. The horse screamed in pain and ran faster; the Wurm was snake swift itself, but too huge to pass down the narrow trail without crushing the undergrowth, and that slowed it. Karl whooped like a boy as he ducked and wove to avoid the branches that might have swept him from the saddle. Another blast of fire—hot enough to singe his hair where it escaped under the edge of his helm, hot enough to dry the last water out of his cloak and set the padded gambeson beneath his hauberk steaming. Yet it was not as large and did not reach as far as the first blast. *Praise be to God,* Karl thought. He would have spurred the horse, except that it could run no faster. The last section of trail was straight and broad. He could hear the earthshaking beat of the Wurm's feet behind him.

Now. The trail and the ground vanished beneath the

horse's feet. It did not jump, simply ran out into empty space. That was enough to take them two lengths out into the river; Karl parted company with the saddle in midair. By luck he landed clear of the thrashing hooves, although he lost his helmet to the waters. They were deep enough for him to claw fingers into the mud and be well hidden. Even through the water he could see the shadow of the Wurm as it tumbled into the steep riverbank. Too heavy to jump, as he'd thought. And—

A scream, loud even through the waters. Steam exploded off their surface as the stricken monster crashed down; around him the river went from ice chill to warm in an instant. When Karl surged up through the surface, the mist still boiled, but only a trickle of flame came from the Wurm's jaws as it thrashed. The stub of his lance protruded from its side, driven in to the very crossbar by the Wurm's own weight. Only such force could have pierced that armored hide, which was why he'd braced it beneath the riverbank where the Wurm must come, if it followed him.

"Haro! Haro!" Karl shouted—half wheezed—as he drew his sword and darted in.

Beyond expectation, his war-horse came to the call. The huge beast reared and chopped down at the crippled Wurm. Ironshod hooves struck bone, and one clawed leg dangled limp. The Wurm tried to breath fire again, but only a trickle came forth, enough to burn his eyebrows dry and no more. Two-handed, he swung. Sparks rang, but the fanged head juddered to the shock. There was an old scar along the left side of the face, ending in a ruined eye; his blow reopened that old wound, and blood spattered out to hiss and steam on the wet rocks of the riverbed. Karl roared his triumph and stepped close, raising his sword above his head to drive it into the eye socket and the brain beneath.

"Die, beast!" he shouted. The long years fell away; he was the emperor's paladin, young and strong and victorious, the future open before him in blood and fire and gold.

Blackness struck.

Ermenagarde lowered her bow. The range was close, no more than twenty paces, but she'd never expected to strike so well. Karl von Obersberg stood like a statue with his sword raised and the arrow quivering in the base of his skull. His victory shout was still echoing as he toppled forward rigid as a tree and splashed down on the stones. His sword rang and sparked on river stones.

"Father!" Gudrun called, running forward and kneeling by the Wurm's head. "Father! Are you all right?"

The huge scaly muzzle moved feebly, and one forelimb pawed the air.

More practical, Ermenagarde looked around for the war-horse. Trained war steeds were the most valuable part of a knight's plunder, if the most difficult to sell, and Lord Widukind had a deplorable tendency to devour them if not reminded. The beast had retreated a hundred paces or so; she advanced slowly, with soothing words. The horse had had time to grow used to her voice, and to the taint of magic that hung about her. She got within arm's reach, took up the reins, and looped them firmly about an oak limb.

Gudrun's scream brought her about. Her eyes widened as she dashed to the other woman's side. The Wurm—Lord Widukind—was...

Molting, she thought in amazement.

The armor of brazen scales dropped from his sides like rain, plashing into the water like rain or tinkling on the rocks, then dissolving into dust. Steel bone and stony flesh melted, like sand in the purling water. Wriggling out of the mass, like a snake out of last year's skin, came... a man. A man she had not seen since she was an infant; not since the night they fled from a burning hold and the swords of the Franks.

"Father," Gudrun wept. "Father."

Lord Widukind, last overlord of the Saxons, staggered to his feet and stood with the water rippling around his bare knees. He was tall and fair-haired, with the massive scarred body of a fighting man of seven-and-thirty years. One arm hung limp, and a wound gouged up the side of his face to take his left eye, but he smiled—grinned and shouted for joy:

"The curse is broken!" He embraced his daughter with his good arm. "And Gudrun—I see you with a man's eyes, a father's eyes." He looked around in wonder. "How different the world is…" Down at himself. "I'm older. Well-a-day, that comes to us all."

Ermenagarde slung her bow and knelt, heedless of the water. "My lord," she said, breathless. "My lord."

Widukind raised her. With one hand he parted the silver collar about her neck. "Keep this as a gift," he said, handing it to her. "For your loyalty."

He looked down and pulled the dead knight onto his back. The face held no pain, only a look of transcendent happiness. "I know this man," he said slowly. "Not his name or his deeds, but I know him. Somewhere—"

"His name was Karl von Obersberg," Ermenagarde said.

Widukind shook his head. "*I curse you until the circle is broken,*" he quoted softly. "So the priest said. Hengst said the magic could be turned on itself, but only when the two were one. He was the one I taught at the last battle, when the temple burned."

The three looked down on the body. Widukind spoke at last. "Come. We will give him burial; he was a brave man, and a great warrior. And we will splint this arm, and rest before we go north."

"North?" Gudrun asked, wiping at the tears of joy on her cheeks.

"To the Dane king's court," Widukind said, wincing. The pain of his wounds was returning. "We won't lack for a welcome, with the gifts we bring."

Ermenagarde trudged through the water to retrieve the fallen knight's sword. *Twenty-seven swords,* she thought. Mostly with full sets of armor to accompany them, and other gear besides—a fair number of knights had passed by over the years, and few had been able to resist her story of Gudrun's looks.

"I'll cut the splint," she said, and headed for the woods.

TAKING FREEDOM

Adelia the sorceress was an uncommonly proud woman. This was obvious from her fine dress, a king's ransom of green satin, tucked and ruched, bright with ribbons and glittering with gold lace. Her thick brown hair, beautifully coiffed, was held in place by a gold net glittering with jewels, and in one richly gloved hand she bore a delicate little peacock feather fan.

She was certainly pretty enough to carry off these fripperies without looking ridiculous, which couldn't be said of every finely dressed lady at the fair. But it wasn't merely her appearance that made Adelia vain. The lady was a sorceress of note, an accomplishment which made her a person greatly to be feared as well as admired.

Adelia wore the signal of her achievement upon her smooth white brow, an illusion which the uninitiated saw only as a spot of flame. But the adept could read her capabilities there and know that she was both skilled and very powerful indeed.

The sorceress moved through the fair with her glossy head held high, ignoring the wary, often unfriendly stares of the folk around her. Ignoring as well the embarrassing meeping and cringing of her servant Wren, whose shyness had the wretched girl well on the way to panic. Wren had dropped the parcels she carried into the dust and the mud twice after a meaningless sight or sound had startled her; once, a cat sleeping on a window sill, then a dog barking in the street.

Listening to the sniveling and the whimpering behind her, Adelia rolled her eyes. *I should never have made her from such a pathetic creature in the first place! What was I thinking? A wren is the very essence of shyness. If I'd made her from a nightingale, she'd still be shy, but at least she could sing.* Suddenly she turned on her servant, glaring at the small, brown-haired girl in her plain dress. Wren froze, her mouth agape, panting in unabashed terror.

"Return to our room at the inn, Wren," Adelia commanded. "I shall come when the sun is *there*," the sorceress indicated a spot just above the western horizon. "Have a hot…have a *warm* bath prepared for me."

The last time she'd ordered a "hot" bath, Adelia had raised a blister on the foot she'd so incautiously plunged into the near-boiling water.

Wren gaped and panted.

"Do you understand me?"

Wren nodded.

"Then go!" Adelia pointed in the direction of the inn.

The little servant girl turned and bolted through the crush of people, trying to go in a straight line and calling out in little shrill peeps when she couldn't.

Some of the surrounding crowd cast a surreptitious glare in Adelia's direction, and she couldn't blame them. There was every appearance of a girl broken by ill treatment. But the truth was that Adelia never abused Wren; there would be no point.

Existing is punishment enough for that poor creature. With a tsk of disgust she continued on her way alone. It might be best to simply unmake the girl. Adelia was not quite ready to take that step just yet. Though admittedly, after this afternoon she was much closer to it than she had been.

Perhaps, she mused, *I would have better luck if I began with a bolder creature.* Adelia paced on. *A stallion?* The thought brought a smile to her face as she walked along. Then, with a sigh, she dismissed the idea. A stallion's size and aggression would be as difficult to manage in their own way as poor little Wren's terror. *Pity.*

At last her walking had taken her to the far end of the fair, where the animals were kept. Here at the leading edge of the animal market were smaller, less offensive creatures, and she passed by cages of dogs and ferrets and even monkeys.

Adelia paused to examine the capuchin monkey in its little velvet vest and fringed cap, sitting on its master's shoulder. But something almost human in its hands turned her away with a shudder.

That won't do, she thought with a grimace. *If I wanted something almost human, I could pick up any urchin off the streets.* And she moved on.

At last the sorceress came to the sellers of birds, and her steps slowed. Her experiment with Wren had been an almost total failure. The girl that had resulted from her spells ate worms, feared everything, and had to be constantly coaxed down from the rafters. But some part of Adelia resisted giving up.

Here, she knew in her heart, was the answer. Birds. They pleased her so, their beauty, their grace, their freedom.

She longed to possess that freedom, or at least to take it; on the theory that if you could take something from an entity, then in some measure what you had taken became yours.

She passed the song birds, lingered by the rare parrots. They were far more intelligent than the finches, she could see, but none of these had the fire she sought.

At last she came upon the hunting birds; some in cages glaring boldly out between the bars, some, hooded, sat upon their perches.

Yes! Adelia thought triumphantly. *A predator!* Just like herself. *This is what I need.*

"You there," she called imperiously. "Are these yours?" A gesture encompassed all the falcons of every variety.

The man she'd called looked up from his bargaining to note the lady sorceress. He bowed, and the man he'd been speaking with murmured that he'd return later and made off.

"Tell me about these," Adelia demanded.

The man was tall and hazel-eyed, with a shaggy beard streaked with gray. His craggy face fought a frown and Adelia wondered at it. Did the creature dare to think of denying her whatever she asked for?

"My Lady Sorceress," he said at last in a voice deep and quiet. "Is it your pleasure to hunt with hawks?"

"My pleasure," she said stiffly, "is to know about these birds. Instruct me in their character."

It seemed to the hawk seller that the flame on her brow burned brighter for a moment, and he bowed his head, leading her over to the cages.

"Their character, Lady?" He pursed his lips. "It varies from one to the other, just as character varies in people," he said at last. "Here," he said, pointing to a tiny kestrel, bright as a songbird, "this little lass, perfect for a lady…"

"No!" Adelia exclaimed contemptuously. "Nothing so small will do. And I want a male," she added on impulse.

"Females are preferred in falconry, Lady Sorceress," the man assured her. "The males are smaller, you see."

"Hmm," Adelia murmured. As she looked around, she spied a handsome blue-gray bird perched on a block, a curious leather mask over its head. Its color pleased her, and the size was just about what she wanted. "Tell me about this one," she said eagerly.

"He…"

"Ah!" she said approvingly. "He!"

"Yes, my Lady Sorceress. He is a goshawk. And…" the hawk seller paused. "And if the Lady Sorceress is unfamiliar with falconry, he would be a very poor choice to begin with."

Adelia leaned in close to the bird, studying its plumage; it had a clean, spicy fragrance. Suddenly she blew hard against its breast and the bird started with a sharp cry, then settled.

"I like him," she said decisively. "How much?"

The hawk seller's mouth dropped open. He looked at her, then at the bird, then drew himself up, like a man facing an angry mob.

"I cannot sell him to you, my Lady Sorceress. Unless, of course, you have some servant skilled in the ways of hawks."

She was utterly astonished at his audacity. Fortunately for the hawk seller, Adelia chose to find his response interesting.

With narrowed eyes she asked him, "Do you imagine that anyone in this whole fair will so much as touch this bird when I have expressed an interest in him?"

With a bow, the hawk seller replied, "The Lady is undoubtedly correct. If I do not sell him to you, he will not be sold."

Adelia studied him; he would not meet her eyes, and she detected a fine sheen of sweat forming on his brow. Clearly, he feared her.

"Then why will you not sell me this bird?" she said at last.

"Goshawks are the most difficult of hunting birds to bond with, my Lady. They are sensitive and wild and are considered utterly indifferent to the falconer. Some think them quite mad. And this fellow is not even fully trained, my Lady Sorceress. Let him fly, and he will leave you. And… in panic, to which goshawks are inclined, he may harm you."

"Then *why* is he here for sale?" Adelia demanded in exasperation.

"Because, my Lady, many falconers prefer to train their own birds."

She frowned. All this talk of training was unexpected, and indeed was useless since she never intended to hunt with the bird. Still, as a predator, it might need specialized care. Certainly it would need more than a seed cup and a little water. With a deep sigh, she resolved to pay heed to the hawk seller's concerns. Besides, she would need a male slave on hand, she might as well get some use out of him.

"Where might I find a servant skilled in the ways of hawks?" she inquired.

The hawk seller gave her directions and she tsked in disgust. The slave mongers were on the opposite side of the fair from the animal sellers.

One would think that they would keep all the livestock together, Adelia growled within her mind.

In less than two hours she returned with her purchase. The man she had bought was in his mid-twenties, only a little taller than herself, but with a muscular warrior's build. He had a thick head of rough-cut black hair and a short, curly beard. It was his shrewd, narrow, sherry-wine eyes that had decided her to buy him, though, over the older fellow the slave dealer told her was also familiar with hawks. Around his neck hung a relsk stone, the spell that rendered him obedient despite the pride with which he carried himself.

"My name," he murmured to her as they approached the hawk seller, "is Naim."

His name is Naim, she thought, amused. Naim was a word in the ancient tongue meaning an amount so small as to be nothing at all.

She walked up to the hawk seller and, ignoring the customer he'd been speaking with, the one she'd interrupted twice now, announced, "I believe that this person should satisfy you. Ask him what you will of caring for hawks." She glanced at Naim. "And he'd better satisfy you." She deliberately left it unclear as to whether this was a threat against Naim or the hawk seller.

She wandered idly around, examining the little kestrel that had first been shown to her. A pretty thing, but, she sniffed, female. Adelia listened without much interest as the two men talked, exchanging terms like "creance" and "tiercel." At last they settled down to dicker on price. Adelia crossed her arms beneath her breasts and raised one brow. Still, though she had not given him permission to do so, she allowed Naim to speak for her in obtaining the bird.

At last the two men shook hands. Naim turned to her to obtain money, while the hawk seller went into his little booth and returned with a heavy glove, a perch, and what looked like a leash.

Naim put on the glove and touched the back of the hooded hawk's ankles. The bird stepped back automatically, caught his balance, and settled on this temporary perch.

"I wanted to carry him," Adelia complained, chagrined.

"Of course, my Lady," Naim said soothingly. "But he's heavy, perhaps two pounds in weight, and he *is* a bird. I should hate to see him soil your beautiful gown."

She smiled slightly at the manipulative courtesy of his response and wondered where he'd learned it.

"No matter," she said with a shrug, and led the way to the inn proud as a queen at the head of a procession. Being followed by a handsome young man carrying a hawk was far more in keeping with her vanity than the attendance of the wretched Wren. *I shall definitely have to do something about her,* the sorceress thought.

Wren began to scream the moment they brought the hawk into the room. To scream and to leap from chair to bed to table to chair. Had it been open, she'd have gone straight out the window. As it was, she bounced off the shutters more than once. And she kept up the cacophony until Adelia threw the bedquilt over her, whereupon Wren dropped to the floor and lay silent and panting.

"Obviously someone will have to sleep in the barn tonight," Adelia snarled.

Naim bowed.

"Not you! That's a valuable bird," she said. "I won't risk its being stolen. "And don't get any ideas," Adelia warned him as she noted a flicker of interest spark in those sherry-brown eyes. "You will only be here to see that this bird is well tended."

The sorceress turned and contemplated Wren where she lay quietly beneath the blanket, then the gently steaming tub of scented water, and finally she turned back to look into the interested eyes of her falconer.

"Put that down," she said, indicating the goshawk. "Then go and tell the landlord that I'll need a curtain set up to run across the room. If we can keep Wren from seeing the bird, she should keep quiet."

She could have created some sort of barrier magically, but Adelia never wasted *power* if there was a more mundane way of doing things. Particularly if the doing required no effort on her part.

Naim settled the hawk on its perch, bowed, and left the room. Adelia smiled, pleased with her purchases. She could hardly wait to see what he and the hawk combined would become.

Now I think on it, the girl I combined with Wren was a coward. She remembered the pale, tear-stained face with disgust. The spell had been designed to put the bird personality uppermost, but the shy little bird and the cowardly girl had only accentuated each other's defects. *This time,* she thought happily, *I should have* much *better results.*

Adelia carried her hawk on her wrist for the first few miles of the journey home, wearing the too large gauntlet over her own exquisitely embroidered glove.

Wren, blindfolded, rode behind her, clutching the high rim of the sidesaddle and trying not to slide off. Every now and again, Naim, walking beside them, put a hand beneath the girl's foot and hoisted her back up.

"Should we feed him?" Adelia asked Naim.

"Nay, my Lady. From the look of his crop, he'll be all right for a while. And the hawk seller told me he hadn't been trained. While I'm sure he could find himself some dinner with no problem, getting him back to hand would be impossible."

She looked down on him and allowed herself a very small smile.

"I can do many things that others consider impossible, Naim. You would do well to remember that."

He bowed, and she laughed at his ridiculous courtly manners. Then she pulled up her horse.

"You were right, the bird grows heavy. Take him." She lowered her arm, and raised her brows when Naim sought to remove the glove with the bird. "Take him, I said," Adelia commanded.

The relsk stone did its work and Naim brought his bare hand up immediately and touched the hawk behind the ankles. As soon as its talons clamped down on the man's arm, blood began to flow.

"Ah," she said, stripping off the glove and dropping it. Immediately it filled as though an arm were wearing it and it floated into position behind the hawk. When the bird had stepped onto it, she said, "Now put your arm inside the glove."

Wincing, Naim did so. She rode on, unconcerned.

"Have you a shed where we can keep the bird, my Lady?" he asked, his voice thick with pain.

"Yes, but why can we not keep him in the house?"

"He is still half wild and would be frightened to be among us. The dark and quiet of the shed will be soothing for him, and he will learn that when I come, there will be food and something to relieve his boredom. These are the first steps to forming a bond." The hawk shifted, and Naim drew in a rasping breath.

Adelia frowned. "I do not like it that he should be fearful."

"It is his nature, my Lady. Those creatures that do not fear humans don't live to breed."

She laughed at that, then fell silent for a while. "When we return home," she said at last, "I will have Wren tend to your hand." She couldn't use wounded flesh in her experiments. Still, by the time she'd gathered the needed ingredients, these slight punctures should be healed.

A week later Adelia flung down Naim's hand in disgust.

"Why are these wounds not healed?" she demanded.

"They're very deep," Naim answered. "One of the punctures went right to the bone, I'm sure."

She glared at him, hands on her hips. "Well, this is very inconvenient!" He bowed and she spun away from him with an impatient tsk! "I detest delay," she snapped. "Absolutely detest it!"

Naim opened his mouth to speak, closed it, frowned, then licked his lips. "My Lady," he said at last, "I must speak to you on a matter of some concern to me."

Adelia cast a disdainful glance over her shoulder and asked, "Of what matter could a *matter* of concern to you, be to me?"

He bowed, and her brows snapped down into a frown. She decided that she didn't like all this bowing. *A mere nervous tic,* she thought contemptuously. A habit, like clearing one's throat before speaking or always saying, "therefore." *It is an imperfection. And I do not like it that my subject should have an imperfection.* Working with imperfect material had created the disaster that was Wren.

"I am the son of Baron Tharus of Arpen. If you will but send to him, he will ransom me, I know. Whatever price you ask, he will pay it." Naim gazed at her most earnestly.

"Hmph," she said, turning to look at him. "You are the son of a baron?"

"Yes, my Lady."

"*Don't* bow," she cautioned him. "So you are familiar with the use of a sword and lance?"

"Yes, my Lady."

Oh, excellent! she thought, hugging the information to her.

I must translate those skills to my new creature. I knew I'd made the right choice in this slave!

"And how did the son of a baron come to be in a slavepen?" she asked in idle curiosity.

"I was kidnapped," he replied, "and carried over the border."

"Oh, really? Well," she said, and brought her hand to her face, "I don't imagine your father wants you back, then."

"I promise you that he does," Naim insisted, somewhat piqued. "I am his only son and his heir."

"Then don't you find it odd that your kidnappers never applied to your doting papa for this ransom you so confidently promise? I doubt the slave dealer gave them as much as I paid for you, and I assure you, Naim, you weren't very expensive." She smiled, knowing by the look in his eyes that she'd shaken him, at least for a moment, and it amused her tremendously.

"I gave an enemy who may have paid them to do it," he said slowly.

In a sudden shift of mood Adelia became bored by the subject, and she cut him off with a graceful gesture.

"It doesn't matter!" she said dismissively. "I don't need your pathetic *ransom*. I can provide for myself very well. And have I not said that I detest delay? I don't need gold, I need you. So put any thought of leaving here out of your head." Adelia spun on her heel and moved toward the door of the parlor.

"Wren told me what you did to her," Naim shouted.

Adelia stopped like one struck in the back by a dagger, and looked toward the kitchen as though she could see through the wall. Then slowly, she turned toward him.

"Wren speaks?" she said in astonishment.

"Aye," he said defiantly. "Just not to you."

"Huh," she said, and quirked her lips downward. "And your point is?"

"My point is that I am a nobleman! It cannot be that I am

meant to be destroyed by your evil magic!" he cried. "There are standards in the treatment of noblemen that every right-thinking king or duke will acknowledge. You have no right to do this to me!"

"But, Naim," she said gently, taking a step toward him, "you aren't a nobleman. You are a slave. And I have every right to do with my property whatever I wish. As every *right*-thinking king or duke would agree." Adelia gave him a taunting smile. "Did you not have slaves in your father's house, Naim?"

He glared at her, breathing hard.

Adelia enjoyed his obvious anger, and his helplessness to act upon it.

"No doubt you embraced them as your brothers, treated them as equals. What a paradise your father's house must have been," she sneered, spreading her arms wide, "with everyone living in perfect harmony."

Naim lowered his eyes, his cheeks flushed with fury or shame.

"Oh, no?" Adelia stepped closer, lowered her head in an attempt to look into his eyes. "Did you beat them? Humiliate them? Let them go hungry?"

"Yes," he whispered.

"And yet you expect better." Adelia quirked the corners of her mouth downward. "I fear you will be disappointed, Naim."

He merely glared at her from under lowered eyebrows.

"Go," she said. "Tend my hawk. Feed it, make friends with it, do whatever you must to keep it alive and healthy."

Naim gave her a surly glance, then stomped out of the room. Ruefully, she watched him go.

So Wren can speak, Adelia thought. *And she knows and understands, at least a little, what's happened to her. Hmph. Well, that's useful to know, but somewhat annoying, too.* Naim might well prove a handful over the next few days if he believed she intended to destroy him. *I would rather he had remained ignorant of his fate.*

Not that knowing it would change anything. Adelia gave a little huff of annoyance. Then decided that she would keep Wren a little longer. The girl was hopeless at most things. *But she does my hair so beautifully.* Doubtless a carryover of her nest-building abilities.

Well, there were worse reasons to keep someone alive.

She contemplated the necessary delay while Naim continued healing and sighed. *A few days shouldn't make that much difference,* she thought. Adelia calculated planetary influences in her head and frowned, not greatly liking the results. There would be ample power to draw on, but nothing that especially favored *her;* ever the most important part of the equation where the sorceress was concerned.

"I want you to show me my hawk," Adelia said, coming up behind Naim.

He started and turned, frowning, made a slight move as though to bow, thought better of it and did not.

"He has only seen me for days now, my Lady," Naim said. "It would not be good for his training to introduce a new person into his life just now."

Adelia smiled brightly and nodded.

"I don't care," she said. "I have never seen my hawk without that stupid-looking *thing* on its head, and I want to look at it."

"It would cause delay, my Lady."

She stepped close to him and held his gaze with her own. "Are you trying to manipulate me, Naim?"

"No, my Lady." He seemed genuinely confused.

Ha, so it really would affect the hawk's training. How very fortunate that it doesn't matter.

She gestured for Naim to take her to the shed, and they moved off.

"Have you given any further thought to what I told you,

my Lady?" he asked as they walked along.

"Of course not, Naim. And we will not speak of it again."

Naim compressed his lips and walked on. He opened the door and stood aside for her.

"Oh!" Adelia gasped in astonished dismay.

At her entrance the tethered hawk had flattened the feathers on its body, but those that framed its head flared in a sunburst around its staring, blood-red eyes. The hawk's beak gaped half open as though eager to rip at her flesh.

She took a step backward and looked at Naim in horror.

"Its eyes are *red?* The other hawks didn't have red eyes! This is most unexpected." *That rotten-hearted hawk seller never mentioned those freakish eyes.* "What's wrong with it?" she demanded of Naim. *I'll give that hairy fool red eyes if he's sold me a sick bird! I'll pluck them out and feed them to him!*

"The bird is perfectly normal, my Lady. His eyes will darken as he ages, but all goshawks have red eyes." Naim couldn't help the superior little smile that twitched at the corners of his mouth. The lady sorceress was so very startled.

Adelia looked up at him, gazing into his eyes intently as though searching for some great meaning there. Pleased, he turned the full force of his very charming smile upon her.

I'll have to keep Naim's eye color, she thought. *Size. Size will be a consideration as well. Hmm. Perhaps I'll import Naim's eyes entirely, just as they are.* But she was not pleased. She'd hoped to use the hawk's vastly superior vision, but... the hideous color and freakishly large orbs would be impossible to live with.

Adelia sighed, and Naim closed his eyes and lowered his head, seeking her lips.

"*Back!*" she snapped, her voice like a whip-crack.

Naim almost leaped away from her, his eyes wide.

"What is the matter with you?" She looked at him as if he'd gone mad. "Is this some ploy to get me to send you back to your *papa?*"

"No, no," he stammered. "It's… when you looked into my eyes like that…"

"By all that lives," she said in wonder, "you are a vain and foolish little man." Then she laughed. *Oh, dear,* she thought. *I do hope he'll be as amusing when I've changed him.*

And laughing, she walked back to the house, where Wren stared in wonder at her as she came through the door.

"Ah. So you're here," Adelia said, smiling. "The time has come at last."

Naim stood in the door of her spell-casting chamber, his face somewhat pale.

"Go away, Wren."

The servant girl, who'd summoned Naim at Adelia's command, gave him one last, desperate look and flitted off. Adelia grinned conspiratorially at him.

"She spoke to me, you know. On your behalf." She was genuinely delighted to have heard Wren's voice, which was high and sweet. "She wished me to spare you. And I'm so pleased that she dared to speak up that I've decided I shall. Come in," she gestured him forward.

"Do… do you mean it?" he asked, looking very young in his relief.

"Yes," she said, bustling about. "Sit there." She indicated a chair set within a complicated design. "Step through the break I've left in the pattern."

He looked nervously at the chair and then back at her where she mixed something in a cup. The hawk, hooded, sat on its perch inside an identical design.

"You're going to let me go?" he asked.

"No, of course not." Adelia glanced over her shoulder at him. "I told you to sit down."

Naim simply stood and stared at her. He swallowed visibly, looking stunned.

"Sit!" she told him in a voice of command.

Naim took a deep breath and then reluctantly, fighting the compulsion of the relsk stone around his neck, moved to the chair.

"I don't understand," he whispered, his voice thick with tears.

"You have been well fed, you have enjoyed Wren." She grinned at his shock. "Don't look so surprised. I know everything that happens in my house or on my land. It accorded with my wishes, and so I've allowed it." She moved toward him, cup in hand.

"You said that you would spare me." His eyes were pleading.

"And I will." Adelia held out the cup. "There is no reason for you to be awake while the transformation takes place. Apparently that was the worst of it for Wren, and so I shall spare you that." She smiled. "Drink."

"I do not want to be transformed!" Naim shouted. "I merely wish to go home," he said softly.

The sorceress closed her eyes and took a very deep breath.

"By the same token," she said crisply, after a moment's pause to hold onto her temper, "there is no need for you to be asleep either. You can sit here screaming your head off, totally aware the whole time of what is happening to you, or you can sleep through it." She held the cup out to him. "It's entirely up to you."

"Can I say nothing that will change your mind?" he pleaded.

"This is your last chance," Adelia said through clenched teeth.

Looking her straight in the eye, he took the cup. Then he flung back his head and drank it all in three great swallows.

"Excellent," Adelia said with a nod, taking back the cup.

She knelt and completed the open space in the pattern around his chair. Then placing the cup outside her circle, she completed all the spaces left undrawn, picked up her wand,

and began to work the spell she'd labored over so long.

Adelia called upon forces and elements and gods so old they barely knew themselves that they existed. Her long hair belled out around her head with the discharge of power, and the words she spoke made no sound though she shouted them. She gestured with her wand and the words that she wrote on the air hung there, palpable, but invisible, yet squirming with a life of their own.

Naim's head dropped to his breast, his breathing the slow, regular rhythm of deep sleep; even as the goshawk screamed and bated, beating its wings frantically as it sought to escape whatever *thing* crawled insidiously beneath its feathers.

At the appointed moment Adelia spoke a word, and the air boomed like a thunderclap. The man and the bird began to stream toward each other in thin ribbons, meeting and mixing over a complex pattern in the center of the design. Faster and faster the elements of their being mingled and solidified into one mass, until the jesses hung empty and the man's clothes collapsed with a small sound like a sigh.

When the shape that hung over the design was complete, the sorceress called out again and silence fell so sharply it stung like a slap.

Adelia fell to her hands and knees, drooling with exhaustion and nausea. She fell onto her side, panting, and stared up at what she'd created.

The man who stood over her had hair of a curious gray-blue shade, and proud, imperious features. His chest was broad and muscular as were his arms. His legs, though, were thin and his feet curiously bony. But the eyes were Naim's.

We can do something to build up his legs, Adelia thought. *I am pleased.*

"There are clothes for you, there," she croaked, gesturing at a table in the corner.

The man looked down at her, then went to the table and began to dress.

She'd chosen black for him, trimmed in blue. It went very well with his odd hair color.

He picked up the sword, drew it partway from its sheath, and smiled at the quality of the blade. Then he wrapped the sword belt around his slim hips as he walked back to where she lay.

With difficulty Adelia hoisted herself onto one elbow and reached up to him.

"Help me up," she commanded.

"I think not," he said, his voice a sharp tenor. "There is no relsk stone on me to bind me, nor am I blindfolded." He smiled down at her, flashing white teeth. "And you are far too weak to command me, sorceress."

Adelia blinked.

"As Naim, I would have done anything you asked to stay as I was. I'd have done twice that for my freedom. As a hawk, all I knew was that I wanted to fly free. And you would have taken that hope from both of us. You meant to meld us into one earth-bound creature tied to your will. Didn't you, sorceress?"

She dropped onto her back and licked dry lips.

"You are bound to me," she said.

He smiled again.

"No, I am not." He looked down at her, examining her with cold but interested eyes. "I am my own. More than I have ever been."

He drew his sword and stroked the flat of it over her cheek.

"What you have made of me, sorceress, is a better predator than I have ever been. The hawk in me thanks you for that. And the man in me," he drew the sword down her neck and across her breast to her heart, "he sees great possibilities. The man in me knows that he doesn't need to fear the sorceress; your powers are spent. The hawk in me knows that I need not fear the stranger; you lie there panting like a rabbit broken in the hunt."

He grinned, most joyfully, and pressed the point of his sword onto its target.

"Good-bye, Adelia."

LOST LEGION

"**S**hit," Captain McNaught said.

The map room of Firebase Villa had been dug into the soft friable rock with explosives, then topped with sheet steel and sandbags. It smelled of sweat and bad coffee and electronic components, and the sandbags in the dogleg entrance were still ripped where a satchel charge—a stick grenade in a three-pound ball of plastique—had been thrown during the attack six months ago.

"Captain?" the communications specialist said.

"Joy, wonder, unconfined happiness, *shit*," the officer snarled, reading the printout again. "Martins, get in here!"

Lieutenant Martins ducked through the entrance of the bunker and flipped up the faceplate of her helmet. The electronics in the crystal sandwich would have made the bunker as bright as the tropical day outside, but also would have turned her face to a nonreflective curve. Human communication depends on more than words alone to carry information, as anyone who meets face-to-face for the first time after telephone conversations learns.

"News?" she said.

"Look." He handed over the paper.

"Aw, *shit*."

"My comandante, is this the right time for the raid?"

Miguel Chavez turned and fired a long burst. The muzzle blast of the AK-74 was deafening in the confined space of the cave. The other guerrilla's body pitched backwards and slammed into the coarse limestone wall, blood trailing down past fossilized seashells a hundred and twenty million years old. Pink intestine bulged through the torn fatigues, and the fecal odor was overwhelming.

None of the other guerrilla commanders moved, but sweat glistened on their high-cheeked faces. Outside the sounds of the jungle night—and the camp—were stilled for an instant. Sound gradually returned to normal. Two riflemen ducked inside the low cave and dragged the body away by the ankles.

"The Glorious Way shall be victorious!" Chavez said. "We shall conquer!"

The others responded with a shout and a clenched-fist salute.

"I know," Chavez went on, "that some of our comrades are weary. They say: *The colossus of the North is reeling. The gringo troops are withdrawing.* Why not hide and wait? Let the enemy's internal contradictions win for us. We have fought many years, against the compradore puppet regime and then against the imperialist intervention force.

"Comrades," he went on, "this is defeatism. *When the enemy retreats, we advance.* The popular masses must see that the enemy are withdrawing in *defeat*. They must see that the People's Army of the Glorious Way has *chased* the gringos from the soil of San Gabriel. Then they will desert the puppet regime, which has attempted to regroup behind the shelter of the imperialist army.

"Our first objective," he went on, "is to interdict the resupply convoy from the coast. We will attack at—"

"Yeah, it's nothing but indigs," Martins said, keeping her

voice carefully neutral. "The indigs, and you and me. That's a major part of the problem."

Will you look at that mother, she thought.

The new tank was huge. Just standing beside it made her want to step back; it wasn't right for a self-propelled object to be this big.

The Mark III was essentially a four-sided pyramid with the top lopped off, but the simple outline was bent and smoothed where the armor was sloped for maximum deflection; and jagged where sensor-arrays and weapons jutted from the brutal massiveness of the machine. Beneath were two sets of double tracks, each nearly six feet broad, each supported on eight interleaved road wheels. Between them they underlay nearly half the surface of the vehicle. She laid a hand on the flank, and the quivering, slightly greasy feel of live machinery came through her fingerless glove, vibrating up her palm to the elbow.

"So we don't have much in the way of logistics," she went on. *Try fucking none.* Just her and the captain and eighty effectives, and occasionally they got spare parts and ammo through from what was supposed to be headquarters down here on the coast. "Believe me, up in the boonies *mules* are high-tech these days. We're running our UATVs"—Utility All-Terrain Vehicles—"on kerosene from lamps cut with the local slash, when someone doesn't drink it before we get it."

The tank commander's name was Vinatelli; despite that he was pale and blond and a little plump, his scalp almost pink through the close-cropped hair. He looked like a Norman Rockwell painting as he grinned at her and slapped the side of his tank. He also looked barely old enough to shave.

"Oh, no problem. I know things have gotten a little disorganized—"

Yeah, they had to use artillery to blast their way back into New York after the last riots, she thought.

"—but we won't be hard on your logistics. This baby has

the latest, ultra-top-secret-burn-before-reading-then-shoot-yourself stuff.

"Ionic powerplant." At her blank look, he expanded: "Ion battery. Most compact power source ever developed—radical stuff, ma'am. Ten years operation at combat loads; and you can recharge from *anything*, sunlight included. That's a little diffuse, but we've got five acres of photovol screen in a dispenser. Markee"—he blushed when she raised a brow at the nickname—"can go anywhere, including under water.

"We've got a weapons mix like you wouldn't believe, everything from antipersonnel to air defense. The Mark III runs its own diagnostics, it drives itself, its onboard AI can perform about fifteen or twenty combat tasks *without* anybody in the can. Including running patrols. We've got maps of every inch of terrain in the hemisphere, and inertial and satellite systems up the wazoo, so we can perform fire-support or any of that good shit all by ourselves. Then there's the armor. Synthetic molecules, long-chain ferrous-chrome alloy, density-enhanced and pretty well immune to anything but another Mark III."

Bethany Martins ran a hand through her close-cropped black hair. It came away wet with sweat; the Atlantic coast lowlands of San Gabriel were even hotter than the interior plateau, and much damper, to which the capital of Ciudad Roco added its own peculiar joys of mud, rotting garbage, and human wastes—the sewer system had given up the ghost long ago, about the time the power grid did. Sweat was trickling down inside her high-collared suit of body armor as well, and chafing everywhere. Prickly heat was like poverty in San Gabriel, a constant condition of life to be lived with rather than a problem to be solved.

She looked around. The plaza up from the harbor—God alone *knew* how they'd gotten the beast ashore in that crumbling madhouse, probably sunk the ships and then drove it out—was full of a dispirited crowd. Quite a few were gawking at the American war-machine, despite the ungentle urging of squads of Order and Security police to move along. Others were concentrating on trying to sell each other bits and pieces of this and that, mostly cast-offs. Nothing looked new except the vegetables, and every pile of bananas or tomatoes had its armed guard.

Her squad was watching from their UATVs, light six-wheeled trucks built so low to the ground they looked squashed, with six balloon wheels of spun-alloy mesh. The ceramic diesels burbled faintly, and the crews leaned out of the turtletop on their weapons. There were sacks of supplies on the back decks, tied down with netting, and big five-liter cans of fuel.

At least we got something out this trip.

"What I'd like to know," she said to Vinatelli, "is why GM can build these, but we've got to keep a Guard division in Detroit."

"You haven't heard?" he said, surprised. "They pulled out of Detroit. Just stationed some blockforces around it and cut it loose."

Acid churned in Martins' stomach. Going home was looking less and less attractive, even after four years in San Gabriel. The problem was that San Gabriel had gone from worse to worst in just about the same way. The difference was that it hadn't as far to fall.

"We're supposed to 'demonstrate superiority' and then pull out," Martins said. "We kick some Glorio butt, so it doesn't look like we're running away when we run away."

The twisting hill-country road looked different from the height of the Mark III's secondary hatch. The jungle was dusty gray thorn-trees, with some denser vegetation in the low valleys. She could see it a lot better from the upper deck, but it made her feel obscenely vulnerable. Or visible, which was much the same thing. The air was full of the smell of the red dust that never went away except in the rainy season, and of the slightly spicy scent of the succulents that made up most of the local biota. Occasionally they passed a farm, a white-washed adobe shack with a thatch or tile roof, with scattered fields of maize and cassava. The stores in the few towns were mostly shuttered, their inhabitants gone to swell the slums around the capital—or back to their home farms out in the countryside, if they had a little more foresight.

Everyone was keeping their distance from the Mark III, too, as soon as it loomed out of the huge dust-cloud. *So much for stealth,* she thought, with light-infantry instincts. *The Glorious Way will be laughing fit to piss their pants when we try to catch them with this mother.*

"Only thing is," Martins went on, "we don't need a Mark III to kick Glorio butt. We've been doing it for three years. Maybe they could send us some *replacements*, and a couple of Cheetah armored cars, like we used to have, or some air support, or decent *supplies* so we didn't have to live off the local economy like a bunch of goddamn feudal bandits. All of which wouldn't have cost half as much as sending this hunk of tin down to roar around the boonies looking purty and scaring the goats."

The rest of the convoy were keeping their distance as well. Her UATV was well ahead, willing to take point to keep out of the dust plume. The indig troops and the supplies were further back, willing to eat dust to keep away from the churning six-foot treads. Kernan's rig was tail-end Charlie, just in case any of the indigs got ideas about dropping out of the convoy. Not that she'd mind the loss of the so-called government troops, but the supplies were another matter.

She looked down. The newbie was staring straight ahead in his recliner, two spots of color on his cheeks and his back rigid.

"Hell, kid," she said. "I'm not mad at you. You look too young to be one of the shitheads who poured the whole country down a rathole."

He relaxed fractionally. "Maybe things'll get better with President Flemming," he said unexpectedly. "He and Margrave are pretty smart guys."

"And maybe I'm the Queen of Oz," Martins said. *This one still believes in politicians?* she thought. *God, they are robbing cradles.*

Or possibly just being very selective. You got enough to eat in the Army, at least—even down here in San Gabriel, admittedly by application of ammunition rather than money. Maybe they were recruiting extremely trusting farmboy types so's not to chance another mutiny like Houston.

Christ knew there were times when she'd felt like mutiny herself, if there had been anyone to mutiny *against* down here.

She put her eyes back on the surroundings. More thornbush; she clicked her faceplate down and touched the IR and sonic scan controls. Nothing but animal life out in the scrub, and not much of that. Certainly no large animals beyond the odd extremely wary peccary, not with the number of hungry men with guns who'd been wandering around here for the last decade or so.

"Why don't you shut the hatch, ma'am?" Vinatelli said.

"Because I like to see what's going on," Martins snapped. "This is bandido country."

"You can see it all better from down here, El-Tee," he urged.

Curious, she dropped down the rungs to the second padded seat in the interior of the hull. The hatch closed with a sigh of hydraulics, and the air cooled to a comfortable seventy-five, chilly on her wet skin. It smelled of neutral things, filtered air and almost-new synthetics, flavored by the gamy scent of one unwashed lieutenant of the 15th Mountain Division. Her body armor made the copilot's seat a bit snug, but otherwise it was as comfortable as driving a late-model Eurocar on a good highway. Martins was in her late twenties, old enough to remember when such things were possible, even if rare.

"Smooth ride," she said, looking around.

There were the expected armored conduits and readouts; also screens spaced in a horseshoe around the seats. They gave a three-sixty view around the machine; one of them was dialed to x5 magnification, and showed the lead UATV in close-up. Sergeant Jenkins was leaning on the grenade launcher, his eggplant-colored skin skimmed with red dust, his visor swiveling to either side. There was no dust on it; the electrostatic charge kept anything in finely divided particles off it.

"Maglev suspension," Vinatelli said. "No direct contact between the road-wheel pivot axles and the hull. The computer uses a sonic sensor on the terrain ahead and compensates automatically. There's a hydrogas backup system."

He touched a control, and colored pips sprang out among the screens.

"This's why we don't have to have a turret," he said. "The weapons turn, not the gunner—the sensors and computers integrate all the threats and funnel it down here."

"How d'you keep track of it all?" she asked. "Hell of a thing, trying to choose between fifteen aiming points when it's hitting the fan."

"I don't, anymore'n I have to drive," Vinatelli pointed out.

It was then she noticed his hands weren't on the controls. Her instinctive lunge of alarm ended a fraction of a second later, when her mind overrode it.

"This thing's steering itself?" she said.

"Yes, ma'am," he said. "Aren't you, Markee?"

"Yes, Viniboy," a voice said. Feminine, sweet and sultry.

Martins looked at him. He shrugged and spread his hands. "Hey, it's a perfectly good voice. I spend a lot of time in here, you know?" He waved a hand at the controls. "Best AI in the business—software package just came in, and it's a lot better than before. Voice recognition and tasking. All I have to do is tell it who to shoot and who to like."

"I *hope* you've told it to like me, Corporal ," she said flatly.

"Ah—Markee, register Martins, Lieutenant Bethany M, serial number—" he continued with the identification. "Lieutenant Martins is superior officer on site. Log and identify."

Martins felt a brief flicker of light touch her eyes; retina prints. The machine would already have her voiceprint, fingerprints, and ECG patterns.

"Acknowledged, Vini. Hello, Lieutenant Martins. I'm honored to be under your command for this mission. What are our mission parameters?"

"Getting home," Martins said shortly. Talking machinery gave her the creeps.

"Acknowledged, Lieutenant Martins. I will help you get home."

Vinatelli noticed her stiffen. From the tone of his voice, it was a familiar reaction. "It's just a real good AI, El-Tee ," he said soothingly. "Expert program with parallel-processing learning circuits. It's not like it was alive or anything, it just sort of imitates it."

The machine spoke: "Don't you love me anymore, Vini?" The sweet husky voice was plaintive.

Vinatelli blushed again, this time to the roots of his hair. "I put that in, ma'am. You know, I spend—"

"—a lot of time alone in here," Martins filled in.

"Hey, El-Tee," the young noncom said, in a voice full of false cheerfulness. "You want a Coke?"

"You've got Coke in here?" she asked.

He turned in his seat, pushing up the crash framework, and opened a panel. "Yeah, I got regular, classic, diet, Pepsi, and Jolt. Or maybe a ham sandwich?"

Fan-fucking-tastic, Martins thought. She looked again at the screen ahead of her; Jenkins was taking a swig out of his canteen, and spitting dust-colored water over the side of the UATV. Chickens struggled feebly in the net-covered baskets lashed to the rear decking. She felt a sudden nausea at the thought of being in here, in with the screens and the air conditioning and fresh ham sandwiches. The thing could probably play you 3-D'ed ancient movies with porno inserts on one of the screens, too. *Damned if I can see what it's got to do with fighting.*

"I'm bailing out of this popcan," she said. "Unit push." Her helmet clicked. "Jenkins, I'm transferring back to the UATV."

She heard a Coke can pop and fizz as she slid out of the hatchway.

"What's it like?" the big noncom said. He didn't face around; they were coming up on the Remo bridge, and all three of the soldiers in the back of the UATV were keeping their eyes on station. So were the driver and those in the front.

"It's a fucking cruise ship, Tops. Economy class, there's no swimming pool."

"Big mother," Jenkins said; his position at the rear of the vehicle gave him a view of the one hundred and fifty tons of it. Even driving at thirty miles an hour they could feel it shaking the earth as it drove. "Surprised it doesn't make bigger ruts."

"Lot of track area," Martins said. "Not much more surface pressure than a boot. Though goddamn me if I know what we're going to do with it. It isn't exactly what you'd call suitable for running around forty-degree slopes and jungle."

"Hey, El-Tee, neither am I," Riverez said, from the other machine-gun.

"Shut up, Pineapple," she said—the gunner was named for his abundant acne scars.

"Hell, we can run air conditioners and VCRs off it," Jenkins said. "Christmas tree lights. Dig a swimming pool. Maybe rig up a sauna."

"Can it, Tops," Martins said.

The road was running down into one of the steep valleys

that broke the rolling surface of the plateau. There was a small stream at the bottom of it, and a concrete-and-iron bridge that might be nearly a century old. The air grew damper and slightly less hot as they went under the shelter of the few remaining big trees. There were a few patches of riverine jungle left in the interior of San Gabriel, but most—like this—had been cut over for mahogany and tropical cedar, and then the slopes farmed until the soil ran down into the streams. Really thick scrub had reclaimed the valley sides when the peasants gave up on their plots of coffee and cannabis. Although the latter was still cheap and abundant, one of the things that made life here possible at all.

"Oh, shit," Martins said suddenly, and went on the unit push. "Halt. Halt convoy. *Halto.*"

As usual, some of the indigs weren't listening. The Mark III provided a more than usually efficient cork, and this time they didn't have to worry about someone driving an ancient Tatra diesel up their butts. Silence fell, deafening after the crunching, popping sound of heavy tires on gravel and dirt. The dust plume carried on ahead of them for a dozen meters, gradually sinking down to add to the patina on the roadside vegetation.

"What's the problem?" Jenkins asked.

"The bloody Mark III, that's the problem," she replied, staring at the bridge.

"Hell, it hardly tears up a dirt road," the sergeant protested.

"Yeah, it distributes its weight real good—but it's still all there, all 150 tons of it. And no way is that pissant little bridge going to carry 150 tons. Vinatelli!"

"Yes, ma'am?"

"You're going to have to take that thing and go right back to Ciudad Roco," she said. *What a screwup.* She must be really getting the Boonie Bunnies to have forgotten something like this. "Because that bridge isn't going to hold that monster of yours."

"Oh, no problem, El-Tee ," Vinatelli said.

His voice was irritatingly cheerful. The voice of a man—a boy—who was sitting in cool comfort drinking an iced Coke. A boy who'd never been shot at, who hadn't spent four years living in the daily expectation of death; not the fear of death, so much, as the bone-deep conviction that you were going to die. Who'd never fired a whole magazine from an M-35 into the belly of a Glorio sapper and had the bottom half of the torso slide down into the bunker with her while the top half fell outside and vaporized in a spray of fluids and bone-chips when the bagful of explosives he was carrying went off…

"Yeah, well, I'll just drive down the bank and up the other side," he went on. "Lemme check. Yes ma'am, the banks're well within specs."

Martins and Jenkins looked at each other. "Corporal," the lieutenant went on, "the water's about sixteen feet deep, in the middle there. The rains are just over."

In fact, it would be a good time for an ambush attack. Luckily the Glorios had been pretty quiet for the last three months. Doubtless waiting for the 15th to withdraw, so they could try final conclusions with the indigs. So that what was left of them could.

"That's no problem either, ma'am." A slightly aggrieved note had crept into the newbie's voice. "Like I said, we're completely air-independent. The sonics say the bottom's rock. We'll manage."

"How come everything's screwed up, but we can still build equipment like that?" Jenkins said.

Martins laughed. "Great minds," she said. "Fuck it, we've got a *spaceship* ready to blast off for the moons of Jupiter, and the government's lucky if it collects taxes on three-quarters of the country. They can't get their shit together enough to pull us out."

The Mark III was edging down the bank of the river. The banks were steep, in most places; right next to the first abutments of the bridge they'd been broken down in the course of construction, and by erosion since. Still fairly rugged, a thirty-degree angle in and out. A UATV would be able to handle it, and even swim the river gap against the current—the spun-alloy wheels gripped like fingers, and the ceramic diesel gave a high power-to-weight ratio.

The tank wasn't using any particular finesse. Just driving straight down the slope, with rocks cracking and splitting and flying out like shrapnel under its weight. Into the edge of the water, out until the lower three-quarters of the hull was hidden, with the current piling waves against the upstream surface—

"Lieutenant Martins," the oversweet voice of the AI said. "I detect incoming fire. Incoming is mortar fire."

A section of Martin's mind gibbered. *How?* The hills all around would baffle counterbattery radar. The rest of her consciousness was fully engaged.

"Incoming!" she yelled over the unit push. All of them dropped down into the vehicle's interior and popped the covers closed above them. The driver turned and raced the UATV back down the length of the convoy, past ragged indig troopers piling out and hugging the dirt, or standing and staring in gap-mouthed bewilderment.

Then the bridge blew up.

"Eat this!" Jenkins screamed.

The 35mm grenade launcher coughed out another stream of bomblets. They impacted high up the slope above. Return fire sparked and tinkled off the light sandwich armor of the UATV; a rocket-propelled grenade went by with a dragon's hiss just behind the rear fender and impacted on a cargo truck instead. The indig troops hiding under the body didn't even have time to scream as the shaped-charge warhead struck one of the fuel tanks built into the side of the vehicle. Magenta fire blossomed as the pencil of superheated gas speared into the fuel. Fuel fires rarely cause explosions, contrary to innumerable bad action shots. This was the rare occasion, as the ripping impact spread droplets into the air and then ignited them with a flame well above even the viscous diesel fuel's ignition point. A ball of orange fire left tatters of steel where the truck had been, flipped over the ones before and behind, and nearly ripped over the racing UATV.

The little vehicle's low wheelbase and broad build saved it. It did slow down, as the driver fought to keep control on the steep slope above the road.

"Now!" Martins shouted, rolling out the back hatch. Riverez followed her, and they went upslope at a scrambling run until the trunk of a long-dead tree covered them. She knew that the bruises along her side would hurt like hell when she had time to consider them, but right now there were more important matters.

Shoonk. Shoonk. Shoonk.

The mortar fired again. The result was the same, too. Not much of the Mark III showed above the water and the tons of iron and shattered concrete which had avalanched down on it five minutes before. One set of 5mm ultras was still active, and it chattered—more like a high-pitched scream, as the power magazine fed slugs into the plasma-driven tubes. Bars of light stretched up, vaporized metal ablating off the depleted-uranium bullets. There was a triple crack as the mortar-bombs exploded in midair—one uncomfortably close to the height that its proximity fuse would have detonated it anyway. Shrapnel whamped into the ground, raising pocks of dust. Something slammed between her shoulder blades, and she grunted at the pain.

"Nothing," she wheezed, as Riverez cast her a look of concern. "Armor stopped it. Let's do it."

It would be better if this was night; the Glorios didn't have night-vision equipment. Even better if this was a squad; but then, it would be better still if the Company was at its regulation hundred and twenty effectives. *Best of all if I was in Santa Fe.*

She and the other Company trooper spread out and moved upslope. Martins had keyed the aimpoint feature of her helmet, and a ring of sighting pips slid across her faceplate, moving in sync with the motions of her rifle's muzzle. Where she put the pips, the bullets from the M-35 in her hands would strike. Sonic and IR sensors made the world a thing of mottles and vibration; it would have been meaningless to someone untrained, but to an expert it was like being able to see through the gray-white thornbush.

"Left and east," she whispered, sinking to hands and knees. The heat signature of the ancient .51 heavy machine-gun was a blaze in the faceplate, the barrel glowing through the ghostly imprints of the thornbush. It was probably older than she was, but the Soviet engineers had built well, and it was still sending out thumb-sized bullets at over three thousand feet per second. They would punch through the light armor of the UATVs without slowing. The AKs of the guerrilla riflemen supporting it were vivid as well; the men were fainter outlines.

"Pineapple."

"In position."

"Now."

She slid the sighting ring over the gunner a hundred meters away and squeezed her trigger. *Braaaap.* The burst punched five 4mm bullets through the man's torso. The high-velocity prefragmented rounds tore into his chest like point-blank shotgun fire, pitching him away from his weapon and spattering blood and bits of lung over his loader. The other guerrilla was fast and cool; he grabbed for the spade grips and swung the long heat-glowing barrel towards her. *Braaap.* A little high that time, and the Glorio's head disintegrated. He collapsed forward, arterial blood and drips of brain sizzling on the hot metal.

The riflemen were firing at her too, and she rolled downslope as the bullets probed for her. It was about time for—

Thud-thud-thud. Pineapple's grenade launcher made its distinctive sound as it spat out a clip of bomblets. They were low velocity, and there was an appreciable fraction of a second before they burst among the enemy. Fiberglass shrapnel scrubbed green leaves off the thorny scrub; it also sliced flesh, and the riflemen—the survivors—leaped up. Perhaps to flee, perhaps to move forward and use their numbers to swamp the two members of the 15th. Martins fired until the M-35 spat out its plastic clip. The UATVs were shooting in support from the edge of the road, effective now that the Glorios were out of their cover. By the time she slapped in another 50-round cassette of caseless ammunition, they were all down, caught between the two dismounted troopers and the machine-guns from the road.

The wild assault-rifle fire of the fifty or so indig troops with the convoy may have been a factor, but she doubted it.

"Get those turkeys to cease fire!" she snapped through the helmet comm to Jenkins. It took a moment, and another burst from the UATVs machine-gun—into the ground or over their heads, she supposed, although it didn't much matter. "We got the others to worry about."

The Glorio mortars had made three more attempts to shell the convoy. Pretty soon now they were going to get fed up with that and come down and party.

A dot of red light strobed at the bottom left corner of her faceplate, then turned to solid red.

"Makarov?" she asked.

"Took one the long way," Corporal Kernan said laconically.

Damn. The big Russki had been a good troop, once he got over his immigrant's determination to prove himself a better American than any of them, and he'd done that fairly quick—down here in San Gabriel, you were pretty sure of your identity, Them or Us. More so than in any of the Slavic ghettos that had grown up with the great refugee exodus of the previous generation. *Damn.* He'd also been the last of their replacements. In theory the whole unit was to be rotated, but they'd been waiting for that for over a year.

"The Mark III's moving a little," Jenkins said.

She could hear that herself, a howling and churning from the streambed a thousand meters to her rear; it must be noisy, to carry that well into the ravines on the edge of the stream valley.

"Fuck the Mark III—" she began.

A new noise intruded onto the battlefield. A multiple blam sound from the riverbed, and a second later the distinctive surf-roar of cluster bomblets saturating a ravine two ridges over from the road. Right after that came a series of secondary explosions, big enough that the top of a ball of orange fire rose over the ridgeline for a second. Echoes chased each other down the river valley, fading into the distance.

"Well," she said. "Well." Silence fell, broken only by the rustling of the brush and the river. "Ah, Pineapple, we'll go take a look at that."

Somehow she didn't think there would be much left of the guerrilla mortars or their operators. "Pity about that Mark III. Looks like it might have been good for something at that."

"Vinatelli, come in," Martins said, perched on one of the bridge pilings.

Close up, the Mark III looked worse than she'd thought. Only the sensor array and two of the upper weapons ports showed. The bulk of the hull was buried under chunks of concrete, wedged with steel I-beams from the bridge. Limestone blocks the size of a compact car had slid down on top of that; the Glorios had evidently been operating on the assumption that if one kilo of plastique was good, ten was even better. She couldn't argue with the methodology; overkill beat minimalism most times, in this business. Water was piling up and swirling around the improvised dam, already dropping loads of reddish-brown silt on the wreckage. With the water this high, the whole thing would probably be under in a few hours, and might well back up into a miniature lake for weeks, until the dry season turned the torrent into a trickle.

"Vinatelli!" she said again. If the radio link was out, someone would have to rappel down there on a line and beat on the hatch with a rifle-butt.

The newbie had come through pretty well in his first fire-fight, better than some... although to be sure, he hadn't been in any personal danger in his armored cruise liner. It was still creditable that he hadn't frozen, and that he'd used his weapons intelligently. He might well be curled up in after-action shock right now, though.

"Lieutenant Martins," the excessively sexy voice of the tank said. *Christ, how could Vinatelli do that to himself?* she thought. The voice made *her* think of sex, and she was as straight as a steel yardstick. Mind you, he was probably a hand-reared boy anyhow. Maybe a programming geek made the best rider for a Mark III.

"*Vinatelli!*" Martins began, starting to get annoyed. Damned if she was going to communicate with him through a 150-ton electronic secretarial machine.

McNaught's voice came in over the Company push. "Martins, what's going on there?"

"Mopping up and assessing the situation with the Mark III, sir," Martins said. "It's screwed the pooch. You'd need a battalion of engineers to get it loose."

"Can you get the UATVs across?"

"That's negative, sir. Have to go a couple of clicks upstream and ford it. Double negative on the indig convoy." Who had cleared out for the coast as soon as they'd patched their wounded a little; so much for the supplies, apart from what her people had on their UATVs… supplemented by what they'd insisted on taking off the trucks.

"What if you shitcan the loads, could you get the UATVs across then?"

"Well, yeah," she said, her mind automatically tackling the problem. Use a little explosive to blow the ends of the rubble-pile, then rig a cable… the UATVs were amphibious, and if they could anchor them against being swept downstream, no problem. "But sir, we *need* that stuff."

"Not anymore we don't," McNaught said grimly. She sat up. "Just got something in from Reality."

That was the U.S. Martins extended a hand palm-down to stop Jenkins, who was walking carefully over the rocks toward her. The captain's voice continued: "The President, the Veep, the Speaker, and General Margrave were on a flight out of Anchorage today. A Russian fighter shot them down over the ocean. No survivors."

"*Jesus Christ,*" Martins whispered. Her mind gibbered protests; the Russians were a shell of a nation, and what government they had was fairly friendly to the U.S.

"Nobody knows what the hell happened," McNaught went on. "There's some sort of revolution going on in Moscow, so *they* aren't saying. The East African Federation has declared war on North Africa and launched a biobomb attack on Cairo. China and Japan have exchanged ultimatums. There are mobs rioting in DC, New York, LA—and not just the usual suspects, in Seattle and Winnipeg too. General mobilization and martial law've been declared."

Martin's lips shaped a soundless whistle. Then, since she had survived four years in San Gabriel, she arrowed in on practicalities: "How does that affect us, sir?"

"It means we're getting a tiltrotor in to collect us in about six hours," he replied. "CENPAC told the 15th HQ element at Cuchimba to bring everyone in pronto—they want the warm bodies, not the gear. We cram on with what we carry and blow everything else in place. They're sending heavy lifters to pick up what's left of the division and bring us home from Cuchimba. If you read between the lines, it sounds like complete panic up there—the Chiefs don't know what to do without Margrave, and Congress is meeting in continuous session. Much good that will do. Sure as shit nobody cares about San Gabriel and the Glorios anymore. Division tells me anyone who isn't at the pickup in six hours can walk home, understood?"

"Sir, yes sir," Martins said, and switched to her platoon push.

"All right, everyone, listen up," she began. "Jenkins—"

"*What* did you say?"

"This unit is still operable," Vinatelli's voice replied.

My, haven't we gotten formal, Martins thought furiously. "I told you, newbie, we're combat-lossing the tank and getting out of here. *Everyone* is getting out of here; in twenty-four hours the only Amcits in San Gabriel are going to be the ones in graves. Which will *include* Corporal Vinatelli if you don't get out of there *now.*"

Behind her the first UATV was easing into the water between the two cable braces, secured by improvised loops. The woven-synthetic ropes were snubbed to massive ebonies on both banks, and with only the crew and no load, it floated fairly high. Water on the upstream side purled to within a handspan of the windows, but that was current. The ball wheels spun, thrashing water backward; with his head out the top hatch, Jenkins cried blasphemous and scatological encouragement to the trooper at the wheel and used his bulk to shift the balance of the light vehicle and keep it closer to upright. Most of the rest of her detachment were out in overwatch positions. Nobody was betting that the Glorios wouldn't come back for more, despite the pasting they'd taken.

You could never tell with the Glorios; the death-wish

seemed to be as big a part of their makeup as the will to power. Revolutionary purity, they called it.

"Lieutenant," Vinatelli said, "this unit is still operable. Systems are at over ninety-five percent of nominal."

"Jesus fucking *Christ*, the thing's buried under four hundred tons of rock! I'm combat-lossing it, Corporal. Now get out, that's a direct order. We're time-critical here."

"Corporal Vinatelli is unable to comply with that order, Lieutenant."

"Hell," Martins said, looking down at the top of the Mark III's superstructure, where fingers of brown water were already running over the armor.

It looked like she was going to leave two of her people here dead. The lad had frozen after all, only it took the form of refusal to come out of his durachrome womb, rather than catatonia. Frozen, and it was going to kill him—when the ham sandwiches and Coke ran out down there, if not before. There was certainly nothing she could do about it. Sending a team down with a blasting charge to open the hatch didn't look real practical right now. Even if they had time, there was no telling what someone in Vinatelli's mental condition might do, besides which the tank was programmed to protect its own integrity. And she certainly had better things to do with the time.

A *whump* of explosive went off behind her; Kernan making sure the captured Glorio weapons weren't any use to anyone.

"Max units, pull in," she said, and began climbing back to the cable anchor point to board Kernan's UATV. Behind her, a thin muddy wave washed across the top surface of the Bolo Mark III.

"Comrades, we have won a glorious victory!" Comandante Chavez shouted.

He was standing in front of the crater where the guerrilla

mortars had been. For sixty meters around, the trees were bare of leaves and twigs; they sparkled in the afternoon sunlight, a fairy garden of guttering glass fibers. The crater where the ready ammunition had gone off was several meters across; the enemy had arranged the bodies of the crew—or parts thereof—in more-or-less regular fashion, the better to count them. Nothing useable remained.

"The giant tank filled some of our weaker comrades with fear," Chavez went on. The ground that he paced on was damp and slightly greasy with the body fluids of several Glorios, and the bluebottles were crawling over it. "They wanted to run and hide from the monster tank!

"Yet we—mere humanity, but filled with the correct ideological perspective—triumphed over the monster. We buried it, as the Glorious Way shall bury all its enemies, all those who stand between suffering humanity and Utopia!"

With several of the comandante's special guards standing behind him, the cheering was prolonged. And sincere; they had destroyed the tank that had been like nothing anyone had ever seen before. Now it was just a lump in the river below the fallen bridge.

"Onward to victory!" Chavez shouted, raising his fist in the air.

The Caatinga River was powerful at this time of year, when the limestone soil yielded up the water it had stored during the brief, violent rains. Maximum flow was in May, well after the last clouds gave way to endless glaring sun and the fields shriveled into dusty, cracked barrenness where goats walked out on limbs to get at the last shoots.

Now it backed at the rock dam created by the bridge. The lower strata were locked together by the girders, and the upper by the weight of the stone and the anchoring presence of the tank; its pyramidal shape made it the keystone. Water roared over the top a meter deep, and the whole huge mass ground and shifted under the pounding.

"Vini, the water will help," the Mark III said. "I'm going to try that now."

Mud and rock and spray fountained skyward, sending parrots and shrikes fleeing in terror. Boulders shifted. A bellowing roar shook the earth in the river valley, and the monstrous scraping sound of durachrome alloy ripping density-enhanced steel through friable limestone.

"It's working."

"Talk about irony," Jenkins said.

"Yeah, Tops?" Martins replied.

Jenkins had had academic ambitions before the university system pretty well shut down.

"Yeah, El-Tee. Most of the time we've been here, the Mark III would have been as useful as a boar hog to a ballerina. The Glorios would have just gone away from wherever it was, you know? But now we just want to move one place one time, and they want to get in our way—and that big durachrome mother would have been *real* useful."

"I'm not arguing," she said.

The little hamlet of San Miguel de Dolorosa lay ahead of them. The brief tropical nightfall was over, and the moon was out, bright and cool amid a thick dusting arch of stars, clear in the dry upland air. In previous times troops had stopped there occasionally; there was a cantina selling a pretty good beer, and it was a chance to see locals who weren't trying to kill you, just sell you BBQ goat or their sisters. Right now there were a couple of extremely suspicious readings on the fixed sensors they'd scattered around in the hills months back, when they decided they didn't have the manpower to patrol around here anymore.

Suspicious readings that could be heavy machine-guns and rocket launchers in the town. There were no lights down there, but that was about par for the course. Upcountry towns hadn't had electricity for a long time, and kerosene cost real money.

"It's like this," Martins said. "If we go barreling through there, and they're set up, we're dogmeat. If we go around, the only alternate route will eat all our reserve of time—and that's assuming nothing goes wrong on that way either."

Jenkins sighed. "You or me?"

Somebody was going to have to go in and identify the sightings better than the remotes could do it—and if the Glorios were there, distract them up close and personal while the UATVs came in.

"I'd better do it, Tops," she said. The squad with the two vehicles was really Jenkins'. "I'll take Pineapple and Marwitz."

Half the string of mules were in the water when the Glorio sergeant—Squad Comrade—heard the grinding, whirring noise.

"What's that?" he cried.

The ford was in a narrow cut, where the river was broad but shallow; there was little space between the high walls that was not occupied by the graveled bed. That made it quite dark even in the daytime. On a moonless night like this it was a slit full of night, with nothing but starlight to cast a faint sparkle on the water. The guerrillas were working with the precision of long experience, leading the gaunt mules down through the knee-deep stream and up the other side, while a company kept overwatch on both sides. They were not expecting trouble from the depleted enemy forces, but their superior night vision meant that a raid was always possible. Even an air attack was *possible*, although it was months since there had been any air action except around the main base at Cuchimba.

When the Bolo Mark III came around the curve of the river half a kilometer downstream, the guerrillas reacted with varieties of blind panic. It was only a dim bulk, but the river creamed away in plumes from its four tracks, and it ground on at forty kph with the momentum of a mountain that walked.

The sergeant fired his AK—a useless thing to do even if the target had been soft-skinned. A bar of light reached out from the tank's frontal slope, and the man exploded away from the stream of hypervelocity slugs.

A team on the left, the western bank, of the river opened up with a four-barreled heavy machine-gun intended for anti-aircraft use. They were good; the stream of half-ounce bullets hosed over the Mark III's armor like a river of green-tracer fire arching into the night. The sparks where the projectiles bounced from the density-enhanced durachrome were bright fireflies in the night. Where the layer of softer ablating material was still intact there was no spark, but a very careful observer might have seen starlight on the metal exposed by the bullets' impact.

There were no careful observers on this field tonight; at least, none outside the hull of the Mark III. The infinite repeaters nuzzled forward through the dilating ports on its hull. Coils gripped and flung 50mm projectiles at velocities that burned a thin film of plasma off the ultradense metal that composed them. They left streaks through the air, and on the retinas of anyone watching them. The repeaters were intended primarily for use against armor, but they had a number of options. The one selected now broke the projectiles into several hundred shards just short of the target, covering a dozen square yards. They ripped into the multibarrel machine-gun, its mount—and incidentally its operators—like a mincing machine pounded down by a god. Friction-heated ammunition cooked off in a crackle and fireworks fountain, but that was almost an anticlimax.

"Cease fire! Cease fire!" Comrade Chavez bellowed.

It was an unnecessary command for those of the Glorios blundering off into the dark, screaming their terror or conserving their breath for flight. A substantial minority had remained, even for this threat. They heard and obeyed, except for one team with the best antiarmor weapons the guerrillas possessed, a cluster of hypervelocity missiles. One man painted the forward tread with his laser designator, while the second launched the missiles. They left the launcher with a mild chuff of gasses, then accelerated briefly with a sound like a giant tiger's retching scream.

If the missiles had struck the tread, they would probably have ripped its flexible durachrome alloy to shreds—although the Mark III would have lost only a small percentage of its mobility. They did not, since the tank's 4mm had blown the designator to shards before they covered even a quarter of the distance to their target. The operator was a few meters away. Nothing touched him but one fragment tracing a line across his cheek. He lay and trembled, not moving even to stop the blood which flowed down his face from the cut and into his open mouth.

Two of the missiles blossomed in globes of white-blue fire, intercepted by repeater rounds. A third tipped upwards and flew off into the night until it self-destructed, victim of the laser designator's last twitch. The fourth was close enough for the idiot-savant microchip in its nose to detect the Mark III and classify it as a target. It exploded as well—as it was designed to do. The explosion forged a round plate of tungsten into a shape like a blunt arrowhead and plunged it forward with a velocity even greater than the missile's own.

It clanged into the armor just below the muzzles of the infinite repeaters, and spanged up into the night. There was a fist-sized dimple in the complex alloy of the tank's hull, shining because it was now plated with a molecule-thick film of pure tungsten.

"Cease *fire*," Chavez screamed again.

The Bolo Mark III was very close now. Most of the mules had managed to scramble up on the further bank and were galloping down the river, risking their legs in the darkness rather than stay near the impossibly huge metal object. Men stayed in their positions, because their subconscious was convinced that flight was futile. The tank grew larger and larger yet; the water fountained from either side, drenching some of the guerrillas. Comrade Chavez was among them, standing not ten feet from where it passed. He stood erect, and spat into its wake.

"Cowards," he murmured. It was uncertain exactly who he was referring to. Then more loudly: "The cowards are running from us—it fired at nobody but those actively attacking it. Fall in! Resume the operation!"

It took a few minutes for those who had stayed in their positions to shake loose minds stunned by the sheer massiveness of the thing that had passed them by. Collecting most of the men who'd fled took hours, but eventually they stood sheepishly in front of their commander.

"I *should* have you all shot," he said. A few started to shake again; there had been a time when Chavez would have had them shot, and they could remember it. "But the Revolution is so short of men that even you must be conserved—if only to stop a bullet that might otherwise strike a true comrade of the Glorious Way. Get back to work!"

Bethany Martins gripped the bowie in hatchet style, with the sharpened edge out. The blackened metal quivered slightly, and her lips were curled back behind the faceplate in a grimace of queasy anticipation. The weapon was close to the original that Rezin Bowie had designed, over a foot long and point heavy, but the blade was of an alloy quite similar to the Mark III's armor. It had to be sharpened with a hone of synthetic diamond, but it would take a more than razor-edge and keep it while it hacked through mild steel.

The Glorio sentry was watching out the front door of the house. She could tell that from the rear of the building because it was made of woven fronds, and they were virtually transparent to several of the sensors in her helmet. She could also tell that all the previous inhabitants of the three-room hut were dead, both because of the smell and because their bodies showed at ambient on the IR scan. That made real sure they wouldn't blow the Glorio ambush, and it was also standard procedure for the Way. The inhabitants of San Miguel had cooperated with the authorities, and that was enough. Cooperation might include virtually anything, from joining a Civic Patrol to selling some oranges to a passing vehicle from the 15th.

Generally speaking, Martins hated killing people with knives although she was quite good at it. One of the benefits of commissioned rank was that she seldom had to, anymore. This Glorio was going to be an exception in both senses of the word.

Step. The floor of the hut was earth, laterite packed to the consistency of stone over years of use, and brushed quite clean. A wicker door had prevented the chickens and other small stock outside from coming in. There was an image of the Bleeding Heart, unpleasantly lifelike, over the hearth of adobe bricks and iron rods in the kitchen. Coals cast an IR glow over the room, and her bootsoles made only a soft minimal noise of contact

Step. Through behind the Glorio. Only the focus of his attention on the roadway below kept him from turning. He was carrying a light drum-fed machine-gun, something non-standard—it looked like a Singapore Industries model. Her body armor would stop shell fragments and pistol-caliber ammunition, but that thing would send fragments of the softsuit right through her rib cage.

Step. Arm's length away in pitch blackness. Pitch blackness for *him*, but her faceplate painted it like day. Better than day...

Martins' arm came across until the back of the blade was touching her neck. She slashed at neck height. Something warned the man, perhaps air movement or the slight exhalation of breath, perhaps just years of survival honing his instincts. He began to turn, but the supernally keen edge still sliced through neck muscles and through the vertebrae beneath them, to cut the spinal cord in a single brutal chop. The sound was like an axe striking green wood; she dropped the knife and lunged forward to catch the limp body, ignoring the rush of wastes and the blood that soaked the torso of her armor as she dragged him backwards. The machine-gun clattered unnoticed to the ground.

The lieutenant dragged the guerrilla backward, then set him down gently on the floor. Only a few twitches from the severed nerve endings drummed his rope-sandaled heels against the floor. She paused for a moment, panting with the effort and with adrenaline still pulsing the veins in her throat, then stepped forward into the doorway.

"Jenkins," she murmured. A risk, but the Glorio elint capacity had never been very good and had gotten worse lately. "I'm marking the heavy stuff. Mark."

From point-blank, the shapes of machine-guns and rocket launchers showed clearly. She slid the aiming pips of her faceplate over each crew-served weapons position, then over the individual riflemen, the second-priority targets. Each time the pips crossed a target she tapped a stud on the lower inside edge of her helmet, marking it for the duplicate readout in Jenkins' helmet. The guerrillas had tried their best to be clever; there were low fires inside a number of the houses, to disguise the IR signatures, and as backup there were bound civilians grouped in what resembled fire teams around pieces of metal—hoes, cooking grills, and the like—to fox the sonic and microradar scanners. Some of them were so clever that she had to spend a minute or two figuring them out. When in doubt, she marked them.

It occurred to her that an objective observer might consider the technological gap between the Company's troopers and the Glorios unfair. Although the gross advantage of numbers and firepower the guerrillas had these days went a long way to make it up.

On the other hand, she wasn't objective and didn't give a damn about fair.

"Got it," Jenkins said.

"Pineapple, Red?" she asked. Short clicks from Riverez and Marwitz. She slid her rifle around, settling down to the ground and bracing the sling against the hand that held the forestock. The aiming pip settled on the rear of the slit trench that held the .51. Four men in the trench…

"Now." Diesels blatted as the UATVs revved up and tore down the road toward the village. She stroked her trigger, and the night began to dissolve, in streaks of tracer and fire. A cantina disintegrated as Pineapple's grenade launcher caught the RPG team waiting there.

"Shit, why *now?*" Martins said.

Captain McNaught's voice in her ears was hoarse with pain and with the drugs that controlled it. He could still chuckle.

"… and at the worst possible time," he said.

Firebase Villa was on fire this night. The mortars at its core were firing, their muzzle flashes lighting up the night like flickers of heat lightning. *Shump-shump-shump,* the three-round clips blasting out almost as fast as a submachine-gun. The crews would have a new set of rounds in the hopper almost as quickly, but the mortars fired sparingly. They were the only way to cover the dead ground where Glorio gunners might set up their own weapons, and ammunition was short. Bombardment rockets from outside the range of the defending mortars dragged across the sky with a sound like express trains. When the sound stopped there was a wait of a few seconds before the *kthud* of the explosion inside the perimeter.

The pilot of the tiltrotor cut into the conversation. "I got just so much fuel, and other people to pull out," he said. His voice was flat as gunmetal, with a total absence of emotion that was a statement in itself.

"Can you get me a landing envelope?" he said.

"Look, we'll cover—" Martins began.

A four-barreled heavy lashed out toward Firebase Villa with streams of green tracer. Yellow-white answered it; neither gun was going to kill the other, at extreme ranges and with both firing from narrow slits. The Glorio gun was using an improvised bunker, thrown up over the last hour, but it was good enough for this. Parts of the perimeter minefield still smoldered where rockets had dragged explosive cord over it in a net to detonate the mines. Some of the bodies of the sappers that had tried to exploit that hole in the mines and razor wire still smoldered as well. Many of the short-range guns around the perimeter were AI-driven automatics, 4mm Gatlings with no nerves and very quick reaction times.

"Hell you will, Martins," McNaught wheezed. "There's a battalion of them out there. I think—" he coughed "—I think Comrade Chavez has walked the walk with us so long he just can't bear the thought of us leaving at all." The captain's voice changed timbre. "Flyboy, get lost. You try bringing that bird down here, you'll get a second job as a colander."

"*Hell,*" the pilot muttered. Then: "Goodbye."

Martins and McNaught waited in silence, except for the racket of the firefight. The Glorios crunched closer, men crawling forward from cover to cover. Many of them died, but not enough, and the bombardment rockets kept dragging their loads of explosive across the sky.

It's not often you're condemned to death, Martins thought. Her mind was hunting through alternatives, plans, tactics—the same process as always. Only there wasn't anything you could do with seventy effectives to attack a battalion of guerrillas who were hauling out all the stuff they'd saved up. Even if it was insane, insane even in terms of the Glorios' own demented worldview.

"Bug out," McNaught said in a breathless rasp. "Nothing you can do here. They're all here, bug out and make it back to the coast, you can get some transport there. That's an order, Lieutenant."

If there was anything left to go back north for. The latest reports were even more crazy-confused than the first.

"Save your breath, sir," she said.

The Company had been together down here for a long time. They were all going home together. One way or another.

"Movement," someone said. She recognized the voice of the communications specialist back in Villa. Like everyone else, she doubled in two other jobs; in this case, monitoring the remote sensors. "I got movement… vehicle movement. Hey, big vehicle."

Nobody said anything for a minute or two, in the draw where the two UATVs waited.

"That's impossible," Martins whispered.

The technician's voice was shaky with unshed tears. "Unless the Glorios have a 150-ton tank, it's happening anyway," she said.

They were a kilometer beyond the Glorio outposts in the draw. The river ran to their left, circling in a wide arch around Firebase Villa. Water jetted in smooth arcs to either bank as the Mark III climbed through the rapids. In the shallow pools beyond the wave from the treads was more like a pulsing. Then the tank stopped, not a hundred meters from the UATVs' position.

"Vinatelli," Martins breathed. "You beautiful little geek!"

The tank remained silent. Another rocket sailed in, a globe of reddish fire trough the sky.

"What are you waiting for?" Martins cursed.

"I have no orders, Lieutenant," the newbie's voice said. "Last mission parameters accomplished."

Something dead and cold trailed fingers up Martin's spine. *He's gone over the edge,* she thought. Aloud, she snapped:

"Fight, Vinatelli, for Christ's sake. Fight!"

"Fight whom, Lieutenant?"

"The *Glorios*. The people who're attacking the firebase, for fuck's sake. Open fire."

"Acknowledged, Lieutenant."

The night came apart in a dazzle of flame.

"I think I know—I think I know what happened," Martins whispered.

Nothing moved on the fissured plain around Firebase Villa, except what the wind stirred, and the troopers out collecting the weapons. It had taken the Mark III only about an hour to end it, and the last half of that had been hunting down fugitives. The final group included Comrade Chavez, in a well-shielded hillside cave only three klicks away, which explained a great deal when the tank blew most of the hillside away to get at it. He'd been hiding under their noses all along.

She slung her M-35 down her back and worked her fingers, taking a deep breath before she started climbing the rungs built into the side armor of the Mark III. Some of them were missing, but that was no problem, no problem… The hatch opened easily.

Vinatelli must have had his crash harness up when the bridge blew. From the look of the body, he'd been reaching for a cola can. His head must have been at just the right angle to crack his spine against the forward control surfaces.

"So that's why Vinatelli didn't want to come out," she said.

McNaught was watching through the remotes of her helmet. "So it is alive," he said.

Martins shook her head, then spoke: "No." Her tone shifted. "Markee. Why didn't you go back to the coast?"

"Mission parameters did not require retracing route," the tank said, in the incongruously sultry voice. "Last established mission parameters indicated transit to point Firebase Villa."

"What are your mission parameters. Correction, what were your mission parameters."

"Lieutenant Bethany Martins is to go home," the machine said.

Martins slumped, sitting on the combing. The smell inside wouldn't be too bad, not after only six hours in air conditioning.

"It was Vinatelli," she said. "He was the dreamy sort. He had it programmed to do a clever Hans routine if an officer started making requests when he was asleep, and reply in his own voice."

"Clever Hans?" the captain asked.

"A horse somebody trained to 'answer' questions. It sensed subliminal clues and behaved accordingly, so it *looked* like it understood what the audience was saying. You can get a good AI system to do the same thing, word-association according to what you say. You'd swear it was talking to you, when it's really got no more real comprehension than a toaster."

"Why did it come here?"

"That was the last order. Go to Firebase Villa; it's got enough discretion to pick another route out of its data banks. And to shoot back if attacked in a combat zone. But that's all, that's all it did. Like ants; all they've got is a few feedback loops but they get a *damned* lot done."

She rose, shaking her head.

"Which leaves the question of what *we* do now," the captain said.

"Oh, I don't think there's much question on that one," Martins said.

She pulled off her helmet and rubbed her face. Despite everything, a grin broke through. *Poor ignorant bastard,* she thought, looking down at Vinatelli. *The tank was everything you said it was.* She'd been right too, though: a newbie was still cold meat unless he wised up fast.

"We're *all* going home. With Markee to lead the way."

ANCESTRAL
VOICES

"Shall I provide a map display of the tactical situation?" The Bolo Mark III sounded slightly hopeful.

"Who needs maps?" Lieutenant Martins said. "Take a goddamn piece of paper, crumple it up, and you've *got* a map of this goddamn country, and the towns are worse."

"My optical storage capacity extends to 1:1 mapping of this entire hemisphere," the tank said.

It didn't add that the street-maps of this particular Central American city were hopelessly obsolete. Unchecked fires and squatters almost as destructive had altered it beyond recognition over the past decade.

The Bolo Mark III still used the sultry-sweet female voice poor Vinatelli had programmed in; Martins told herself that the hint of injured pride was her imagination. The plump newbie's bones were pushing up the daisies—or bougainvillea—back in the Company's old firebase in the now-defunct Republic of San Gabriel a few hundred miles to the south, but the Mark III was still with them. Being sent a giant state-of-the-art tank had seemed right on schedule with the general madness and decay, a couple of months ago. They'd been virtually cut off from even routine resupply, and then the Pentagon had delivered a mobile automated firebase instead of ammunition or replacements. Now...

If the Company had any chance of getting back to what was left of the USA, the Bolo would be the key. It was also much more comfortable than sitting outside in a UATV, an Utility All-Terrain Vehicle. A nice soft crash-couch, surrounded by display screens that could register data in any format she chose; there was even a portapotty and a cooler, although the supply of Jolt had given out. You could fight a major battle in this thing without even cracking a sweat—and with 150 tons of density-enhanced durachrome armor, about as much risk as playing a video game.

Bethany Martins hated it. She hadn't joined a light infantry unit to sit in a cramped moving fort. Still, you used what you had. She shifted in the crash-couch restraints at the next message.

"Target two hundred sixty degrees left, range one thousand forty-three, target is bunker. Engaging."

A screen slaved to the infinite repeaters showed an aiming-pip, sliding across the burning buildings. Bars of light snapped out as the coils gripped the depleted uranium slugs and accelerated them to—literally—astronomical speeds. Where they struck, kinetic energy flashed into heat. What followed was not technically an explosion, but the building shuddered and slid into the street like a slow-motion avalanche.

The Company's troopers advanced across the shifting rubble. Screens focused on them, or showed the jiggling pickups of the helmet cameras. Part of that was the ground shaking under the Bolo as it advanced, maneuvering with finicky delicacy.

"Give me a scan of the area right of our axis of advance," she said to the machine. "Sonic and thermal." The computer overlaid the visual with a schematic, identifying sources of heat or hard metal, sorting shapes and enhancing. Martins nodded to herself and switched to the unit push.

"Right four-ten, Captain," Martins said. "Heat source."

She could see the M-35 in the commander's hands turn.

Then the picture tumbled and the weapon went skidding across the stones, catching on a burning window frame. Bullets flailed the ground around the Americans, and a hypervelocity rocket streaked out at the Bolo. Intercepted, it blew up in a magenta globe of flame halfway across the street. The first screen showed a tumbling view of dirt as someone dragged the Company commander backwards.

"Captain's hit, Captain's hit—medic, medic!" a voice was shouting.

"Suppressing fire!" Martins shouted, cursing herself. *It's not alive.* But it gave such a good imitation you could forget it had no judgment.

"Acknowledged," the tranquil sex-goddess tones replied.

BRAP. That was audible even through the armor; the main ring-gun mounted along the axis of the vehicle cutting loose. The impact was half a mile away; evidently the machinery had detected something important there. The infinite repeaters opened up all at once, threading with needle accuracy around the pinned-down troopers of the Company. Enemy fire shredded and vanished.

"McNaught's out cold, broken leg, doesn't look too bad otherwise," a voice said. Sergeant Jenkins, the senior NCO.

Martins nodded. "We're pulling out, Tops. Northwest, transmission follows." She traced the Bolo's idea of the optimum path, then transmitted it to Jenkins' helmet display with a blip of data.

Silence for a moment. Then: "Ma'am—" That was a bad sign, Tops getting formal. "—we're awful short of supplies, fuel too, and there's nothing much there."

That was why the captain had taken the chance of coming into an urban area; better pickings. The problem was that pickings attracted predators.

"Do it, Tops. We've got enough firepower to level this place but we don't have enough troopers to *hold* it long enough to get what we need."

The Mark III turned and headed northwest. A building was in the way, but the great vehicle only heaved slightly as it crushed its way through in a shower of beams and powdered adobe. The sensation of power would have been more intoxicating if Bethany Martins hadn't been quite so hungry.

Two days later, she popped the hatch and stuck her head out. There was no point in talking to an AI, after all; it wasn't conscious, just a bundle of reflexes. Although a very *good* bundle of reflexes.

For once the air outside wasn't too hot; they'd climbed a ridge above the jungle and they were a couple of thousand feet up. The line of volcanoes ahead of them shimmered blue and green in the morning light, densely forested, patches of mist on their sides. This forest smelled different from the dry scrub and limestone back in San Gabriel, intensely green with an undertang like spoiled bread or yeast. It reminded her of childhood, the time her father had tried making beer in the basement. The barrel had shattered in the night, leaving the floor two inches deep in half-fermented suds, and the smell had never come out of the concrete. The jungle smelled a little like that.

There was the odd patch of smoke, too, where the locals burned off the cover to plant their crops. Her tongue touched her lips. Supplies were short, now that they'd gotten out of the inhabited country.

"Anything new on the net from back home?"

That was Captain McNaught. He was sitting in one of the UATVs, a light six-wheeled truck built so low to the ground it looked squashed, with six balloon wheels of spun-alloy mesh. His splinted foot rested on the dashboard, beside the muzzle of his M-35.

"Nothing I can make sense of, Captain," she said. "California just left the Union. San Francisco just seceded from California. And that's not the worst of the weird shit coming down."

They'd called the United States *Reality* back in San Gabriel, while they'd been fighting the Glorious Way guerrillas. Since the recall order, that was beginning to look like a very sick joke. Things had been going to hell *before* some crazed Russian shot down the President, the Veep, and the Chairman of the Joint Chiefs over Alaska.

"Well, if you can bear to leave the air-conditioned comfort—" McNaught said.

"Yeah," Martins muttered, tucking the printout into a shoulder pocket of her armor and picking up her helmet and M-35.

The climb down was a long one. The Mark III weighed 150 tons, and looked it—the Bolo was essentially a four-sided pyramid with the top lopped off, bent and smoothed where the armor was sloped for maximum deflection, jagged with sensor-arrays and weapons. Two sets of double tracks underlay it, each nearly six feet broad and supported on eight interleaved road wheels, underlying nearly half the surface of the vehicle. She dropped to the ground with a grunt—her body-armor weighed about a tenth of her mass—and walked over to the commander's vehicle.

The ten UATVs of the light infantry company were parked around the perimeter of the scrubby clearing. They'd all turned off their ceramic diesels, and the loudest noises were the buzzing of insects and the raucous cries of birds. Everyone was looking at her as if she knew a solution to their problems; all seventy-five of the troopers, and the half-dozen or so hangers-on, mostly girls. Everyone looked hungry. They *were* hungry.

"There *was* a road through here," she said to McNaught. "Problem is, I don't think anyone's used it since before either of us was born. Since things started going bad—and they went bad there first."

"Big Brother can use the route?" Sergeant Jenkins flipped up the faceshield-visor of his helmet. The path behind them was crushed flat and hard; the Bolo pulped hundred-foot trees as if they were stalkes of cane.

"Oh, sure—but if there isn't enough traffic to keep it open, where are we going to get food or fuel?"

The Mark III was powered by ionic batteries; it could travel thousands of miles on one charge, and carried acres of monomolecular solar film in one of its dispensers. The UATVs were combustion powered; their ceramic diesels would burn anything from raw petroleum to bathtub gin, but they needed *something*. So did their passengers.

The three leaders looked at each other. McNaught had freckles and thinning reddish hair, and a runner's lanky body; Jenkins was the color of eggplant and built like a slab of basalt; Martins was wiry and olive-skinned, with short-cropped black hair and green eyes. All of them had been together through the Glorio war and its aftermath; they could communicate without much need for words. *We can't go back.* They'd left a hornet's nest behind them, one way and another, and gringos had never been too popular down here. *We can't stop.* This jungle wouldn't feed a coatimundi, much less ninety human beings.

"*Why* do the locals keep fighting us?" McNaught asked.

Because they're starving themselves, Martins thought irritably, then forced herself to relax. The captain was hurting and pumped full of painkillers. The locals were hurting too; first the worldwide collapse, a slow-motion catastrophe that had gone berserk in the last year. Chaos with that, and the famine that usually followed anarchy, harder than any drought. At that, things seemed to be going down the tube even faster back home. When worst came to worst people around here could go back to being subsistence farmers, and try conclusions with the hordes of cityfolk-turned-bandits. That wasn't much of an option in the USA.

They were going home because there didn't seem to be much alternative. And they couldn't go forward without something to run on.

"Hey, Tops," Martins said meditatively. "Doesn't Carmody's squeeze come from around here?"

The big black man frowned, then grinned. "Now that you mention it, El-Tee, she does. Most recent intelligence we're likely to get."

"Lord of the Mountain, First Speaker of the Sun People, there is no doubt."

The cool whitewashed room was empty save for the old man and the messenger. The man who had once been Manuel Obregon leaned back in his chair and examined the youngster who sank to one knee before him, still panting with his run, trim in cotton culottes and sandals. Seven-Deer was one of his best; a steady young man, and reliable.

"Go on," Obregon said, stroking his chin reflectively.

Pleasant sounds drifted through the tall arched windows; masons' chisels, the clack of a loom, a woman singing. There were smells of tortillas cooking, flowers, turned earth, and underneath it a faint sulphur reek. He used them to cut free of worry and thought, making his mind a clear pool for the scout's words. He would absorb it, and then analyze.

"Sixty, perhaps seventy of the *yanqui* soldiers, and with them some *Ladino* women from the south. A dozen little trucks with six wheels each, some pulling carts."

"They are *yanqui*, beyond doubt? Not government soldiers of San Gabriel, not terrorists of the Glorious Way?"

"No, Lord of the Mountain, First Speaker of the Sun People." Seven-Deer touched the jade plug in his lower lip for emphasis. "The farmers I spoke with saw them closely and heard them speak English. Also…"

He hesitated, his eyes sliding aside for the first time. "Go on," Obregon said, schooling impatience out of his voice.

"They said the *yanquis* had with them a mountain that walked."

Obregon's age-spotted hands tightened on the arms of his

chair. The scout swallowed: "I only repeat—"

"Yes, yes."

The old man stood and walked to the window. Across the plaza and the town, over the patchwork fields of the basin, a thin trickle of smoke rose in the air from the notched summit of the Smoker.

"I saw myself great tracks and crushed jungle," the scout went on, gathering confidence. "Like this." He unfolded a paper.

So. A tank, Obregon thought, surprised. It had been a very long time since heavy war vehicles came into these remote uplands. Then he caught the neatly drawn scale. Each of the tread-tracks was wider than a man was tall, and there were four of them impossibly close together.

"A mountain that walks," he said to himself—in Spanish, not Nahuatl. "But does it *burn?*"

Seven-Deer's eyes flicked sideways to the sky-pillar of dark smoke that reached upward from the mountain, and he shuddered with awe and fear and worship.

"Your orders, Lord of the Mountain, First Speaker of the Sun People?"

"Report to One-Coyote that the Jaguar Knights are to be mobilized, and the border guards strengthened. We cannot allow outsiders to prey upon our people."

"Lord of the Mountain, First Speaker of the Sun People," Seven-Deer said, greatly daring, "they are only *Ladinos* beyond the mountain—and perhaps the *yanqui* will turn aside before the pass."

Obregon nodded. "Yet they pay us tribute," he said. "And their blood is ours." His own face showed more Europoid genes than the scout's did, or than most of the people in the valley. "In time, they will return to the ways of the Ancestors; as we did, after many years of following the false gods of the *Ladinos.* This valley is our base, not our prison—we must be ready to expand beyond it. Now go."

And, Obregon thought, looking up at the darkening sky, *Venus is nearing the holy place.* The favor of the gods was not bought cheaply. The *yanqui* troops could be valuable, in their way.

Outside, the masons shouted cheerfully to each other as they worked on the last level of the stepped pyramid—small, but brilliant with whitewash, gaudy along its base with murals in the ancient style he had reconstructed from books and disks. It would be ready soon.

And in the end you must go, he thought regretfully, looking at that library. In a way, he would miss the ancient videos more than the anthropological texts. The latter held the voice of the ancient gods, but they would live—live more truly—when they existed only as words spoken among the people. The videos were his only vice; he was not a man who needed much in the way of women or wealth or luxury. In a way, it was sad to think that they must die with him… for he too could never really be a part of the world he was bringing to birth.

He selected his favorite; viewing it would calm him, and it was a minor indulgence, after all.

"*The Wicker Man,*" he read from the spine, as he slid the chip into its slot and pulled the goggles over his eyes.

Me and my big mouth, Martins thought. The problem was that she *was* the best one for the job; her Spanish was better than Jenkins', since she'd grown up in Santa Fe.

The view through her faceshield was flat and silvery, as the sandwich crystal picked up the starlight and amplified it. The fighting patrol eeled through the undergrowth from tree to tree, their heads turning with lizard quickness as the sensors in their helmets filtered light and sound. These were *big* trees, bigger than she'd thought survived anywhere in the isthmus. Not too much undergrowth, except where one of the forest giants had fallen and vines and saplings rioted. Not much light either, stray gleams through the upper canopy, but the faceshield could work with very little. The Americans moved quickly; every one of them had survived at least three years in the bad bush, where you learned the right habits or died fast.

Martins made a hand signal, and the patrol froze. They went to ground and crawled as they neared a clearing. Thick bush along the edges, then scattered irregular orchards of mango and citrus and plantains. She felt saliva spurt over her teeth at the sight, and somewhere a cow mooed—steak on the hoof. And where there were people and food, there would be some sort of slash; distilling was a universal art. The UATVs could run on that.

"Careful," she whispered on the unit push. "We don't want to off any of the indigs if we can avoid it."

Not that lifting their stuff was going to make them feel very friendly, but there was no need to put them on a fast burn.

Planted fields, maize and cassava and upland rice. Then a village, mud-and-wattle huts with thatch roofs. It smelled cleaner than most, less of the chicken-shit-and-pigs aroma you came to expect. Nothing stirring; through the walls she could see the faint IR traces of the sleeping inhabitants. A man stumbled through one door, fumbling with the drawstring of his dingy white-cotton pants. A trooper ghosted up behind him and swung his arm in a short, chopping arc. There was a dull sound—a chamois bag full of lead shot does not make much noise when slapped against a skull—and the indig slumped into waiting arms.

"*Proceeding,*" she whispered on the unit push. Captain Mc-Naught would be watching through the helmet pickups.

She wasn't quite sure which was worse: being out here at the sharp end, or being stuck back there helpless with a broken leg. Call-signs came in as the squad-leaders took up position.

"Right." She raised her M-35 and fired a burst into the air, a short sharp *braaap* of sound.

Voices rose; a few at first, enquiring. Then a chorus of

screams. Martins sighed and signaled; a flare popped into being high overhead, bathing the village in actinic blue-white light. That was for the benefit of the locals, to let them see the armed soldiers surrounding them.

"Out, out, everybody *out!*"

That and slamming on doors with rifle-butts was enough to get them moving. Martin's mouth twisted with distaste. *Robbing peasants wasn't what I joined up for either.* There had been altogether too much of that, back in San Gabriel, after the supply lines back to the US broke down.

Although when it came down to a choice between stealing and starving, there wasn't much of a dispute.

The noise died down to a resentful babbling as the two hundred or so of the little hamlet's people crowded into the dirt square before the ramshackle church. Very ramshackle; the roof had fallen in, and goats were wandering through the nave. That was a slightly jarring note; mostly the people in this part of the world took churches seriously. And it wasn't one of the areas where everyone had been converted by the Baptists back in the '90s, either.

Jenkins trotted up, flipping up the faceshield of his helmet. There was a slight frown on his basalt face.

"Not a single goddamn gun, El-Tee."

She raised a brow, then remembered to raise her visor in turn. A village without a few AKs was even more unusual than one that let its church fall down.

"Not just rifles—no shotguns, no pistols, *nothing.*"

Something coiled beneath her breastbone. They might have hidey-holes for the hardware that would defeat the sonic and microray sensors in the Americans' helmets, even the scanner set Sparky was packing, but they wouldn't have buried every personal gat and hunting shotgun. In fact, since they hadn't known the soldiers were coming, they shouldn't have hidden anything. You keep a gun for emergencies, and a gun buried ten feet deep is a little hard to get to in a hurry.

She looked at the peasants. Better fed than most she'd seen over the past half-decade, and almost plump compared to what had been coming down recently, with the final collapse of the world economy.

"If the indigs can't defend themselves, bandits should have been all over them like ugly on an ape," she said meditatively.

"Right," Jenkins said. Which meant that the locals—or somebody—*had* been defending this area.

The locals were murmuring louder, some of them trying to sneak off. She was getting hard stares, and a few spat on the ground. That was wrong too. Far too self-confident...

Well, I can fix that, she thought, keying her helmet.

"Front and center," she whispered.

It took a while for the sound to register over the frightened, resentful voices. When it did it was more of a sensation, a trembling felt through the feet and shins. A few screams of *earthquake!* died away; the ground was shaking, but not in quite that way. Harsh blue-white light shone from the jungle, drawing their eyes. Trees shivered at their tops, then whipped about violently and fell with a squealing, rending crackle. What shouldered the forest giants aside like stems of grass was huge even in relation to the trees. The steel-squeal of its four treads grated like fingernails on a blackboard, crushing a path of pulp stamped harder than rock behind it. The snouts of weapons and antennas bristled....

Now the villagers were silent. Martins walked up to the huge machine and swung aboard as it slowed, climbing the rungs set into the hull until she stood at its apex. When it halted, she removed her helmet.

When she spoke, her voice boomed out like the call of a god:

"BRING ME THE *JEFE* OF THIS VILLAGE!"

Best to strike while the iron was hot. Eyes stared at her, wide with terror. A whisper ran across the sea of faces; *the mountain that walks.*

"I don't like it."

Martins also didn't like the way McNaught was punishing the tequila they'd liberated; the bottle wavered as he set it down on the rough plank table beneath them. Liquor splashed onto the boards, sharp-smelling in the tropical night. Big gaudy moths fluttered around the sticklight she'd planted in the ceiling, taking no harm from its cold glow. A few bugs crawled over the remnants of their meal; she loosened the tabs of her armor, feeling it push at her shrunken and now too-full stomach.

He'd always been a good officer, but the news from the States was hitting him hard. Hitting them all, but McNaught had family, a wife and three children, in New Jersey. The broadcasts of the bread riots—more like battles—had been bad, and one blurred shot of flames from horizon to horizon before the 'casts cut off altogether.

"Plenty of supplies," he said carelessly. Sweat trickled down his face and stained the t-shirt under his arms, although the upland night wasn't all that hot. "More than we can carry."

"It's the indigs," Martins said, searching for words. "They're... not as scared as they should be. Or maybe not as scared of *us*. The Mark III sure terrifies the shit out of them."

McNaught shrugged. "It usually does; whatever works."

Martins nodded. "Sir." Somebody had to be boss, and her misgivings were formless. "We'd better scout the basin ahead; according to the maps there's a fair-sized town there, San Pablo de Cacaxtla. We won't get much fuel here, but there should be some there even if the town's in ruins."

McNaught shrugged again. "Do it."

Six hundred men squatted together in the circular ball-court, ringed by the empty seats, a stone loop at each end where the hard rubber ball would be driven during the sacred game. Now it served as a rallying-ground. They were young men mostly, leanly fit, their hair bound up on their heads in topknots; they wore tight uniforms of cloth spotted like the skin of jaguars. Those and the hair and the jade plugs many wore in lips or ears gave them an archaic cast, but the German-made assault rifles and rocket launchers they carried were quite modern. So was the electronic equipment hung on racks at one end of the enclosure.

One-Jaguar finished his briefing; he was a stocky-muscular man, dark and hook-nosed, still moving with the stiffness of the professional soldier he had been. He bowed with wholehearted deference as Obregon stood, and gestured to his aides to remove the maps and display-screens from the stone table.

Obregon was in ceremonial dress this time, feathered cloak, kilt, plumed headdress, pendants of jade and gold. He raised his hands, and absolute silence fell.

"Warriors of the Sun," he said. The armed men swayed forward, eyes glittering and intent. "When the mother of our people, the holy Coatlicue, was pregnant with Left-Handed Hummingbird, his four hundred brothers conspired to kill him—but Standing Tree warned him. As Seven-Deer has warned me of the approaching enemy."

In the front rank of the Jaguar Knights, Seven-Deer looked down at the ground, conscious of the admiring eyes on him.

Obregon continued: "And Left-Handed Hummingbird— Huitzilopochtl—was born in an instant; his face painted, carrying his weapons of turquoise; he had feathers on the sole of his left foot, and his arms and thighs were striped with blue. He slew the four hundred Southern Warriors, and our people worshipped him, and he made them great."

A long rolling growl of assent. "That was in the day of the Fifth Sun. Huitzilopochtl showed us how to greet enemies—

and made us great. Yet when the new invaders came from the sea, the First Speaker of the Sun People, Montezuma was weak. He didn't take up his weapons and kill them, or send them as Messengers. So the Fifth Sun was destroyed. Now the Sixth Sun has been born here; we have returned to the ways of our ancestors. While all around us is starvation and desolation, we grow strong.

"Will we follow the word of Left-Handed Hummingbird? Will we kill the invaders?"

This time the growl grew into a roar, a savage baying that echoed back from the empty seats of the auditorium.

"Before we go into battle, we must appeal for the help of the gods of our people. Seven-Deer, bring out your beloved son."

The young scout bowed and walked to the entranceway. His role was symbolic, like the cord that ran from his hand to the prisoner's neck; two priests held the bound captive's arms, their faces invisible behind their carved and plumed masks. The prisoner was a thin brown man with an acne-scarred face, naked and shivering. His eyes darted quickly around the amphitheatre, squeezed shut and then opened again, as if he was willing the scene before him to go away. He was neither old nor young, wiry in a peasant fashion, a farmer from the lowlands driven into banditry by the collapse.

"Come, my beloved son," Seven-Deer said, his face solemn. "Hear the messages you must take to the land beyond the sun. Be happy! You will dwell as a hummingbird of paradise; you will not go down to Mictlan, or be destroyed in the Ninth Hell." He bent to whisper in the man's ear.

Evidently the lowlander spoke a few words of Nahuatl, or he recognized the stone block for what it was, because he began to scream as the Feathered Snake priests cut his bonds and stretched him out over it on his back. That too was part of the rite.

Obregon—*Lord of the Mountain, First Speaker of the Sun*

People, he reminded himself—stepped up and drew the broad-bladed obsidian knife from his belt. There had been enough practice that he no longer feared the embarrassing hacking and haggling of the first few times. His original academic specialty had been geophysics, not anatomy, but the sudden stab down into the taut chest was precise as a surgeon's. There was a crisp popping sound as the knife sliced home, its edges of volcanic glass sharper than any steel. Ignoring the bulging eyes of the sacrifice, he plunged his hand into the chest cavity, past the fluttering pressure of the lungs, and gripped the heart. It beat one last time in his hands like a slippery wet balloon, then stilled as he slashed it free of the arteries.

Blood fountained, smelling of iron and copper and salt, droplets warm and thick on his lips. He raised the heart to the Sun, and felt the pure clean ecstasy of the moment sweep over him. The Jaguar Knights gave a quick, deep shout as he wheeled to face them, red-spattered and gripping heart in one hand, knife in the other.

"We have fed the Sun!" he proclaimed. "And so shall you, Our Lord's knights, be fed." The priests were already taking the body away, to be drained and butchered. "Our Lord Smoking Mirror shall fill you with His strength, and you will destroy the enemy—take many prisoners for the altar. Victory!" The Knights cried him hail.

"Looks good," Martins murmured under her breath.

The jungle thinned out around them as the UATVs struggled up the switchback road. Grassy glades and forests of pinion pine and oak replaced the denser lowland growth; the temperature dropped, down to something that was comfortable even in body armor. After years in the steambath lowland heat, it was almost indecently comfortable. The air carried scents of resin and cool damp soil and grass; for a moment she was back in the Sangre de Cristo, longing like a lump of scar-tissue beneath her breastbone. Then she caught a rotten-egg tang underneath it.

"Air analysis," she keyed, on the Mark III's frequency.

The tank was back downslope with McNaught and the other half of the Company, but it should be able to tell her something through the remote sensors she carried.

"Variations from standard: excess concentrations of sulphur, sulphur dioxide, dilute sulfuric acid compounds, ozone," the Bolo said. "Seismic data indicate instabilities." A pause. "My geophysical data list no active vulcanism in this area."

Which means it's as out of date as the street maps, Martins thought.

She leaned a hand against the rollbar of the UATV, the long barrel of the autocannon on its pintle mount swaying about her, tasting the dust and sunlight, eyes squinting against it. The landscape looked empty but not uninhabited; the grass had been grazed, and there was animal dung by the side of the road—goat and cattle, from the look of it. It was a different world from the ghost-gray limestone scrub of San Gabriel, or the thick moist jungles they'd been passing through since. Telltales in her faceplate gave a running scan of the rocky hillsides. No indications of metal concentrations, no suspicious E-spectrum radiation. She cracked one of the seals of her body armor to let in the drier, cooler air.

"Our athlete's foot and crotchrot will die if we're not careful, El-Tee," Jenkins said. "Doesn't look like much else in the way of danger so far."

Martins nodded. "Objective A deserted," she broadcast.

That was a small town near the top of the pass; a couple of thousand people once, maybe more in shack-tenements at the edges that had long since slumped into weed-grown heaps. There was the wreckage of an old colonial Baroque church and town hall near the center, and both might have been impressive once. The snags of two modest steel or concrete structures stood nearby. The buildings looked positively crushed, as if toppled by earthquake, but they had also been quite comprehensively looted. Stacks of girders and rebar hammered free from the concrete stood in orderly piles; there wasn't much rust on cut ends and joints, which meant the work had been going on until the last few weeks. Rubble had been shoveled back out of the main street.

"Halt," she said. *This is serious.* Bandits would steal food and jewelry, but this was *salvage.* That implied organization, and organization was dangerous.

"Take a look. Make it good, troopers."

She collated the reports. Everything gone, down to the window-frames. Truck and wagon tracks...

"You," she said. It was her private name for the Bolo; she couldn't bring herself to give it the sort of nickname Vinatelli had. "How many, how long?"

"I estimate that several thousand workers have been engaged in the salvage operation for over a year, Lieutenant Martins."

Martins' lips shaped a soundless whistle.

"You catch that, Captain?"

He grunted. "We need more data."

"*Damn,* that's impressive," Jenkins said.

The cut through the lava flow wasn't what he meant, though it showed considerable engineering ability. The view of the valley a thousand feet below was. The road switchbacked down forest slopes; much of the forest was new, planted. The valley floor beyond was cultivated, with an intensity she hadn't seen in a long, long time. A rolling patchwork quilt of greens and yellows and brown volcanic soil rippled with contour-plowing. She cycled the magnification of her visor and saw the crops spring out in close view; corn, wheat, sugarcane, roots, orchards, pasture. There were people at work there, some with hand-tools or oxen, but there were tractors as well. Irrigation furrows threaded the fields, and so did power-lines.

"Damn," Martins echoed. "They've got a grid, working

down there."

"Geothermal plant, I think," Jenkins said. "Over there by the town."

There were several villages scattered through the valley, but the town was much larger. It lay in a semicircle around the base of the conical mountain, tiny as a map from this height. The usual *hispano* grid centered on a plaza, but very unusual otherwise. The buildings were freshly painted, and there was *new* construction off to one side, a whole new plaza ringed by public structures and some sort of monument, a stone heap fifteen meters on a side and covered in scaffolding.

"Well, we ought to be able to get fuel here, right enough," McNaught's voice said in her ear, watching through the helmet pickups. "All we want. Maybe even spare parts."

"If they'll give us what we need," Martins said slowly. They looked as if they could afford it, much more so than anyone else the Company had run across. But it was her experience that the more people had, the more ready they were to defend it. "I wish we could pay for it."

"Maybe we can," McNaught said thoughtfully. "I've been thinking… the computer capacity in the Beast is pretty impressive. We could rest and refit, and pay our way with its services. Hell, maybe they need some earth-moving done. And if they won't deal—"

Martins nodded. "Yessir."

We have the firepower, she thought. Using it hadn't bothered her much before; the Company was all the friends and family she had. These people looked as if they'd hit bottom and started to build their way back up, though. The thought of what the Mark III could do to that town wasn't very pleasant. She'd seen too many ruins in San Gabriel, too much wreckage on the way north.

"Well, we'd better go on down," she said. "But carefully. One gets you nine they're watching us with passive sensors; Eyeball Mark One, if nothing else."

"No bet," Jenkins said, his voice returning to its usual flat pessimism.

"Right, let's do it." She switched to the unit push. "Slow and careful, and don't start the dance unless it looks like the locals want to try us on. We fight if we have to, but we're not here to fight."

"Surely you see that precautions are reasonable," the old man said to her. "In these troubled times."

He looked to be in his seventies, but healthy; white haired and lean, dressed in immaculate white cotton and neat sandals. The "precautions" consisted of several hundred mean-looking *indios* spread out along the fields behind him, digging in with considerable efficiency and sporting quite modern weapons, along with their odd spotted cammo uniforms. The helmet scanners had detected at least one multiple hypervelocity launcher, and the Mark III thought there was an automortar or light field-piece somewhere behind.

This close the town looked even better than it had from the pass. The additions upslope, near the black slaggy-looking lava flows, looked even odder. The building beneath the scaffolding was roughly the shape of her Bolo; a memory tugged at her mind, then filtered away. There was a delegation of townsfolk with the leader, complete with little girls carrying bouquets of flowers. It made her suddenly conscious of the ragged uniforms patched with bits of this and that that her Company wore. The only parts of them that weren't covered in dust were the faceshields of their helmets, and those were kept clear by static charges.

The spruce locals also made her conscious of the twenty-odd troopers behind her in the UATVs; if the shit hit the fan the rest of the outfit and the Mark III would come in and kick butt, but it could get very hairy between times.

"Hard times, right enough, *señor*," she answered politely. Some of the crowd were murmuring, but not in Spanish. She caught something guttural and choppy, full of *tz* sounds.

"You've done very well here," Martins went on, removing her helmet. A face generally looked less threatening than a blank stretch of curved synthetic.

The old man smiled. "We seek to keep ourselves isolated from the troubles of the world," he said. "To follow our own customs."

Looking around at the rich fields and well-fed people, Martins could sympathize. The well-kept weapons argued that these folks were realistic about it, too.

"You've also got a lot of modern equipment," she said. "Not just weapons either, I'd guess."

The *jefe* of the valley spread his hands. "I went from here to the university, many years ago," he said. "There I had some success, and returned much of what I earned to better the lives of my people here. When the troubles came, I foresaw that they would be long and fierce; I and my friends made preparations. Luckily, the eruption sealed the main pass into the valley of Cacaxtla when the government was no longer able to reopen it, so we were spared the worst of the collapse. But come, what can we do for you?"

That's a switch. "We're traveling north, home," she said. "We need fuel—anything will do, whatever your vehicles are running on—"

"Cane spirit," the local said helpfully.

"—that'll do fine. Some food. We have spare medical supplies, and our troops include a lot of specialists; in electronic repairs, for example."

Actually the self-repair fabricators of the Mark III were their main resource in that field, but no need to reveal everything.

"You are welcome," the *jefe* said. "The more so as it is wise to—how do you say in English—speed the parting guest." He looked behind the brace of UATVs. "I notice that not all your troops are here, señora , or the large tank."

Large tank, Martins thought. *Nobody really believes in that mother until they see it.*

She inclined her head politely. "Surely you see that precautions are reasonable," she said. "In these troubled times."

The *jefe*'s laugh was full and unforced. "I am glad that we understand each other, *teniente* Martins. If you will follow me…"

Fearless, he stepped into her UATV; the children threw their bouquets into it, or hung necklaces of flowers around her neck and those of the other troopers. Martins sneezed and looked around. The *jefe* noted her interest.

"As you say, a geothermal unit," he said, pointing out a low blocky building. "The waste water is still hot enough for domestic use, and also for fishponds and other uses. Very simple. We have a few shops, as you see, and small workshops to make what household goods we need."

There were actual open shops along the streets, selling clothing and leather goods, tools and food—something she hadn't seen for years. And people selling *flowers.* That shook her a bit, that anyone could still devote time and energy to a luxury like that.

"We issue our own money, as a convenience for exchange; but everyone contributes to things of public worth," he went on. "As our guests, your needs will be met from the public treasury; and first, since you have traveled far, baths and refreshment. Then you must join us for dinner; tomorrow, we will see to the fuel and traveling supplies you need."

Martins and Jenkins looked at each other and the spacious, airy house the Americans had been assigned.

"Is it just my sour disposition, Tops," she said meditatively, "or does what looks too good to be true—"

"—probably too good to be true, El-Tee," the sergeant said.

"See to it."

"All right. Listen up, shitheels! Nobody gets out of reach of his weapon. Nobody gets out of sight of his squad—washing, crapping, I don't care what. Nobody takes more than one drink; and you keep it in your pants, I don't care what the local señoritas say, understand me? Michaels, Wong, you're first guard on the vehicles. Smith, McAllister, Sanchez, overwatch from the roof. Move it!"

"Omigod," Jenkins muttered. "*Beer*. Real, actual, honest-to-God-not-pulque-piss *beer*."

The *jefe*—he'd answered to Manuel Obregon, but the locals called him by something unpronounceable—smiled and nodded and took a swallow from his own earthenware pitcher. There were more smiles and nods from all around, from the tables set out across the plaza. Much of the town's population seemed to be taking this chance for a *fiesta*. They were certainly dressed for one, although the clothes were like nothing she'd seen in the back-country, and very fancy. The food was good enough that she'd had to let out the catches of her armor—nobody had objected to the troopers wearing their kit, or seemed to notice their M-35s and grenade launchers—roast pork, salads, hot vegetable stews, spicy concoctions of meats and tomatoes and chilies.

Obregon sat at their table, and quietly took a sampling of everything they were offered, testing before they did. Martins appreciated the gesture, although not enough to take more than a mug or two of the beer; Jenkins' eagle eye and the corporals' made sure nobody else did either. It was intoxicating enough just to feel *clean*, and have a decent meal under her belt.

"I notice you don't seem to have a church," she said.

Obregon smiled expansively. "The Church always sat lightly on the people here," he said. "When the *campesinos* prayed to the Virgin, they called her Tonantzin, the Moon. Always I hated what the foreigners—the Spaniards—had done here. Since my people made me their leader, I have spoken to them of the old ways, the ancient ways of our ancestors; what we always new , and what I learned of the truth in the university in my youth, things which the *Ladinos* and their priests tried to suppress."

Can't argue with success, Martins thought.

The helmet beside her on the table cheeped. She took another mouthful of the coffee, thick with fresh cream, and slid it on.

"Lieutenant Martins," the Mark III's voice said.

"What *now?*" she snapped. *Damn, I'm tired.* It had been a long day, and the soak in hot water seemed to be turning her muscles to butter even hours later.

"Please extend the sensor wand to the liquids consumed."

Nothing showed on Martins' face; except perhaps a too-careful blankness, as she unclipped the hand-sized probe and dipped it into the beer.

"Alkaloids," the computer-voice said calmly. "Sufficient to cause unconsciousness."

"But the *jefe*—"

"Partial immunity through sustained ingestion," it said. "Have you any instructions, Lieutenant Martins?"

Bethany Martins tried to shout and pull the knife sheathed across the small of her back in the same instant. Somewhere a single shot cracked; she was vaguely conscious of Jenkins toppling over backwards, buried under a heap of locals. Her tongue was thick in her head, and hands gripped her. Obregon stood watching, steadying himself with one hand against the table, his eyes steady.

"Basser sumbitch," Martins slurred. "*Help*—"

The helmet came off her head, with a wrench that flopped her neck backward. Blackness.

A confused babble came through the pickups. Captain McNaught stiffened in the strait confines of the Mark III's fighting compartment. His leg knocked against a projecting surface in a blaze of pain.

"Get through, get me through!"

"None of the scouting party are responding, Captain," the tank said in its incongruous sex-kitten voice.

The pickups from the UATVs showed bustling activity, and a few bodies in American uniform being carried by, unconscious or dead—until thick tarpaulins were thrown over the war-cars. The helmets showed similar blackness; IR and sonic gave the inside of a steel box and nothing more. Until one was taken out.

"Greetings, Captain," Manuel Obregon's voice said.

His face loomed large in the screen, then receded as the helmet was set on a surface and the local chieftain sank back in a chair. The voice was slurred, but with tongue-numbness, not alcohol, and his black eyes were level and expressionless as a snake's.

"Release my troops and I won't kill anyone but you," McNaught said, his voice like millstones. "Harm them, and we'll blow that shit heap town of yours down around your lying head."

Obregon spread hands. "A regrettable ruse of war," he said. "Come now, *mi capitán*. I have more than a third of your personnel and equipment, and your second-in-command. It is only logical, if distressing from your point of view, that you listen to my terms. I cannot in all conscience allow a large armed body—which has already plundered and killed—to operate in the vicinity of my people."

"I repeat; release them immediately. You have no conception of our resources."

"On the contrary," Obregon said, his voice hard and flat. "You have forty men, light weapons, and one large tank—which must be short of fuel. Abandon the vehicles and the tank, taking only your hand weapons, and you will be allowed to leave, with your advance party. For every hour you refuse, one of the prisoners will die. And, *Capitán*—do nothing rash.

This valley is protected by forces which are stronger than anything you can imagine."

Flat sincerity rang in the old man's voice.

Something seemed to have crawled into Martins' mouth and died. She tried to sit up and stopped, wincing at the pain, then doggedly continued. She was lying in a row of bodies, some of them groaning and stirring. They were all wearing white cotton tunics; a quick check showed nothing else underneath. The room was bare and rectangular, with narrow window-slits along one wall and a barred grillwork of iron at the other end, the holes barely large enough to pass a human hand and arm. Fighting weakness and a pain that made her sweat, she staggered erect and groped along one wall to the end. Beyond the grillwork was a plain ready room, with a bench and nothing else except a barred window and steel-sheet door.

And a guard in the jaguar-spot local uniform, with an assault rifle across his knees. He gave her a single glance and turned his eyes back to the wall, motionless.

Oh, this is not good. Not good at all, *Bethany,* Martins thought to herself.

More groans came from her troopers where they lay like fish on a slab—an unpleasant thought she tried to shed. Jenkins was sitting with his head in his hands.

"Goddamn native beer," he said, in a painful attempt at humor.

"Check 'em, Tops," she said.

A minute later: "Wong's missing."

Martins chewed a dry tongue to moisten her mouth, striding back to the grillwork and trying to rattle it.

"I demand to speak to your leader," she said in a calm voice, pitched to command. "Where is Private Wong?"

The guard turned, moving very quickly. She was just quick enough herself to get her hand mostly out of the way of the fiber-matrix butt of the man's weapon, and take a step back sucking at her skinned knuckles.

Jenkins unhunched his shoulders as she turned. "What's the word, El-Tee?"

"For now, we wait until the captain and the Beast get here," she said quietly. "We—"

A rising swell of noise from outside interrupted her, muffled by the high slit windows. Then it cut off, replaced by chanting. One commanding voice rose above the rest. Then a scream; words at first, in English, followed by a high thin wailing that trailed off into a blubbering *don't... don't...* and another frenzied shriek.

Jenkins bent and cupped his hands. Martins set a foot in the stirrup and steadied herself against the wall as he straightened, then raised his hands overhead until her compact hundred-and-twenty pounds was standing on his palms. That put the bars on the slit windows just within reach. Grunting and sweating with the effort and the residual pain of the drug, she pulled herself up.

Brightness made her blink. They were on one side of Cacaxtla's new square, the one with the odd-looking building. Her mind clicked, making a new association; the one with the unfinished stepped pyramid. Because it was unfinished, she could see quite clearly what went on on the flat platform atop it, over the heads of the crowd that filled the plaza below and the gaudily costumed priests on the steps. When she realized what was happening, she wished with all her heart that she could not. A dry retch sent her tumbling toward the floor; Jenkins' huge hands caught her with surprising gentleness.

"What's going on, Lieutenant?" he said—the formal title a sign of *real* worry.

"Wong," she said. "They've got him on the top of that pyramid thing. They're—" She swallowed, despite years of experience in what human beings could do to each other. "They're skinning him."

"Enemy in blocking positions two thousand meters to our front," the tank said. "Shall I open fire?"

Captain McNaught felt cold sweat leaking out from his armpits. The narrow switchback up to the pass had been bad enough, but the passage through the recent lavaflow was worse, barely any clearance at all on either side of the Mark III. Every once and a while it scraped the cutting, and sent showers of pumice rock bouncing downslope toward the UATVs.

"Not yet, we'll wait until we can do 'em all at once," he said, and switched to the unit push. "Take up covering positions."

Damn, damn. It was his fault. He'd let things slide, gotten apathetic—and the wound was no excuse. There *were* no excuses. The Company was his.

Obregon's voice came though. "This is your last warning," he said.

"Fuck you."

If they thought an avalanche would stop the Mark III, they could think again. Or an antitank rocket. They might damage one of the treads, but that was a worst-case scenario; there was no precipice they might hope to sweep the tank off, not here.

"Follow when I've cleared the way," he went on to the waiting troopers. Some of the guilt left him. He might be behind a foot of durachrome alloy, but he was leading from the *front*, by God.

The tank trembled. "Seismic activity," it said helpfully. "Instructions?"

"Keep going! Bull through. We're going to rescue Martins and the others *at all costs*. D'you understand, you heap of tin?"

"Acknowledged." Rock ground by, pitted and dull, full of the craters left by gas-bubbles as it hardened. "Anomalous heat source to our left."

There was no view, but the rumbling underfoot grew louder.

"What the hell are they doing?"

"Insufficient data," the tank said. "Estimated time to firing position—"

Obregon's voice: "You are in the hands of Xotl-Ollin," he said regretfully. "Feel his anger while I dance for Xipe Totec. Better if this had been a Flower War, but the god's will be done."

The indig chief had clearly gone nuts. The problem was that the world seemed to have done so too. The restraints clamped tighter around McNaught as the Mark III shook. Rocks and boulders and ash cataracted down around it, muffled through the armor but thunder-loud in the pickups until the guardian AI turned it down. Something went off with a rumbling *boom*, loud enough for the noise alone to make the tank vibrate slightly.

"What was that, what was that?" McNaught shouted.

"No weapon within known parameters," the Mark III said. "Searching."

At first McNaught thought that the wall of liquid was water, or perhaps thick mud. It wasn't until he saw patches of dried scrub bursting into flame as it touched them that he recognized it. That was when he screamed.

It was not entirely the lava that made him bellow and hammer with his hands at the screens. The one slaved to Martins' helmet was showing a visual; it was showing Obregon. He was dancing, and he was covered in skin—Trooper Wong's skin, skillfully flayed off in one piece and then sewn on to the old man like an old-fashioned set of long-johns. Hands and feet flopped empty as he shuffled and twirled, his eyes staring through holes in the sagging mask.

The molten stone swept over the Mark III in a cresting wave.

The guard proved unbribable, to anything from promises of gold to offers of more personal services; and he never came within arm's reach of the grillwork.

The attendant who brought them water did. Martins' eyes met her NCO's; from the man's frightened scurry, they both did an identical, instant evaluation of his worth as a hostage. He was old, older than Obregon and withered with it, nearly toothless.

Somewhere between nada and fucking zip, Martins decided.

"*Agua ,*" he said.

Martins crouched to take the canteens through the narrow slot near the floor.

"*Gracias,*" she whispered back.

That seemed to make the man hesitate; he glanced over his shoulder, but the guard was staring out the window at the pyramid. The screaming had stopped long ago, but the chanting and drumming went on.

"It is a sin against God," the servant whispered fearfully. "They worship demons, demons! It is lies, but the people were afraid—are afraid, even those who don't believe in Obregon's lies."

"Afraid of what?" Martins whispered back, making the slow drag of the canteens on the rock floor cover the sound. "His gunmen?"

"The Jaguar Knights? No, no—they fear his calling the burning rock from the mountains, as he has done. As he did to cut us off from the outside world."

Oh, great, one sympathizer and he's another loony, Martins thought.

The man went on: "It is lies, I say. I saw the machines he brought, many years ago—machines he buries all about the valley. He says they are to foretell earthquakes, but he lies; he *makes* the earth shake and the lava come! It is machines, not his false gods!"

The guard shouted in the local language, and the servant cringed and scurried out.

"What'd he say?" Jenkins asked.

"We're in the hands of the Great and Powerful Oz, Tops," Martins said with a bitter twist of the mouth. "But I don't think this one's a good guy—and this sure isn't Kansas, anyway."

"No shit."

This is where we're supposed to make a rush, Martins thought. *If this were movieland. One of us would get a gun …*

She'd seen an old, old vid about that once—some snotnose got a vid hero into the real world, and the stupid bastard got himself killed, or nearly.

In reality, a dozen unarmed soldiers with automatic weapons pointed at them were simply potential hamburger. The door in the grillwork was too narrow for more than one person to squeeze through at a time, and there were grenade launchers stuck through the high slit windows on either side of the prison chamber.

Jenkins muttered under his breath: "We could crap in our hands and throw it at them."

"Can it, Tops. Wait for the captain. I got us into this, no reason more should get shorted than have to."

Although it was taking an oddly long time for the Mark III to make it. The ground had trembled after Wong… died… and then nothing, for hours.

She walked out from the huddle of prisoners. Hands pulled her through the slit door and clanged it behind her, pulled off the tunic and left her nothing but a loincloth. Others bound her hands behind her back and led her out.

The sun was blinding; no less so was the fresh paint on the pyramid, the feathers and jade and gold and bright cloth on the priests. She ignored them, walking with her eyes fixed on the horizon and the smoking volcano above the town. Her heart seemed to beat independently of herself.

Crazy bastard, she thought, as she trod the first step. The stone was warm and gritty under her feet; twenty steps up it started to be sticky. She could smell the blood already, beginning to rot under the bright sun, and hear the flies buzz. Sheets and puddles of it lay around the improvised altar; she supposed they'd build something more imposing when the pyramid was finished, but the block of limestone would do for now.

At the top, Obregon waited. They'd washed the blood off him—most of it—when he shed Wong's skin.

Like a snake, she thought, lightheaded.

"Lord of the Mountain," she said in a clear, carrying voice. He frowned, but the chanting faded a little—as it would not have for screams. "The Mountain that Walks will come for me!"

Obregon gave a curt sign, and the drums roared loud enough to drown any other words. Another, and the priests cut her bonds and threw her spread-eagled back across the altar, one on each limb pulling until her skin creaked. Her skin... at least they didn't have the flaying knives out.

"You are brave," the old man said as he stepped up to her, drawing the broad obsidian knife. "But your tank is buried under a hundred feet of lava, and the valley sealed once more." The plumes nodded over his head, and his long silver hair was streaked and clotted with crusty brown. "Tell the Sun—"

"That you're a fucking lunatic," Martins rasped, bending her head up painfully to look at him; the sun was in the west, and she could just see Venus rising bright over the jagged rim of the valley. "Why? Why the lies?"

Obregon replied in English, slowly raising the knife. "My people needed more than tools and medicines. More even than a butterfly-effect machine that could control venting. They needed to *believe* in their guardian." A whisper: "So did I."

The knife touched the skin under her left breast and then rose to its apogee.

Braaap.

The ultravelocity impact that smashed Obregon's hand cauterized the wound. It twirled him in place like a top, until his head sprayed away from the next round.

One of the priests released her left foot and snatched for his own knife. Martins pivoted on the fulcrum of her hip and kicked the other at her feet in the face. Bone crumpled under the ball of her foot. Something smashed the man with the knife out into the shadows of gathering night. One hand slacked on her wrist; she wrenched it free with a brief economical twist and flipped erect, slamming the heel of her free hand up under the last priest's nose. He dropped to the blood-slick stone deck, his nasal bone driven back into his brain.

Martins stood and walked to the head of the steep stairway down the pyramid, the only living thing on its summit. Below her the crowd screamed and milled, and behind them...

Mountain that Walks. It looked it, now, with the thick crust of lava that covered it from top deck to the treadguards. Cooling and solidifying, smoking, whirled and dripping like hot wax. A few antennae poked through, and the muzzles of the infinite repeaters.

Two treads were gone, and the machine kept overcorrecting for their loss.

"Light," she whispered.

Actinic glare burst out from the Bolo, making it a hulking black shape that ground forward and shook the earth. The same searchlight bathed her in radiance; she couldn't see much detail of the square below, but she saw enough to know that townsmen and Jaguar Knights alike had fallen on their faces.

Bethany Martins raised both hands, fists clenched, her body spattered with blood and bone and brains. She remembered treachery, and Wong screaming. One word, and everyone in ten miles' space would die.

She remembered famine and bandits, and bodies in ditches gnawed by rats or their own kinfolk.

"They do need a guardian they can believe in," she muttered to herself. "A sane one." Whether she was still entirely sane was another matter, but she had more to think of.

A statue stood at the base of the stairs, squat and hideous. Her right fist stabbed at it, and stone fragments flew across the square, trailing sparks. It was important to know when to stop. The rest of the Company wouldn't take much talking around—and it was best to get things straight with the locals right from the beginning. Hit 'em hard and let 'em up easy, as her father had always said.

"Amplify."

"YOU HAVE FOLLOWED FALSE GODS," her voice bellowed out, relayed at an intensity enough to stun. "BUT THERE WILL BE MERCY."

The people of Cacaxtla shuddered and pressed their heads to the ground, and knew that a god—a goddess—stronger than the Lord of the Mountain had come.

He had brought fire from the stone. She had made stone walk.

THE SIXTH SUN

The American soldiers gathered at the base of the sacrificial pyramid. Morning sun shone bright on the fresh-cut limestone, and on the bougainvillea that was already beginning to curl up from the base. Two months had washed away the last lingering traces of the smell of rotten blood, leaving only the scents of dust and people and growing things in the plaza. Around them the town of Cacaxtla was bustling to life, a group of children on their way to school, farmers heading out to the fields. The *put-put* of a methane-fired tractor slapped back from the walls of the buildings around the plaza.

That was louder than the burbling of the ceramic diesels in the UATVs waiting to leave; the little six-wheeled jeeps were almost hidden under sacks and crates of supplies, netting bags of squirming live chickens and bunches of bananas.

"Sure you're not coming?" Captain McNaught asked. His freckled brow wrinkled. "I've got a feeling we're going to need every good soldier we can find back home."

Lieutenant Bethany Martins smiled and shook her head.

"There's no home back there, at least not for me, Captain," she said.

"Me neither, sir," Company Sergeant Jenkins—Tops—

agreed. "Bad's it was in my neighborhood, I think I'm happier rememberin' the way it was than seein' it the way it is."

Behind the big black NCO, privates Michaels, Smith, McAllister, and Sanchez nodded solemn agreement. They'd been down in the Republic of San Gabriel for years, and the news out of Reality—the United States—had gotten steadily worse every one of them.

McNaught's eyes narrowed. "Maybe you're right. Maybe there's nothing left to go home to. But I've got to know."

Bethany winced and looked away from the bright sunlight. The captain had a wife and three kids in New Jersey. Had. Who knew now, with the way things were back in Reality.

But there was no one waiting for her, or the others. "These folks need us too," she said, waving a hand out over the upland valley drowsing in the sun. "We ran out those lunatics who were running the place."

A vivid flash came to her, the feather-decked Jaguar Knights and the rough grit of the altar against her skin as they bent her back and raised the obsidian knife to cut out her heart. Political scientists were bad enough, but an anthropologist run amok on Identity Politics was something else again.

"If we all leave, seven different brands of bandit will be all over them like ugly on an ape—they'll be dead or starving in a month, like everyone else down here."

Like everyone else everywhere, she thought but did not say.

"All right," the captain said, his eyes distant, as though already seeing the Jersey shore. "I won't force it. You people've got a right to your own lives. You've been good soldiers. It's been an honor serving with you." He drew himself up to attention, his clean but ragged uniform loose on his thin frame, and snapped them a salute straight out of West Point.

Martins, Tops, and the rest answered him in the same brisk, professional manner. Then the captain went down the row shaking hands.

When he got back to Bethany he said softly: "I'll miss you, Lieutenant."

Bethany felt a lump in her throat. She whispered hoarsely, "I'll miss you too, sir." Her throat was tight. "Damn, it would be good to see Santa Fe again."

"Not too late."

"Too late years ago."

She swallowed and the pain seemed worse for it, hot and tight, beginning to rage out of control. She whimpered. *I will not cry,* she told herself. *I will not!* The pain spread, clawing at her vitals, spreading remorselessly until it filled her, left her standing dumbstruck and immobile as the captain drove away.

She closed her eyes and gasped. When she opened them, her eldest son was smiling down at her, standing awkwardly with his hat clenched in his hands. The big master bedroom of the *jefe*'s house was shuttered, and dim, light slashing in as hot bars between the louvers of the blinds. There was a sickbed smell of medicine, and her canes stood in one corner. Her M-35 was neatly racked above it, oiled and immaculate though she hadn't carried it in... how long? A decade?

"You slept Mom, almost an hour, I think."

She drank in his face; he looked so much like his father. Her breath rasped in her throat and her mouth was dry. She didn't ask for water. Swallowing was agony.

"Mama?" said a voice from the opposite side of the bed.

She turned, and there was her youngest, James, a wet cloth in his hands. He placed it between her parched lips, and as she sucked the moisture from it she thanked him with her eyes.

She gritted her teeth and swallowed, tried to suppress her moan. When James took the cloth away she was panting as though she'd run a race.

It was time.

"Boys," she smiled briefly. *They were not boys any longer, but married men.* "My sons," Bethany began again, pride in her voice even now. "I want to talk to the Beast. Take me to it."

"Mother," Joseph said, just a hint of asperity in his tone. "We can't move you. You're too sick." He frowned. "I can bring you a helmet…" he added reluctantly.

"Mom?" James' lips drew back from his teeth in a parody of a grin as he struggled not to cry, his eyes were awash with tears. "Mom?" he said again.

"Yes," she said gently. "I need to go." She was panting again. "Maybe—in some way—it can help. The autodoc…" Her voice faded away.

James nodded helplessly, beyond speech.

"All right," Joseph said at the end of a long, drawn-in breath. "It's worth a try."

They lifted their mother with the featherbed she was lying on. The brothers' eyes snapped up and met in consternation. She was so *light!* They might have been lifting the bedding alone.

"Move it!" Bethany snarled, partly to break the moment, partly to disguise her pain as they shifted her.

The brothers smiled fondly at the tone of command. That was more like the mother they knew.

Silently, the brothers carried their mother into the street. The people of Cacaxtla had been waiting all day, some for days before that; they gave way silently, many kneeling to pray and crossing themselves, many weeping. It had been thirty-five years since the lieutenant came, a generation of peace and plenty for Cacaxtla, amid a chaos which had eaten whole continents.

Across the plaza the Bolo loomed above their heads like a mountain, its hundred and fifty tons stretching twenty-four feet in height. The late evening light threw the crags and hollows of its surface into high relief, emphasizing the brutal power of the great war-machine; the heavy crusting of hardened lava gave it a primeval look, like the spirit of some god of war. Behind it stretched the marks of its four treads, ground into the paving stones the day the captain had driven it to rescue the soldiers—and Cacaxtla—from the Jaguar Knights and the First Speaker, the man who'd brought the Old Faith back to bloody life here. It hadn't moved since that day.

The people of Cacaxtla had painted its entire exterior surface with colorful depictions of that rescue, what had led to it and what had come after; it might have been a natural pyramid... except for the cannons.

The three of them stared up the rough, bright side of the Bolo.

"How're we going to get you up there, Mom?"

Joseph had known it would be a struggle, but now he was here, he knew it to be plain impossible. He imagined ropes, and pulleys. "Maybe we could get some help." He looked away from his mother's contemptuous stare.

"Don't even think it," she warned. "I don't want this—turned into—a circus." Bethany Martins lay gasping, her breath spent; her hatred of her own helplessness was a tangible force in the gathering night, like hot light on their hands.

Joseph glared off into the darkness.

"Mom," James leaned over her. "If I tie the featherbed around me and carried you up that way... would it hurt you too much?"

She shook her head. "At least *one* of you knows how to get things done," she rasped. "Do it, boy."

James climbed as gently as he could, unnerved by the hot, light weight of his mother curled against his back. His heart thudded, fear making his palms wet and slippery against the lava and durachrome. Catching his breath on a sob, James gritted his teeth, unwilling to put his mother through the shaking she'd get if he broke down and cried. He looked up at Joseph, who was just reaching the hatch.

"Mom," Joseph said softly, "it won't open for me."

"Markee," came Bethany's muffled voice. "Open the hatch."

With a sigh of hydraulics the hatch came up, releasing the scent of stale, dry air. A light went on below to guide their way down into the cramped interior.

Joseph knelt on one crash-couch and carefully caught his mother as James untied the ends of the featherbed from around his shoulders and waist. Then he laid her gently on the other seat, propping her up against its straight back, though she winced with pain as he did so.

"Markee," Bethany said hoarsely.

She coughed once, then stopped herself, knowing how easily she could lose control and never stop. The bright smooth surfaces of the interior shone back at her, the flat-screen displays and touch-controls like a breath from the past. *Thirty years*, she thought. Thirty years of adobe and stone, wood and woven cotton... the high-tech womb was so strange, now....

"These are my sons. Register Martins, Joseph A., the village *jefe* and senior civilian on site. Log and identify. Say hello, Joseph."

"Hello," Joseph said awkwardly. He sensed a flicker of light, touching his eyes too briefly for certainty.

Bethany took a few moments to recover; her face was slicked with sweat, but the pain, for the moment, seemed to be abating. As much as it ever did.

"Register Martins, James Q., he is the senior..." She pursed her lips in doubt. James had no official title, for all the village acknowledged his position in practice. "He's captain of the village militia." She grinned briefly to think of a lieutenant appointing her son a captain. "Log and identify."

"Hello, Markee," James said.

Bethany smiled, a rictus of thin lips over teeth. He was quick, her James.

"Acknowledged," the Bolo said in a voice as sweet as warm honey. "Hello Jefe, hello Captain. I'm honored to make your acquaintance."

James blinked. He'd spoken to the Bolo once or twice, to

obtain information, or to report in from a distant site, asking the Bolo to relay a report. But this was different. The machine was acknowledging him personally. *An interesting legacy, Mother.*

"It will recognize your authority now," Bethany said. "Leave now, come back for me later."

"We can't leave you alone, Mother," Joseph said, his eyes wary.

She looked at him. "I'm going to take off my shirt—for the sensors," she replied. "Half an hour, come back. I'll let you know if I'm ready." She sat drawing deep breaths, her gaze steady.

Joseph had never been able to outstare his mother and he couldn't now. He turned his head and sighed, then turned and began to climb up the handholds to the hatch above.

James leaned over her and whispered. "I don't want to go." His eyes pleaded to stay, to keep her safe, to help—somehow.

"Go."

He kissed her cheek and stood, his lips pressed into a straight white line.

Bethany waited until the hatch sighed shut before speaking.

"Markee bring up the autodoc, tell me what you see."

"Blood pressure…"

"In plain English."

There was a pause. "You are in the last stages of terminal cancer. Six to eight weeks before complete failure of essential functions."

That long! Six to eight weeks of *this*. Bethany remembered her mother describing how grandfather had died, how at the end he would beg for the painkillers even though they couldn't touch his agony. *And we've got nothing that strong*, she thought, her heart giving a little bump of panic. Eight weeks, losing her dignity, crying and screaming… and the pain. She swallowed hard and winced. It was already as much as she could bear. She imagined herself mewling and writhing—her sons' horrified, helpless faces.

"Is there any medication left?" she asked.

"Negative, Lieutenant. All that remains in the pharmacy is a single shot of fast acting poison to be used to avoid capture."

Bethany closed her eyes in relief. *Good,* she thought.

"I have instructions for you," she said.

"Waiting."

"I want you to defend the people of Cacaxtla from any outside aggressors. Someone from outside—comes here, kills and steals—you destroy them."

"Understood, Lieutenant. What about aggressors from inside Cacaxtla? My programs indicate that there are often internal pressures in a community that might lead to aggression."

"Let the people work it out for 'emselves. Can't protect people from—stupidity. Just don't let 'em be—victimized by outsiders."

"Yes, Lieutenant."

"I want that shot now." Bethany closed her eyes, breathing hard and waited.

"You are in danger of capture?" the Bolo asked. "I detect no enemy activity." The machine could not *sound* confused... Bethany smiled again through the pain, remembering the computer-geek corporal who'd first programmed in that sultry voice. Vinatelli was thirty years dead, but the Bolo Mark III still bore the mark of his lonely fantasies. "You entered with family members."

"In danger of extreme torture," Bethany said.

"From outside the community?"

"From inside me!" Bethany snapped, knowing the autodoc would confirm that she was telling the truth. "Give me the damn shot. Now!"

There was a slight hiss, but no prick of a needle. Then she felt a warmth begin to flood her veins, followed by cold. It became a little harder to breathe, her heart faltered. Bethany gasped and widened her eyes. Breathed out once more and slumped unblinking in the command chair.

The brothers had been pacing for over an hour. The mountain air was becoming distinctly chill, and still the people waited behind them, some wrapped in shawls or blankets, others simply standing.

"Maybe she's fallen asleep," Joseph said. He frowned. "I wouldn't want to wake her."

He and James looked at each other.

"Markee," James said, "is Lieutenant Martins asleep?"

"No, Captain."

It was their mother's voice, younger and stronger than they'd heard it in years. Both men straightened and stared at each other in astonishment, hopeful smiles beginning to curl their lips.

"Mom," Joseph said, and began to climb.

"You're all right, Mom?" James said, his heart lifting, trying not to hope too much.

This time it was the sultry sweet voice of the Bolo that answered. "Lieutenant Bethany Martins cannot answer at this time."

Joseph froze on the ladder and James slapped the side of the tank like an angry child.

"What do you mean she can't answer?" he demanded. "If she's not asleep why can't she?" His eyes widened. "Does she need help?"

"No sir," Bethany's voice answered, "no help is required."

Joseph climbed back down and slumped against the side of the Bolo.

"She's dead," he said flatly.

"What are you talking about?" James snapped. "She sounds

fine." *She does!* he insisted to himself, ignoring the inner voice that told him she wasn't making sense. He started up the Bolo's craggy side.

"Markee," Joseph said, "please confirm. Is Lieutenant Bethany Martins dead or alive?"

"Lieutenant Bethany Martins is dead, sir," the Bolo murmured in its soft voice.

James' breath exploded out in shock, as if he'd been punched in the gut, up under the breastbone. His body hunched around the pain. He turned to stare down at his brother who stood with his face buried in his hands, shoulders shaking.

He stumbled back down, almost falling off. James started to walk away, numb with shock when Joseph's hand stopped him.

"We've got to bring her out," Joseph said, his voice high and tight.

James flung off his brother's hand.

"She didn't even say goodbye," he snarled, his face red with fury. "She knew she was going to do it and she didn't even say goodbye."

Joseph's face was white and blank.

"You think she committed suicide?" The idea had obviously never occurred to him. "She tricked us into bringing her here for help… and then…?"

James continued as though he didn't hear him: "She didn't trust us, dammit! She wanted to come here so bad, let her stay here. Let her rot here! I don't want to see her face again."

"We can't just…"

"Yes we can. Let the damn thing be her tomb! Can you think of a better one? And while we're on the subject of the Bolo, why the hell was that thing talking in our mother's voice? Huh? Why would she *do* that to us?" James' eyes were bright with tears and the certainty of betrayal.

"The stories… Remember? The guy who first programmed it had it fixed to answer certain questions put to it by superior officers in a way that would make them think he was awake and sober. Apparently when we—superior officers—asked the right questions it supplied pre-programmed answers."

"Yeah?" James growled. He strode to the Bolo and shouted up at it. "You are never to use Bethany Martins' voice again! Is that understood, Markee?"

"Affirmative, Captain."

"And you are never to speak to *anyone* again unless you are directly spoken to and required to answer. Do you understand?"

"Affirmative, Captain."

Then James spun on his heel and stopped at the staring eyes. The crowd was looking at him, and he could see their bewilderment and fear. He drew a deep breath.

"Lieutenant Martins is dead," he said. A murmur went through the crowd like a giant's sigh, louder than a wail might have been. He licked dry lips. *What would Mom have said?* "We'll carry on."

Unit #27A22245 Mk. III
Communications—negative broadband scan.
Systems check. 03/02/2045; 0700 hours.
Power: 99.3% capacity. Nominal.
Mobility: restricted. Tread 12 broken; treads 11, r1, r2 jammed. Drive and suspension, nominal.
Weapons: main gun — nominal.
　　　　　　infinite repeaters — units 1-7 nominal.
　　　　　　　　　　— units 7-12 nonoperational.
Sensors: 32.3% capacity.
AI: 97.3% optimum. Nominal.
Query: resume standby yes/no.
: [decision tree]—affirmative.
Unit #27A22245 Mk. III resuming standby status.

"We thought it was the end," Tops said, his voice only slightly cracked with age.

The sun felt good, though. He could feel his bones creak as he stretched and the waiting circle of children leaned forward for the end of the story. Wryly, he flexed his great knobby hands. *Hell, who'd have expected me to live long enough to die of old age?* A few of the youngsters shifted restlessly. He looked up at the bulk of the pyramid, shaggy under its coating of green, and continued:

"The Glorios were all around us and throwing everything they'd been saving up our way. It wasn't enough for them that we were pulling out of San Gabriel; they wanted our heads. When the 'plane came to take us home there was no way that flyboy could land and Captain McNaught told him: 'Get away from here, you can still save some others.' And that was a hard thing to hear…"

"Sergeant Jenkins," a boy called. "I have some questions."

Tops sighed in weary irritation. It was Bethany's grandson, Paulo. Who was ten, the age of extreme obnoxiousness.

"What is it?" he asked warily.

"Why do they call the Bolo 'the Mountain that Walks,' when it can't even move?" Paulo paused long enough that Tops had opened his mouth to answer when he asked: "Or why is it called the Beast, when it's not alive and never has been?"

Tops tried to wait him out, but the smaller children who'd been listening to his story began to get restless.

Just as he started to speak, Paulo, his young face as innocent as a puppy's, said, "And why, please tell me, is it called the Beautiful One, when, even with the paintings, it's ugly as sin?"

"It's called the Beautiful One for its voice, Paulo," James said from behind him.

Paulo gasped and spun around guiltily.

"Please excuse my son, Tops. He doesn't want answers, he wants to get out of his lessons."

Paulo's face turned red.

"As you don't want to study, Paulo, come with me. I'm going

on patrol and you can do the camp chores for me. Perhaps when we get back you'll be more appreciative of the opportunity to study with Sergeant Jenkins, eh?"

Well, that's some punishment, Tops thought. You could see the kid trying not to skip as his father led him away. *Maybe I'm turning into a boring old fart.* Maybe he should tell his war stories less often. He shifted to a sun-warmed bit of the Bolo he was leaning against; the heat soothed the stiffness in his back.

"All right boys and girls, let's get back to work," he said.

Seven-Deer danced. Though he was almost fifty his battle-scarred body was lean and muscular, lithe and graceful in the dance. It was a rare strand of silver that marred the jet black of his gleaming hair and his grimly set face bore few marks of age.

As he danced he sang the sorrows of his people, his voice rough with grief. The children sat enraptured, their dark eyes glowing as he unfolded the history of the people of the Sixth Sun. How the First Speaker had brought them back to truth and the rightful ways of service to the gods, after the *Ladinos* brought disaster on the world by leading the people astray, making them serve Quetzalcoatl-Jesus. How the First Speaker had led them to the upland valley where his command of the volcano kept them safe.

He told of the coming of the evil *yanquis,* who invaded their valley, which was like a paradise. And, being greedy and cruel as the four hundred Southern Warriors who had sought to slay their brother Huitzilopochtl—Left-Handed Hummingbird—they fell upon the people of Cacaxtla and slew the First Speaker of the Sun. Cowards, they hid behind the bulk of their war-machine that was like a mountain. Evil, they would not accept the honored place of a Beloved Son sent as messenger to the gods.

The children gasped in horror at this part—always—as though

their innocent minds could not accept such wickedness.

Seven-Deer sang on, his voice moving from sadness to the joy of victory as he told of how the exiles descended the mountain and how the Jaguar Knights had fallen upon their enemies like the wrath of the Sun. Thus making a safe place for the people here in the lowland jungles, taking some of their enemies as slaves to serve them, but sending most as messengers to the Sun to plead for aid.

He spun and leapt and the children's small chests swelled with pride to think of the victories of the valiant Jaguar Knights. Every boy among them dreamed of a place in that ferocious company.

Then Seven-Deer danced the promise. All who left the Valley of Cacaxtla, the place like paradise, were exiled princes whose time of vengeance would come. All who remained in the valley were traitors whose blood would nourish the gods, food waiting for the harvest.

It was their duty and privilege to prevent the destruction of the Sixth Sun as the Fifth had been destroyed. For it had been blotted out by indecision and faithlessness as much as by foreign greed.

He finished his performance on this solemn note and stood straight and tall, his breathing only slightly heavier than normal. Servants wiped the sweat from his face and body, naked save for a loincloth; the heat beat down through the steamy lowland air, making water run over his brown skin. One of the priests brought the feathered cloak and another the elaborate headgear that marked him as First Speaker of the Sun People.

"Three-Coyote," he intoned. "Bring forth your beloved son."

A stocky warrior led a bound and naked man to the altar. The prisoner glared defiantly and spit at the people where they knelt around the earth and timber mound. He was an escaped slave, one who had unwisely behaved like a warrior and now would pay the price.

Behind his impassive face Seven-Deer sneered. It was disgraceful that they should be forced to send a mere slave as a messenger. It smacked of impiety.

Four priests grasped the prisoner, who had begun to struggle, and slammed him onto the altar, stretching his limbs so that his chest arched upward drum-tight. The man cursed them and spat in Seven-Deer's face as he raised the knife.

It was with rather more anger than was proper that the First Speaker plunged the knife downward.

Smack!

"Jesus! Will ya look at the size of this thing?"

Gary Sherman thrust the bloody corpse of the insect under Pasqua's nose.

"Oh, for God's sake!" she snarled, pushing his hand away. "I'm driving, Gary, show some sense."

The road they were on was muddy, slippery, and narrow. In fact it all but vanished in the thick, steaming greenery that slapped the sides and rollbar of the jeep. The jungle smelled *thick*, like spilled beer on a hot day, or wet rotting bread.

Gary glared at his partner, an attractive woman in her late twenties; straight, shoulder-length black hair held back by a yellow scarf, almond-shaped green eyes hidden by dark glasses.

This woman is not good for my ego. He doubted she'd look at him twice if he was on fire. Not that he was much to look at, he admitted self-pityingly, with his hair creeping towards the back of his neck and a stomach that made it look like he was smuggling kettle-drums.

He sighed dramatically as he rubbed his hand against his thick khaki-covered thigh to scrape off the squashed mosquito.

"Will you tell me what the fuck we're doing out here in the green hell?" He watched her from the corner of his eye as she pursed her—*luscious,* he thought—lips.

"Language, Gary," she admonished. "In answer to your question, *you're* here because you wanted to be. If you'll recall, you insisted on coming along. To help."

"Yeah, to help," he said impatiently.

Actually, he'd been hoping that the jungle at night, the howling of the monkeys, the roar of the jaguar, the creeping of the jeep-sized insects, might loosen her up a bit. God knew, *he* could use some cuddling after four days of this shit.

He should have known better. From what little she'd let drop she'd spent her early years hangin' with the Giacano Family, the Dukes of New Orleans. An old-fashioned bunch whose reputation made the jungle at night seem safer than your own living-room. Pasqua had to have crossed 'em. What else would a beauty like this be doing scraping a living as an arms dealer in darkest Central America? This place made the East Coast baronies look like civilization.

"*I* am here pursuing a hot lead that might help us get rid of that damned railgun you bought," she continued.

"That gun's a beauty," Gary said defensively.

"That gun's a white elephant," Pasqua sneered.

"It's also the best weapon we've got," he insisted. "XM-17 Railgun, yessir. That baby'll take out a Bolo. You know that?"

"Yeah, and I know how common Bolos are in Central America, too. Every piss-ant town's got one in the plaza. It's amazing we haven't sold it yet."

"Sarcasm doesn't become you, baby."

Pasqua braked hard, put the car in park, and turned slowly towards him.

"We've discussed this before, Gary."

He could almost feel those hidden green eyes melting holes in his face. Her right hand twitched slightly, and he remembered the *jefe* of the port town. His successor had been perfectly willing to do business on an impersonal level, after

Pasqua shot his predecessor.

"Aw, Pasqua! C'mon, you know I dint mean anything." He looked at her, trying to keep his face innocent. Then he rolled his eyes, looked out his window into the jungle.

While she waited.

"Okay," he turned back to her, "I'm sorry that I called you baby and there's a guy behind you with a gun."

"What?"

"Behind you. A-guy-with-a-*gun*."

She turned in slow, graceful stages to look out her side of the jeep. It was hard to see the man at first. He wore a tight-fitting brown uniform dotted with black splotches. His face had broad black stripes around the eyes and mouth, accented by more dots, his black hair was pulled up into a topknot.

Very, very slowly, Pasqua took off her sunglasses so that he could see her eyes.

His own eyes were calm and cold. He stood absolutely still, his M-35 pointed at the center of her chest.

"*Hola*," she said, and saw him stiffen. She took a closer look and saw that under the war-paint the man was an *indio*. *Bingo*, she thought. If the rumors back in Puerto Zacarta were right. She marshalled her few words of Nahuatl and tried again. "*Greeting, warrior. We seek your First Speaker.*"

Apparently it was the right move. Now she could see a dozen of the leopard-spotted men as they moved closer.

There was a brief conference, their eyes never leaving Pasqua and Gary; the language had far too many consonants for her taste.

"Weapons," the man grunted.

Not without a pang, Pasqua lifted the PPK from the holster at her belt; it was a Family heirloom. Tradition had it that her great-grandfather had killed a Cajun detective with it, right after the Collapse. The *indios* took it, and Gary's antique Glock, and the M-35 from the rack behind the driver's seat, and their machetes. Fortunately they missed the switchblade tucked into the back of her pants; that was an heirloom too. A Giacano without a switchblade was naked.

The… soldiers, she supposed… arrived at a decision and the others melted into the jungle again, leaving their original captor behind. He motioned them out of their jeep. Pasqua dragged a folder out with her and he raised the gun threateningly.

"First Speaker," she said, holding it up to show that it could never be, or hide, a weapon.

He jerked his M-35 down the trail and Pasqua and Gary started walking.

"And why did you not bring this with you," Seven-Deer asked contemptuously, tossing the pictures Pasqua had brought with her into their faces.

Pasqua and Gary were on their knees, their hands tied before them, broad sticks thrust behind their elbows. "You may not even have such a thing." He stalked like a panther to the low dais where his throne, a wide chair covered with deerskins, sat. "It would not be the first time our enemies, the *Ladinos,* thought us such fools, too weak in the head to know any better."

The situation's a little extreme, Gary thought, *but I know a bargaining ploy when I hear one.* Except for the occasional Nahuatl word, they'd been speaking in Spanish.

"Pitch!" he whispered to Pasqua who turned to him with frightened eyes. "He's interested. Or we'd be dead. Pitch!"

"The only reason you are alive," Seven-Deer said as he lounged back, "is that you spoke a few words in a civilized language. Enough to pique my curiosity. And the woman wears the color of the Sun."

Pasqua blinked. *My scarf?* she thought.

This bunch of indigs were crazier than most, but they had a pretty big stretch of territory marked out and a lot of it was farmed. They probably *could* pay a reasonable price for the

XM-17, in goods that would be valuable back in the north, in the Duchy of New Orleans, to the Caquique of Florida, to one of the seven kings of Cuba, or any of the Duchies from Charleston north. Timber, grain, rum, coffee, slaves, you name it.

"Speak! Why have you not brought this 'tank-killing' gun with you for me to see with my own eyes?"

"It…" Pasqua choked on a dry throat and had to begin again. "It is too big for us to bring, *Uetlatoani*," Pasqua said obsequiously. "It is as big as a mountain and would take a great truck…" She realized these people had nothing like that and hurried over what she feared they might see as an insult: "…or many men to move it. Surely you can understand that I would not make such an effort if you were not interested?"

Seven-Deer, the First Speaker of the Sun People, straightened slowly and rose from his throne, his obsidian eyes gleaming.

"As big as a mountain," he whispered.

A smile spread slowly across his face and leapt like a spark to the faces of the Lords and Generals and Ladies around him. The people murmured the words, "… as big as a mountain…" over and over again, turning it into a chant, clapping their hands and stamping their feet joyously.

Seven-Deer stabbed a finger at his prisoners like a spear.

"You will take us to this wonder!" he shouted, and the room erupted in cheers.

When the *yanqui* woman had said the words "… as big as a mountain" to him, a fire had been lit below Seven-Deer's heart. Now, in the awesome presence of the giant gun he felt elevated, touched with the Sun's own power, mind and heart and soul blazed together with purpose. And that purpose was *vengeance!*

"It's called the XM-17 Railgun," Pasqua was saying as she escorted-shooed him to the gunner's seat and urged him to

take the control yoke in his hands. "This is a computer-gener-
ated holographic magnifying sight." She flipped a couple of
switches and the village down the road from their compound
sprang into view, hovering before Seven-Deer's astonished
eyes in every known shade of bilious green. This red dot,"
she pointed at a dime-sized red dot in the upper corner of
the holo, "shows where the gun is pointing. To move the dot,
move the control yoke."

Seven-Deer cautiously did so and the dot jiggled its way
down to the center of the scene in the holo. He laughed like
a child.

"Isn't that neat?" she said, smiling and nodding like this was
a perfectly normal presentation.

"How does it work?" Seven-Deer growled.

"When it's fired, two charged bars come together to shoot
out a rod of depleted uranium sheathed in steel."

"The rods're only about a foot long," Gary said, moving
up to his other side. "But when ya press the firing stud it's
like, slam! bam! thank you, ma'am!" He slapped his hands
together and laughed heartily. Until he saw the First Speaker's
expression.

"How does it fire?" Seven-Deer asked through gritted
teeth.

Pasqua and Gary looked at each other nervously.

"We only have twelve rods, and can't afford to waste any, so
I'm afraid we can't allow you to test fire it." The First Speaker
stared at her disdainfully and she sighed. "When you have the
right target in view," she said emphatically, "press the firing
studs at the top of the hand grips on the control yoke. Here
and here."

"Eexxcellent," Seven-Deer said like a man being told "yes"
by a reluctant lover.

He centered the sights on the village church, a small stone
building at the center of the plaza. He powered up the gun,
the bars began to charge with a low hum that quickly escalated

to a piercing whine.

"What are you doing?" Pasqua asked. But she knew and she was numb with horror.

"Testing your merchandise," Seven-Deer answered. He pressed the firing studs, the bars clanged together with a scream of electronic excitement and the depleted uranium rod emerged with a supersonic *crrraaaaccckkk!* that numbed their ears.

In the holo the village church burst apart into a blizzard of gravel. An instant behind, the sound of the explosion reached them and looking up they saw a gray-brown plume boiling into the sky.

"He fired the bastard," Gary said in disbelief.

"You…" Pasqua began and stopped. Around her Seven-Deer and his followers were cheering and dancing in delight. Instinctively she stepped back, flight on her mind, when Seven-Deer's hand flashed out and caught her wrist.

"Oh, stay," he said grinning, "you would not wish to miss the ceremony."

Several of the *indios* had grabbed Gary and were dragging him to the front of the gun. Seven-Deer dragged her along behind them and when they had Gary spread-eagled at the base of the railgun he flung her into the arms of a group of his followers. Who twisted her arms up behind her and bound her hands, then pushed her to her knees in the dirt.

"You can't do this," Gary was shouting in panic. The front of his khakis were stained dark. "You want the gun, take it," he said frantically, his eyes bulging as he watched Seven-Deer approach, leisurely drawing a long obsidian knife. "Please don't," Gary said.

Pasqua was so terrified she couldn't even scream. Her traitorous mind filled with all sorts of babble. *I told you not to buy that gun, Gary.* And *Please don't, no, please!*

Gary's last desperate scream began when the knife went up, but it didn't end for a surprisingly long time after the knife came down.

She saw Seven-Deer lift a bloody heart high and thought inanely, *So you did have one after all, Gary.* Then she blacked out.

When she came to, Seven-Deer's blood-smeared face was smiling into hers, his black eyes dancing with a mad glee. He trailed one blood-wet finger down her face and she whimpered with terror.

"And when we retake the valley of Cacaxtla," he said, "we will send you back to the Sun. For surely you are his servant. How he will smile to see you again."

Seven days of chores, James thought. *And not a whimper.*

Either Paulo was becoming a stoic, or he'd learned that pouting and complaints would get him nowhere. Probably the latter; the kid was smart—he knew that this was the best way to make his father feel like a heel. It was even working, sort of.

He snapped the bolt back into the M-35, sipping at a final cup of coffee as he watched his son carefully tamping down the campfire with water and entrenching-tool loads of dirt. The upland forest was chilly in the morning; they were a thousand meters above the valley floor, and it was never really hot here. A clean crisp smell of pine filled the air, and he could see for miles across tumbled blue hills. From what his mother had said, back in the old days—before her time, even—most of these hillsides had been logged off or burnt off and then farmed. He shook his head in wonder, trying to imagine that *many* people in the world.

Paulo was frowning seriously as he policed up the campsite, checking that nothing was left or out of place. It gave his face a look of his mother. Maria used to say that Paulo could wrap James around his little finger. His smile faded. It had been four years since his wife's death, four years of trying to be mother and father both, trying to anticipate what Maria would have said or done. In a way it helped to keep her close to him.

Paulo suddenly looked up and grinned at him. James nodded solemnly and slung his rifle, turning to the UATV.

"You can fix it, can't you?" Paulo stood across from him looking serenely confident.

"I think so. This time."

The UATVs were incredibly hardy machines, capable of running on almost anything combustible, with six spun-alloy wheels that never seemed to show wear. Even the engine parts were incredibly durable... but when they wore out, you were in trouble. Nobody made things like that anymore; there were machine-shops in the valley, but they worked with metal, not fiber-bound ceramics.

"This is the compressor," he began.

Paulo leaned close, and James remembered the same expression on his own face as his mother ran him through the checklist. She'd been a tougher disciplinarian than he ever could be, though. *I suppose because she'd spent so long with her life depending on the equipment,* he thought. Her life and others. James had drifted into command of the valley militia, but there hadn't been anything more than a skirmish with wandering bandits since he was Paulo's age.

I try to remember it's not a game, he thought.

"I don't think she's got much longer though," he concluded.

Paulo's head came up and he looked around, a puzzled frown on his young face.

"What?" James said.

"Listen..." After a moment Paulo said, "It sounds like men singing."

"Or mourning," James murmured. And there were a *lot* of them.

He slipped on the helmet, buckled on his equipment belt and the body armor that never quite fit; none of Bethany Martins' original platoon had been quite his size. His M-35 suddenly felt more serious in his hands.

"Stay here," he said to Paulo. "I'll be right back." Powering up the helmet, he trotted off into the trees.

Paulo frowned after his father. *Why do I have to stay behind?* he asked himself. *I'm not a baby. And besides, I heard them first.* Whoever *they* were. Paulo chewed his lip thoughtfully. Fair was fair, he had a right to take a look.

Paulo reached into the UATV, grabbed his slingshot and bag of stones—in case—and padded into the woods after his father.

He moved quickly, but kept some attention on where his feet were going; Dad had taught him that, and he was good at it. And... yes, there was a shape in camouflage-mottled fatigues and helmet. *He's* really *quiet,* Paulo thought, impressed. James turned around suddenly and he froze, though his cover was only a screen of thorny bushes. His father had told him that motion in such a circumstance was as bad as being in plain view. After a quick glance down his back-trail, James hurried on. Paulo found it hard to suppress his delighted laughter.

Dad doesn't even know I'm here! he thought in wonder. *It works!*

Paulo ghosted onward, silent—although his grin was the facial equivalent of a shout.

The farther he went, the louder the singing became. James still couldn't make out any words, but thought there must be many, many voices to make that sound. His mouth was dry; he took a quick swig from his canteen and went down on one knee, acutely conscious of the sweat trickling down his flanks under the armor. *What was it Mother said...* Ah, yes. He licked a finger and checked the wind direction; very slow, but from the low ground up to him. *In case they have dogs.* He was approaching an overlook on the old road leading out of the valley; he dropped to his belly and leopard-crawled to the lip of the cliff. In response to his whisper the helmet-visor supplied times-four magnification, making everything nearby jerk and quiver disorientingly with each motion of his head.

He grunted in surprise and felt his jaw drop. Below him, down below the boulder-strewn hillside and the sparse trees, was an *army*.

An army of sweating men, perhaps as many as seven hundred, yoked to an enormous gun with long sisal ropes. Other men in tight, spotted-brown uniforms moved up and down the line of chanting pullers striking them ferociously with whips. He could see one stagger and fall; the uniformed men closed in, kicking and striking with the butts of their rifles—good rifles, M-35s like the one across his back, not the single-shot black-powder models the traders brought around these days. One of them stood back and fired a burst into the fallen laborer.

I guess that means they're not volunteers, James thought.

There was—he called for more magnification from the crystal-sandwich visor—a bound woman spread-eagled at the base of the cannon. Just above her head sat a man in an elaborate feather headdress and very little else, pounding an enormous drum.

They'll never get that thing into the valley, he thought incredulously. The road was completely blocked by the old lava flow. Though thirty years had gentled its contours considerably, *still*, they couldn't possibly…

He winced as he watched one of the spotted slave-drivers whip a cut right through one man's shirt. *And skin*, James thought as the blood began to flow. Yes, they did think they could get into the valley on this road. *And with that kind of brutality they may be right.*

"Unit push," he whispered, though he doubted the strangers would hear him over the mournful singing. "Conito, come in." No answer. Someone was *always* supposed to man communications, but over time people grew lax. He'd skin the bastard who'd left the comm empty today. "Record," he ordered.

"There's something weird here… and dangerous…"

The world flashed white. There was a moment of dazzling pain, and then blackness.

Paulo knew this place. It was near the cliff that overlooked the ancient road. He watched his father drop to his belly and crawl forward. Looking around he spotted a suitable tree and climbed. When he'd lodged himself comfortably in the crook of the tree Paulo looked out over the old road and lost his breath.

Never had he seen or imagined anything like this. People were dragging a big, *huge* gun up the road. And other people were *hitting* them to make them do it! Paulo's stomach clenched and his mouth watered, he felt like throwing up. He closed his eyes and took deep breaths like his father had told him. And did feel a little better.

He looked out over the road again, a flicker of movement caught his eye, something closer. Something *close.*

A man was standing behind his father, one of the spotted men. A long shape was in his hand, a sort of wooden paddle with edges of shiny black rock. The blade shattered on the durachrome, but the helmet flew off and clattered down the steep hill. James' head dropped to the dirt.

Paulo felt his mouth drop open, and his hands trembled for an instant. Then he fumbled for his slingshot, loaded it with the heaviest stone that came to hand, whirled it around his head and let fly with a snapping twist of his body and arms. The same motion he used to hunt ducks…

The club was raised for a killing blow when Paulo's stone struck the man's temple. The *thock* sound was clearly audible even twenty feet away, and he dropped limp across James' unconscious body.

Paulo didn't see him fall, as he half slid, half fell out of the tree, his palms burning from scrapes as he scrabbled to save himself. Then he was racing towards them, his skin icy cold, his heart beating until his throat felt like it was being squeezed shut. Paulo's sight tunneled in on his father's boots where they stuck out from beneath the other man's body.

"Dad!" he said, his voice shrill with alarm. "Dad?" he said again, touching the blood in James' hair warily. His father moaned softly. Paulo sprang up and began trying to move the man who lay across him, thinking he must be smothering his father.

He yanked and pushed frantically, sobbing with frustration as the body refused to budge. The man's dead weight was so *heavy!* Finally Paulo sat down and kicked him off, the limp form rolling heavily against his sandals.

James moaned again. *Good! That must have been the right thing.* Paulo pulled off his shirt and began to wrap it snugly around his father's head.

"Dad?" he kept calling softly. "Dad?"

James suddenly lifted his head with a gasp.

"What... happened?"

"This guy came up behind you and clobbered you with a club, so I beaned him with my slingshot," Paulo babbled. "He's right there."

Paulo's father turned to him, head wobbling, his eyes unfocused and looking odd somehow. Then Paulo realized what it was, one pupil was noticeably larger than the other. *Concussion! Oh no.*

Tops taught everyone about concussion in survival class. This was serious, maybe life-threatening. He held up two fingers.

"How many fingers am I holding up?"

His father looked at him owlishly.

"Two," he said.

Paulo let out his breath in a rush of relief. "Then you're okay. You can see all right."

"No. People always hold up two fingers."

"Daaa-ad."

His father dropped his head and moaned again. This time it was echoed by the man who'd hit him. Paulo froze.

"Dad?" he said, his lips stiff with terror. "Dad? He's alive."

Wake up! James shouted in his own mind. The voice sounded like his mother's.

Get moving, c'mon, on your feet, soldier!

He fought the nausea that struck him every time he lifted his head and struggled to coordinate his limbs—which moved slowly and clumsily, however hard he willed them to obey.

"Daaa-ad!" Paulo said, panic creeping into his voice. "He's waking up, Dad. What do I do?"

Paulo pressed his lips firmly together as he looked frantically from his prone father to the stirring enemy beside him. He started looking around for a big rock. *Too small, too small.* Unngghh! *Too big. Rotten stick. I don't believe this!* he thought. *All I want's a damn rock!*

James lifted his head and the world spun, grimly he pushed himself up on his elbows and waited for the dizziness to subside. He took deep breaths and the nausea abated somewhat. His head throbbed, and he tried to ignore the pain. He opened his eyes. The world was doubled, sometimes tripled and blurred. He might as well be blind. He closed his eyes.

"Paulo. Help me up, son."

Paulo was beside him in an instant, heaving like a hero. James laughed, and stopped when that made the world spin.

"Easy, boy. I'll end up in a tree. Slow and easy does it. I can't see real good, so we've got to take things one step at a time."

"Okay, Dad." But Paulo was anxiously watching the man on the ground. He wasn't moving much, he rocked a little, and twitched his hands and feet, but his eyes were still closed, so Paulo didn't know whether he was coming to or dying.

Once on his feet, James swayed for a moment, his balance uncertain. Then he steadied, as much from sheer will as receding trauma. He fumbled at his equipment belt and pulled the bowie knife from its sheath. It was over a foot long and point heavy, and felt good in his hand. His mother had taught him how to use it, though he'd never had to, and had given it to him when he went on his first patrol.

"Son," he said. "Lead me to him." *I don't want to do this in front of you,* he thought. *I don't want to do this at all, but we have to. Better me than you.*

Paulo took his hand and put it on the stricken man's body. James felt his way to the man's throat. He placed the knife carefully, making sure his other hand was out of the way of the razor-sharp edge of the blade. Pressing his lips together he applied pressure and dragged the knife towards him.

There was a bizarre and ugly sound from the severed windpipe and hot fluid cascaded over his free hand.

James gasped and fell back on his heels.

"C'mon, son," he said, "let's get back to the UATV. We've got to warn the village."

Paulo was staring at the dying man. *There's so much blood,* he thought. He'd seen animals die, he should have expected it, but… His mind whirled and for a moment, the man's throat seemed to be the only thing visible at the end of a long tunnel. He'd never missed his mother more, he wanted to feel the safety of her arms around him, lifting this horror out of his mind forever.

"Son!"

Paulo stared at his father's blood-drenched right hand, reaching out for his.

"Here I am," he said, and took it.

We might as well be advancing in the damned Bolo! James thought as he noisily stumbled for perhaps the fortieth time.

"I'm sorry, Dad!"

"It's all right, son, it's not your fault. Let's rest a moment." He started to squat when Paulo yanked at his arm.

"Not there, Dad." He pulled his father away from the anthill. "Here's okay."

James sank down with gratitude, feeling weak and cold. *Maybe a little shocky,* he thought, wishing he could sleep for a few hours.

"How close are we?" he whispered.

"Not far," Paulo said. "Just down there." He pointed, then whipped his arm down, blushing. "And through some trees," he added hastily to cover his error.

James thrust his chin forward and put his hand on Paulo's shoulder. "Son," he said, "I'm… going to send you on ahead to scout. I'm making too much noise and that guy back there must have friends. So I want you to sneak up on the UATV, wait for a few minutes to see if there's anybody around—do *not* break cover—and report back to me. Can you do that?"

"Yessir. I'll be careful," he said quickly, anticipating his father's next words.

"See that you are," James growled.

Paulo looked back from the bend of the trail to where his father sat waiting, his arms loosely draped over his knees, eyes closed, his face gray with fatigue. *Should I go back and hide him?* he wondered. Dad looked so vulnerable. Paulo wavered, looked down the trail towards the UATV. *No, he'll say I'm wasting time, or something. And he'll be embarrassed.* Resolving to hurry, Paulo moved on.

Paulo knew they were there before he saw them. The spotted men were talking and laughing like they had no reason not to. They were speaking pure Nahuatl, he realized, unmixed with English or Spanish as it was in Cacaxtla.

Paulo dropped and began to crawl. Sneaking-through-the-woods was the best part of school, and he'd always done well on the tests. He peered through the bushes, keeping his head low to the ground.

There were five of them, stripping the UATV with surprising

efficiency for men who were making so much careless noise. *I wish they were as clumsy as they are stupid,* Paulo thought bitterly. He didn't understand this. Why were they being so obvious? Surely they knew someone would be coming back for the vehicle.

Then realization hit him with a chill like snow down his back. "The answer is implicit in the question," his father was fond of saying. "Your grandmother taught me that." This was a trap. Their noise was intended to draw someone carelessly into the open, too intent on the outrage before them to think about an ambush.

He almost panicked. That meant that somewhere around him were other men in spotted uniforms. Deliberately he squeezed his fear into a small box inside himself. *Later,* he promised himself, *later.* Then, moving with exquisite care, he hurried back to his father.

"Damn!" James smacked his fist into his other hand, and swore more ripely and bitterly inside his mind. "So now our second line of communication is cut off." *There's only one thing left to do,* he thought. *Paulo will have to go alone.* Given a day and a half, cutting directly across the hills and moving as fast as he could go, James figured the boy could reach the village with a warning.

No, that's too optimistic. Two days. Maybe. At least the gun people won't be able to move too fast. That ought to give us some time to prepare.

He wondered if the Bolo could still defend itself, let alone the people of Cacaxtla, neglected as it was.

"Son," he said, and reached out for Paulo, who grasped his hand. "We've got to warn the village, so they have time to prepare for this." He paused, his face set.

"I know, Dad." Paulo looked at him warily, wondering what was coming.

"You've got to go alone. I'll only hold you back…"

"No!" Paulo snatched his hand away in horror. Leave him? Leave his own father out here *blind* and all alone. "I can't."

"You have to. The village is more important than any one person," James said calmly.

"No. I mean I can't. I don't know the way."

James frowned. "The valley's not that big, son. I don't think you can get lost."

"Dad, it's huge. And this is only my second time on patrol with you, I've been this far from the village only once before. And I didn't pay that much attention, I mean, I didn't know I'd have to. Honest, Dad, I'll get lost. Don't make me do this, please." He was panting when he finished speaking and shaking with pure terror. He knew that leaving his father alone out here would be like killing him. And he couldn't bear to lose his father, too.

"Son…"

"I can't. You know the landmarks, you can guide me. We'll go together."

For a moment there'd been something so like his grandmother in Paulo's voice that James blinked.

"Okay," he said slowly. "Then we'd better get started." James pulled some of his makeshift bandage down over his eyes. It was easier that way, without the blurring, shifting light to confuse him.

"First, look for the peak of the old volcano. Can you see it from here?"

Seven-Deer had taken upon himself the task of feeding the servant of the Sun. It pleased him mightily that Tezcatlipoca had chosen a *yanqui,* one of those who had brought about the downfall of his people, as an instrument of vengeance. He took it as a sign of favor that the god would make such a joke. Smoking Mirror had a sense of humor; it made Seven-Deer slightly ashamed that he'd never been able to emulate his god in that.

"A full bowl," he said, and the cook-slave dipped his ladle once more.

The First Speaker of the Sun threaded his way through the encampment; it was crowded and noisy, inevitable with so many slaves along. The stink was not as bad as it would have been down in the lowlands. They must have climbed at least five hundred meters already; the air began to remind Seven-Deer of his youth in the cool uplands of Cacaxtla.

"I have brought food," he said, as he gracefully mounted the gun carriage, disdaining to use his hands for climbing. The rungs that led up the side of the wheeled gun's boxy mounting were cool beneath his iron-hard soles, not like metal or stone.

"I'm not hungry," Pasqua said coldly.

"You will like it," he said cheerfully, sinking into a crouch beside her head. "It comes from my own table." He filled the spoon and thrust it at her mouth.

Pasqua turned her head away and the spoon relentlessly followed. She turned to glare at him and he smiled benevolently.

If she'd had appetite, the sight of him would have killed it. He still was smeared with Gary's blood, his hair was caked with it and the sweetish smell of rot was thick on his hands.

She opened her mouth to say, "I don't want it," and Seven-Deer thrust the spoon home. Immediately she spat it out. Not on him, though she'd have liked to, but she didn't want to inspire him to anything too creative. The Duke of New Orleans had some *extremely* creative people on his staff, and she'd had to attend those events as a child, like anyone in the Family.

"I'm nauseous," she snapped. "I can't eat, okay? You wouldn't want me to choke on my own vomit before you get to cut my heart out. Now would you, babe?"

Seven-Deer's face stiffened with offense. To be refused thus by this ignorant *yanqui* slut was... a test perhaps. The Sun sought to determine his worthiness. He placed the bowl down gently near her bound right hand.

"Very well," he said quietly. "Let the insects have it. And may its scent torment you. Perhaps tomorrow you will have a better appetite."

He rose and descended the steep gun carriage as gracefully as he'd come. Pasqua would have paid any price to see him slip and fall flat on his face.

Her lips and the inside of her mouth were burning fiercely from the spoonful of food he'd forced on her. It brought tears to her eyes. She waited; the camp grew quieter, fires died down, only a few sentries moved. Her mouth still burned.

Jeez, she thought, *that stuff would burn through steel.* She turned her head and looked consideringly at the abandoned bowl. *You don't suppose…*

Her numb hand plopped into the bowl and scooped up some of the contents, bending her wrist as far as she could. Pasqua slid the mess onto the vegetable fiber ropes that bound her. "Whoooo!" she yelped as the chili sauce penetrated to burn the chafed and bleeding skin below. Which motivated her to yank her bound hand frantically.

Maybe it was the grease, maybe it was because the rope was thoroughly wet, maybe it was because she was so desperate to get that stuff *off*, but this time her hand, and not a little skin, came free.

She rubbed her wrist off on her shirt; it didn't stop the burning. Frustrated, she turned to free her other hand. Bound as she was she could barely reach the knot. It had tightened with her struggles and with bearing her weight all day. A fingernail bent back and she suppressed a yelp of pain. She sucked the finger, then spat as her tongue began to burn again. The need to swear seemed almost as imperative as the need to breathe.

With a sigh, Pasqua scooped up a handful of her supper and dumped it over her other wrist.

After she'd freed her feet, Pasqua snatched the yellow scarf from her hair and rubbed off as much sauce as she could from her wrists and hands, though the flames were dying now. Then she tossed it aside, glad that her shirt and slacks were gray and unlikely to call attention to her in the darkening jungle.

She moved carefully and quietly, keeping low, sometimes on hands and knees. The slaves were sleeping all around the gun carriage, so thickly that it was difficult to step between legs and arms and heads. In their exhaustion they slept through her quiet passage, even when she accidentally touched one of them.

Her eyes were on the jungle when a man sat up and looked at her. Pasqua froze, a nasty, almost electrical shock frissoned over her and her breath stopped in her throat. The man's face was blue-gray in the darkness, his eyes black pits. He stared at her unmoving. Then he smiled, and silently, he lay back down.

Thank you, God, Pasqua thought. As she moved into the jungle she made vague, but fervent, promises about being a better person hereafter.

Sometimes, just before turning in, Sergeant Jenkins liked to wander around the village, to settle his mind and his aching bones for sleep. And on nights like this one when he was feeling especially solitary he'd stop to have a few words with the Bolo.

Since Lieutenant Martins' death no one spoke to Markee. And occasionally Tops felt a little guilty about it. He knew that the Bolo wasn't lonely, didn't feel neglected or slighted being ignored by the populace, didn't feel anything at all in fact. It was as empty of self-awareness as a toaster.

But when it spoke it sometimes seemed so like a person that he made a point of visiting from time to time. And if he took solace in knowing that it had seen him young and bore memories of his old comrades, well, so what? Besides, sometimes it picked up a faint radio broadcast from back in Reality and he enjoyed hearing them, weird as they were. The Lord of Philly had declared war on the Jersey Barons? Either that was a sports broadcast, or things had gotten unreal in Reality.

"Good evening, Markee," Tops said, settling himself on a familiar outcropping on the Bolo's lower surface. "Tell me what's new with you?"

"I've received a most disturbing message from Captain Martins, Sergeant. As follows…"

James Martins' voice came from the Bolo's speakers, weakly, as though over some distance. "Unit Push. Conito, come in." There was a pause and then an impatient sigh. "Record. There's something weird here… and dangerous…" There was a sparkle of static and then nothing.

"That's it?" Tops asked.

"Yes. It has been ten hours and thirty-four minutes since I received this message. Nothing at all since. This is unlike Captain Martins, who is punctilious about following up on his recorded messages."

"Hmph. Any other chatter on the unit push?"

"Negative, Sergeant. As far as I can tell Conito has yet to hear this message."

Tops straightened his spine, his eyes blazing with outrage. Lord knew Conito had his problems. His wife had died in childbirth leaving him with twin babies to take care of. But this kind of neglect was unheard of.

"These damn kids," Tops muttered. "They're spoiled is what. We did our job too good. Think the world's their friend, never going to do 'em any harm." He stood up. "I'll see to it, Markee. Keep an ear out for the captain."

"Yes, Sergeant."

Joseph opened his door to find Tops on the doorstep, standing in the halo of bugs that orbited around the methane lantern above the door.

"Hello, Tops," he said, surprised. "It's late," he said doubtfully.

And the old man was in uniform, from boots to helmet.

"I know what time it is, Jefe. I have something to tell you." Tops pushed past Joseph and into the house, then turned to face him.

"James is in trouble," he said shortly. "The Bolo intercepted a partial message from him. He said, 'there's something weird here, and dangerous,' then nothin' but static. That was over ten hours ago. Markee hasn't heard anything since."

"Conito hasn't reported…"

"Conito hasn't accessed his messages yet. Anymore than he's been monitoring the unit push. I heard the recording. It was broken off. He's in trouble."

Joseph looked at him doubtfully. He licked his lips and looked away, then back again. "What do you expect me to do?" he asked.

"I *expect* you to send help." Tops began to do a slow burn as the Jefe's eyes flicked away again.

"Don't be lookin' away like I've done somethin' socially unacceptable. Your brother was cut off in mid-report and hasn't been heard from in hours. You have the power, and the responsibility, to send help." He stood glaring at Joseph. "And that's what I expect you to do."

Joseph rolled his eyes. "Probably the UATV broke down. That one's on its last legs. And the helmet comms aren't much better. What's more," he said, spreading his hands and smiling reasonably, "the Bolo's in even worse shape than the UATV. It might have misheard James."

"I heard the recording myself," Tops said through clenched teeth. "With my own ears. It was very distinct, Joseph. You could access that recording yourself if you wanted to."

Joseph's shoulders slumped and his mouth twisted impatiently.

"*Querida?*" a voice called from the hall stairs above. "*Mi corazón?*"

"It's late…"he began.

"Either you send someone to check this out or I'm going," Tops said fiercely, his breath beginning to come hard.

"Will you relax, old man," Joseph said, putting his hand on Tops' shoulder and guiding him to the door. "There's nothing we can do tonight anyway. It'll have to wait till tomorrow."

Tops' big fist flashed out and caught the *jefe* on the side of the head like a five-pound maul.

Joseph heard the sound through the bones of his skull. It didn't hurt; mostly he was conscious of outrage, and surprise that the old man could still move that fast. He was older than Mother. *But I can't hit him back—*

It was then that he realized he had dropped bonelessly to the floor. He thrashed helplessly in slow motion until the sense returned to his eyes, and the pain began. Then he stared up at the elderly man who'd flattened him.

"That was from the El-Tee," Tops said furiously. "'Cause she'da given you one those for even *thinkin'* about leaving one of your people hangin' fire after a message like that. Let alone your own brother."

Tops' eyes flashed in the candlelight, yellow around smoky black irises.

"You listen to me, little boy, it's a bad ol' world out there. And there's always a chance that trouble will find its way to your door. Now, to me it sounds like trouble is knockin', and it's knockin' real loud." He pointed one massive finger in Joseph's face. "Now you send someone out there to help your brother!"

Joseph glared at him, rubbing his jaw and wondering if he should have Tops thrown in jail. Tops glared back with an outraged sincerity that finally penetrated the Jefe's hurt pride.

"You're right," Joseph said grudgingly. "It does bear investigating." He picked himself up and headed for the door. "You needn't worry," he said over his shoulder as Tops started to follow him, "I'll see to it. They'll leave tonight."

The woman's voice called again from upstairs. Tops flexed

and shook his right hand as he walked out into the street and closed the door; it was lucky he hadn't popped a knuckle doing that. Normally he didn't believe in hitting a man with his bare hands, not unless he was naked and had his feet nailed to the floor… but you did have to make allowances for the El-Tee's son.

Paulo's whole body burned as his father's weight dragged at him again. It was so dark now he could barely see and he was trembling with exhaustion, as sweat-sodden as his father, sick with listening to the rasping breath of pain above him. He wanted to stop, to eat, to take a sip of the little bit of water in his father's canteen. He wanted to sit down and cry like a little kid. *But I can't. Dad's hurting worse than me. I've got to keep up.*

As it had grown darker Paulo had concentrated on the ground before them, avoiding rocks and roots and vines with considerable efficiency, considering the gloom. Besides, tired as he was his head just naturally tended downward. The noises of the insects and frogs lulled at him, like he was home and had the window open, looking out at the moon…

BONK!

"Aaauggh!"

James' head had connected solidly with a low-slung branch. The pain from his forehead telegraphed itself to the wound on the back of his skull and the agony washed back and forth like reciprocal tidal waves. He fell to the ground uttering a shrill, almost silent, scream.

Paulo fell to his knees beside his father. "Dad!" His hands hovered uncertainly over the writhing form and tears began to fill his eyes. "Dad?" he said again, his voice tight with desperation and tears. "I'm sorry, I'm so sorry." He broke down and began to cry, ashamed and unable to stop. He pushed his hands against his mouth to stifle the uncontrollable sobs. If he could stop them his eyes would quickly dry, he knew.

Suddenly his father rolled to his knees and began to retch; straining mightily to no effect as his stomach was utterly empty. At last the spasm passed and he rolled to his side, groaning.

"Dad?" Paulo's voice was very small.

"S'all right," James said, panting. "C'mere." He lifted his arm and Paulo collapsed next to him.

James folded his arm around his son. "Not your fault, kid. You're doin' okay."

The pain was receding to an echoing ache and he was horribly aware of his own pulse as it beat through his head. White dots sparked behind his eyelids and the nausea was definitely back to stay for a while.

"Gotta rest," he said quietly. Shame brought heat to his cheeks as he realized he had to place yet another burden on Paulo's shoulders. "You've got to find us some shelter, son. Doesn't have to be much. Just good cover, with maybe a wall at our backs. Don't go far."

He tightened his arm at the thought of losing his son out here in the dark. "If you don't find something quickly, come back, we'll just spend the night here."

Paulo sat up. "Okay, Dad."

"Here," James said. "Take a drink," and he passed over the canteen.

Paulo took it gratefully and allowed himself two swallows, holding the second in his mouth a moment to saturate his dry tongue.

"I'll be quick," he said, and leaned forward to kiss his father's cheek, startling him.

He hasn't done that since his mother died, James thought as the sound of Paulo's footsteps faded away.

It seemed only an instant later that Paulo shook his sleeve, "Dad. I've found it," he said.

James struggled to his feet and Paulo led him, being particularly careful to watch above as well as below this time.

A short distance later Paulo drew them to a halt.

"There's these bushes," he explained, "you have to crouch down and crawl. But it's like a hollow behind 'em and there's a wall with an overhang. It's almost like a cave," he ended eagerly.

"Good job, son," James said. "You go first." He got on his hands and knees and followed his son through the bushes. "This is good," he said once inside the hollow, noting the dryness of the thick bed of leaves and the absence of any musky animal smell. "You rest."

"You need to rest more'n I do," Paulo protested, determined to stay on guard all night if necessary.

"I couldn't, son. My head won't let me." James knew that Paulo was at the end of his strength and would soon be asleep whether he wished to be or not. Besides, once they got within sight of an unmistakable landmark, if his eyes were still useless, he intended to send Paulo on alone. The boy would need his strength for that. "Go to sleep."

With a relieved sigh, Paulo surrendered and lay down on his side, curling up as comfortably as he could.

James heard his son's breathing change to the rhythm of sleep and then he knew no more.

Moving quickly, but quietly, Pasqua pressed on. She was half in a dream state, but breathing comfortably and moving efficiently, body wolf-trotting without being told to. A method one of her father's bodyguards had taught her, part of her survival training. She was skirting the trail that led into the valley, approaching only close enough to see it every two hundred paces, then fading back into the jungle. Woods, actually. They were pretty high up here. The weather was nice, not like the steambath down below; that had been as bad as summer back home. This was like October on the Bayou Teche, or over in the piney woods on the Gulf Coast; the Family had hunting lodges there.

If I warn whoever's in the valley about the Knave of Hearts and his laughing boys, I'm a hero, she reasoned. *If I try to get back to the coast I run into the very unhappy people he's run that* damned *gun over and I'm toast. Tough choice.*

She shrugged mentally. *The weather's better up here anyway.* Later, she could loop around and back to the coast and pick up her stuff. Nobody would have touched it; not when her name was Giacano. Even if she'd severed formal connection with the Family, nobody had put an open contract on her. And nobody would want one of the Duke's schooners to pay a visit, which they would if news came back that she'd been ripped off. Just on general principles, mind, not out of familial affection.

Pasqua gauged her level of exhaustion and decided to find somewhere to sleep for a couple of hours. She slowed down and almost immediately her limbs felt weighted with sand, her chest aching with the effort of breathing the thin upland air. *Sleep,* she thought, *what a concept.*

AAWwwnkkk!

My God! She froze, but her heart went into overdrive. She could almost feel it on the back of her tongue.

AAWwwnkkk!

Snoring! But was it human?

Creeping forward, though her gut insisted she should run, Pasqua came upon a lush growth of bushes pressed against an overhang.

If I were a bear, she thought, *this is where I'd sleep.* Did they have bears in this country?

AAWwwnkkk!

Human, she thought and straightened, her mouth a grim line. The switchblade went *snick* in her hand, oiled deadliness. *Maybe one of the Lord of Multiculturalism's merry crew.* Cautiously she began to move back. The satisfaction of giving one of them an extra mouth wasn't worth the risk.

"Daaaa-ad," a sleepy child's voice said. "Y'r snorin.'"

A grin spread slowly across Pasqua's face and her eyes

gleamed. *Hunters maybe,* she thought. *Definitely not Jaguar Knights.* Maybe marks.

"Hey," she whispered, and could almost feel them come aware. "I need help."

"Hey! Conito!" Tops trotted out into the road and the UATV stopped. He suppressed a smile at the sight of Conito's weary face and the carload of militia around him.

Hey, poetic justice, pal, he thought, pleased at how the punishment fit the crime.

Conito was looking at him dubiously. "You can't come with us, Sergeant Jenkins." His voice was respectful, his attitude courteous.

Tops was surprised at how good the respect felt. *Has it been that long since someone talked to me like I'm a grown man?* Still, he was being brushed off, told to go away like a good little nuisance so the responsible people could get their work done. This from *Conito!* A guy who'd never finished anything except getting his poor wife pregnant. The guy who'd left the unit push unmonitored probably since James had gone out.

"Well, thank you for the invite, son, but I've got some sleep to catch up on." Conito's tired eyes narrowed slightly. "Maybe some other time. What I wanted was to give you this." He held up his own helmet. "I've been workin' on it and it's probably the best one in the village right now. It's also hooked into the Bolo."

Conito had taken the helmet with pleasure and had passed his own, marginally working one to his second. But his head came up at that.

"Why's that?" he asked. "Nobody talks to the Beast."

Tops forced himself not to be sarcastic. It was an honest question, nobody had spoken to the Bolo for years. He set his hands on his hips and looked down at Conito, just a bit longer than was comfortable for the younger man.

"I don't know why we didn't think of it before," Tops said mildly, "the Bolo can monitor the unit push twenty-four hours a day. If something urgent comes through it can set off an alarm. Oh, yeah, the Beast says the last transmission came from the cliff that overlooks the old road out of the valley." He turned and headed back to his house.

"That oughta make it easier to find 'em," he said over his shoulder. He didn't grin at Conito's stupefied expression until he'd turned his head away.

Tops was halfway up the Bolo's craggy side when a child's voice asked severely, "Where are you going, Sergeant Tops?"

Startled he looked down into the big brown eyes of Joseph's youngest daughter. Catherine was frowning fiercely, her arms crossed over her chest, one pudgy bare foot tapping impatiently.

"What are you doing out here so late?" he countered, keeping his voice low.

"You had a fight with my daddy," she accused. "You woke me up and I couldn't sleep anymore."

"Does he know you're out here?" Tops whispered. *Quiet down kid, you'll wake up the whole town.*

She looked disconcerted, but her head went down like a little bull's. "Where are you going?" she repeated.

"Shhhhh! I'm going to visit your grandma," he said.

A look of absolute horror went over the little face.

"Are you going to die?" Her eyes were huge.

He barked a laugh, he couldn't help it. "Naw. Not for a long time. I'm just goin' for a visit."

"You promise?"

Tops smiled, touched. *She's loud, but she's really a nice little kid.*

"I'll not only promise that, I'll promise not to tell anyone I saw you out so late. If," he held up one finger, "you promise not to tell anyone you saw me up here."

"Okay," Catherine said cheerfully, "I promise."

"You go home now," Tops, said and nodded.

"Okay." She turned and padded off into the darkness. Halfway down the street she turned and waved, smiling sweetly, then hurried on. He watched her open her door, she looked up and waved one more time, then entered.

Yeah, and I'll bet if I hadn't been watchin' you'd've bopped off into the night on some business of your own, wouldn't cha? The kid was just like the El-Tee, stubborn and fearless. He shook his head and resumed his climb.

He paused at the top and bit his lip, feeling like he was violating a tomb. Then he had to grin as he imagined Bethany Martins turning to just stare at him as if she'd known his thoughts. He shook his head.

"Open the hatch, Markee," he said.

The rush of cool dry air that flowed over him smelled every bit as bad as he'd expected. Like a long dead corpse to be exact. He wrinkled his nose disgustedly. *This ain't going to be no day at the beach,* he thought.

The near-mummified corpse in the command chair looked nothing like his old friend. *Thank God for small favors,* he thought. If anything he was surprised at how small it was. The El-Tee loomed much larger in his mind's eye.

He spread one of the blankets he'd brought over her and very gently began to pry her off the seat. It felt like moving furniture, there was nothing human-feeling about the shape under the blanket at all. Thank God they still had a few of the body bags left; they folded down to handkerchief size, but they sealed air-tight.

A gruesome few minutes later, a clean blanket covering the command seat, he sat down gingerly. "Key in the view from that helmet, Markee," he said. With a nervous glance at the body-bagged form beside him Tops settled in for his vigil.

In the "I need help," Olympics these indigs have got me beat, Pasqua decided. *Why me?* she wondered as her heart sank. *A guy who's effectively blind and a scared kid. Does someone plan these disasters for me? Has Grandfather got the squeeze on God or something?*

The thing to do was cut and run, she could think up a dozen plausible excuses without breaking a sweat. Some of them were even true.

"What did you say his name was?" the man—James—said.

He was lighter than the average around here, and spoke English with a mixture of accents, local and what sounded like old American. Crisper than her own Canal Street dialect. Good-looking guy in his early thirties, broad shoulders and a working-man's hands. Wearing an old United States uniform, of all things; Pasqua recognized the body armor. The Family had... inherited... a lot of Army equipment during the Collapse, and still had it stockpiled.

"It's got too many notes for me to say, but it comes out as Seven-Deer," she said cautiously.

Something about the man said he wasn't a friend of the Jungle Cardiac Removal League. The way both of them paled at the name confirmed it. The boy looked up at the man, and he put an arm around his son's shoulders.

"Okay, I'll help you get back home," Pasqua said, not believing the words as she heard them coming out of her own mouth.

She looked out at the tumbled mountains, at the tall volcano standing white-topped to the west. Above it a face seemed to loom in her mind's eye. Her father's.

"The last thing a Giacano needs," he'd said the last time she'd seen him, his dead-fish eyes weighing her like so much meat, "is a fuckin' conscience."

She'd flown to Central America the next day, losing herself down here and never expecting to see home again. Not wanting to, once she realized she was free.

James' mind went over and over the woman's story. When he'd heard her voice in the night he'd feared for a moment that it was some trick. Then she'd explained her presence.

"…Seven-Deer…"

His head had come up with a jerk that hurt him and he could feel the blood draining from his face. Paulo took his hand and squeezed it tightly and he'd been ashamed of his own fear. To the valley's children Seven-Deer was the bogeyman.

"You're sure his name was Seven-Deer?"

"Yes." Her voice was cautious, as though she feared they might be allied with him. "Why?"

He'd told her and then insisted that they begin walking. The urgent need to warn his people burned within him.

Seven-Deer has a very old grudge. Not that he needed the excuse.

Pasqua was so thirsty she didn't think she could even cry. And she was tired enough to want to. They'd been walking, or rather, stumbling all day and the sun was beginning to set. *God, I never imagined a path could be a luxury. Just to be able to walk five paces without tripping,* she thought, suppressing a groan, *I'd pay for the privilege.* How could country with this much rainfall not have springs or rivers?

"Because we're sticking to the ridgelines," James said.

She started, realizing she'd spoken the last thought aloud. *I must be more worn down than I realized.*

"Stop," James said quietly, holding up his hands.

Pasqua looked back at him; from the way he held his head it was apparent he'd heard something. She looked around, straining her ears. All she could see were pine trees, scrubby on the upper slopes; further down were tropical oak, and a tormenting sound of rushing water. Sweat dried on her face and body, the rest letting her realize that although the sun was fierce the air-temperature wasn't much above seventy. Wind soughed through the trees, cool and fresh-smelling. She pushed away knowledge of aches and sore feet and paper-dry tongue. At last she heard a faint yipping.

"Coy-dogs?" she asked.

His lips pressed thin and he shook his head, then winced. His hand brushed his forehead.

"Voices," he said, very quietly.

Just then a stray breeze brought the sound of laughter and she stiffened. Her eyes flicked to Paulo but his expression was the same he'd worn all day, frightened and determined.

"We'd better keep moving," she said.

James shook his head and winced again.

"Will you just *say* things and quit wagging your head around," she said impatiently. "Why not keep moving?"

"They might be valley people," he said. "In which case we should warn them. They might even be looking for me… and Paulo," he added.

"In which case we should avoid them because they're making enough noise to attract Seven-Deer's whole cavalcade of fun. Or it could be a trap."

"Then we'd better find out," James said. "They might have water…" He let the thought dangle.

If she weren't so thirsty, Pasqua might have smiled. *The man's a manipulator,* she thought. *A clumsy one, but when you have the right hook you don't have to be an artist.* She licked dry lips and Paulo mirrored her action.

"Okay," she said. "Let's go."

The closer they got, the more obvious it became that there was some sort of sick celebration in progress. Sound echoed off the oaks, through the screens of hanging vines. The yipping and the laughter were interspersed with conversation and screaming; a hummingbird went by her head and hovered over a flower in cruel obliviousness. Pasqua grabbed James' arm.

"These are not your friends," she whispered urgently. "We've got to get out of here!"

"I need to know," James said, and started forward.

"No, you don't," she insisted. "If you want to know what's going on I can tell you. They're killing people! Okay? And they'll be happy to kill us too. Now that you know that, can we go?"

She yanked at his arm but he balked.

"We need to know how many there are and how they're armed," he persisted.

"I can tell you that too," Pasqua snapped. "I was their prisoner, remember. There'll be fifteen of them and they carry M-35s just like you do, as well as obsidian swords and knives. Let's *go.*"

"No," Paulo said unexpectedly. He took his father's hand. "Those are our friends. Maybe we can help."

"Help!" Pasqua squeaked, but she was talking to their backs. For a moment she stood there, immobilized, half of her wanting to head for the inner valley and the village, half wanting to follow.

"Shit," she muttered, and started after them. *If they do happen to make it back to the village I won't win any hearts for having deserted them out here.*

Right now, she needed friends… and these two weren't fit to be allowed out alone.

With a shrill, yipping cry the Jaguar Knight plunged the ball down on to a sharpened stake planted in the ground.

That's not a ball! Paulo thought, and gagged. It was a head, still encased in its helmet.

The stake was surrounded by the dead bodies of the Cacaxtla militia. The Jaguar Knights, yipping out their victory, did a little impromptu dance around the pile, then leaping and prancing they went to a UATV and one by one got in. One of them stood on the back, waving his M-35 and jigging enthusiastically until the UATV started and he tumbled backwards into the laps of his laughing fellows.

"What's happening?" James ground out, his face grim.

"I'm going to assume the UATV is the valley's," Pasqua began.

"They're dead," Paulo near shouted, tears running down

his cheeks. "They're all dead!"

James pulled his son into his arms, and brushed his free hand over the boy's hair.

"Hush, son. There may be listeners."

"They're all dead," Paulo insisted. Then he sniffed and rubbed his nose. "Those men rode off in the UATV. There isn't anybody here but us. Dad," he went on in a small voice, "they cut off somebody's head."

James hung his head. "Who, son?"

"I don't know, it's still got a helmet on."

James stiffened. "We've got to get that helmet," he said. "Then we can warn the others."

"Very noble of you," Pasqua drawled, knowing he wouldn't be the one to retrieve it. "But as you've already suggested they may have left watchers behind."

"Why watch the dead?" Paulo sneered, stung by her tone.

"To see if anyone approaches them," Pasqua answered through clenched teeth. "They know someone will come looking eventually. Why else make such a big deal out of this?"

"To intimidate us," James suggested, then he sighed. "We still need that helmet," he said firmly. "We can't count on our luck, such as it is, holding."

Pasqua made a sour face.

"I'll go," Paulo said, anger and pride in every syllable.

"Don't be ridiculous," Pasqua snapped. "You stay with your father." Then she dropped to her stomach and crawled off into the surrounding bushes.

James listened for a moment, and under the concealing bandages his brows went up in surprise. "She's good," he commented.

Paulo gave a little growl. "Well, I don't like her," he muttered.

James smiled. "Sometimes, son, people I haven't liked at first turned out to be my best friends."

Paulo stayed silent. He was in no mood for a little homily

on understanding. Paulo wasn't going to like her.

He looked out over the field again, to where the bodies were piled and fury rose within him. These were people he knew! Familiar faces that he'd seen every day of his life. How *dare* they hurt them? He balled his hands into fists until the knuckles turned white and ground his teeth, his eyes blazing. If he could, he'd show them, he'd hurt them like they'd hurt the valley people. Worse! He'd...

One moment the head on the stake wore a helmet, the next it was just a head on a stake. Paulo turned away, feeling sick again.

James felt the tension in his son's body change.

"What is it?" he asked.

"She's got it," Paulo answered, then he turned his back on the bloody field.

Half an hour later Pasqua stood up and walked towards them, the helmet swinging by one strap.

"I'm *not* putting this on," she said.

"Give it to me," James said. Taking it he pulled off his bandage and wiped the wet inside of the helmet. Then he inverted it and put it very carefully on, wincing when it came into contact with his wounds.

"Unit push," he said.

"Go ahead, Captain Martins," replied the lush voice of the Bolo.

"Markee?" James was astonished.

"Never mind Markee," Tops said. "Where the hell are you?"

The squad of fifteen knelt before him, heads bowed, one fist and one knee on the ground, radiating shame as the Sun did heat. Seven-Deer stood before them, resplendent in jade nose and lip plugs, gold rings weighing down his ears, arms crossed over his brawny chest. His face was implacable, but a fear from the World Beyond the World tickled the back of his neck like a chill breeze.

The servant of the Sun had vanished. Oh, not vanished really, escaped. But it should not have been possible. Too many things had gone awry to allow that escape. She got free of her ropes, with no one noticing. She climbed down from the gun carriage, with no one noticing. She walked through the crowd of sleeping slaves, with no one noticing. And she slipped through the squad of fifteen kneeling before him… with no one noticing. As if she'd had supernatural help. Perhaps the people of the Sun were being led to their destruction?

Tezcatlipoca is a trickster, he thought. *Smoking Mirror does what he does and no man can understand him.* Seven-Deer had thought that he understood the will of Tezcatlipoca. *Perhaps… perhaps it was a lesson, intended to punish my pride in thinking so.* After all, the girl was not important now that they had the gun.

The tension within him released slowly. If this was true then he should not punish the men before him. This was also a relief. The people of the Sun were few and every man was needed. Nevertheless, Smoking Mirror's power must be acknowledged.

"Look at me," he said to the kneeling men. "It is not I who must be propitiated. The gods demand their due." He looked into each man's eyes and saw that he was understood. "You shall give blood to Tezcatlipoca, but you may not impair your battle-worthiness. One of your number, a volunteer, or one selected by vote, will be permitted the honor of giving more on behalf of all."

The men looked at one another, then one by one they pointed until all were pointing at the same man, the squad leader, Water-Monster.

He rose with pride and stepped forward to stand at attention before Seven-Deer.

Two priests came forward in their stinking black robes; one bore a thin-bladed knife, the other a basket. The first gave the knife to Water-Monster, who bowed as he accepted the blade. Water-Monster took the blade and sang out a prayer, then he grasped his tongue in one hand and plunged the blade through its center with the other.

Blood ran down his chin and splattered his chest. His eyes filled with water, though he allowed no tears to fall, pupils contracted to pinpoints and his breath came fast.

The other priest came forward and presented the basket. Without taking his eyes from Seven-Deer's, Water-Monster's hand fumbled within it and caught the end of a rope studded with thorns. He fitted it carefully into the slit he'd made and began drawing the rope through. His face and body were slicked with a cold sweat and he trembled from the agony as foot by foot he dragged the lacerating rope through his tender flesh.

He bore the pain well, though to his shame he gagged once or twice. Behind him, his squad took out their knives and slit their ears, singing a song in praise of Tezcatlipoca.

"Tops? What—"

"Where *are* you, James? We've got a search party out looking for you."

"Where we are is too far from Cacaxtla to do any good," he said. "I've got bad news, Tops. The UATV you sent out… they won't be coming home."

There was silence for a moment. James could almost feel Tops' mind clicking into gear, long-disused reflexes opening smoothly. Then: "What are we up against, Captain?"

"Seven-Deer," James said succinctly. "And at least two hundred Jaguar Knights. In addition, they've got upwards of six hundred… slaves, I guess."

"Slaves?"

Why are you surprised? Tops asked himself. *This is Seven-Deer we're talkin' about.*

"They're dragging a weapon, Tops. It's a massive cannon.

The chassis is mounted on eight balloon wheels, about chest height on me. The gun itself is strange," he paused. "It's about twenty feet long with two rectangular bars bracketing its entire length. And it's thin, looks more like a pipe than anything else. There's a seat for a gunner behind it. I'm assuming that the chassis contains some sort of mechanism for positioning the gun. That about wraps it up. I don't know how they expect to get it into the valley, but if they do, I think we're in deep trouble."

A good assessment, Pasqua thought. Even though James couldn't see her she kept her face immobile.

Tops sighed. "I can't even picture it, Captain. Did it look like something they cobbled together from parts?"

"Excuse me, Captain, Sergeant," the Bolo interrupted. "From the description I would say that the enemy have obtained an XM-17 Railgun. It was an experimental model that was undergoing its final testing phase just before this unit was dispatched to San Gabriel. At that time there were no plans for bringing one this far south."

"That's all you can say?" Tops asked.

Then, with an inward curse over the literal-mindedness of the Bolo, he asked: "What capabilities?"

"The XM-17 Railgun is capable of penetrating the armor of any known self-propelled vehicle at a distance of fifteen hundred meters."

After a long moment he asked carefully: "Including yours?"

"Yes, Sergeant," the Bolo said in its cheerfully sexy voice.

"Can you defend yourself against it?" James asked urgently.

Paulo stared at the dark, curved surface of the helmet's face plate and wished he could hear what was being said to his father. James' hands were bunched into fists and his voice was tight with anxiety.

"In my present state of repair, Captain, I would estimate

that I have only a twelve percent chance of successfully defending myself. That estimate is my most optimistic, based on the assumption that the railgun will be facing me head on, giving my own guns a direct shot at it. I cannot turn, nor can I deploy my infinite repeaters owing to the heavy coating of lava stone on my chassis."

"Tops…"

"You don't have to say it, Captain. We'd better get the whole village busy chippin' that stuff off."

Tops was sweating now, though it was still cool and dry inside the Bolo. "We should have done it years ago—"

"—but as my mother always said, if wishes were horses there would be even more horseshit in the world than there is."

"Can you get us more information, sir? Where the main body of 'em are, their direction and speed so I can tell Joseph and the council. And if you can, slow 'em down."

"Tell him your condition," Pasqua said suddenly, prompted by a sick suspicion.

"Will do," James said. "Out."

"Will do what?" she demanded, dread sitting in her stomach like raw dough.

"Find 'em, find out how fast they're moving, slow 'em down if we can."

"*What?*" She exploded. "Are you crazy? Did that knock on the head kill more brain cells than we realized? Why didn't you *tell* him that you're as good as blind and being assisted by a ten-year-old and a civilian? What are you going to do, throw spitballs, tie a rope across the trail and trip all six hundred slaves? What are your plans, generalissimo? I can't wait to hear."

"Lady, you can leave any time you want to," Paulo said, eyes blazing. "My father and I can handle it ourselves."

"Ah, glorious!" she sneered. "I'm in the company of heroes."

"No," James replied with strained patience, "you're in the company of people with family and friends who are in the path of terrible danger. That head down there belonged to a friend of mine. I'm not going to let those spotted thugs kill his children."

Paulo threw Pasqua a look of smug contempt.

She hissed in exasperation. *I hate this!* she thought vehemently. *Playing hero's one thing, actually becoming one is* not *something I want to do!*

More hateful still was the blood-freezing realization that she wasn't going to leave them to it, but was going with them… to help them in any way she could. There wasn't even the possibility of profit in it.

Father had been right. She *was* crazy.

Tops leaned back in the command seat and ran his hands nervously over his short white hair. *Seven-Deer! My God! I'd hoped that bastard was dead.* He slid a glance over to the body-bagged form beside him.

"El-Tee, I like your oldest boy, I really do. But Joseph's the kind thinks if you postpone trouble it's bound to solve itself." Tops thought he knew Bethany Martins well enough that she'd agree with his assessment, and that she'd agree with what he planned to do now.

They'd see combat soon. He sighed, and the adrenaline hummed and sparked along his nerve endings. He hadn't missed the feeling at all, hadn't wanted his own children to ever know it.

So much for that blind hope. He smiled; that was something the El-Tee would have said. He gave himself a little shake, being right beside her body wasn't good for him. Next thing he knew he'd think she was talking to him.

"Markee, do you have a view on the plaza?"

"Negative, Sergeant. Those cameras not damaged by the lava were covered by it."

Oh well. "Open up your P.A. system," he ordered. "Good'n loud, but not painful."

"Ready, Sergeant."

"Attention people of Cacaxtla."

He leaned forward as he spoke.

"We are in an emergency situation. There is an invading force on its way into the valley, composed of approximately two hundred hostiles." He'd considered telling them who it was, but didn't want to send the whole town into a blind panic. "Children and noncombatants are to be evacuated. All able-bodied persons are to report to the Bolo immediately to begin clearing it of debris so that it will be combat ready."

He paused. "Can you hear how they're taking it, Markee? I don't want a panic."

There was a moment's silence, then, "The consensus seems to be that you've lost your mind and are reliving the glory days of your youth," the Bolo reported.

Damn! He hadn't expected that.

"The Jefe is approaching and is demanding that you come down," Markee continued. "The Jefe's authority exceeds your own, Sergeant," the Bolo observed. "I must request that you leave now."

"Whose authority exceeds the Jefe's?" Tops asked desperately.

"The captain's would, as military authority would always exceed civilian in the deployment of this unit."

"Then get on to him. Ask for his orders. This is an emergency, Markee, if I go out there it's over. For all of us."

A moment later James' voice came through, sounding weary but determined.

"Attention, please. This is Captain Martins speaking. The valley is under attack. The UATV that was sent out to assist me and my son has been overwhelmed, the crew killed and the vehicle stolen. An escaped prisoner of the hostiles has informed me that Cacaxtla is their destination..." He paused. "And that Seven-Deer is their leader. Follow Sergeant Jenkins' instructions; he is acting with my authority. Jefe, I expect you to offer him your complete cooperation. Markee, you will follow Sergeant Jenkins' orders as though they were my own. Martins out."

"What's happening?" Tops demanded. "Open up a channel to the outside, Markee, I need to know what's goin' on."

Joseph stood outside the door of the *jefe's* house and slowly closed his mouth.

"Oh, I wish he'd really finally gone crazy," he whispered to himself.

People were boiling out of their homes, some with their napkins still tucked into their collars. Children were crying—adults, too—and a babble of voices rose higher and higher. Lanterns came on outside the homes and shops, turning evening into daylight as if for a fiesta, Christmas or Lieutenant Martins' birthday.

This is a hoax. Something they cooked up before James went out.

The thought still echoed in his mind and he stood paralyzed by doubt. The sense of being the butt of some military joke brought a flush to his cheeks, he could feel the warmth of it.

No. James was a careful planner and a considerate man. If he had something like this in mind surely James would have discussed it with him. Suddenly he felt a horror more real than his own embarrassment, more immediate than the terrible knowledge that everyone would be looking to *him* to do something.

Eventually, a panicked corner of his mind screamed. *This is real! Seven-Deer is coming.* Joseph thought of his wife and daughters. *He'll kill us all.*

He looked around. "Enrique, Hernando, Susan," he said, beckoning to the three. "Gather up all the tools you can find that might be used to chip off this rock. Consuela, Perdita, Joan, put together some teams to organize an evacuation..."

Joseph's mind clicked into another level of awareness, wherein he organized and ordered even as another part of his mind made plans. Men and women flew to undertake the tasks he assigned them and there was room for pride in his busy mind.

We'll be all right, he assured himself. *If we can just hang on, like this, we're going to be fine.*

"*Unngghh!* This, *ungh*, is, *ungh*, ri-dic-ulous." Pasqua continued applying pressure to the lever planted under the boulder James had selected even as she protested.

"This won't, unngghh, slow them down by more than a couple of hours." The huge stone was rocking and she expected it to give momentarily.

"Keep pushing," James said, heaving on the lever beside her.

Slowly, almost with grace, the boulder toppled to the sound of pebbles cracking under its great weight. Then faster and faster it roared down the slope, slapping tons of loose dirt and smaller stones free from the slope to accompany it down to the road. Dust rose in a choking cloud, and bits of vegetation were thrown back at them with the dirt.

Pasqua stood panting, her hands on her knees as she watched it. Then she straightened and wiped the sweat from her face with her sleeve and sneezed. She'd never worked this hard in her life. They'd already cut down two massive trees with James' flex-saw.

When he'd handed her one of the toggles at the end of the durachrome coil of toothed wire she'd been astonished.

"Where'd you get this?" she asked, wondering who her competitor was.

"Part of my mother's kit," he'd answered calmly. "You ready?"

And suddenly she was a lumberjack.

She didn't know how long she could keep this up. There'd been nothing to eat for two days now and she was thirsty beyond belief. Her lips were cracking and her head ached terribly. Pasqua shot a glance at James. He was gray-faced, his jaw slack, he sat with his hands limp beside him, drawing in great gulps of air. If she was hurting, he must be half-dead. She frowned, ashamed of her selfishness and moved to pity by James' condition and to admiration for his uncomplaining strength.

He'll kill himself if I don't stop him. She wondered who the hell his mother had been.

Then she cursed herself mentally. "Heroes live short lives," her father used to say, with a snake-cold smile implying the brevity was deserved. And that he'd implemented Fate's sentence himself fairly often.

I should leave them, she scolded herself. *They're going to get themselves killed.*

All she had to do was get across the valley and out again. Seven-Deer hadn't indicated any particular ambitions beyond taking Cacaxtla. Even if he chose to hunt her down he wouldn't be able to until he'd subdued these people.

Which won't be easy, she thought, stealing another glance at James and levering herself painfully back to her feet. Paulo scooted closer to his father, looking worried, and she closed her eyes at the expression on his face.

"We'd better get moving," she said through clenched teeth. "The noise and the dust are going to bring the Nahuatl Strength through Joy brigade running."

James nodded, exhausted, and heaved himself to his feet, one trembling hand lifted to his forehead. Then he put his arm around Paulo's slim shoulders and let his son lead him away.

Seven-Deer trembled with rage as he stood on the worn surface of the road. Gullies and undergrowth creeping over the ancient pavement were bad enough.

Another road block. And the perpetrators gone like smoke. He drew in a deep breath and held it, while his dark eyes blazed like fire.

"Find them!" he roared, and his hand flashed out, pointing to two captains of fifteen. "GO!"

The men turned and vanished into the trees, their squads leaping after them. They disappeared at a steady ground-devouring lope, fanning out until they were lost among the trees and brush.

Seven-Deer watched them go, fury bringing a slaver of foam to his lips. And underneath, inching its way to the surface, as a snake works its way up from the underworld, fear crawled. He cast his eyes over the slaves that labored on the road, dragging boulders and baskets of dirt away.

There. That one was taller than the rest, and despite hunger and days of dragging the gun he still looked fit. Seven-Deer motioned to the feather-decked priests behind him.

"We will send a messenger," he told them. "I fear we offended Tezcatlipoca and I would win his favor again."

He watched the priests move off to gather up the sacrifice, then turned his eyes to the surrounding cliffs. Not wondering at the fact of resistance, but at the curious weakness of it.

James struggled to speak, to report on their most recent delaying tactic, a pile of brush they'd heaped in the center of the road and set on fire. He'd envisioned it much larger, but Pasqua and Paulo hadn't been able to drag the enormous limbs needed into the road. As for himself, he could barely lift a hand. *Hell... I can hardly talk.*

Suddenly the helmet was lifted off his head. The cool air and the sense of space around him made his head spin. "Hey!" he snapped.

"Take a break, soldier," Pasqua sneered.

"Dad, I found a spring. Here."

And there was the canteen at his lips. He pawed at it eagerly, too weak to support it himself, sucking down the icy cold liquid. The tissues of his mouth seemed to expand and his throat felt more like flesh than rock once again. It almost hurt to drink, but he kept on.

Paulo held the canteen for his father and looked him over critically. *This is it,* he thought. *Dad can't do any more.* Unformed lay the thought, *I won't sacrifice him.* The village meant nothing if his father didn't survive. He glanced over at Pasqua who was walking off a ways, the helmet in her hand. *I can't believe she's still with us. Y'can tell she'd rather be anywhere else.*

Though he didn't much like her, Paulo was grateful that she'd stayed. He swallowed convulsively at the thought of being alone, nobody to help his father but himself.

Pasqua drifted out of earshot of the man and boy and, with a moue of distaste, put the helmet on. It was a standard model, as expected, and she quickly activated it.

"Listen up," she snarled. "We've bought you all the time we can. Martins is injured and the boy and I are exhausted. Seven-Deer's about two miles from the old lava flow. What they'll do when they get there is anybody's guess. But he *is* coming and we can't stop him."

"Who the hell is this?" Tops demanded.

"Name's Pasqua. I'm that escaped prisoner Martins told you about."

There was a pause, then: "How bad is he?"

"He's concussed and has been for at least three days—I think he hit his head again after the first injury. He can't really see, his vision's doubled, and we haven't been getting enough water. And we haven't eaten for two days." *And then it was rotten fruit.*

"How's Paulo?"

"Spunky, doing a grownup's job, but wiped out. We're coming in." She could feel her face settle into grim determined lines. An expression few people would argue with. *Pity he can't see it,* she thought.

"We're evacuating the village," Tops said. "By the time you

get here the noncombatants will be hiding out in the hills. Tell James they're hiding by the thermal pool." Tops paused, then asked: "Is he… able to… is he coherent?"

"Yes. Or has been. But right now he's dangerously exhausted for a man in his condition."

"Okay." Tops' mind was working overtime. "Listen, there's a cave a half-mile from the old lava flow. It's well hidden and there's even a small cache of emergency rations. It's a good place to rest. Can he make it that far?"

Two and a half miles? Pasqua chewed her lower lip. *Not bloody likely.* Part of the problem was they were starving. James especially would need the food before he could make the walk.

"No," she said aloud. "But if I can retrieve those supplies, maybe."

Tops gave her directions, hoping she was the kind of person who could visualize what he was describing. He made her repeat them until he was satisfied and she was obviously annoyed.

"I'll contact you when I've got something to report," she said tartly, and broke contact.

"You do that, honey," Tops muttered unhappily. He sighed deeply, rose, and began to climb from the Bolo's innards, reluctantly about to add to Joseph's burdens.

The cave was almost cozy; five feet by ten, a volcanic bubble in the dark basaltic lava of the ridges that surrounded the valley. With the radiant heater and thermal-film blankets in the cache—more Old American stuff—it was even comfortable, compared to what she'd been going through lately.

"You need more rest," she said to James.

"We need more time, but we haven't got it," he said.

Reluctantly she nodded; he was well enough to see that, at least. "Yeah, that was them at the spring." Not while she was there, thank God, but who else would leave a flake of volcanic glass? Even after the Collapse, most people didn't make knives out of obsidian; they hammered them out of old car springs or rebar, like sensible people. Besides, the urge to spy on the gun convoy ate at her like acid, and she knew better than to press her luck that far.

James' sight was working its way back to normal, though his vision was still poor, and the headache was bearable. He felt almost cheerful.

"Let's set up a nice little booby-trap for them," he suggested. "It might make 'em a little slower to follow us."

Pasqua grinned. "Or that much more eager. Remember, we're not dealing with normal people here."

"Well, I think it's a good idea," Paulo said defiantly, tired of the way Pasqua always seemed to disparage his father's notions.

"It is," Pasqua said holding her hands out, still smiling. "I was just making an observation."

"We'll set it up like we're still here," James said. "Son, you can make up dummies and put one of the thermal-film blankets over them. We'll scatter some of the empty packets around and maybe leave a small fire smoldering…"

"You're an artist," Pasqua said.

"Thank you, ma'am. Got it from my mom."

"She sounds like an interesting lady," Pasqua said. "Wish I could have met her."

James turned and looked at her for a moment, blinking and squinting. "You know, lady, I think you and she would have gotten along fine… or one of you would have gotten killed."

Pasqua chuckled, looking around the cave with a considering eye. *Damn! Why am I feeling so good?* It wasn't as if this was a pleasure cruise up the Mississippi to pay a social call on the Despot of Natchez and get in a little roulette, after all. But she felt more cheerful than she had in years.

James went on: "Um. I can't do the close work on setting up the explosives, Pasqua, but I can talk you through it. There's nothing to be afraid of, we're not going to be doing anything too radical." *Not with the materials we've got anyway.*

"*Pphhh!* Teach your grandmother to suck eggs," she said. "I'll tell you how to set a booby trap."

She plucked one of the grenades from his utility belt and held it up.

"What would really be great is if we had some plastique to wrap around this little darling. There's nothing like a little MDX," she said wistfully. "Gives it a nice explosive bonus. I remember one time, Guido gift-wrapped a grenade that way and planted it under this guy's car seat—he'd been muscling in on Giacano territory over in the Atacha. BLAMMO! That sucker went off like an ejector seat, right through the roof of his car and he didn't have a sun roof until that moment."

She smiled nostalgically. "Anyway, getting down to business. You anchor one end of a wire, thread's no good—breaks too easy—about two inches above the ground, right in the path of your target. You attach the other end to the pull ring. Then, you tease these little flanges open, juuust enough to loosen the pin, but tight enough so that it won't fall out, then…"

Pasqua continued to describe the proper method of setting a man-killing trap wearing the happy, innocent expression of a woman explaining her favorite recipe.

She was about to conclude with one of Guido's favorite expressions, *And den ya watch da pieces fly upward*, when she noticed their faces. Both their jaws had dropped and their eyes stared unblinking at her.

Uh oh. "Y'know," she chirped, "I never noticed before how much alike you guys look. Paulo, you're going to grow up to be just as handsome as your father."

They both blushed, glanced at each other, then looked away, turning their attention to preparing the campsite.

Whew! she thought. *I've got to watch my big mouth.*

The fire in Water-Monster's wounded mouth burned as hot

as the fire in his heart each time he thought of his shame at allowing the servant of the Sun to escape. A shame his whole squad shared, but blamed exclusively on him. He could barely speak with his tongue so swollen and the frown of confusion on his second's face drove him to fury.

"Th tacka! Ya ool. Wa da th tacka ay?"

"Captain," the second's eyes slid rapidly north and south as he desperately tried to decipher Water-Monster's lispings. Inspiration struck before the captain did.

"The trackers have found a definite trail leading from a small spring to a cave a half-mile away, lord."

Water-Monster's smile of pleasure was like a spurt of venom.

"Ooh ow!" he bellowed.

The second's brows went up and he gritted his teeth, as behind the Captain's back he frantically signaled the puzzled troops to move out as commanded.

They approached the cave with caution, ghosting through the twilight, moving as silently as the jaguar from whom they took their name despite the steep slope and the loose volcanic scree underfoot. It was quiet. Birds and insects stilled their cries in alarm as the men passed.

Water-Monster frowned. It was possible that cave was deserted; their quarry might have rested and gone. The tracker had stated that the trail he followed was at least a day old. His nose flared. Yes, the unmistakable scent of woodsmoke. Their quarry had grown careless, building a fire that was too large and not made of thoroughly dry wood. His eyes scanned. Yes, a trace of smoke rising dark against the dark stone of the cliff ahead.

Suddenly his second was beside him, whispering.

"There are three, Captain, sleeping near a small fire."

Water-Monster's heart leapt. "A ga?" he asked.

"No, lord, no guard." The second smiled too, pleased at the

ease of capture.

Water-Monster moved up to where the foremost of his troops were and looked into the cave. He could see three humped shapes behind a very smoky fire. *How can they stand it?* he wondered. Down in the lowlands, it might have been a smudge fire to drive off mosquitoes. But why here, in these cold uplands? He gestured four of his men to move up and into the cave.

They moved forward with exaggerated care, around piles of leaves and other debris, delicately placing their feet on the few spots of bare ground. They entered the cave like shadows, hugging its walls as they moved towards the sleepers.

When they were well inside, Water-Monster rose and followed them. Striding arrogantly through brittle leaves and crackling brush he anticipated their quarry's horror when the noise of his passage woke them and they stared up into the implacable faces of his warriors.

This pleasant image accompanied him to the underworld as the grenade beneath his feet went off, shredding his body before he could even cry out. The impact was less on the men farthest from him. They were able to scream again and again as ricocheting fragments of rock and metal tore through them.

Water-Monster's second and two others came running, peering into the smoking interior of the cave just in time to receive the full blast of the second grenade, set to go off five seconds after the first.

"Do you think it worked?" Paulo asked for perhaps the hundredth time, as they lurched down the slope.

James looked wearily down at his son, who was gazing adoringly up at Pasqua. He stifled a spurt of jealousy. Ever since she'd allowed Paulo to help her set the booby trap for Seven-Deer's troops the boy's attitude towards her had changed drastically. *I always thought I'd be the one to teach you the "arts of war" as Mom used to call 'em.* He sighed, and Paulo looked up at him. James' eyesight had improved to the point where he could read the worry in his face.

"It's nothing, son. I was just thinking about how you're growing up."

Paulo looked puzzled, and cocked his head dubiously, as though wondering where *that* had come from.

"You have grown, you know," Pasqua said. "An experience like this changes you." She made herself stop talking before she annoyed everybody, including herself.

They turned a corner. She stopped with an involuntary gasp. Both the others looked at her.

"It's *beautiful*," she said.

The valley was like a bowl—a bowl with a broken rim, a rim of forested hills, rising to one tall volcanic peak to the west. Rivers ran through it, silver in the evening light. Fields were squares of color, like a quilt ranging from yellow-gold wheat through infinite shades of green, from pasture to orchards and patches of woodlot. Tile-roofed, whitewashed houses stood scattered amid the fields; a larger clump made the village, around the open plaza and the vine-grown shape of the pyramid; the gardens and trees were splashes of color dividing the buildings. The scene breathed peace to her, like something from before the Collapse—long before.

A second look revealed things even more unusual than the undisturbed pastoral scene.

"You've got a power grid!" she said.

"Well, of course," Paulo said. "We're not *savages*."

James smiled. "Geothermal," he said. "Enough for essentials."

Pasqua nodded soberly, impressed. The duchy was wealthy, but there was little electricity there outside the houses of the Family and the *caporegime* and *consigliere* class. This *was* something out of the ordinary, and to find it here, lost in the mountains...

"The thermal springs are there," James said, pointing.

"Unca Jamie!" a child shrieked.

Pasqua jumped and her brows went up as a little yellow-dressed, dark-haired cannonball slammed into James, nearly knocking him off his feet.

"Pick me up! Pick me up!" the little girl shouted and James stooped to comply.

"This is my niece, Catherine," he said as the little girl rained kisses on his cheek. She turned to gaze at Pasqua with bright eyes.

"Hi," Pasqua said.

"Are you a fairy princess?" Catherine asked seriously.

"Uh, no." *Mafia princess maybe.* Pasqua couldn't help smiling at the little girl. It was nice to be asked.

"Captain!" A man in a camouflage uniform emerged from the trees, relief writ large on his homely face. "Good to see you, sir."

"Good to see you too, Zapota. How's it going?"

"Well, sir. Everyone's bivouacked around the old thermal pool and the work in town is progressing." His eyes flicked to Pasqua and back to the captain.

Introductions followed; they turned a corner on the well-graveled road, past an old but well-maintained blockhouse, and into a clump of whitewashed houses. The smell of roasting meat drifted by, and Pasqua heard her stomach growl.

"I want to eat, I want to bathe, I want to sleep."

"No problem," Zapota said smiling. "My little helper there can guide you."

"This way!" Catherine shouted, pointing imperiously. James winced slightly as she tugged at his hair, but he was smiling as he followed the chubby finger.

Pasqua wiped the sweat from her forehead and chin with the end of her scarf, then looked wryly at her battered hands.

This was far more like honest labor than anything she'd ever done before, and while the experience was interesting she couldn't see making a habit of it. It was a bit of a consolation that so many others were doing exactly the same work, but not much.

Getting this damn pumice off the damn tank is practically a war in itself. The Family had a couple of Mark IIs in storage, but they were no preparation for the sheer *size* of this thing. It was difficult to convince your emotions that this was a machine, not part of the landscape.

A familiar voice caught her attention and she looked down. Far below her James conferred with his brother, the Jefe of the village. She smiled slightly. A few days rest and some food had put him back on his feet and she had to admit, he was pretty. Pretty impressive, and just *pretty.* Straight features, olive tan, white teeth when he smiled, level brown eyes. *Nice butt, too,* she decided, then reflected that a couple of days rest and food had done *her* a world of good, too.

"Yes, it's an assumption," James said. "But it's an educated guess. The gun was a prototype, they can't have much in the way of ammunition for it. Which means that we need that wall around the village."

It was a mere palisade, constructed of raw trees and fence posts, but better than the nothing they'd started with. Joseph had fought them over every inch of it.

"If we get the Bolo up and running the wall is irrelevant," Joseph insisted. "That's where we should concentrate our efforts."

James turned and stared at him. "I've said it before, I'll say it again. One lucky shot and we don't *have* a Bolo." The two men glared at each other. "We're building the wall." James stalked off, leaving civilian authority stymied and enraged behind him.

Pasqua's eyes met Tops' where he was engaged in a more delicate bit of chipping around the Bolo's infinite repeater ports. She smiled ruefully. "I'll bet the old girl loves to hear stuff like that," she said.

Tops chuckled. "*It* doesn't mind," he said. "Markee, you don't take that kinda talk personally, do you?"

"The captain has made an accurate evaluation of our situation, Sergeant Jenkins. If I were capable of taking offense I cannot imagine why the truth should cause it."

"Be nice if people were that reasonable," Pasqua said.

"Sergeant," the Bolo interrupted. "I have received a report from our scouts on the valley's perimeter. Seven-Deer is over the barrier. If he continues at this rate he should be here in two days."

Fear rang like a silver bell, shrill and cold along her nerve endings.

"Damn," Tops swore. "How'd they get through the lava so fast? Must be thirty, fifty feet thick."

"Hypervelocity shot, Sergeant. They have expended three rounds."

Pasqua redoubled the speed of her chipping.

Seven-Deer gazed down from the pass at the village of Cacaxtla and sneered at the pathetic palisade that now surrounded it.

It was a flimsy thing, backed by earth only in places. The great gun would sweep it aside like an anthill. His eyes lifted to where, in the center of the plaza, the Mountain that Walks was partially visible behind the buildings that surrounded it. It sat like a spider in its web. He squinted; attendants crawled over the spider's great body, doing things he couldn't discern at this distance.

It is useless anyway, he thought smugly, *whatever you are doing. Soon your blood shall slake Tezcatlipoca and Xipe Totec's thirst.* A huge grin split his face. Tomorrow at dawn they would wheel the great gun into place and destroy the Mountain that Walks. And then…

Ah, revenge is so sweet that even anticipating it is pleasure. The evening breeze lifted his hair and he inhaled deeply of its freshness.

He turned back to his campsite; where screams indicated that they had begun to slaughter the slaves, lest their great numbers prove an inconvenience in the morning. Besides, his men were hungry. The gods would take the blood and hearts that were their due, and the Sun People the remainder.

And Seven-Deer had always preferred liver, in any case. Grilled over an open fire, with some chilies and wild onions... delicious.

That the attack would come in the morning everyone knew, with an instinct as sure as that which told them the sun would rise.

Pasqua tossed and turned on her pallet in the women's great tent. She'd been put in with the combatants; those with young children were still up by the thermal springs. It was a compliment, in a way. It hadn't even occurred to anyone that she wanted to run. Finally she rose—exasperated and exhausted—but with energy thrumming through her body like a low-voltage electrocution.

She slipped from the tent and the camp with no one the wiser, heading for the village and the command center, through the chill night. Sentries were no problem; one of them was smoking as he walked his rounds. Simply freezing in place was enough to send them on their way regardless.

Jeez, she thought, *if he wanted to, Seven-Deer could cut every throat in camp and nobody'd notice.*

These people were so good, so kind and wholesome. *And so bloody helpless! It's going to be a slaughter in the morning.* Maybe that wasn't fair. James was one tough hombre, if he was more typical than his brother...

When did you ever see a place where the Jameses outnumbered the Josephs? she sneered.

She stopped just outside the palisade, her palms sweating, heart beating frantically.

I should run, she told herself. *I should grab some food and a canteen and get the hell out of here.* Staying was suicide. No sensible person would place themselves in danger for the benefit of strangers. She could picture the weary, disgusted look in her father's eyes if he but knew, and blushed with shame.

She frowned. *But he doesn't know. And Paulo and James are hardly strangers. More importantly, their danger is my fault.* She squared her shoulders and stepped forward.

"*Alto!* Who goes there?"

"A friend," she said. Take me to Captain Martins."

"You *what?*"

James' cry echoed back from the plastered walls of the room; from the looks of it, it had been his living room before the emergency. Maps and documents covered everything now, except a charcoal portrait of a smiling dark-haired woman. *Paulo's mother, I suppose,* Pasqua thought

She held her hands up placatingly. "We owned the gun, but he stole it from us," she insisted.

"But you were going to sell it to him. Isn't that right?"

She put her hands on her hips and bit her lip, closing her eyes to avoid his.

"We were arms dealers. Yes—we would have sold it to him. Just as we would have sold it to you."

"But *he* is an insane mass murderer bent on conquest and bloodshed, while *we* are farmers who only want to live and work in peace." James glared at her.

"Well," she said, still not meeting his eyes. "Arms dealers *are* known for their flexible attitude and lack of curiosity about end-use intentions."

He turned from her with a sound of disgust and Pasqua thanked heaven that she'd asked to see him alone. *If the others were here I'd be dancing at the end of a rope by now.*

He ran his hands through his hair. "Why are you telling me now?" he asked, with his back to her.

She pressed her lips into a tight line, then forced herself to speak calmly. "He fired off a shot to test the gun the day he stole it. I think it's probable that he used it to clear the road when he got to the lava flow—the Bolo thinks so, too. Three shots should have been enough. Which leaves him with eight."

He turned and slumped into his chair, then he glanced at her guilty face. "It would have saved some arguing with my brother if I'd known that," he muttered sardonically. "It's nice to know that his resources are limited, but otherwise…" He made a gesture implying the irrelevance of the information.

"Know your enemy," she quoted.

"Yeah," he said, narrowing his eyes. "Sometimes it's a little hard to identify 'em at first."

"I'm not your enemy," she said through gritted teeth. "I just wanted to make a clean breast of things."

"I look like a priest to you?"

"Dammit, James! I want to help."

"Oh you will, lady. You're going to be right by my side when Seven-Deer and his men come pouring over the hill. For now," he said rising and taking her arm, "go and get some rest."

"I'm sorry," she said impulsively. "I am so sorry."

He smiled tiredly. "Sometimes you can find absolution under fire. My mother used to say that."

The remaining fifty slaves and even some of the Jaguar Knights heaved on ropes fed through massive pulleys anchored to huge posts they'd driven into the ground. The slaves, though few, were the strongest and their will to live was evident in the way they struggled to pull the great gun to the top of the ridge. The balloon tires turned slowly, inch by inch, dragging the weight of synthetic and metal forward. The turbogenerator whined, burning the last of their cane-spirit and pumping the capacitor full of energy.

Seven-Deer smiled benignly. He had ordered the slaves whipped, and the Jaguar Knights assisting them, so that their blood might be a gift to Tezcatlipoca, earning his good will. When the gun was in place, the rest of the slaves would be destroyed.

"Pull!" he shouted. "Bring forth the instrument of our vengeance so that our enemies' hearts may rot within them. Know, my people, that this dawn will be our enemies' last!"

The Jaguar Knights cried out in exultation, and smiling at their acclamation, Seven-Deer turned and stood with his arms crossed on his breast, legs apart, his head high and a smile of victory already brightening his face.

The railgun rose over the hill, haloed by the sun. The long thin tube, bracketed by the two rails, looked unimaginably strange as it seemed to pierce the ball of the sun.

"Does that thing have a body?" one of the men asked.

"Jeez, Hernando, I thought you said you had the biggest equipment around," a woman commented to general laughter.

James powered up his helmet. "Tops," he said, "can the Bolo tell where that thing is going to hit?"

"You'll have to ask the Beast that," Tops answered. "It knows what it can see."

James scowled, he didn't like talking to the Bolo. "Markee, can you see where they're aiming?"

"Yes, Captain."

"Can you advise us in time for us to move out of the way?"

"Negative, Captain. The XM-17's aiming system is very simple to operate, a target can be obtained in seconds. I believe there would be insufficient time for humans to react to my warnings."

"We needn't stand on the wall while they're shooting," Pasqua said. "I'd stake my life on it that they won't come down here until the Bolo's out of commission."

He turned to look at her. Her eyes slid away from her reflection on his faceplate's opaque surface.

"Good suggestion," he said. "Unit push. Stand down from the wall. They probably won't charge until and unless the Bolo's destroyed. No sense in risking our necks for nothing. Fall back to the first row of houses, take shelter in the basements. Avoid the ones between the gun and the Bolo; I think we can assume they'll be casualties."

James held his position and Pasqua stayed beside him as she'd promised Paulo.

"If I can't be there you have to be," he'd insisted fiercely. He'd met her just outside the women's tent in the blue-gray light just before dawn. "Dad's making me stay here," Paulo muttered resentfully. "He needs someone to watch his back." He'd glared at her then, dark eyes glittering with unshed tears, silently demanding her word.

"I'll do it," she'd said simply, and he'd nodded once and walked away.

"It isn't necessary for you to stay," James said quietly.

"I want to see."

They turned and trotted back, through the vegetable gardens and the flowers, into the courtyard of a building and down into the cellar. Above was a distillery; the fruity-sugar smell of rum was strong from the wooden vats behind them. As one, they stepped up to a shelf that gave them a view through the narrow ground-level windows.

After that they were silent. Their bodies tense as drawn wire, the mounting horror of the giant gun being brought into position bearing down on them like a physical weight.

"Tops, how's it going?" James asked suddenly, breaking the long silence.

Tops paused; they could hear a rasping sound as he raised his visor and wiped the sweat from his forehead.

"I've got the infinite repeater ports clear," he reported. "The

Bolo says it can use 'em. But," he paused and licked dry lips, "it can't turn and it can't walk. And you'll have noticed, sir, that bastard's comin' up from behind."

"Thanks, Tops. Martins out." James turned back towards the ridge and found himself staring into the barrel of the railgun. "Shit!" he snarled, and grabbing Pasqua around the waist, dove from the wall just before it disintegrated.

The impact of the blast knocked the breath from their bodies and carried them for yards, before the giant, invisible fist that had smacked into them allowed them to fall. Dirt and fragments of wood pummeled them where they lay, writhing as their stunned lungs refused to take in air. Beams sagged into the cellar as the endless rumble of falling stone from above avalanched down.

At last, with a painful spasm, James was able to draw breath, only to cough uncontrollably as he inhaled the dust that was still settling around them. Pasqua gasped and began hacking a moment later.

"Tops," James croaked, "what's happening?"

"Oh, thank God," Tops said. "I thought you were dead for sure, sir. They're dancing around and slapping themselves on the head up there, yellin' and singin' from the sound of it."

The buzzing in James' ears was fading and he could indeed hear, very faintly, what sounded like singing.

"It would be really nice if Markee could return the favor," James prompted.

"Workin' on it, Captain."

Yeah, workin' on it, Tops thought as he and his crew hammered desperately at rock that had flowed deeply into the Bolo's crevices, freezing it in its current position. *Why didn't we do something about this before?*

He knew the answer, of course. They didn't want to admit that a day like this would come. *I'm as spoiled as any of the kids who were born here,* he castigated himself. *Only I don't have an excuse, because I knew better than to believe we were safe.*

Somewhere behind him a house rose like a flock of startled birds, broke apart in midair and fell into a pile of rubble. The shockwave smacked his ears painfully and he felt the heat of the blast on his skin, though the explosion was a quarter of a mile behind him.

He hammered, they all hammered and prayed that they'd free the Beast in time.

Seven-Deer's joy was like a swelling sun in his chest. He grinned as the wall blew apart and the first row of houses disintegrated. Fire began to spread from the demolished buildings and he was certain that they had killed at least two of the defenders.

Tezcatlipoca, he prayed, *such sacrifices I shall give you! The ground will flow with a river of blood, all offered for your pleasure.*

Carefully he aligned the red dot on the next row of targets, the last row of buildings between the gun and Mountain that Walks.

"Soon," he crooned softly. "Soon you will die, monster."

James levered a beam aside. They both stuck their heads through, coughing at the thick smoke that was beginning to spread. He stared up the slope, through the ruins of his town at the gun that was tearing his world apart. He looked at Pasqua, prepared to hate her, only to find a pitifully shaken woman. Her green eyes were wide with shock and horror, pale lips trembling.

"I swear to God," she said, "I will never sell another gun as long as I live."

"Better late than never," he muttered. The ground quaked as another shot hit home. Anything solid enough to slow the ultradense material of the penetrator caused it to give up every erg of energy it possessed... and at those speeds, the kinetic force involved was *huge*. More buildings fell. The dust and smoke made it as hard to see as it was to breathe, but James knew that the Bolo was now fully exposed to Seven-Deer's gun.

There seemed to be a long breathless pause. No sound of triumph came from the ridge. Only the clatter of settling rubble or the sound of flames taking root in the houses around them was to be heard in the town.

Pasqua found James' hands with her own and he clasped them, pressing them to his chest as they watched the distant figures on the hill. They were fanning out, shaking themselves out into combat formations and coming down.

Seven-Deer didn't seem to think there would be much resistance. James wished he didn't agree.

"Sergeant," the Bolo said in its incongruously sweet voice. "You and the rest of the crew should seek shelter now. The enemy is targeting this unit."

Tops glanced behind him and froze. All that stood between him and the tank killer was an impenetrable cloud of dust.

He stood and shouted. "Everybody off the Bolo, get to cover!" Then he leaped himself, wincing at the pain in his ankles and knees as he struck the paving stones. Long time since he'd done that. It didn't stop him running as fast as he could; men and women dropped their tools and scrambled down the sides of the tank, moving with desperate speed around him.

A bolt pierced the drifting cloud of smoke and dirt. Far too fast to see, but the incandescent track it drilled through air and dust was solid as a bar for an instant, burning a streak across his retinas.

A flash like a dozen bolts of lightning burned through his closed eyelids and upraised hand. Heat slapped at his face, as the hypervelocity shot liberated *all* its energy. A plasma bloom of vaporized uranium and durachrome washed halfway across the plaza, burning everything it touched to ash. A hundred and fifty tons of war-machine rocked with the blow, surging backward on maglev suspension, wheeling in a three-quarter circle as the off-center impact torqued against the enormous weight of the Bolo. Lava stone fell from her sides like rain and clouds of electric sparks burst from her.

Tops rolled to a halt in the shadow of a house and turned to watch, sick with dread.

But the Bolo was not shattered. A disk twelve feet broad on its surface was *clean*, polished as if by a generation of sand-blasters to a mirror finish. The rest of it looked different too; it took a moment for his blast-stunned mind to grasp why.

Pasqua leveled her M-35 and stroked the trigger. *Braaaap.* The 4mm slugs whipped away downrange. A Jaguar Knight tumbled; perhaps her fire, perhaps someone else. She spat aside to clear her mouth of some of the gritty dust and blinked at the rubble and smoke before her.

"It's been good to know you!" she shouted over the noise.

James nodded without looking around. Mortar shells began dropping on the rubble at the edge of Cacaxtla; the Knights had their heavy weapons in operation.

Move, baby, Tops thought. *Move!*

He held his breath and watched the huge machine. Under the impact of the railgun shot the whole surface of the du-rachrome armor had *flexed*. The lava that had covered it was gone, blasted away in molecular dust, coating the plaza stones for hundreds of yards in all directions.

But there were also electrical fires on the Bolo's surface, and the bright dished spot in the armor glowed, the heat cycling down from white towards a sullen red.

Move, he thought as despair washed over him, along with the conviction that the Bolo was dead.

"Markee!" he shouted. And waited. No answer.

But in the silence the sound of shouting men grew, and he didn't need the captain's voice to tell him what was happening.

"They're coming!"

The Jaguar Knights pounded down the hill, literally screaming for blood. James Martins fired again and again, but he could feel the small hairs along his spine lifting at the sound of their gleeful shrieks.

Pasqua envied him his preoccupation, as she snapped out orders and offered encouragement. She could only kneel, dry-mouthed, clutching her M-35 and watching death come bellowing down the hill after her.

"All right, aim and shoot, aim and shoot, people," James said. *I wonder how many of us will be able to aim today.* They'd all been hunting, most were pretty good shots, but they hadn't been firing on men. *Or under the stress of attack, with our houses burning behind us.*

"Damn," he said.

"What?" Pasqua said.

James tapped the side of his helmet. "They're not just charging in. Mortar teams moving forward, and they're swinging around to flank us. We've only got about twenty assault rifles, and not all that much ammunition. They've got two hundred. The rest of us…"

Not far off, a Cacaxtlan raised her rifle and fired over a hill of rubble. Gray-white smoke jetted out, marking her position; she rolled down the rubble as bullets spanged and sparked off the spot she'd been occupying, struggling with the lever of her weapon. It gave, and a brass cartridge popped out. She fumbled another free of the bandolier across her chest, and thumbed it home into the breech. Another smack of the lever closed it, and she began to crawl toward another pile of broken stone.

"We don't have the firepower to stop them. *Down!*"

He caught Pasqua and flattened himself. A mortar landed not ten yards away, and fragments whined viciously about them. Their strained faces were inches apart, and James opened his mouth to speak.

An earsplitting scream of tortured metal stopped the words. Something made the earth shake beneath them, an endless droning, creaking rumble. Time slowed. Pitching and swaying with the uneven stress of advancing on three treads, the Bolo surged forward to fill the gap in the center of the villagers' line. Rock crackled beneath it, louder than gunshots; rock crunched and bled out of its road wheels.

Many of the villagers screamed at the sounds and spun 'round with their M-35s leveled at the Bolo, only to start laughing as the Bolo swept towards them, moving to fill the gap in the gate.

Seven-Deer screamed hatred as the Bolo moved across the holographic sight-image.

"I killed you!" he shouted. "I will kill you again, and again!"

His hands gripped the control yoke. His thumbs stabbed down on the firing button.

Status: weapons 27%, sensors 38%. Severe degradation of function due to kinetic-energy round impact. Power reserves 64%. Forward sensors at 3% optimum. 51% of drive units inoperable due to surge overload. Main data processors secure. Infinite repeaters nominal. Main armament nominal.

Mission priorities: fire support to Cacaxtla forces defending position; as per, orders, Martins, Lieutenant Bethany, 01/07/2040.

Threat envelope: enemy infantry, small arms.

enemy infantry, mortars.

enemy antitank gun, towed, manned.

:[decision tree]—priority. Query.

Query: continue fire support mission/interrupt.

:[decision tree]—maintain unit integrity/vital assigned mission parameters.

Priority: threats to unit integrity. Threat is antitank gun.

distance/bearing/wind factors/weapons selection/ status

:[decision tree]—main gun.

Bearing. Fire as you bear.

Fire.

Enemy damage assessment.

:[decision tree]: resume fire support mission.

The process had taken quite a long time; Unit #27A22245, Mk III, was in grossly suboptimal condition. Fully 1.27 seconds elapsed before the coils energizing the Bolo's main gun activated.

James and Pasqua stood, the muzzles of their rifles drooping earthward as they watched the fireball climbing into the sky as Seven-Deer met the Sun. The flash made their eyes wince and water, but they could already see that nothing remained of the railgun—nothing remained of the *ridge*, either; there was a great big semicircle taken out of it, like a bite. The muzzle of the Bolo's long main cannon throbbed blue-white, a deep humming through the air as it cooled.

For a moment silence fell over the battlefield, broken only by the crackling flames and the screams of wounded humans. Then another tortured squeal of metal came as the Bolo lurched forward. Fire stabbed out from it, and the next flight of mortar bombs exploded in midair. The infinite repeaters sounded again and again; smaller globes of fire marked the sites where the mortars had been. Again, and Jaguar Knights exploded into mists of fractionated bone and blood. They threw down their weapons and fled, screaming as loud in terror as they had in bloodlust. Again…

James ran forward. "Cease fire!" he shouted. "Cease fire!"

The low sweet voice of the war-machine sounded in his ears. "Mission priority is to protect the valley from exterior aggressors, Captain," it said. Men died. "Are my mission parameters to be changed?"

"No! But let them surrender—that's an order, Markee!"

"Yes, Captain."

A voice spoke, louder than a god; James threw his hands to his ears in reflex, shouting with pain even though the cone of sound was directed up the slope. The Voice blasted again, in the guttural choppy sounds of Nahuatl. Then in Spanish, and English.

"THROW DOWN YOUR WEAPONS AND PLACE YOUR HANDS BEHIND YOUR NECKS. SURRENDER AND YOU WILL NOT BE HARMED. RESISTANCE IS DEATH. THROW DOWN—"

A Jaguar Knight raised his M-35. For an instant a bar of light seemed to connect him to the Bolo, and then his body *splashed* away from the contact. All except for his legs; those fell outward, one to the left and one to the right.

The Knight beside him bent and laid his rifle on the ground.

"God," James murmured. He looked around at the town, at the charnel house spread out on the slopes above it. "God."

"Which one?" Pasqua said, coming up beside him.

James found Pasqua watching the celebrations from the shadow of a neighbor's wall. She looked different in a flounced skirt and bodice… He handed her a beer and took his place beside her.

"You don't dance?" he said.

She shrugged.

"Are you staying?" he asked, watching the dancers whirl and clap their hands, sweat glistening on happy faces.

Her brows went up and she turned to look at him.

"Would I be welcome?"

James grimaced slightly. "I'm the only one who knows everything and I'd say you'd balanced things out over the last week."

Tell that to Gary, she thought.

"Yeah," he continued, "you'd be welcome. I... you'd be welcome, sure."

Beside him she inhaled deeply and straightened. *Oh, God,* he thought. *What's coming now?* That was the way she'd looked at the *last* confession.

"I think you should know that my name is Giacano," she said.

"Instead of Pasqua?"

"I'm Pasqua Giacano," she snarled.

She obviously expects a comment on that, he thought.

"I like it. It's very musical."

She gaped at him. Then a slow smile took possession of her face, one that she couldn't have suppressed to save herself from torture.

Musical! My relatives started out as extortionists, pimps, and murderers. They moved up to slaving and grand-scale tyranny; and this guy thinks my name is musical? She could have hugged him. *I could be my own person here! No vile expectations, no fearful gasps of recognition. I won't have to be ashamed of not making my bones.*

"If I can stay, I'd like to," she said in a choked voice. "I think I'd like it here."

James shifted into a more comfortable position against the wall and sipped his beer.

"Oh, you will," he assured her confidently. "Hey, let's go punish the buffet—the *carne advodada* is to die for."

Tops settled himself on an outcropping in the Bolo's side, a beer in his hand and a smile on his face. In the distance the villagers danced and sang around bonfires in the plaza.

"You did good, Markee," he said.

"Actually, Sergeant Jenkins, I have been derelict in my duty."

He looked up at the Bolo towering over him, his eyebrows raised.

"That's a little harsh for a Bolo that just saved all our asses," he observed.

James and Pasqua passed near him, heading for the buffet with their heads together. Tops smiled and eased the splint around his broken arm more comfortably in the sling. There was something a little strange about Pasqua Giacano... but then, you could say that about all of them.

"I'd say you did pretty good," he went on, patting the dura-chrome beneath him.

"Lieutenant Bethany Martins ordered me to defend the valley from external aggression," it said. "But when the invasion came I was virtually unable to defend myself. I should have recognized my diminished capacity and asked that something be done about it."

"We could have seen it for ourselves, honey."

What the hell, why not surrender to it, this tank's a she.

"I guess we were all just hoping that we'd never need you and kept putting the job off. We'll just have to go on from here." He took a sip of his beer. "And we'll be better prepared next time," he promised grimly.

Paulo was watching him; the boy waved, and ripped off a salute to the Bolo. Behind him, the dance went on.

THE APOTHEOSIS OF MARTIN PADWAY

"This is the *right* vector," the computer insisted.

"If you say so," Maximus Liu-Peng replied. *Insolent machine,* he added to himself. *Still, there's something fishy here. Some sort of temporal loop?*

Luckily, the passengers were too occupied oohing and ahing at the screens to notice the interplay. The big holographic displays around the interior of the compartment showed a blinking succession of possible cities, all of them late-sixth-century Florence; cities large, small, burning, thriving, an abandoned one with a clutch of Hunnish yurts...

They wavered, then steadied to a recognizable shape; recognizable from maps, from preserved relics four hundred years old, and from the general appearance of an Early Industrial city.

Classical-era buildings sprawled across a set of hills with a river winding through it, all columns and marble around the squares and squalid tenements elsewhere; old temples had been converted into churches; city walls torn down and replaced by boulevards and parks; and a spanking-new railway station on the outskirts had spawned a clutch of factories with tall brick chimneys and spreading row housing for the workers.

"How quaint!" gushed somebody's influential cousin, officially an observer for the Senatorial Committee on Anachro-Temporal Affairs.

Maximus controlled his features. Several of the scholarly types didn't try to hide their scorn; either safely tenured, naive, or both. A coal-black anthropologist cleared her throat with a *hrrrump*.

"You're certain this is our *own* past?" she said.

The operator's poker experience came in handy again. "That's a"—*bloody stupid question*—"moot point, *Doctore Illustrissimo*," he said. "It's definitely a past with Martinus of Padua in it. There are no other lines within several hundred chronospace-years that show a scientific-industrial revolution this early. Quantum factors make it difficult"—*fucking meaningless*—"to say if it's *precisely* the line that led to us."

"But will *He* be here?" an archbishop said.

That required even more caution. "Well, Your Holiness, that's what we'll have to find out. This *is*—" he pointed to the July 14, 585 A.D. readout "—the traditional date of the Ascension."

"I am not worthy to witness a miracle," the cleric breathed. "Yet that is why we have come—"

"We're here to find final proof of the Great Man theory," a historian answered, and they glared at each other. "Not to indulge in superstition. It's only natural that primitives, confronted with one of history's truly decisive individuals, should spin a cocoon of myth as they did with Alexander or Manuel—"

"Nonsense," the anthropologist said. "Martinus was merely there at the right time. Socioeconomic conditions were obviously—"

"I just drive this thing," Maximus muttered as the argument went into arm-waving stalemate, and checked the exterior deflector screens. It wouldn't do to have any of the natives see them floating up here....

Lieutenant Tharasamund Hrothegisson, *hirdman* in the Guards of Urias III, King of the Goths and Italians and Emperor of the West, looked carefully at each man's presented rifle as he walked down the line.

Then he called his troop to attention, drew the long *spatha* at his side, turned to face his men and stood at parade rest, with the point of the blade resting lightly on the pavement between his feet. The street was flat stones set in concrete—nothing but the best for the capital of the Romano-Gothic Empire!—but not too broad, perhaps thirty feet from wall to wall counting the brick sidewalks.

"All right, men," he said, raising his voice. "This shouldn't be much of a job. Wait for the word of command, and if you have to shoot to kill, shoot low."

There were nods and grins, quickly stifled. Tharasamund had spoken in Gothic; that was still the official language of the army—though nowadays only about a fifth of the men were born to Gothic mothers, even in a unit of the Royal Guards, and that was counting Visigoths. There were plenty of Italians, other Romans from Hispania and Gaul and North Africa, Burgunds, Lombards, Franks, Bavarians, Frisians—even a few Saxons and Angles and Jutes, a solitary Dane, and a couple of reddish-brown Lyonessians from beyond the western sea.

None of them were unhappy at the thought of taking a slap at a city mob, though, being mostly farmers' sons or lesser gentry themselves. Good lads, but inclined to be a bit rough if they weren't watched.

"Deploy in line," he said, looking back over his shoulder at the guns for a moment.

There were two of them: old-fashioned bronze twelve-pounders, already unhitched from their teams and pointing forward. *And may God spare me the need to use them,* he thought. They were obsolete for field use, but as giant short-range shotguns with four-inch bores they were still as horribly efficient as they'd been in the Second Greek War, when they were a monstrous innovation and surprise.

The soldiers trotted quickly to make a two-deep line across the street, identical in their forest-green uniforms and cloth-covered steel helmets. The city was quiet—far too quiet for Florence on a Saturday afternoon, even with the League play-offs sucking everyone who could afford it out to the stadium in the suburbs. The wind had died, leaving the drowsy warmth of an Italian summer afternoon lying heavy; also heavy with the city smells of smoke and horse dung and garbage. The buzzing flies were the loudest sound he could hear, save for a distant grumbling, rumbling thunder. Shopkeepers had pulled down their shutters and householders barred window and door hours ago.

"Load!"

The men reached down to the bandoliers at their right hips, pulled out cartridges and dropped them into the open breeches. They closed with a multiple *snick-snick-snick*.

"Fix bayonets!"

The long sword-knives went home below the barrels with another grating metallic rattle and snap.

"Present!"

The troops advanced their rifles with a deep-throated *ho!* That left a line of bristling steel points stretching across the street. With any luck…

Tharasamund took off his helmet and inclined his head slightly to one side. *Yes, here they come,* he thought.

He replaced the headpiece and waited, *spatha* making small precise movements as his wrist moved, limbering his sword arm. The first thing he saw was a man in the brown uniform of the city police. He was running as fast as he could—limping, in fact—and blood ran down his face from a scalp bare of the leather helmet he should have worn. When he saw the line of bayonets, he stopped and started thanking God, Mary, and the saints.

"Make some sense, Sathanas fly away with you," Tharasamund snapped.

He was a tall, rangy, blue-eyed man a few years shy of thirty himself, with a close-trimmed yellow beard and mustaches and shoulder-length hair a shade lighter, but his Latin was without an accent—better than the rather rustic Tuscan dialect the policeman spoke, in fact. Still, his uniform and Gothic features calmed the Italian a little. They represented authority, even in these enlightened times of the career open to talents.

"My lord," he gasped. "Patrolman Marcus Mummius reporting."

"What's going on?"

"My lord, the Carthage Lions triumphed!"

Tharasamund winced. "What was the score?" he asked.

"Seventeen-sixteen, with a field goal in sudden-death overtime."

Oh, Sathanas take it, he thought, restraining an impulse to clap his hand to his forehead and curse aloud.

The Florentine mob *hated* losing, even when times were good—which they weren't. When times were bad, they were as touchy as a lion with a gut ache. For some reason they thought being the capital city entitled their team to eternal victory, and this was just the sort of thing to drive them into a frenzy. Particularly with defeat at the hands of an upstart team like the Carthage Lions, only in the League a few years—North Africa hadn't been part of the Western Empire until the war of 560, twenty-five years ago.

"We tried to keep everything in order, but when the Carthaginian fans stormed the field and tore down the goalposts, the crowd went wild. They would have killed all the Lions *and* their supporters if we hadn't put all our men to guarding the entrances to the locker rooms. Then they began fighting with all the men from other cities, shouting that foreigners were taking all the best jobs, and—"

"Sergeant, give this man a drink and patch him up," Tharasamund said, ignoring the Italian's thanks as he was led away.

There were thousands of out-of-towners around for the playoffs, plenty of material for a riot with the bad times of the last year—the papers were calling it a *recession*, odd word.

The first spray of hooligans came around the corner two hundred yards south, screaming slogans, banging on shop shutters with rocks and clubs. *They* were wearing leather helmets, the sort actual footballers used, but painted in team colors and with gaudy plumes added, and the numbers of their favorite players across their chests.

Their noisy enthusiasm waned abruptly as they saw the soldiers; then a deep baying snarl went up, and they began to edge and mill forward towards the line of points.

Tharasamund winced. That was a *very* bad sign.

"I've been too successful for too long," Martinus of Padua said as he lit a cigarette and leaned back for a moment in his swivel chair, looking at the neat stacks of paper that crowded his marble-slab desktop.

"On the other hand, consider the alternative," he told himself.

His voice was hoarse with age and tobacco smoke; the precise Latin he spoke was a scholar's, but it bore the very faint trace of an accent that was—literally—like none other in the whole world. He'd been born Martin Padway, in the United States of America during the first decade of the twentieth century, but even he hardly ever thought of himself by that name anymore; it had been fifty-two years since he found himself transported from Benito Mussolini's Rome to the one ruled by Thiudahad, King of the Goths and Italians, 533 A.D.

He gave a breathy chuckle; the city fathers of Padua had

even erected a monument to his supposed birth in their fair town, and it attracted a substantial stream of tourists. Quite a lucrative little business, all built on a linguistic accident—any native Latin speaker would hear *Padway* as *Paduei,* "of Padua." The chuckle became a rumbling cough, and he swore quietly as he wiped his lips with a handkerchief. The years had carved deep runnels in his face, leaving the beak of a nose even more prominent, but he still had most of his teeth, and the liver-spotted hands were steady as he picked up a file from the *urgent* stack.

He took another drag on the cigarette, coughed again, flipped the file open and read:

Item:

The East Roman armies looked like they'd finally broken the last Persian resistance in Sogdiana, what Padway mentally referred to as Afghanistan.

Damn. I was hoping they'd be pinned down there fighting guerrillas forever. The way the Byzantines keep persecuting Zoroastrians and Buddhists, they deserve it. Plus the Sogdians are even meaner than Saxons. Oh, well. Might be good for trade if they settle down peacefully.

The East Roman Emperor Justinian was even older than Martin Padway, and he'd never stopped hating the Italo-Gothic kingdom—what had become the reborn and expanded Empire of the West. The more it grew, the more bitter his enmity. Despite the fact that he personally would have been long dead without the doctors Padway had supplied, and never would have beaten the Persians or pushed the Byzantine frontier far north of the Danube without the gunpowder weapons and telegraphs and steamboats his artisans had copied from the models Padway had "invented."

That made absolutely no difference to Justinian's intensely clever but even more paranoid mind; he probably thought he'd have done it all anyway if Padway hadn't shown up. Or even more.

Maybe his grandnephew will be more reasonable. The old buzzard can't last forever… can he? Note to State Department: get the spies working double-time to see if the Byzantines start shifting troops west to the Dalmatian frontier. He'd love to take another slap at us.

Item:

Riots between pagan and Christian settlers had broken out again in Nova Eboracum, over in Lyonesse; what in another history had been called New York.

Maybe I was a bit too clever there.

Diverting the Saxon migrations from Britannia to the Americas had taken care of their land hunger and gotten a lot of inveterate pirates out of the Channel. It had even introduced them to the rudiments of civilization, since the new colonies were more firmly under the Empire of the West's control than the North Sea homelands.

What it hadn't done was lessen their love of a fight; "Saxon" meant something like "shiv-man," and the tribal ethnonym was no accident. These days they were just using different rationalizations, stubborn Wodenites bashing enthusiasts for the White Christ and vice versa and the Britanno-Roman and Gallo-Roman and Iberian settlers rioting against them all.

The current financial crisis didn't help either. People here just weren't used to the idea of market fluctuations—bad harvests and famine, yes, the trade cycle, no. FDR hadn't been able to cure the one at home, and Padway hadn't found any way to do it here either, except spread a little comfort money around and wait.

Note to Royal Council: send a couple of regiments to Lyonesse. Not ones with a lot of Saxons or Frisians in the ranks. Push the troublemakers up west of Albany into the frontier townships and give them all land grants.

Then the transplanted Saxons could take out their pugnacity on the Indians. The British Empire had used that trick with the Scots-Irish, in Ireland and America both.

Item:

The Elba Steel Company was complaining about competition from the new mills in the Rhineland. *Nothing much I can do about that.*

Italy just didn't have much basis for heavy industry, and now that the Rhone-Rhine canal and railway were working... But the Elba Company *did* have a lot of important Italian and Gothic aristocrats on the board of directors. *They* had pull in the House of Lords. Plus he'd advised many of them to put their serf-emancipation compensation money into Elba stock, back when. Italian industry had spent a generation or two booming, because it was the only game around. Now the provinces were starting to catch up and all the established balances were shifting.

Wait a minute. We'll throw them some government contracts, and they can use the profits to tempt some of the new Gallic and Britannic steel firms to agree to cross-shareholdings. That would ease the transition—and keep those important votes sweet.

Item:

Down in Australia—

A knock came at the door, and his secretary Lucilla stuck her head through. "Quaestor," she said, having always refused to call him "excellent boss" like everyone else. "Your granddaughter is here."

"And it's my *birthday*, Grandfather!" Jorith said, bursting through and hurrying forward. He rose—slightly painfully—and returned her enthusiastic hug.

His daughter's youngest daughter was just turned eighteen. She took after her father's side of the family in looks; he was the third son of King Urias I. She was nearly up to Padway's five-foot-six, which made her towering for a woman of this age and area, with straight features, long dark-blonde hair falling past her shoulders, and bright green eyes.

Actually, she reminds me of her father's mother, Padway

thought. *Just as gorgeous a man-trap, and just as smart. Doesn't have Mathaswentha's weakness for lopping off people's heads, though.*

At one point, he'd come within an inch of marrying Mathaswentha himself. Urias' uncle Wittigis had tried to marry her by force, during the first Byzantine invasion, a few months after Padway was dropped back into Gothic-era Rome; as a princess of the Amaling clan, she made whoever married her automatically eligible for the elective Gothic monarchy. That was one reason he'd pushed the Goths into accepting a pure eldest-son inheritance system; it cut down on succession disputes.

Padway had rescued Mathaswentha from a forced marriage at the very altar, and for a while he'd been smitten with her, and vice versa.

Brrrr, he thought; the memory of his narrow escape never failed to send a chill down his spine. Luckily he'd wised up in time, and had had Urias on hand—a Goth smart enough and tough enough to keep that she-leopard on a leash, and a good friend of Padway's.

Gentle, scholarly Drusilla had been much more the American's style.

"Pity your parents couldn't get back from Gadez," he said, feeling slightly guilty.

The truth was he'd never much liked his daughter Maria. That was unjust. It wasn't *her* fault that Drusilla had died in childbirth. He'd tried to be a good father anyway, but between that and the press of business, she'd mostly been raised by relatives and servants. Jorith was the delight of his old age.

And doesn't she know it, he thought indulgently.

They walked out together through the Quaestor's Offices, her arm linked around his left elbow. He was slightly—resentfully—conscious of the fact that she was walking slowly and ready to catch him if he stumbled, despite the cane he used with his right hand. He was in his mid-eighties now. Moving hurt. He'd spent nearly six decades back here, and he wasn't that spry, brash young archaeologist anymore.

Not even the same person, really. A few weeks ago he'd tried to make himself *think* in English, and found it horrifyingly difficult.

I should be grateful, he thought, as they walked down corridors past offices and clerical pools, amid a ripple of bows and murmurs. *I'm not senile or bedridden.* Or dead, for that matter. And he'd done a lot more good here than he could have in his native century; nobody who'd seen a real famine close up, or what was left of a town after a sack by Hun raiders, could doubt that.

He ignored the quartet of guards who followed, hard-eyed young men with their hands on the hilts of their swords and revolvers at their waists. *They* were part of the furniture. Justinian and assorted other enemies would *still* be glad to see him go. He chuckled a little as they came out into the broad marble-and-mosaic foyer of the building.

"What's so funny, Grandfather?" Jorith said.

"That there are still men prepared to go to such efforts to kill me," Padway said.

"That's *funny?*" she said, in a scandalized tone.

"In a way. If they'd killed me right after I arrived here, they might have accomplished something—from their point of view; stopped me from changing things. It was touch and go there, those first couple of years. It's far too late, now…"

"But not too late for the theatre," Jorith said. "It's a revival of one of your plays, too—*A Midsummer Night's Dream…* what are you laughing at *this* time, Grandfather?"

"There's nothing here," the archbishop fretted.

"Well, the Cathedral wasn't built until the 700s," the historian pointed out with poisonously sweet reasonableness.

The field wasn't empty, strictly speaking. There was a big two-story brick building, so new that the tiles were still going on the roof. The rest of it was trampled mud, wheelbarrows, piles of mortar and brick and timber and boards, and a clumsy-looking steam traction engine.

"But why should... marvelous are the works of the Lord," the archbishop said. "If His Son could be born in a stable, a saint can rise to heaven from a building yard."

"We're redirecting traffic, my lord," the policeman said, walking up to the door of the carriage.

"What for?" Padway said. *Mustn't get testy in my old age,* he thought. *And it was a pretty good performance.* Thank God for a good memory; he'd managed to put down something close to Shakespeare's text.

"There are rumors of riots," the policeman said, sweating slightly. Nobody liked having the Big Boss suddenly turn up on their beat when something was going wrong. "Riots among the football spectators, my lord."

"Oh. Well, thank you, Officer," Padway said. As the carriage lurched into motion, he went on: "I keep outsmarting myself."

Jorith giggled. "Grandfather, why is it that all the other politicians and courtiers are dull as dust, but you can always make me laugh?"

It does sound funnier in Latin, he thought. Plus he'd gotten a considerable reputation as a wit over the past fifty years by reusing the clichés of the next fifteen hundred years. He chuckled himself.

And Drusilla swooned over things like parting is such sweet sorrow, *too.* That brought a stab of pain, and he leaned out the window of the carriage.

"What I mean," he went on, "is that I introduced football to quiet people down. Didn't think anyone could get as upset about that as they did over chariot races."

"I've never seen the point, myself," Jorith said. "Polo is much more exciting."

Padway grinned to himself. The Gothic aristocracy had taken to *that* like Russians to drink. In fact, they'd virtually reinvented the game themselves, with a little encouragement and some descriptions from him.

They remind me of horsy country-gentleman-type Englishmen, he thought, not for the first time. *Particularly now that they've taken to baths and literacy.*

They were out of the theatre crush now, the carriages moving a little faster as they moved downhill. The clatter of shod hooves on pavement was loud, but at least most of them had rubber wheels these days, which cut down on the shattering racket iron-clad ones made on city streets. He stopped himself from making a mental note to look into how automobile research was coming.

Leave it to the young men, he thought.

There were enough of them coming out of the universities now, trained in the scientific worldview. In the long run, it would be better *not* to intervene anymore, even with "suggestions." There were enough superstitions about "Mysterious Martinus"; he wanted the younger generation to learn how to think rationally, and for themselves.

He smiled, thinking of the thrill he'd had the first time a young professor had dared to argue with him about chemistry—and the whippersnapper had turned out to be right, and Padway's vague high-school recollections wrong, too. And after that…

Jorith was smiling at him indulgently. He blinked, realizing he'd dozed off, lost in half-dreams of decades past.

"Sorry," he said, straightening on the coach's well-padded seat, wincing a little at the stiffness in his neck.

"You deserve to be able to nap when you feel like it, Grandfather," Jorith said. "It's a sin, the way you work yourself to a nub, after all you've done for the kingdom. Why, I remember only last month, how everyone cheered in the Senate when you made that speech—the one where you said we had nothing to fear but fear itself—"

A short crashing *baaammm* rang out ahead. Padway's head came up with a start, the last threads of dream slipping away. He knew that sound of old—was responsible for it being heard a millennium or so early.

Rifles, firing in volley…

"*Fire!*" Tharasamund said reluctantly.

The sound of fifteen rifles going off within half a second of each other battered at his ears. The front rank reloaded, spent cartridges tinkling on the pavement, and the sergeant bellowed:

"Second rank, volley fire present—*fire!*"

Dirty-white powder smoke drifted back towards him, smelling of rotten eggs and death. Ten yards away the crowd milled and screamed, half a dozen lying limply dead, twice as many more whimpering or fleeing clutching wounds or lying and screaming out their hurt to the world. The rest hesitated, bunching up—which meant a lot of them were angry enough to face high-velocity lead slugs.

"*Cease fire!*" he said to his men, with enough of a rasp in it to make them obey. To the mob, he went on in Latin.

"Disperse! Return to your homes!" he called, working to keep his voice deep and authoritative, and all the desperation he felt out of it. "In the Emperor Urias' name!"

"Down with the Goths!" someone screeched. "Down with the heretics! *Dig up their bones!*"

"Oh-oh," Tharasamund said.

That was call to riot, an import from Constantine's city…. The religious prejudice was home-grown, though. Most Goths were still Arian Christians—heretics, to Orthodox Catholics—and the Western Empire enforced a strict policy of toleration, even for pagans and Jews and Nestorians, and for Zoroastrian refugees from Justinian's persecutions.

I hate to do this. They're fools, but that doesn't mean they deserve to be sausage meat. Drunk, half of them, and a lot of them out of work.

"Clear firing lanes!" he rasped aloud.

The soldiers did, shuffling aside but keeping their rifles to the shoulder to leave a line of bright points and intimidating muzzles facing the crowd. The artillerymen stepped aside from their weapons—they'd recoil ten feet each when fired, on smooth pavement—with the gun captains holding the long lanyards ready. Those four-inch bores were even more intimidating than rifles, if you knew what they could do.

"Ready, sir," the artillery noncom said. "Doubled-shotted with grape."

Tharasamund nodded. "Disperse!" he repeated, his voice cutting over the low brabbling murmur of the crowd. "This is your last warning!"

He heard a whisper of *Why give them any fucking warnings?* but ignored it; there were some times an officer was wise to be half-deaf.

The noise of the crowd died down, a slow sullen quiet spreading like olive oil on a linen tablecloth A few in the front rank tossed down their rocks and chunks of brick, turning and trying to force their way back through the crowd; the slow forward movement turned into eddies and milling about. He took a long breath of relief, and felt the little hairs along his spine stop trying to bristle upright.

"I should have stayed home in Campania and raised horses," he muttered to himself. "But no, I had to be dutiful…"

He half-turned his head as he sheathed his sword; that let him catch the motion on the rooftop out of the corner of his eye. Time froze; he could see the man—short, swarthy, nondescript, in a shabby tunic. The expression of concentration on the man's face as he tossed the black-iron sphere with its long fuse trailing sputterings and blue smoke…

"*Down!*" Tharasamund screamed, and suited action to words—there was no time to do anything else.

Someone tripped and fell over him; that saved his life, although he never remembered exactly what happened when the bomb fell into the open ammunition limber of the twelve-pounder.

"What was *that?*" Jorith exclaimed, shock on her face.

Neither of them really needed telling. *That* was an explosion, and a fairly big one. The driver of the carriage leaned on the brake and reined in, but the road was fairly steep here—flanked on both sides by shops and homes above them. Padway leaned out again, putting on his spectacles and blinking, thankful that at least the lens grinders were turning out good flint glass at last. Then another blast came, and another, smaller and muffled by distance.

"Goddamn that bastard Justinian to *hell,*" he growled—surprising himself by swearing, and doing it in English. Normally he was a mild-mannered man, but...

"Grandfather?" Jorith said nervously; she wasn't used to him lapsing into the mysterious foreign tongue either.

"Sorry, kitten," he said, then coughed. "I was cursing the Emperor of the East."

Her blue eyes went wide. "You think—"

"Well, we can produce our own riots, but not bombs, I think," Padway said. "Dammit, he can try and kill *me*—he's been doing that for fifty years—but this is beyond enough."

Shod hooves clattered on the pavement outside. One of the bodyguards leaned over to speak through the coach's window.

"Excellent boss," he said. "There are rioters behind us. We think it would be best to try and go forward and link up with the soldiers we heard ahead, and then take the Equinoctal Way out to the suburbs. There will be more troops moving into the city."

"As you think best, Hermann," Padway said; he'd commanded armies in his time, but that was forty years ago and more, and he'd never pretended to be a fighting man. He tried to leave that to the professionals.

Tharasamund shook his head. That was a bad mistake; pain thrust needles through his head, and there was a loud metallic ringing noise that made him struggle to clap hands to his ears. The soft heavy resistance to the movement made him realize that he was lying under several mangled bodies, and what the sticky substance clotting his eyelashes and running into his mouth was. He retched a little, gained control with gritted teeth and a massive effort of will, and pushed the body off. Half-blinded, he groped frantically for a water bottle and splashed the contents across his face while he rubbed at his eyelids. The blood wasn't quite dried, and the flies weren't all that bad yet; that meant he hadn't been out long. A public fountain had broken in the blast, and water was puddling up against the dam of dead horses and men and wrecked equipment across the road.

As he'd expected, what he saw when he *could* see properly was very bad. Nobody looked alive—most of the bodies weren't even intact, and if one of the field guns hadn't taken some of the blast when both limbers went off, he wouldn't be either. Nobody but the dead were here—a tangle of the mob around where the last of his soldiers had fallen. All the intact weapons were gone, of course, except for his sword and revolver; he'd probably looked too thoroughly like a mangled corpse to be worth searching by men in a hurry. The fronts of the shops on either side were smashed in by the explosion and by looters completing the work; a civilian lay half in and half out of one window, very thoroughly dead.

"Probably the shopkeeper," Tharasamund muttered grimly, his own voice sounding muffled and strange. The pain and the ringing in his ears were a little better, but probably he'd never have quite the keenness of hearing again.

That was another score to settle, along with the cold rage at the killing of his men. He staggered over to the fountain and washed as best he could; that brought him nearer to consciousness. The first thing to do—

He hardly heard the coach clatter up, but the sight brought him out into the roadway, waving his sword. That brought half a dozen pistols in the hands of the mounted guards on him, and a shotgun from the man beside the driver. The men were in civil dress, country gentleman's Gothic style, but they were a mixed lot. Soldiers or ex-soldiers, he'd swear; from the look of the coach, some great lord's personal retainers. None of them looked very upset at the carnage that was painting the coach's wheels and the hooves of their horses red… best be a little careful.

"Tharasamund, Captain in the *Kunglike-hird*, the Royal Guard," he snapped, sheathing the blade. "I need transport, and I call on you to assist me in the Emperor's name."

"Straight-leg, we don't stop for anyone," the chief guard said—he had a long tow-colored mane, a thick bull-neck, and an equally thick growling accent in his Latin: Saxon, at a guess. "The only thing I want to hear from you is how to get our lord to someplace safe."

Tharasamund looked around. He could hear distant shouting and screams and the crackle of gunfire. That meant they were *loud*. And he could see columns of smoke, too. It might be an hour—or four or five—before enough troops marched in from the barracks outside town, between the built-up area and the royal palace, to restore order. Someone had screwed up royally; he'd be surprised if there wasn't a new urban prefect soon.

Not that that will be much consolation to the dead, he added to himself.

He was opening his mouth to argue again—he had to get back to regimental HQ, to report this monumental ratfuck, and get some orders—when a young woman leaned out of the half-open carriage door.

Not just any young woman. Her gown and jewels were rich in an exquisitely restrained court fashion, but that face would have stopped him cold if she were naked—*especially* if she were naked. His gesture turned into a sweeping bow.

Wait a minute. They said their lord, *not their* lady.

The girl's eyes widened at the sight ahead, and she gulped. Then she fought down nausea—he felt a rush of approval even in the press of emergency—and looked at him. There was a faint feeling like an electric-telegraph spark as their eyes met, gray gazing into blue, and then she was looking over her shoulder.

"Grandfather," she said, in pure upper-class Latin. "There's been a disaster here."

"There's been an attack on Imperial troops here," Tharasamund said firmly, pitching his voice to carry into the interior of the vehicle. "I must insist, my lord—"

It seemed to be a day for shocks. The man who leaned out in turn, bracing himself with a grimace, certainly looked like a grandfather. Possibly God's grandfather, from the wrinkles; he'd never seen anyone older and still alive. The pouched eyes behind the lenses and big beak nose were disconcertingly shrewd. It was a face Tharasamund had seen before, when his unit was on court duty; anyone who saw magazines and engravings and photographs would have recognized it as well, these past two generations and more.

Martinus of Padua. Quaestor to three Emperors of the West; kingmaker, sorcerer or saint, devil or angel—some pagans thought him a god—and next to Urias II, the most powerful man in the world. Possibly more powerful. Emperors came and went, but the man from Padua had been making things happen since Tharasamund's grandfather was a stripling riding to his first war, when the Greeks invaded Italy in Thiudahad's day.

Tharasamund saluted and made a deep bow. "My apologies, my lord. I am at your disposal." He managed a smile, a gentleman's refusal to be disconcerted by events. "And at yours, my lady."

"Jorith Hermansdaughter, noble captain," she said, a little faintly but with courtly politeness. A princess, then, and the old man's granddaughter.

This *definitely* took precedence over his own troubles....

Ouch, Padway thought, pushing his glasses back up his nose and giving thanks, for once, for the increasing shortsightedness of old age. He'd seen worse, but not very often.

"Captain, pleased to see you," he said. "What happened here?"

"My lord," the young man said crisply. He looked suitably heroic in a battered way, but it was a pleasure to hear the firm intelligence in his voice. "A detachment of my company was ordered by General Winnithar of the Capital City garrison command to suppress rioters in aid to the civil power. We were doing so when a bomb thrower dropped a grenade into the ammunition limber. I suspect the man was a foreign agent—the whole thing was too smooth for accident."

As he spoke, another explosion echoed over the city. Padway nodded, looking like an ancient and highly intelligent owl.

"Doubtless you're right, Captain. Do you think the Equinoctal Way will be clear?"

Tharasamund made a visible effort. "It's as good a chance as any, my lord," he said. "It's broad—rioters generally stick to the old town. And it's the best way to get to the garrison barracks quickly."

Broad and open to light, air and artillery, Padway thought—a joke about the way Napoleon III had rebuilt Paris, and part of his own thoughts over the years planning the expansion of Florence.

"Let's go that way," he said. "Hengist, head us out."

"I never wanted to have adventures," Padway grumbled. "Even when I was a young man. *Certainly* not now."

Jorith looked at him and gave a smile; not a very convincing one, but he acknowledged the effort.

"This is an adventure?" she said. "I've always *wanted* adventures—but this just feels like I was walking along the street and stepped into a sewer full of big rats."

"That's what adventures are like," Padway said, wincing slightly as the coach lurched slowly over something that went *crunch* under the wheel and trying not to think of what—formerly who—it was, "while you're having them. They sound much better in retrospect."

The young guardsman—Tharasamund Hrothegisson, Padway forced himself to remember—chuckled harshly.

"Oh, yes," he said, in extremely good Latin with only the faintest tinge of a Gothic accent, then added: "Your pardon, my lord."

Jorith looked at him oddly, while Padway nodded. He might not have been a fighting man himself, but he'd met a fair sample over the years, and this was one who'd seen the elephant. For a moment youth and age shared a knowledge incommunicable to anyone unacquainted with that particular animal. Then a memory tickled at Padway's mind; he'd always had a rook's habit of stashing away bits and pieces, valuable for an archaeologist and invaluable for a politician.

"Hrothegisson... not a relation of Thiudegiskel?"

The young man stiffened. Officially, there had been an amnesty—but nobody had forgotten that Thiudegiskel son of Thiudahad had tried to get elected King of the Goths and Italians instead of Urias I, Padway's candidate; or that he'd gone over to the Byzantines during the invasion that followed and nearly wrecked the nascent Empire of the West.

"My mother was the daughter of his mother's sister," he said stiffly. "My lord."

That didn't make him an Amaling, but...

"Ancient history, young fellow. Like me," he added with a

wry grin. "What are you doing, by the way?"

The young Goth had gotten up and was examining the fastenings of the rubberized-canvas hood that covered the carriage.

"I thought I'd peel this back a bit at the front, my lord—"

"You can call me Boss or Quaestor or even sir, if you must," Padway said. He *still* wasn't entirely comfortable being my-lorded.

"—sir. I'd be of some use, if I could see out."

"Not all the way?"

"Oh, that would never do," Tharasamund said. "You're far too noticeable… sir."

Tharasamund finished looking at the fastenings, made a few economical slashes with his dagger, and peeled the soft material back from its struts, just enough to give him a good view. Warm air flowed in. "Uh-oh," he said.

I know what uh-oh *means,* Padway thought. *It means the perfume's in the soup… or the shit's hit the fan.*

"Give me a hand," he snapped.

Something in his voice made the two youngsters obey without argument. Grumbling at his own stiffness and with a hand under each arm, he knelt up on the front seat and looked past the driver and guard.

"Uh-oh," he said.

"It's in the soup, right enough, excellent boss," Tharasamund said.

One advantage of Florence's hilly build and grid-network streets was that you could see a long way from a slight rise. The view ahead showed more fires, more wreckage… and a very large, very loud mob about half a mile away, milling and shouting and throwing things. Beyond that was a double line of horsemen, fifty or sixty strong. As they watched, there was a bright flash of metal, as the troopers all clapped hand to hilt and drew their *spathae* in a single coordinated movement to the word of command. A deep shout followed, and the horses began to move forward, faster and faster....

"Oh, that was a bad idea. That was a *very* bad idea," Tharasamund muttered.

Sensible young man, Padway thought.

A big man on a big horse waving a sword and coming towards you was an awesome spectacle; scores of them looked unstoppable. Armies had broken and run from the sheer fear from the sight, including one memorable occasion when Padway had been in command, trying to make a mob of Italian peasant recruits hold a pike line against charging Byzantine heavy cavalry.

The problem was...

The horsemen struck. Sure enough, the front of the mob surged away in panic, trying to turn and run. The problem was that there were thousands of people behind them, and they *couldn't* run. There wasn't room. The swords swung down, lethal arcs that ended in slashed-open heads and shoulders, but the horses were slowing as they moved into the thick mass of rioters. Horses were all conscripts, with an absolute and instinctive fear of running into things, falling, and risking their vulnerable legs.

A line of brave men with spears could stop any cavalry ever foaled. A mass of people too big to run away could do the same, in a messy fashion, by sheer inertia.

Padway shifted slightly, keeping his body between Jorith and the results, and noticed that Tharasamund did the same. People stopped running as the horses slowed; they turned, started to throw things, yelled, waved their arms. The cavalry horses were bolder than most of their breed, but they backed, snorting and rolling their eyes; a few turned in tight circles, caught between their riders' hands on the reins and an inborn need to run away from danger. The rain of bits of stone and iron and wood grew thicker; a soldier was pulled out of the saddle....

And at the rear of the mob, a purposeful-looking group was

turning towards the carriage halted at the top of the hill.

"Guards cavalry," Tharasamund said tightly. *They never did know anything but how to die well. Though I grant they* do *know how to do that.*

He looked at Padway, back at the white, frightened, determined face of the girl, then at the mob. "Obviously, there are agitators at work," he said, "not just hungry rioters sparked off by a football game."

Padway nodded. The Saxon chief of his guardsmen bent down from the saddle and pointed to a narrow alleyway.

"That way, I think," he growled. "Liuderis, Marco, get that cart and set it up."

The coachman turned the horses' heads into the narrow, odorous gloom of the alley. The guardsmen grabbed a discarded vendor's pushcart, dumped out its load of vegetables in a torrent of green, and pulled it into the alleyway after the carriage before upending it. Most of them crouched behind it, drawing their pistols.

"We'll hold them here," Hengist said grimly. "Excellent boss, you and this gentleman—" he nodded to Tharasamund "—and the young mistress get going."

Gray eyes met blue, and Tharasamund nodded sharply. Padway seemed about to protest, and the Saxon grinned.

"Sorry, excellent boss, that's not an order you can give me. My oath's to keep you safe—obedience takes second place."

Hengist slapped the rump of the rear horse in the carriage team, leaping back to let the carriage lurch by in the narrow way. Tharasamund lifted a hand in salute, then used it to steady Padway; the Quaestor sat down heavily, sighing. Jorith helped him down, and braced him as they lurched across cobbles and then out into rutted dirt.

Think, Tharasamund, the soldier told himself. They weren't out into the country yet, and wouldn't be for half an hour, but the buildings were very new, some still under construction. No people were about; with a holiday and then a riot there wouldn't be, and this area had few residences, being mostly workshops.

He looked back; nothing to see, but then came a snarling brabble of voices, and a crackle of pistol fire. *By Christ and His mother that's a brave man,* he thought. *And true to his oath. Saxons may not be civilized but they're stubborn enough.*

Jorith looked behind them as well. "Is that—" she said, and swallowed.

Tharasamund nodded. "Yes, lady. They can hold them quite a while, in that narrow way. Not many rioters will have firearms, and there can't be many agents of the Greek emperor. Just enough."

She shivered. "It sounds… different, in the epics. Last stands."

Padway mumbled something in a language Tharasamund didn't recognize, though a couple of the words had a haunting pseudo-familiarity, sounding like oaths. For a moment he thought the old man was dazed, and then he spoke sharply—loud enough for the coachman to hear.

"If any of you get out of this, and I don't, take a message to the king and Council: this means Justinian thinks he's ready for a showdown. I should have—never mind."

There was a mutter of assent. *The Quaestor is a brave man too, in his way,* Tharasamund acknowledged. *He's thinking of the Kingdom's welfare.* And, from the way his eyes darted her way, his granddaughter's.

An idea blossomed. "Sir, I have an idea. Some of those men who turned our way were mounted, and they've identified this coach. What we need to do is to get you to a place of safety for a few hours, until the city's brought back to order. Do you see that half-built whatever-it-is on the hill up ahead? We can…"

"This doesn't look much like what I'd anticipated," the archbishop said, peering at the wide screen.

Maximus snorted. He wasn't an expert, but he *had* scanned the briefing. This was the beginning of the Wars of Reunification; what did the cleric expect, a festival with wreaths and flowers and incense?

The pilot's long nose twitched. There would be incense down there, all right, of a type he'd seen on previous expeditions. Things burning; people too, possibly. That sort of thing happened, if you went this far back. For a long time to come, too.

"There!" he said aloud, and everyone crowded up behind him; he ran a hand through a light-field to make sure nobody tripped a control by mistake. "There, that's *him!*"

The screen leapt, magnification increasing as the computer obeyed his intent—that was a virtue of the more modern types; they did what you wanted them to do, not just what you told them.

A carriage drawn by four matched black horses galloped out of an alley and turned westward, swaying as the coachman stood on his seat and lashed them with a whip. The overhead cover had been partly cut away; Maximus froze a portion of the screen to show the face of an old man. The computer helpfully listed the probability of this being the man they were after. It was as near unity as no matter. This was also the earliest era when photographs of famous men were available, and enough had survived into modern times to be digitized.

Somebody made a half-disgusted sound. "He's so... so *ugly,*" one said. The archbishop made a reproving sound. Maximus nodded, agreeing for once. It wasn't the man's fault that regeneration therapy wouldn't be invented for another two hundred years, or perfected for three. One thing time travel taught you was how fortunate you were to be born in the tenth century A.D.

"And he's stopping!" the historian cried. "I wonder why?"

Maximus hid another snort, and swung the viewpoint. "At a guess, most learned one, because those cutthroats are after him, and he's planning on hiding before they get here."

"Are you sure this is a good idea, Captain?" Padway said.

The young Goth shrugged. "No, sir," he said, helping the older man down from the carriage. "But they ought to follow the coach. It's much more visible."

Padway wheezed a chuckle as they hurried into the unfinished building, around the heaps of sand and bricks and timber; it was always nice to meet a man who didn't promise more than he could deliver. The carriage spurred off, making a great show of haste but not moving as fast as it might. He made two mental notes: one to see that the coachman got something, if he made it out of this, and another to put in a good word for Captain Tharasamund. He'd had a *lot* of experience judging men, and there were never enough good ones around.

The first floor of the building was an echoing vastness smelling of raw brick and new cement, with a concrete slab floor, thin brick walls, and cast-iron pillars holding it all up. A lot of timber was piled about, and a rough staircase led to the second story. Tharasamund and Princess Jorith half-lifted Padway up the stairs and propped him against a pile of sacks of lime mortar; then the Gothic soldier ran to a window, standing beside it and peering out through boards nailed over the unfinished casement.

"Oh, Sathanas take it," he said.

"They didn't follow the coach?" Padway asked.

"Most of them did. Two mounted men are turning in here, and a crowd of what look like ruffians after them. My apologies, sir," he finished, with bitter self-reproach.

"You took a chance. I agreed. If you bet, you lose sometimes."

Tharasamund saw Padway's eyes flick to Jorith's face and then away. His own lips compressed. *Damned if I'll let a mob get their hands on a royal princess,* he thought. *But by all the saints, what can I do about it?*

Fighting was the only thing that came to mind. Tharasamund had a healthy opinion of his own abilities in that line, but fighting off what looked like fifty or sixty men wasn't in the realm of the possible, even with a narrow approach and slum scum on the other side.

"Do what you can, then," he said to himself, looking around.

He had six shots in his revolver, and three reloads in his belt pouches....

He heard voices below and set himself. One of the men he'd seen riding came into view, urging his followers on, a short muscular-looking fellow in respectable but drab riding clothes, with a neatly trimmed black beard. The Goth let the long barrel of his revolver drop over his left forearm, squeezed....

Crack. The man toppled backward, screaming, and then screaming that his leg was broken—screaming in Greek. An educated man's dialect, but a native speaker's, as well. There were such folk in the Western Empire—parts of southern Italy and much of Sicily spoke Greek as their first language—but he would have bet his father's lands against a spavined mule that the man had been born not far from Constantinople.

Tharasamund dodged back as someone emptied a pistol at him; probably the other Greek. Whoever he was, the shooter started exhorting his men to attack; "Gothic heretics" and "two hundred gold crowns for their heads—each" seemed to be about equal inducements. It took a while, and he thought he knew the reason when he heard hasty sawing and hammering sounds.

"They're building a mantlet," he said grimly. At the confusion in the young woman's eyes, he went on: "A wooden shield, the sort they used to use in sieges. Wouldn't do them much good against a rifle, but a few layers of thick planks will turn a pistol ball."

Jorith raised her head. "I know I can rely on you, Captain," she said quietly. Tharasamund winced; he knew what she relied on him to do, and he didn't like it.

Well, that's irrelevant, he thought. *You'll do it anyway, and make it quick.*

Then her eyes went wide. "What's that you're leaning against, Grandfather?" she asked.

"Mortar," Padway said, raising a curious white brow.

"Lime," the girl said. "In the old days, during sieges, didn't—"

"They threw quicklime on men climbing siege ladders," Tharasamund half-whooped, with a strangled shout to keep the rioters and foreign agents below in the dark.

Padway moved himself aside, grinning slightly. Tharasamund moved towards the pile of sacks; Jorith halted him with an upraised hand.

"Wait," she said, and whipped off a gauzy silk scarf. "Those gauntlets will protect your hands, but your face—"

He bowed his head, and she fastened the thin cloth across his face like a mask; with the fabric close to his eyes, he could see out of it well enough. Then he worked, dragging the rough burlap sacks over towards the stairwell, carefully avoiding exposing his body to sight from below.

"Let's see," he muttered. "I'll stack them up here"—he made a pyramid of four, carefully weakening the lacing that held each sack closed at the top—"at the back of the stairwell, so they'll be above and behind anyone coming up the stairs. My lady Jorith? I'm afraid I'll need you to push."

He tried to keep his voice light, but there was a grave knowledge in the way she nodded.

"You up there!" a voice called. "Send us the old man, lay down your weapons, and we'll let you go!"

"And we can believe as much of that as we want to," Tharasamund called back. "No, thank you. Here's our deal: if you run now, before the troops come, I won't shoot you in the back."

"You'll be dead before then, you whipworthy barbarian!" the voice snarled. "You and your drab and the sorcerer too! *Take them!*"

The stairs were steep; Tharasamund had to go down on his belly to reach the upper one without exposing more than his eyes and gun hand. The mantlet—it was a door, with layers of planks nailed across it—came staggering upward. The hale Greek stood behind, firing over his men's heads to keep the Goth's down; he was half-concealed behind an iron pillar, and had his weapon braced against it.

Tharasamund swallowed against a dry throat and ignored him, ducking up to shoot at the feet of the men carrying the wooden bracer instead. Most of the shots missed. The targets were small and moving, and he had to snap-shoot in an instant, with no careful aiming. At last one hit, and the mantlet wavered and stalled as a man fell backward squalling and clutching at a splintered ankle.

"Now, Jorith!" he shouted.

The girl had lain down behind the sacks, with her slippered feet braced against them. She shoved, and they wavered and toppled forward. Momentum took over, and the sacks tumbled down. Acrid white dust billowed in choking clouds, and Tharasamund reflexively threw an arm across his face, coughing. One of the toughs behind the mantlet looked up and shouted, gesturing frantically—and his comrades followed the pointing arm, which was the worst possible thing they could have done.

Screams sounded sweetly, and strangled curses. The mantlet was thrown aside to crash on the hard cement floor beneath, and men ran—up out of the cloud of alkaline dust, or down and away from it. The Goth grinned behind his protecting face mask as he bounded erect and drew his *spatha*. A man staggered up the stairs, coughing and wheezing, his eyes already turning to bacon-rind red.

He swung a club. Tharasamund skipped neatly over it and lunged, his point skewering down over the thug's collarbone; muscle clamped on it, and he put a booted foot on the other's chest and pushed him back onto his fellows. More cursing and crashing; then two came forward, with their handkerchiefs held over their mouths. Both had swords, and one even had some idea of what to do with it. For a long minute it was clash and clatter and the flat unmusical rasp of steel on steel, and then the Goth sheered off half a face with a backhand cut.

"*Ho, la, St. Wulfias!*" he shouted exultantly, then found himself coughing again; some of the dust had gotten through the silk, and his eyes were tearing up as well.

Jorith came up beside him and offered a flask. He drank; it was citron water, and he used some to wash his eyes as well. The acid in it stung, but it would be better than leaving lime dust under his eyelids.

"Saw them off, sir," he wheezed to Padway, and Jorith clapped her hands and rose on tiptoe to kiss him. At another time, he would have paid more attention to that, but...

"For now," Padway said. "But if Justinian didn't send idiots, and his *agentes in rebus* usually are fairly shrewd, they'll—"

The noise below had mostly been bellowing, cries of pain and shrieks of *I'm blind!* and departing footfalls as many of the strong-arm squad decided there were better things to do in a riot-stricken city than have quicklime poured over their heads.

Now a crackling sound arose as well. All three looked at each other, hopelessly hoping that someone would deny that the sound was fire. When smoke began to drift up from between the floorboards, no doubt at all was left.

"Captain," Padway said.

"Sir?"

"I'm going to give you an order," he said. "You're not going to like it, but you're going to do it anyway."

"Sir—"

"Grandfather—"

"Take Jorith and get out of here," Padway rasped. "No, shut up. I'm an old man—a very old man—and I haven't six months to live anyway."

Jorith went white, and Padway waved a hand and then let it fall limp. "Didn't want to spoil your birthday, kitten, but that's what the doctors say. My lungs. Maybe I shouldn't have sent that expedition to find tobacco.... I've lived longer than I ever had a right to expect anyway. Now get out—they won't have enough men to chase you, not when they see I'm not with you. I put my granddaughter in your hands. That is your trust."

A racking cough, and a wheeze: "*Go!*"

Tharasamund hesitated, but only for an instant. Then he brought his sword up in a salute more heartfelt than most he'd made, sheathed it, and put a hand on Jorith's shoulder as she knelt to embrace her grandsire.

"Now, my lady," he said.

She came, half-stunned, looking back over her shoulder. Tharasamund snatched up a coil of rope, made an end fast, looked out to the rear. Padway had been right; there were only two men out there, and they backed away when they saw the tall soldier coming down the rope, even hindered with a woman across his shoulder. He landed with flexed knees, sweeping the princess to her feet and drawing steel in the same motion.

"Follow me... and *run*," he said.

"No!" He turned, surprised that she disobeyed. Then he stopped, forgetting her, forgetting everything.

Light speared his eyes, and he flung up a hand and squinted. Light, not the red of flames, but a blinding light whiter than the very thought of whiteness in the mind of God. In the heart of it, a brazen chariot shone mirror-bright, turning gently with a ponderous motion that gave an impression of overwhelming weight—it must be visible to all Florence, as well.

The roof of the building exploded upward in a shower of red roofing tile and shattered beam, and through it he could see a form rising.

It was Martinus Paduei. It could be nobody else. Borne upward on a pillar of light...

Dimly, he was aware of the remaining rioters' screaming flight, followed by their Greek paymaster. He was a little more aware of Jorith beside him, tears of joy streaming down her face as she sank to her knees and made the sign of the cross again and again. He sank down beside her, holding up his sword so that it also signed the holy symbol against the sky. The light was pain, but he forced his eyes open anyway, unwilling to lose a moment of the sight.

There was a single piercing throb of sound, like the harp of an angel taller than the sky and the light was gone, leaving only the fading afterimages strobing across his vision.

"He was a saint!" Jorith sobbed. "Oh, Grandfather—"

"Yes," the young man said. "I don't think there's much doubt about that now. He *was* a saint."

He looked down into the girl's face and smiled. "And he told me to take care of you, my lady Jorith. We'd better go."

Martin Padway opened his eyes, blinking. For a long moment he simply lay on what felt like a very comfortable couch, looking at the faces that surrounded him. Then two thoughts sent his eyes wide:

I don't hurt. That first. All the bone-deep aches and catches were *gone*, all the pains that had grown so constant over the years that he didn't consciously notice them. Yes, *but* how *I notice them now they're gone!* he thought.

The second thought was: *They're all so* young! There were a round dozen men and women, every color from ebony-black to pink-white via a majority of brown that included several East

Asian types. But none of them looked over twenty; they had the subtle signs—the flawless fine-textured skin, the bouncing *freshness* of movement—that were lost in early adulthood. It was far more noticeable than the various weirdnesses of their clothing.

Behind them were what looked like movie screens showing aerial shots, or various combinations of graphs and numbers, all moving and in different colors.

"Time travelers, right?" he said. *After all, I* know *time travel is possible. I've had going on fifty years to get used to the concept.*

One man—young man—gave a satisfied smile. "Instant comprehension! Just as you'd expect from a superior individual. I told you that the Great Man theory—"

He seemed to be talking upper-class sixth-century Latin, until you noticed that his lip movements weren't quite synchronized with the words and there was a murmur of something else beneath it.

Fascinating, Padway thought. *And that's an academic riding a hobbyhorse, or I was never an archaeologist.* Evidently some things were eternal.

Some of the others started arguing. Padway raised a hand:

"Please! Thank you very much for saving my life, but if you wouldn't mind a little information…"

"Yes, excellent sir," another man said—he was in a plain coverall, albeit of eerily mobile material. "From four hundred years in your future. We are—well, mostly—a study team investigating a crucial point in history… your lifetime, in fact, excellent sir."

"Four centuries in which future?" Padway said. "Gothic Rome, or my original twentieth? Twentieth century A.D.," he went on, to their growing bewilderment.

There was a long moment of silence. Padway broke it. "You mean, you didn't *know?*" he said.

The argument started up again, fast enough that Padway caught snatches of the language it was actually in, rather than the who-knew-how translation. His mind identified it as a Romance-derived language; something like twentieth-century Italian, but more archaic, and with a lot of Germanic loan words and other vocabulary he couldn't identify.

A slow, enormous grin split the ancient American's face. "Fifty years," he murmured.

Fifty years of politics and administration and warfare and engineering. None of them his chosen profession, just the things he had to do to survive and keep the darkness from falling. If this bunch were from only four centuries ahead in the future *Padway* had made, he'd done that, with a vengeance; they were from the date that in Padway's original history had seen the height of the Vikings.

He'd kept the darkness at bay, and now… now he could go back to being a research specialist. The grin grew wider.

Better than that, he'd actually get to *know how things turned out!* Making history was all very well, but he'd always wanted to read it more.

COMPADRES

(WITH RICHARD FOSS)

The man who would be President in half an hour hopped into the open carriage with boyish energy and eyed the still figure who sat waiting for him. The big, somberly dressed man was as quiet as a cat, a relaxation that was complicit of motion, ready without tension.

"Are you ready, Senator?"

"Can anybody ever be ready for something like this?" The soft accent of the southern desert was still strong in his voice. "Twenty thousand people staring at the son of a mule driver while he takes the oath that means he is one heartbeat away from the Presidency?"

The Vice President flashed his famous grin, and the Senator noticed a few more gray hairs in his bushy reddish mustache. "We faced nearly that many at San Juan Hill, or at least it seemed so at the time. The Spanish were better armed, and considering the acumen of Senator Bryan, I should say they were also better led. Buck up, Francisco."

The Senator smiled. "You know, Theodore, you are the only one who calls me that."

"And you are about the only one courteous enough to remember my Christian name as well, no matter how I may correct the others when they shorten it. Back when I was Police

Commissioner a pressman told me that as I was always making news, printing my name in the briefest manner possible saved paper and ink."

I have been called many things, Francisco thought. *All the way back to the day at the mine…*

"Git yo' back into it, y'fuckin' greaser!" The miner rose, slowly. He was a dark young man of medium height, turned browner still by the desert sun. The great open-pit mine around them rang with the sounds of pick and sledgehammer and shovel, with the clang of ore thrown into steel cocopans, with the voices of men and the hooves of mules. Distantly, a *crump!* came as dynamite shattered stone; the air smelled of rock dust, hot stone, sweat. Harsh southwestern sunlight streaked sweat through the white dust on the miner's face, bearing the bitter taste of alkali to his lips; heat reflected back from the white stone in an eye-squinting glare. Those lips quirked in the beginnings of a smile as he thought how it must sting the skin of the foreman, which had turned boil-red and hung in strips despite the wide hat he wore. He was from Alabama, with a cracker's long, lanky build and pale, washed-out blue eyes.

"I cannot haul the cocopan myself, señor," he pointed out reasonably. "And the mules need water and rest."

Then his hand moved with blurring swiftness, up under the rear of the baggy, dirty peon blouse he wore. His face broke into a smile, showing teeth nearly as bright as the stubby-bladed knife now resting in the soft skin beneath the foreman's throat. The tip was right next to the artery, just dimpling the surface, and a bead of sweat curved as it ran past. The dark man's voice sounded as calm and patient as before.

"… And if you call me a fucking greaser again, hijo da puta, I will cut your throat. Do you understand this?"

Hatred glared back at him, through the eyes of a man driven to the edge of madness by prickly heat rash and fatigue. "You're finished here—finished," the man croaked.

"I quit," the miner said succinctly. "And because you are a brave man to speak so, with a knife at your throat, I will let you live this once."

He stepped back and lowered the weapon, looking around at the circle of silence that had fallen among those who could see the little drama.

"Adiós!" he called, grinning at the cheers that rang out; cheers from Hispano and Anglo and the few Chinese as well. Then he cut the mule's traces with a few swift jerks of the steel, vaulted to its back (how unfortunate that it was not a fine stallion with a long sweeping mane), and flourished his sombrero.

"Go with God! I'm going to Cuba!" he called to the miners, and there were cheers as he clapped his heels into the mule's flanks.

The Senator blinked at his friend, shaking off the memory. A long time. Much time, much change since then. The proverb he had heard so often as a child ran through his mind: *Sin Novedad.* May no new thing arise.

But perhaps this should be discarded, this saying. For have not many new things arisen in my life, and most of them fortunate?

One of the horses at the front of the carriage shied as a photographer's flash gun misfired, tossing sparks in all directions. The two men inside looked on approvingly as the driver expertly calmed his team.

"That one would have been an asset at Santiago, when we lost our supplies thanks to bad horsemanship," observed the Senator. "We shall have to see that the army can pay men as good as this one to handle their wagons."

"They just up and died," the young teamster whined, tears in his eyes. "They just up and died."

The officer controlled his own mount with effortless skill, stroking a hand down its arched neck. Sweat lay heavy on its skin, and on his.

This was not like the mesquite country where he had been born. The land south of El Paso was hot, yes; the very anvil of the sun, drying men to jerky and making women old before their time. But at least it was dry. The air sucked the sweat off your skin, and if you drank much you would not die of the sun-fever.

Here… He looked around. Here you felt that something was growing on you, like a mold on a rawhide. The rank green growth around him gave shade that did not refresh; all the trees whose names he did not know were overgrown with shaggy vines, sugarcane rippled in the fields at the height of a mounted man's head, flowers in the ditches beside the rutted mud track flourished in great bursts of purple and crimson.

The air was heavy in his lungs, thick and wet and hot, full of the buzz of insects and the rank smells of lush growth, full of birds with gaudy feathers. Only the houses of the village in the distance had anything familiar about them, tile roofs and whitewashed walls.

Unconsciously, his hand touched the long machete strapped to the left side of his silver-studded charro saddle. The guerilleros were pro-American and anti-Spanish, but they were also half-bandit, and the supply train was a temptation to such starvelings.

And my men are hungry! he thought angrily, and swung out of the saddle. A quick examination of the foundered animals brought his temper to a boil. There were deep weeping harness-galls on their gaunt hides, and the hooves were splintered where the shoes had come off.

"Son of a whore!" he shouted as the wagoneer shrank trembling against the slatted boards of the vehicle. "Don't you know enough to check for footrot? When was the last time you fed these poor beasts?"

He reined in his fury; tongue-lashing the incompetent would not bring the animals back to usefulness. Instead he turned to the patrol that had ridden in with him.

"Sergeant!"

A tall Montanan straightened in the saddle. "L'tenet?" he asked, shifting his quid of tobacco to the other cheek.

"Take five men and go back to the hacienda we passed. There will be animals: horses, mules, oxen. Round them up and bring them here. If there aren't enough, bring the workers in the ingenio; yes, and the hacendado himself. My men will get these supplies, on the Cubans' backs if no other way!"

"Yessir!" the sergeant said, and pulled his Winchester from its saddle-scabbard. "You heard the man, boys! Yo!"

The officer drew his pistol and turned to the horse that lay in the mud before him, its eyes glassy and blank. Some of the others might be saved, but this one he could give only the mercy of a bullet.

The Vice President was speaking, in that high-pitched voice that went so strangely with his burly chest and big-toothed grin:

"We shall see to the army and much more, Francisco, in the next few months. But we shall do none of it if we do not get on our way to the Capitol."

He adjusted his glasses—two small lenses on the bridge of his nose, without earpieces—and directed his attention forward to the driver. "We are ready, sir. Onward to the inauguration!"

Crowds lined the broad avenues of Washington. They cheered as they saw the carriage approach, with its mounted escort before and behind in a glitter of polished brass and steel. The Vice President acknowledged them solemnly, as befitted the occasion. He had gotten his first term because McKinley had fallen to an assassin's bullet, but he had won his second fair and square, after proving that he could indeed uphold the dignity of the office. On this day in 1905, he was more restrained than his usual ebullient self, more formal and proper than anyone had ever seen him.

Yet his companion could sense the coiled eagerness there, the will to command and the certainty of what to command.

Theodore always seems to be urging men forward, thought the Senator. *And because he is who he is, they will follow him, even though the path he leads is through Hell. Now he is urging a whole country forward, and I pity the ones who do not want to go in the same direction. Luckily, I agree with him, at least so far. We have ridden together a long way since the Rough Riders. And now we ride to the White House. If he had not needed an officer who spoke Spanish, where would I be riding now? Among the mesquite and saguaro of home, perhaps fighting the bandit gangs, perhaps joining them?*

Theodore's voice broke in on his thoughts. "Thinking back, Francisco? You have a look on your face that reminds me of the night before the charge."

"Yes, I was there for a moment," the Senator replied. "Seven years ago, and sometimes it seems like yesterday, sometimes another life entirely. We have come far indeed."

"And we shall go farther still once we get to the dais, which I hope we shall by Christmas," Theodore observed flatly. "Driver, your pardon, but what is the reason for this delay?"

The coachman's deferential answer was in such a low tone that Theodore had to lean forward. Francisco leaned back, studying the blustery gray sky. Whoever had suggested the District of Columbia for a capital city had been mad or malevolent, he decided. Too wet in spring, too humid in summer, barely tolerable in fall and hell in winter. It would be better to be fighting in Cuba again than sitting under a blustery March sky in Washington. It would almost be better to be working back at the mine again... no, nothing was worse than that, or he wouldn't have left to join the Rough Riders in the first place.

Such a madly assorted bunch of men those warriors were, roughnecks from the West, adventurers from the East, Englishmen, Germans, Indians, Negroes from both America and Africa, even a few Chinese who held their heads up and fought and cussed just like everybody else. He had come to Theodore's attention thanks to his horsemanship, stayed in his awareness because he, Francisco, had that something that made men follow. He had stayed because Theodore had that something that made even leaders follow, made them glad and grateful to do so.

He had said as much the night before San Juan Hill, the Senator remembered. Francisco had been bent over the hoof of a horse that a picket had found wandering loose when he heard someone coming up behind him.

"Inspecting the animals again, Lieutenant? Bully! Where do you think that one came from, an American unit or Spanish?"

"Local, Colonel Roosevelt, and unfit for anything but pack work as he stands. There isn't a well-shod horse or a well-maintained rifle on this whole island, except the ones we brought with us. Or a well-cooked meal, including the ones we brought with us."

"Blame the outfitters who sold the army that vile tinned beef, not the poor souls who have tried to make something of it. Corporal Hang Ah has thrown away the stuff that came out of the tins green, and he has done all that can be done with the rest."

"I have no doubt he works miracles with what he has, and I will remember to compliment him on his skill the next time I see him."

"You will, Lieutenant, and he will take heart from it. Do you know, you are the only one of my officers who would think to do so. Though you first served me as an interpreter, I will have you know that I consider you an able leader of men, one whose instincts I trust. You have the gift of command, and I shall rely on you to give the men courage tomorrow."

"I will give all that I have, Colonel. I swear it on my honor," Francisco said earnestly.

"That men such as you will take such an oath assures us of victory. It is the job of a commander to inspire competent men, so that the whole army may be led with both valor and skill. God has given me the gift of command, and God or Divine Providence has sent me a man such as you who will be my strong right arm. It could not be otherwise."

"It could have been different, Colonel Roosevelt. Remember, there were two drafts of the treaty after the war with Mexico in my grandfather's time. If the commissioners had signed the other one, with the borderline drawn to the north instead of to the south of Chihuahua, I would have been born on the other side. There are Mexicans fighting us here, you know, volunteers and irregulars. I found one of them dying on the beach yesterday—he begged me for water in a Veracruz accent. Only a hundred miles from where I was born, a hundred miles and a border."

"You have no second thoughts? No feeling of kinship for those with whom your people shared a language and culture?"

"You and I share a language as well, one I have spoken since I was a child. The officers we capture have the accent of Castille , of the grandees who have their position because of their birth, not the plain Spanish my parents spoke in their stables and kitchens. As for culture, Chihuahua was never truly part of Mexico. My father told me tales of the old days; the taxmen everywhere, the police so corrupt that we feared them more than the bandits in the hills. No, I am with you. I will live or die with you, and I will be able to tell my children that I had the honor of riding with Theodore Roosevelt, whom they will call Teddy like everyone else."

A grin stretched the Colonel's red mustache, and he put

out his hand. "And I will be honored to tell mine that I have ridden with Lieutenant Pancho Villa, though tomorrow we shall ride apart. You shall have the left flank, I the right, and I shall meet you atop San Juan Hill."

The carriage was moving slowly, to allow the maximum number of residents and visitors to view the newly elected President. The majesty of the moment affected even the naturally buoyant Roosevelt, who sat erect and waved to the crowd with more restraint than usual. He perked up at the sight of a pair of boys still in the short pants of childhood who shrieked in excitement, evidently as much at seeing the fancy coach and mounted guards as the occupants of the carriage. They ran between the militia who were trying to keep the crowd back, and Theodore laughed at the awkwardness of the police trying to catch them.

"Those boys are as excitable as a pair of freshly minted privates," he chuckled.

"And as much use in a charge," agreed Francisco.

He had expected fear, on the day of battle. He had not expected such confusion. The tall grass on the hill ahead waved in the breeze that blew the smoke of the Americans' black-powder weapons into a haze around the troops. All around him he heard the slow barking of single-shot carbines, the ripping-canvas growl of the Gatlings, the occasional bark of a fieldpiece. The Spanish forces on the ridge above were returning fire with their smokeless-powder Mausers, invisible to eyes or field glasses, the high-velocity bullets passing with a vicious flat whipcrack sound. Over it he could hear men shouting, the horses neighing in terror as they were led over the mushy ground toward territory suitable for a gallop. A few American pickets who had been scouting the area withdrew from the field at something which approached but wasn't quite a dead run.

The flight of the well-dressed soldiers was a marked contrast to the motley but disciplined Rough Riders, who surged forward toward the hidden enemy.

"Forward! *Arriba!*" Francisco shouted.

He raised his voice in a high yipping war-cry and waved his hat towards the Spanish positions. There was fear in his own heart, but pride drove it out as he saw men take heart from his example and surge up the hill behind him. Their eyes upon him did not banish fear, but they made it so much easier to overcome.

The Colonel will not fail me, he thought. *And I will not fail my men.*

The dome of the Capitol came into view, and an instant later they saw the wooden platform which had been erected for the occasion. The black robes of Chief Justice Fuller stood out among the morning coats and striped trousers of the dignitaries and diplomats, the contrast magnified by his shock of white hair waving in the light breeze. Fuller wore his customary air of cool reserve, a marked contrast to the celebratory air of most of the men around him.

One other expression was different—Mark Hanna, the Republican Senator who fancied himself the party's kingmaker, stared at the men in the carriage with unconcealed disgust. When Roosevelt met his eyes, he turned abruptly and started talking to one of his aides.

"Our friend Senator Hanna seems to have eaten something which disagrees with him," mused Theodore happily.

"His hopes, perhaps," suggested Francisco. "He will be an old man in four years, too old to run for President himself, and you will have that time to change this country. You will fight the big corporations and trusts that are dear to him, the railroad barons who are his friends. You will take the country in a direction he does not understand."

"We will do that," exclaimed Theodore, clapping a comradely hand on his shoulder. "Both of us," he affirmed as the carriage came to a stop.

A crush of people surged forward, local dignitaries mixed with Pinkertons, military officers, and a few garishly dressed men with notebooks. In a moment they were surrounded by the crowd. Most converged on Theodore, but one singled out Francisco.

"Mr. Vice President…" he began.

"Not yet, but in a while," replied Francisco.

The man stopped a moment, twisted his long blond mustache thoughtfully, and continued. "Ah, yes, that's right. I ask your pardon. Well then, Senator Villa, I'm Ambrose Bierce of the *Sacramento Bee*, and I'd like to ask you a few questions…."

Both men were distracted as a scuffle broke out nearby. The military police were taking no chances after President McKinley's assassination, and a squad was shoving the crowd back toward the sidewalk.

The reporter hesitated a moment, and Francisco took his hand. "Now is not the time, my friend. Come to my office this afternoon, and I will talk to you then." The reporter nodded gratefully, then hopped toward the sidewalk as a sergeant brandished his baton.

"Making friends with the press?" asked Theodore as the two men walked toward the dais.

"He had good manners, and was the first person to call me Mr. Vice President," answered Francisco. "I have just gotten used to being called Senator, and now I must get used to this new title. Besides, he was a Westerner, and I like them better than the Eastern newspapermen, who are always too cynical."

"Now Francisco, we are one people," chided Theodore gently. "Even if I do agree with you in favoring Westerners, and would take a Colorado farmer or Montana ranch hand over twenty Mark Hannas. Still, I would not have you judge even all Democrats by him."

"There were good men from everywhere at San Juan Hill…." agreed Francisco as they ascended to the platform.

"Now!" cried Theodore, and the bugles blared. The Rough Riders started moving forward slowly, gaining momentum with every step like a tightly wound spring uncoiling. A tall dark Métis trapper who wore a red sash over his uniform whooped as his horse picked up speed, and fired his revolver at the distant Spanish, then jerked back in the saddle as a bullet hit him in the chest. The wet slap of lead on flesh was unpleasantly audible as blood gouted.

A wiry redhead who wore a green bandolier grabbed the reins of the trapper's horse, keeping the animal under control and steadying the wounded man.

"Sure and I have him now, Pancho," the smaller man called in a thick brogue. "You'll have to shoot two for me, then!"

Francisco grinned and waved his hat while deftly maneuvering his horse past a shell crater, then spurred forward, his horse first in the line by a nose, racing toward the barbed wire at the base of San Juan Hill. A bullet went over his head with a flat, ugly crack, and he pulled his pistol and fired in the general direction of the Spanish redoubt without aiming, as a gesture of defiance as much as anything. More shots rang out around him, along with a ragged cheer mixed with shouted slogans, wordless yelps, and Apache war cries.

He joined in with his own yells of "Viva Teddy Roosevelt! Viva los Rough Riders!" and was surprised when the men around him took it up as a cheer.

The House Chaplain had been unusually brief at his oration, a prayer sprinkled with classical references that left a few people on the dais scratching their heads. Chief Justice Melville Fuller was speaking now, his nasal Maine accent making his formal invocation sound like a foreign language. His delivery was so flat that it took a moment after he had finished to realize that his most recent words had been:

"…preserve, protect, and defend the Constitution of the United States?"

Roosevelt's ringing "I shall!" was such a contrast that several people jumped, startled despite the inevitability of the response….

"And furthermore," Roosevelt continued, facing the crowd and projecting his voice in the eager strains which had carried over battlefields, "I shall endeavor to bring about a continuance of the march to greatness that was the mission of my predecessors in the glorious office."

For the first time the applause was more than polite, and the crowd standing below moved forward to hear as he continued his speech. "No people on earth have more cause to be thankful than ours, and I say that reverently, in no spirit of boastfulness of our own strength, but with gratitude to the Giver of Good who has blessed us with so large a measure of well-being and happiness…."

He has them now, thought Villa, *just as he did when we stood at the top of San Juan Hill amid the stink of blood and powder, and I cheered him with the rest of the men. This Easterner with the vigor of the West is going to take this country and stitch it together, from Alaska in the north to Sonora and my Chihuahua in the south, and he will make it one, and make it proud. He is going to take on the best of the Democrats and the worst of his own party, and he will vanquish them both and they will never know why or how, and the most able of them will follow him, will give up everything else as I did, will make themselves better men in the process as I did. When I retire to my hacienda in Chihuahua, as I will someday, flattering men will say I was destined for greatness. The men who remember the miner with the knife, the bandito I once was, they are all dead now, and maybe nobody but me will know that the smooth-talking men are lying. I could have joined the ones in the hills, been their*

Teddy Roosevelt perhaps, worked against all I now hold dear. Whatever I could have been, I am the man you trusted your flank to at San Juan Hill, and I will defend you through shot and shell and congressional committees and whatever else the world sends....

The President finished his speech and paused for effect, his famous grin wide on his face.

And I will hail you in the way of my tradition, so when the news gets back to Chihuahua they will know I have not become entirely a creature of this filthy Northern city of pale people.

Francisco seized Theodore's hand in his own and raised it high, shouting with all his might the same phrase that had rung out over the battlefield by the Santiago road.

"Viva Theodore Roosevelt!"

THE CHARGE OF LEE'S BRIGADE

Brigadier General Sir Robert E. Lee, Bart., had decided that the Crimea was even more detestable than Mexico; even more than Texas, and that was going very far indeed. In all his twenty years of service as a professional soldier, he couldn't recall any place he'd been sent that even rivaled the Crimea—only Minnesota came close, and that only in winter. Even in Minnesota, he'd only had the Sioux to contend with, and not General Lord Raglan, the commander-in-chief of the Imperial expeditionary force.

He sighed, signed the last of the quartermaster's receipts, and ducked out of his tent, settling his sword belt as he did so, and tucking his gauntlets through it. It could have been worse; he might have persisted with his original plan to become a military engineer, and then he'd have been stuck trying to move supplies through the Crimean mud. There were scattered clouds above, casting shadows over the huge grassy landscape about him, with hardly a tree in sight. It reminded him of West Texas, come to that. Although Cossacks and Tatars were more of a nuisance than the Comanche had ever been. Not for want of trying, of course.

I wonder if Father spent as much time on paperwork as I do? he thought. Probably not; "Light Horse Harry" Lee had never commanded more than a regiment in the Peninsula, although he'd added considerable luster to the Lee name there, earned a baronet's title and along the way saved the family estate at Stratford Hall from ruin and bankruptcy. Perhaps the world had been a simpler place then, too, and an officer hadn't had to spend an hour before breakfast catching up on the damned forms and requisitions. Certainly the Iron Duke would never have let a campaign bog down the way Raglan had.

He sat down to breakfast with his aides, and the half hour he allowed himself for personal correspondence. The coffee was strong—Turkish, in fact—and there was a peculiar taste to the local bacon, but his Negro orderly Percy was a wonder as a forager, even when he didn't speak the local languages. The first letter was from Mary. Her joints were still annoying her; he frowned at the news. She was young for arthritis, and the news fanned his disquiet at being so much away; Mary rarely said a word about it, but he knew she'd been much happier when he was stationed near home as colonel of the 1st Virginia. And young Mary had the whooping cough ... Enclosed was the latest from Sitwell, the overseer. There was a certain pleasure to the homely, workaday details of Stratford Hall's operations; so much for guano, an experiment with the new superphosphate, the steam thresher working well, and excellent prices for this year's wheat crop. His brows went up at the figures; a bushel was fetching five shillings sixpence FOB Richmond! Although the harvest wages the freedmen were demanding ate up a good deal of it; the competition from the factories of Richmond and Petersburg was driving wages to ridiculous levels. Unlike many he'd never complained about the Emancipation Act of 1833 (and the compensation had been very welcome in clearing the last of his father's debts) but it did complicate a planter's life. Perhaps he should look into buying the contracts of a few Mexican or Chinese indentured laborers, they were popular in Texas and California these days. With these prices, he could afford to experiment.

War always went with inflation, and the Californian gold wasn't hurting either.

He must have said that aloud. Captain Byrd, the youngest of his aides, replied, "Not only California, sir," and passed over a copy of the *Times*.

"Ah," he said. The story waxed enthusiastic about the new gold discoveries in... *Transvaal?* he thought. Then: Yes—*in the South African viceroyalty, far in the interior.*

"Truly we live in an age of progress," he said. What would his father have thought of great cities and mines springing up even in the heart of the Dark Continent, of railways transporting whole armies a hundred miles in a day? He skimmed another article, this one dealing with the siege of Vladivostok and the progress of the Far Eastern front in the war against Russia. *That might have been more interesting,* he thought. Certainly more mobile; but that part of the conflict was largely Indian troops, and the new Chinese Sepoy regiments. Reading between the lines he suspected that the Queen—God bless her—would be adding another to her list of titles at the conclusion of this war.

"Victoria, by the Grace of God Queen of Great Britain, Empress of North America, Empress of India and the Further East Indies, Sultana-Protectress of the Ottomans, Empress of Japan ... and soon, Empress of China?" he murmured.

"Persia too, I shouldn't wonder," Byrd said with a grin. "Queen of France, for that matter, except in theory."

Lee gave the younger man a frown; the French were touchy about that, and this army did include a large contingent from the Empire's continental satellite kingdom. Not that their sentiments mattered much—they hadn't since Wellington crushed the Revolutionaries and took Paris in '08—but it was ungentlemanly to provoke them. Father, he recalled, had done very well out of the sack of Paris. The Crimea was unlikely to yield any such returns, and in any case, standards of behavior had changed since the raffish days of George III and the Prince

Regent. War in the new era—the Victorian, they were calling it, after the Queen-Empress—was a more staid, methodical, and altogether more respectable affair, as befitted an age of prosperity and progress.

"To business, gentlemen," he said, rising and blotting his lips. He carefully tucked the letter from home into the breast of his uniform tunic.

The regimental commanders of the 1st North American Light Cavalry Brigade waited, as did his orderly with another cup of coffee. "Thank you, Percy," he said, taking it and stepping over to the map table. "Gentlemen," he went on, nodding to the men in the forest-green uniforms of the Royal North American Army.

They stood silent or conversed in low murmurs as he brooded over the positions shown. Balaclava to the south, in Imperial hands now. The Russians were still in force on the rising ground to the north, the Causeway Heights and the Fedoukine Heights beyond the shallow North Valley. More low ground lay to the west, and then the British headquarters on the Sapoune Heights.

The Americans were separately encamped to the south of Sapoune; they were comparatively recent arrivals, and besides that were anxious to avoid the camp fever that was ravaging the rest of the Imperial Army. He looked around at the orderly rows of canvas tents, the picket lines for the horses, the horse-artillery park. Everything was as it should be, smoke from the campfires, the smell of coffee and bacon and johnnycake, the strong familiar scent of horses. The 1st Virginia—Black Horse Cavalry, his own old regiment, now in Stuart's capable hands—the Lexington Hussars from Kentucky, the 22nd Maryland Lights, and the Charleston Dragoons. All Southerners, and he was glad of it; Yankees made fine infantry or gunners, but even their farmers just didn't ride enough to make first-rate cavalry, in his opinion. If a man still had to be trained to keep the saddle when he enlisted, it was ten years too late to make him into a horse soldier. Most of his troopers were from small planter or well-to-do yeoman families, with enough money to keep a stable and enough leisure to hunt the fox.

Most of them had seen service in Mexico too, apart from some recruits they'd picked up in Norfolk while waiting to be shipped across the Atlantic.

"For the present, the situation is static," he said. His finger traced the upper, eastern end of North Valley. "Those people are in strength here, and on the Causeway and Fedoukine Heights to either side. The French and elements of the British light cavalry are further north, skirmishing."

"No more Cardigan, thank God," someone muttered.

Lee looked up sharply, then decided to let the matter pass. Since 1832 Viceroy's Commissions in the forces of British North America had been theoretically equal to Queen's Commissions in the British army proper, but Lord Cardigan apparently hadn't heard the news and had a vocal contempt for all colonials. So had a number of his officers, and there had been unpleasant incidents, a few duels … .

Of course, the man's a snob of the first water. He looked down on all *British* officers who weren't blue-blooded amateurs as well. *A living example of why the British have such superb sergeant-majors.* With officers like Cardigan, you *needed* first-rate NCOs. There were times when he wondered how the Mother Country had managed to conquer half the world.

"Our latest orders are to move up *here*," he went on, putting his finger on a spot in the lowlands where the Causeway Heights most nearly approached Sapoune. "We're to be ready to move in support if the Imperial troops outside Balaclava need us. Any questions?" More silence.

"Please bear in mind, gentlemen, that the reputation of our regiments, our brigade, and the Royal North American Army rests in our hands. I expect brisk work today if those people bestir themselves. Let us all conduct ourselves in accordance with our duties, and our friends and kindred at home shall hear nothing to our discredit."

Stuart looked north, stroking his young beard and tilting the brim of his plumed hat forward for shade. "Can't be worse than Monterrey or Puebla, General," he said.

"Boots and saddles then, gentlemen."

The four regiments of American cavalry made a brave show as they trotted in column of fours past Lee's position; he saluted the flags at the head of each column, the Union Jack, the regimental banners, the starry blue of the Viceroyalty of British North America with its twenty-seven stars and Jack in the upper corner. The men looked fit for service, he thought; not as polished as the British cavalry units with their rainbow of uniforms and plumed headgear, but sound and ready to fight. Every man had an Adams revolver at his belt, a new Swaggart breech-loading carbine in a scabbard at his right knee, and a curved slashing-sword tucked under the saddle flap on his left. Better gear than the British horse; the Americans had stuck with the '97 pattern saber and kept them razor-sharp in wood-lined scabbards. The '43 Universal Pattern sword the British used was neither fish nor fowl in his opinion, and their steel scabbards dulled the blade. Many of the English troopers were still carrying muzzle-loading Enfield carbines or even, God help them, lances.

Even the horses had gotten their condition back, and the commissariat had finally got a supply of decent remounts coming in, Arabs and barbs from Syria—wastage among the horses had been shocking at first.

Lee's head tossed. *I have become a true professional,* he thought. *Logistics have become my preoccupation, and glory a tale for children.*

He stood in the stirrups and trained his binoculars on the Sapoune Heights. The figures of the Russian infantry were still doll-tiny, as they labored to drag away the heavy guns the British had lost to yesterday's assault—the position had been foolishly exposed, in any event. Their gray uniforms were lost against the dry grass and earth of the redoubts; the men were calling the enemy soldiers *graybacks,* in reference to the color of their coats and also to the ubiquitous Crimean lice. He could see one of the steam traction engines as well, bogged down and three-quarters toppled over. They did well on firm ground, but anything softer stopped them cold. *Horses will have to bear with the warlike habits of men awhile longer,* he thought, slapping Journeyman on the neck. The gelding tossed his head and snorted, ready for the day's work, as he might be on a crisp Virginia morning in fox-hunting season.

"Cavalry," he murmured, as morning light broke off lance-heads . "Cossacks, and regulars as well—a regiment at least, in addition to the gunners and infantry. Captain Byrd, what was the Intelligence assessment?"

"Several *Stanitsa* of Kuban and Black Sea Cossacks, sir, Vingetieff's Hussars, the Bug Lancers, and an overstrength regiment of the Czar's Guard cavalry," he said. "Do you think they will attack, sir?"

"The matter is in doubt. I would assume that those people have been given the task of covering the withdrawal of the captured guns, but I am informed that Russian behavior can be somewhat baffling—the Oriental influence, no doubt. Dismount and stand the men easy, Captain, but keep the girths tight."

He steadied a map across his saddle horn and pondered as the orders went out to the regimental commanders; behind there was a long rattle of saddles, boots, and stirrup irons. *That will keep the horses fresh,* he thought.

"Sir."

He looked around. A lone figure was galloping towards the Brigade's position, riding neck-for-nothing over irregular ground. A little closer and he recognized the tight crimson trousers of the Cherrypickers, Cardigan's own lancer regiment. The stiffness of his back relaxed slightly as he realized that it wasn't one of the regiment's regular officers. He recognized the man: one of Raglan's staff gallopers, a colonel. The man had an excellent reputation as a soldier in India—during the conquest of Afghanistan, and in the Sikh War, both of them prolonged and bloody affairs. Queen's Medal and the thanks of Parliament, but Lee thought him a rather flashy and raffish figure, for all his bluff John Bull airs and dashing cavalry muttonchop whiskers. *But he can ride,* Lee acknowledged grudgingly. Even by Virginian standards.

"Sir Robert," the man drawled as he reined in and saluted—public-school accent. *Rugby,* Lee remembered, and some faint whiff of scandal. "Lord Raglan commends your prompt movement, and wishes you to demonstrate before the heights in order to delay the enemy's removal of the guns."

Lee's eyebrows rose, and he tossed his head again. "Demonstrate, colonel? Am I ordered to attack, or not?"

"You are requested to use your initiative, Sir Robert," the staff officer said. "I might add that Lord Raglan is disturbed by the loss of the guns—Wellington never lost a gun, you know."

Lee scanned the written orders. As ambiguous as usual; he was becoming unpleasantly familiar with Raglan's style, and it was no wonder this campaign had taken a year. *We are very fortunate indeed that the Russians are not an efficient people,* he thought.

"Very well," he murmured, looking up at the Russian position again. The terrain and forces ran through his mind, much as a chess game might—except that here both players could move at once, and a piece once taken was unlikely to return to this or any other board.

"You will accompany me, Colonel. We will endeavor to satisfy Lord Raglan."

He cut the man's protests off with a gesture. An eyewitness with Raglan's ear would be able to give a more accurate picture than a written message afterwards.

"Captain Byrd," he went on. "My compliments to Colonel

Stuart, and he is to report immediately."

The Black Horse rode forward in jaunty style, taking their cue from their commander's plumed hat and fluttering crimson-lined cape. Stuart pulled out ahead and cantered down the ordered rows of men, waving his hat as they cheered.

"If you want some fun, jine the cavalry!" one of the troopers called out as Stuart rejoined the colors.

"Walk-march, *trot*," he said, and the buglers relayed it. Not the intoxicating crescendo of the *charge*, the most exciting sound a cavalryman could hope to hear, but good enough. The two years since the Mexican campaign ended had been boring, and chasing guerrillas through the deserts of Sonora was more like being a constable than real soldiering anyway.

The six hundred men and horses stretched out on either side of the regimental banner, pounding along at an in-hand trot. Clods of dark mud flew up where the horses' ironshod hooves broke the thick turf of the steppe, adding a yeasty smell of turned earth to the odors of human and equine sweat, leather and oil. Stuart stood slightly in the stirrups. They were stirring around up there, all right. The hive was active. Closer, closer—four hundred yards, and he could see the crossed chest-belts of uniforms, and the dangling string caps of the Kuban Cossacks.

"Now to sting 'em," he said, and gestured.

The bugle sang, and the whole regiment came to a smooth stop in line abreast; he felt a surge of pride—it took professionals with years of practice to do that under field conditions. Another call and in every second company the men drew the carbines from the saddle scabbards before their right knees and dismounted. One trooper in five took the reins of the others' horses; the other four went forward six paces and sank to one knee.

Stuart listened to the company officers and noncoms: "*Load!*" Each man worked the lever of his Swaggart and the breechblock dropped down. Hands went back to the pouches at their belts, dropped a brass cartridge into the groove atop the block, thumbed it home. A long *click-clank*, as the levers were worked again to close the actions.

"*Adjust your sights, pick your targets. Aim low. Five rounds, independent fire. Ready...fire!*"

BAAAMM. Dirty-white smoke shot out from two hundred and fifty muzzles. Then a steady crackling ripple, experts taking their time and making each shot count. Up among the thick-packed Russians milling among the redoubts, men fell and lay silent or sprattled, screaming. The soft-nosed .45 slugs of the Swaggarts did terrible damage, he'd seen that in Mexico. A round blue hole in your forehead, and the back blown out of your head—exit wounds the size of saucers.

"Remount," Stuart said, as muzzle flashes and powder smoke showed all along the line of the Russian position. *Might as well be shooting at the moon,* he thought. Nine-tenths of the Russian forces were still equipped with percussion smoothbores, muzzle loaders that were lucky to get off two shots a minute and *very* lucky to hit what they were aiming at if it was a hundred yards off. On the other hand, they had artillery up there, and as soon as they got it working...

A long whirring moan overhead, then a crash not far ahead of the line. A poplar of black dirt and smoke grew and collapsed before him. A few horses reared, to be slugged down by their riders' ungentle pressure on the reins. The troopers were swinging back into the saddles, resheathing their carbines, many of them grinning.

"Regiment will retire," Stuart said, smiling himself. Bobby Lee had told him to sting the Russians, and from the noise and confusion up there he'd done that, in spades. "Walk-march, trot."

Every horse wheeled to the left, a hundred and eighty degrees. *That'll give those Englishmen something to think about,* he thought. *Show them some modern soldiering.* The British cavalry reminded him of things he'd read about the Hundred Years' War—only they seemed to have taken the French cavalry as their model.

"Most impressive, Sir Robert," the English colonel said. "Ah… what do you expect Brother Ivan to do?"

"Nothing for a little while," Lee replied, keeping the binoculars to his eyes. "They rarely act in haste, I find. Nor do they coordinate the different arms of their forces well; however, they are formidable on the defense."

That was why he intended to provoke them into an attack, of course. In the next half hour or so the realization that he could sting the Russians any time he chose was going to seep through the thick Slavic skull of the Czarist commander up there. They couldn't leave his force in their front.

Time passed, and the Englishman fidgeted, rubbing at his stomach. Well, half the army had bowel complaints, with the foul water and worse food here—one of the common inglorious realities of soldiering. They'd called it "Montezuma's Revenge" or the "Puebla Quickstep" in Mexico. The ant swarm atop the heights shook itself down into some sort of order, and he could see teams sweating to turn the guns around; heavy guns, four-inch Armstrong rifles for the most part. That could be awkward, and would require him to retire. And… yes. The enemy cavalry were forming up in blocks by regiments—the blue and red of the regulars to the center, the formless gray of the Cossacks to either side. Six or seven thousand men, possibly more. Light broke off the lanceheads in a continuous rippling, and then the sabers of the hussars came out in a single bright flash, coming back to rest on their shoulders.

"Here they come, gentlemen," he said, and began giving orders in a quiet, unhurried voice, aware of the crackling excitement of his aides. *But then, they're young men.* He'd stopped feeling exhilarated at the sound of bullets about his ears well before the first gray appeared in his beard.

"Ah… will you retire, or dismount your men to receive them?" the English staff officer said.

Lee glanced at him. The man's fine English face was red with what looked like anger, but had that been a quaver in his voice? Lee dismissed the thought; the man had been in far worse situations in Afghanistan.

"Neither, Colonel," he said, looking to left and right. "Momentum is all, in these affairs. Prepare to charge," he added in a louder tone.

"But Sir Robert—it's *uphill!*"

A roar came from upslope as the Russian cavalry rolled downward, a mile-long line of blades and glaring bearded faces and red-rimmed horses' nostrils. Hooves drummed like the Four Horsemen riding out on mankind.

Lee smiled. "A good cavalry mount is always part jackrabbit," he said. "And we take care to select the best." He drew his own saber, holding it loosely down by his side.

"Charge!"

The buglers took up the call along the American line, a sweet insistent song. The twenty-five hundred men of the Brigade went forward up the gentle swelling of the hill, building swiftly to a hard pounding gallop. They cheered, not the deep-chested *hurrah* of the British but a wild wailing shriek that rose and fell like nails grating over slate.

You always expect a crash, but you never get it, Lee thought, as the formations met. *Horses have more sense than men; they won't run into an obstacle.*

Instead there was a blurring passage at the combined speed of both formations, enlivened by the tooth-grating steel-on-steel skirl of sabers meeting, the cracking of pistols, the shouting of men and the unbearable shrieking of wounded horses.

A Cossack burst lumbering through the screen of men ahead of Lee, roaring through a beard like a stomach-length mattress that had burst its cover. The little stiff-maned steppe pony beneath him looked almost comically small, but it was fast enough to propel the lance head with frightening speed. Lee had been subliminally aware of the Englishman beside him; then the man was gone. The Virginian spared a moment's glance that almost cost him his life, and saw the British colonel hanging off one side of his horse with a heel around the horn, firing from under its belly, for all the world like a Comanche except for his glaring red face. A soldier's reflexes turned him as much as the shout of the standard bearer beside him, and he beat the lance aside with a convulsive slash. The Cossack went by; then there was another Russian ahead of him, a dragoon drawing back for a cut. Lee thrust, and the point went home. The momentum carried him past and he let it tug the steel free. Then the way ahead was clear, only the rest of the heights and the Russian infantry to face.

A quick glance right and left. The Russians had been rocked back on their heels and split, hundreds dismounted or wounded or dead; the Americans were still in formation, despite a scattering of empty saddles. *Time, ask me for anything but time,* Napoleon had said.

"Rally, left wheel, and *charge,*" Lee said.

The trumpets sang again, and the whole Brigade began to pivot as if it was a baulk of timber and Lee and his staff the pivot. The officers were shouting to their men: the Marylanders in particular were a little ragged.

"Rally by the Virginians!" he heard, and allowed himself a little glow of Provincial pride.

"Charge!"

This time the path was downhill, and the Russian horse was caught in mid-wheel, caught in the flank and rear, nearly stationary. They broke, and he saw dozens going down under hooves and blades. Another halt-and-wheel brought the colonial regiments back to their starting place; he stood in the stirrups to make sure. If the enemy rallied quickly …

"They're skedaddlin," his aide said exultantly.

"That they are, Captain," Lee agreed, nodding soberly and cleaning his saber before resheathing it. The fragments of the Russian force were withdrawing—not even directly north towards the heights, but in clots and clusters and dribbles of men clustering around an officer or a banner. Behind them trailed horses running wild with empty saddles, and a thick scattering of men on foot, running or hobbling or crawling after them.

"Oh, most satisfactory," he said softly, then spurred out in front of the Brigade's ranks. "Well done!" he called. "Splendidly done!"

More cheers came. *"We'll whip 'em for you agin, Marse Bob!"*

"There, you see, Colonel," he said, as he reined in once more. "No harm done—to us, at least."

"No bloody thanks to you!" the man cried.

Lee frowned. *Ungentlemanly,* he thought.

"Guns?" Lee said. "Which guns, if you please, sir?" The new galloper from Lord Raglan seemed to be having a hard time holding his temper. Lee wasn't surprised; the staff around the supreme commander was riddled with factions and quarrels, and Raglan wasn't doing much to control it. The Virginian controlled his own irritation with an effort. He wished Raglan would compose the difficulties among his subordinates; he wished Raglan would take a firmer direction of the campaign. His wishes, however, had little or nothing to do with what Lord Raglan would actually do.

"Lord Raglan requests and desires that you seize the guns, Sir Robert," the galloper said. "Immediately."

Lee's brows rose. At least the order was decisive- ambiguous, but not vague. "I repeat, sir: *Which* guns? The enemy has a good many batteries in this vicinity."

The messenger flung out a hand. *"There,* sir. *There* are your guns."

Lee's face settled into a mask of marbled politeness. "Very

well, Captain. You may assure Lord Raglan that the Brigade will endeavor to fulfill his command."

Whatever it means, he added to himself. He looked north. Up the valley, with massive batteries on either side of it swarming with Russian troops, more guns and earthworks at the head of it, and huge formations of Russian cavalry and infantry in support. Then his eyes swung back to the Sapoune Heights before him, running east and west from the mouth of the valley.

"Messenger," he snapped, scribbling on his order pad as he gave the verbal equivalent. "Here. To Sir Colin, with the Highland Brigade: I request that he be ready to move rapidly in support." The man saluted and spurred his mount into a gallop. "Captain Byrd, the Brigade will deploy in line, with the 22nd Maryland in reserve. Immediately, if you please. The horse artillery battery will accompany us this time."

The regiments shook out to either side of him; he reached out, trying to feel their temper. It reassured him. The men had beaten a superior force that morning; they had a tradition of victory. *If men believe they will conquer, they are more than halfway to doing so.*

This time they were going to *need* every scrap of confidence they could wring out of their souls. He looked left and right, drew his saber again, and sloped it back against his shoulder.

"Brigade will advance at the trot," he said quietly.

Bugles rang, shrill and brassy. The long line of the formation broke into movement, shaking itself out with the long ripple of adjustment that marked veteran troops. Ahead lay the long valley, and the first ranging shots from the Russian batteries on either side came through the air with a ripping-canvas sound—old-fashioned guns, but heavy, twenty-four and thirty-two pounders. Shot plowed the turf, and shells burst in puffs of dirty-black smoke with a vicious red snap at their hearts. One landed not twenty yards to his right, and a section of the orderly front rank of the 1st Virginia was smashed into a bubble of chaos: writhing, thrashing horses screaming like women in labor but heartrendingly loud; men down, one staggering on foot with his face a mask of red and an arm dangling by a shred.

"Steady there, steady."

The voice of a troop commander, sounding so very young. The troopers opened their files to pass the obstacle and then closed again, adjusting their dressing to the regulation arm's length.

"Not up the valley, for Christ's sake!" That was the British colonel.

"Of course not," Lee snapped, letting his irritation out for a moment. Did the man think he was a complete idiot?

"Brigade will wheel to the right," Lee went on. Gallopers fanned out, and bugles sounded. That was a complex maneuver, with so many men in motion. "Right, wheel."

To his left, the 1st Virginia and the Lexington Hussars rocked into a canter. To his right, the Charleston Dragoons reined in, checking their pace. Smooth and swift, the whole formation pivoted until it was facing the junction of the valley with the Sapoune Heights—where neither the Russian batteries nor the captured British guns could fully bear on the North Americans.

Not fully was a long way from not bearing at all, and as the Russian gunners perceived their target he could see muzzle flashes from the heights ahead, and from the batteries behind him came the wailing screech of shells fired at extreme range. *Time to get us across the killing field,* he thought, consciously relaxing his shoulders and keeping his spine straight and easy in the saddle.

"Charge!" he said.

The bugles cried it, high and shrill. This time there would be no retreat, and every man in the Brigade knew it. The troopers were raising their screeching cheer again, a savage saw-edged ululation through the rising thunder of thousands of hooves and the continuous rolling bellow of the Russian barrage. Men leaned forward with their sabers poised, or gripped the reins in their teeth and readied a revolver in either hand. The enemy were closer now; he could see the figures of men as they sweated at their guns. Closer, and they were loading with grapeshot. His face was impassive as he steadied Journeyman with knees and hands; the iron rain would not turn aside if he crouched or screamed. A riderless horse went by, eyes wild and blood on its neck from a graze that had cut the reins.

The grape blasted great swaths through the attackers, and the long war-scream took on an edge that was pain and fear and fury combined. Blades and glaring faces edged up around him, and then they were among the guns. Lee saw a man splash away from the very muzzle of a fieldpiece, and then he was urging his mount up and over in a fox hunter's leap, over the limber of a cannon. A gunner struck at him with a long ramrod, glaring, an Orthodox cross hanging on his naked hairy chest. He threw up his arms with a yell as Lee cut backhanded at him, and then the commander was through. He reined in sharply, wheeling the horse in its own length. Byrd and his other aides drew up around him… no, Carter was gone, and Rolfe was white-faced and clutching a shattered arm.

"See to him," Lee said. The wind was blowing the smoke of the barrage away. "To the regimental commanders—" *or their successors,* he thought, the losses apparent as the struggle around the guns died down tore at him "—dismount the 1st Virginia, the Hussars, the Dragoons and prepare to hold this position until relieved. I expect a counterattack soon. The Maryland Lights to remain mounted in reserve. At once, gentlemen!"

This was a good position. If the Highlanders arrived in time…

The Englishman beside him began to speak. There was a *crack*, and under it a distinct thudding sound. "By God, sir, I think I've been killed," he said with wonder in his voice, pressing his hand over a welling redness on his chest.

"By God, sir, I think you have," Lee blurted. The British colonel slumped to the ground.

Too many good men have died today, Lee thought grimly, and began to position his dismounted troopers. *I hope there was a reason why.*

"Get those guns set up," he snapped. "You"—he pointed at the captain in charge of the field guns—"split up your crews, use volunteers, and see if you can turn some of these pieces around. We can expect a counterattack far too soon."

"By God, Sir Robert," the white-bearded man in the kilt said, removing his bearskin in awe. "Ye've held harrrd, nae doot o' it."

Dead men gaped around smashed cannon; fallen horses were bloating already, adding to the sulfur stink of gunpowder.

"We are most heartily glad to see you, Sir Colin," Lee said hoarsely. He looked northward. The Russians were streaming back as the thin red line of the Highland Brigade advanced. What was left of the 1st North Americans stood about, too stunned to react as yet. Stretcher bearers were carrying men back towards the waiting horse-drawn ambulances.

"Aye, we'll no have trouble takin' the valley now. We enfilade their whole position, d'ye see. 'Twould hae been nae possible if ye'r men hadna taken an' held this position. A direct attack—" He nodded to the open V of the valley. "'Twould hae been a Valley of Death."

The bagpipes squealed out; the sound of glory and of tears.

"It is well that war is so terrible," Lee whispered. "Or we would grow too fond of it."

SOMETHING FOR YEW

"**H**alfway through the twenty-first century," Detective-Inspector Ingmar Rutherston said, his breath showing as white puffs in the raw, chill air.

It was the fifteenth of January in this year of Grace 2050 A.D., and a thin drizzle drifted down from a dark-gray sky to bead on the oilskin outer layer of their anoraks.

"Hurrah. Sir." replied Detective-Constable Joseph Bramble, with a distinct pause between the words. "'Alfway through? I can't wait to get out the other side, if the rest of it's going to be like *this*."

They looked out from the entrance of the railway station over the rain-slick docks of Portsmouth amid the smells of silt and fish and wet cobbles and smoke, horse manure and pumped-out bilges. The bowsprits of scores of ships tied up at the quays speared into the dimness overhead, and masts and spars reached up into the mist like a spiky, leafless winter forest amid the tracery of rigging. Behind them the other passengers were scattering in a flurry of umbrellas, and the streamlined light-metal pedalcar they'd arrived on from Winchester was hitched to a team of British Rail Percherons and drawn away in a crunch of hooves on gravel.

Gaslights glowed through the increasing murk of the

winter's early evening, blurred into smears of light by the wet, and nobody paid two more travelers much attention. The two detectives were in plain clothes. Rutherston had six feet of lean height, with a narrow, clean-shaven beaky face and yellow hair worn rather short, and level gray eyes. Bramble was the same height but stocky and with a longbowman's thick shoulders; he was also very dark for an Englishman, blunt tan features and a mop of curly black hair.

That might have made him stand out anywhere but a polyglot seaport like this… or in the Buckinghamshire parish he came from, where everyone knew the Brambles of Jamaica Farm who'd been there since the resettlement.

"Detective-Inspector Rutherston?"

Rutherston turned. A woman in blue police uniform stood there, with a rain-cloak around her shoulders. She was four inches shorter than him, somewhat older than his thirty-two, and had that look of bone-deep tiredness that took at least a week of inadequate sleep combined with hard work.

"For my sins," he answered, nodding. "Superintendent Arnarsson?" he asked, and went on to introduce Bramble.

"Correct. Mary Arnarsson—"

She pronounced it *Arnson*, changing the Icelandic patronymic into an English family name as many did. The process was often helped along by the second and third generations' desire to fit in; from the slight emphasis she put on it he thought that was the case here, and adjusted his mental file. She went on:

"—general dogsbody and chief lion-tamer to this tide-water zoo, for *my* sins."

They shook hands all 'round; Rutherston offered the superintendent his cigarette case; she accepted one of the *Embiricos* cigarillos and he lit for both of them.

"Partial to rum, I see," she said, looking at the product of Barbados with respect; the tobacco was flavored with it.

"Just doing my bit to support the resettlement program over

there," Rutherston said.

The local went on: "Let's get you out of the wet. What'll it be first, the Scottish corpse or dinner with a garnish of paperwork? Our medical examiner should be along to the murder site soon—delayed by his other hat as a GP."

"Alas, duty calls," Rutherston said.

"Like a crying brat you can't ignore," Bramble sighed. "I could fancy a bite, right now."

The pedalcar was the fastest form of land transport in the world, but British Rail charged extra if you didn't do your share of the pumping at the pedals, and Chief Constable Tillbury in Winchester was notoriously unreasonable about travel-chits which showed you'd gotten your feet up for the trip. That was thirty-four miles of hard labor, and combined with the weather it was enough to give anyone an appetite. Rutherston's lips moved in a quirk of agreement.

Arnson gave a quick nod of approval at their choice, whistled sharply for a porter to carry their bags off to the hostelry, and led the way towards the scene of the crime. The rain was still drizzling down, and it was just cold enough to make cobblestones and paving blocks slippery with a thin film of half-ice. They walked as quickly as they could, the hobnails of their boots grating and their left hands on their sword-hilts, but they still had to be careful. It wasn't very late yet—not more than seven—but winter's early night had fallen hard, with cloud hiding moon and stars.

The gaslights cast enormous flickering shadows on the upper stories of the buildings, and left the masts of the docked vessels to vanish into the misty darkness above; shipyards and workshops and the little factories and foundries had closed, and most of the retail trades, but the taverns and pubs and "pubs" with a suspicious excess of scantily clad barmaids were still doing a roaring business.

"What was that?" Rutherston said quickly, stopping and turning on one heel.

Bramble turned too, and a handspan of steel showed as his right hand closed on the hilt of his blade in the reflex of a soldier, which was what he'd been until last summer.

"Didn't catch it, sir," he said quietly, his dark eyes scanning the alleyway to their right.

"What are you going on about?" Arnson called over her shoulder.

"Thought I saw something," Rutherston said.

He *didn't* add that what he thought he'd seen was someone leaping *across* the gap between two roofs. That was impossible, in this weather.

"It's a busy part of town," Arnson said as they went forward again.

"I didn't see anything," Bramble said. "But I've got that nasty someone-is-watching feeling, roit enough."

Rutherston nodded. Though it *was* busy; dockers were still at work, too, a fresh shift coming off the horse-drawn tramcars, and carts rumbling to and from the warehouses. Portsmouth's trade had been expanding fast of late, faster than piers could be refurbished and modernized. That meant berths were too expensive to sit idle merely because it was dark and dangerous to work; the navigation lanterns of ships waiting their turn glittered dimly from out on the surface of the Portsmouth Water.

"Times like this, I wish I'd taken me mustering-out grant in land. Down Bordeaux way, or Provence, or in Spain, like those lucky sods," Bramble said.

He nodded at the colonists walking up the gangplank of an emigrant ship carrying bundles and children and leading toddlers by the hand. The brig had *Cadiz Merchant* on its stern, and sailors were chanting at the capstan as cargo-nets went by overhead.

"Didn't you say you took me up on joining the police because being a farmer was far too much like hard work?" Rutherston said.

"Roit, sir, but those bastards will get to do it with orange trees an' olive groves."

He grinned as he went on: "And I could tan better than the lot of 'em together, thanks to my granddad Rasta Bob. They'll be sorry they can't, when they're digging and reaping and sizzling and roasting up-country from Lisbon or Cadiz or Casablanca come July, the poor pink buggers."

"True enough," Rutherston said; they both knew the power of the unmerciful southern sun from their Army days.

Rutherston noted the awe on the fresh country faces of the emigrants as they gazed about at their first and last glimpse of Portsmouth.

Probably they've never been out of sight of the steeple of their parish churches before, he thought.

"Meanwhile, here comes another shipload of *them*," Bramble went on, in a half-serious grumble.

He nodded towards the *Prinsessan Birgitta*. The banner that dripped at her stern was yellow with a horizontal red cross, the flag of the friendly and civilized realm of Norland; probably out of the Åland Isles in the Gulf of Bothnia. The people coming down the ramp were fair enough, but not Scandinavians. Sheepskin coats and caps and baggy black trousers, calf-high felt boots or wrapped leggings, kerchiefs on the women's heads and a general pungent odor of damp wool, garlic and old sweat—Poles, at a guess, they'd been trickling in for twenty years or more to take up hard-and-dirty jobs.

"They do jobs in coal mines and clearing squads that Englishmen won't, Constable," Rutherston said, looking at the immigrants charitably; his mother's parents had been immigrants, though that had been in the great influx from Iceland and fifty-one years ago. "And it's not as if we're crowded."

"Easy enough for you to say, Inspector," Arnson said, coming out of her brown study. "They make half my work, even when it's just getting homesick and drinking that vile potato gin and knifing each other. *Or* they break windows and heads over having to use Anglican Rite churches, as if they were more Catholic than the Holy Father. Not to mention every sodding other type of foreigner we get, all with *something* that gets them hot, bothered and bloody. Thank God they don't let Moors settle here to live, and damn the… other party!"

Bramble grinned and Rutherston hid a smile. Officially the police were neutral in politics; in fact, not many were Whigs, even in seaports where the current Opposition's anything-for-the-sake-of-trade platform usually got a lot of votes.

They turned into a narrow road lined by warehouses, dodging loaded carts pulled by damp, discouraged-looking horses, and handcarts and a long line of men wrestling with a huge roll of canvas from a sail-loft. There was a uniformed policeman standing outside the third building in line, and he was leaning on the haft of a billhook—a rarity for the police, issued to signal the gravity of the crime within. The broad steel head glittered wetly above his head in the gaslight, a chopping rectangle drawn out to a spike at the top and a cruel hook at the rear.

On the wall over the doors was a sign: *Vadalà And Sons, Wholesale Merchants.*

"And Sons?" Rutherston enquired. "One of the sons, in charge of their branch here? The report mentioned he was Italian."

Arnson nodded: "Well-established firm, and profitable—we check the books of foreign merchants regularly. No trouble on taxes."

"Superintendent," the man on guard said, straightening up and rapping the butt of his polearm on the pavement in salute.

"How is he, Angus?" she replied.

"Still dead, ma'am, if you mean the kiltie. But Vadalà showed up just a minute ago, and his secretary, and Jock."

"What a happy chance." To the two detectives: "Vadalà's the owner; he lives two streets north, him and his family and clerks and so forth. The secretary actually found the body. We took the initial statements and asked them to drop by later for you. Jock McTavish is our medic, and doubles for forensics work."

They dropped the stubs of their cigarillos, ground them out and went in through one of the great wagon-sized double doors that was open slightly. The interior didn't have gaslight, but the Portsmouth police had lit some of the big alcohol lanterns that hung from rope-and-pulley arrangements on the ceiling. That was high up, iron support beams resting on concrete pillars shaped like giant golf tees, both left over from the old days and reused here.

The isles between the pillars were crowded; there were bundles of carpets, and a rip in the burlap sacking showed they were colorful *frazzate*, done in geometric shapes. There were bundles of rawhides too, but under the odor of the uncured leather were hints of a dozen other things from boxes and bales and sacks stacked high in the gloom and from pyramids of barrels; pickled tuna and artichoke hearts and olives, sweet Marsala wine, brandy, raisins, dried figs and apricots, Deglet Noor dates, flowers of sulfur…

"Don't tell me; Signor Vadalà is from the Kingdom of Sicily," Rutherston murmured.

"Nose like a fox, Inspector Rutherston has," Bramble said.

"Trapani," Arnson said. At their blank looks: "Port on the west coast of Sicily; that's where he comes from. His firm does a lot of business here in the Empire."

They moved over to the open space in the middle of the building; there was a square hole fifteen feet on a side in the ceiling above, with a cargo-hook and pulley system hanging down through it and a geared windlass bolted to the floor. The body lay face-down in the center of the clear space, in the un-lovely sprawl they all recognized. Rutherston leaned forward. The dead man was certainly wearing a kilt, the genuine pleated article though the tartan wasn't one the detective knew, a russet jacket with pewter buttons, a saffron-colored shirt of some rough fabric, and buckled shoes and knee-socks.

There was a young red-haired man bent over the corpse. An older, shorter, portly, black-haired one with a tuft of chin-beard and mustachios waxed to points stood at a discreet distance— too far away to eavesdrop—looking anxious and fingering a hideously lurid purple silk cravat. Standing next to *him* was a younger woman with long dark hair and carrying an attaché case, wearing a smart outfit of dark skirt and jacket and a hat with a slightly damp ostrich feather; at a guess, a secretary or accountant, possibly a mistress as well. Rutherston dismissed them for a moment, focusing on the corpse.

"Now," Bramble said, "did ee jump, or was ee pushed?"

"Neither," the red-haired man said, looking up; he was in his twenties, with a pale, freckled face… and, right now, rubber gloves on his hands. "Stabbed in the back, and then fell."

He straightened. "Artie McTavish, at your service, Detective-Inspector. I'd shake hands, but…"

"But everyone calls you Jock, Jock," one of the uniformed police said.

The young man sighed. "*One* of my grandparents moved south, along with nine-tenths of the folk in the Hebrides. I'm a dead-average Englishman! Why does it have to be *me* who gets called *Jock?*"

"Because you don't hit them often enough?" Bramble said, grinning and holding up a great knobby fist.

"We call you Jock because you moan about it," Arnson said. "And because you're a cheap bastard and have those carrot-shavings on your head. Now, tell us a story, Jock."

Rutherston and Bramble crouched by the body. The dead man had brown hair, worn rather long, shoulder-length, and a mustache that was also long enough to fall past his mouth on either side. There was a pool of slowly congealing blood beneath the corpse, but not as much as might have been ex-pected. Rutherston looked at the face; bleeding from the nose and mouth too, of course, and with a day's stubble or better, and the blotches of postmortem lividity. The staring eyes were a rather pale blue.

"About thirty?" he said, guessing at the dead man's age.

"About that, or a bit younger. He was an outdoor worker," the doctor said.

Which aged the skin. Rutherston went on: "Time of death?"

"He died sometime between nine o'clock and noon today," McTavish said. "Rigor mortis is just setting in—his face is stiff, but the joints are only now losing mobility. The low temperatures would delay onset, of course, but it would also depend on how physically active he was just before death."

"Signor Vadalà's secretary opened up at noon to load cargo for transfer to the railway," Arnson amplified. "She sent for him—we have confirmation on that from the laborers who were with her—he ran to us, and we signaled Winchester over the semaphore when we couldn't identify the dead man. It's not a local killing, or just some ruff-scruff off a tramp freighter."

The origins of the body had been why they'd called in New New Scotland Yard. The thin scattering who'd stayed up in the Hebrides and Shetland and Orkney when the rest of the survivors moved south had done well enough in the generations since, in an oatmeal-potatoes-and-whiskey way. Certainly they'd multiplied energetically. But though formally part of Greater Britain and the Empire of the West they were very out of the way, and largely self-governing.

Meaning, Winchester ignores them and vice versa, Rutherston thought. *Except when one of them gets knocked over the head* down here. *Wouldn't do to offend some powerful clan.*

"Cause of death was a bit puzzling at first glance, Inspector," McTavish said. "But it's this puncture wound, sure enough."

He drew a scalpel from his black bag and widened a slit in a section of blood-soaked cloth on the dead man's back. "See, here—" he used the blade as a pointer. "Just a tiny little pinprick, but I'll wager anything you care to name, it went up under the ribs and across to the heart. I'll know for sure when I've done the autopsy, of course. The entry wound is very neat, completely circular. Certainly not a knife with an edged blade. Stiletto, I'd say."

"*Or* a piece of sharpened wire spoke in a bit of doweling," Bramble said. "I've seen that. Either way, someone knew how to do it."

The medic grunted, Arnson nodded, and Rutherston made a *just-so* gesture of agreement. Killing a man instantly with a single thrust like that was *not* easy. Even a sword through the body usually took longer and involved some thrashing about.

"Then he toppled forward—see the abrasions on the shins—and fell fourteen feet to the floor here. Fractured skull; broke his neck, shoulder and ribs too. All that was postmortem, or nearly, though."

Bramble got up and began quartering the area, then grabbed the rope and swarmed up to the second story arm-over-arm. Rutherston stayed crouched on his hams, sketching the body and its position in his notebook; then he drew rubber gloves of his own, put them on and bent forward.

The dead man was about his own height or Bramble's, six feet. A little over the average for someone of North European descent, which he probably was. Lanky but muscular in a lean fashion, like a man who'd eaten well but worked hard all his life, which was normal enough for someone from a civilized country. Naturally fair-skinned, but not so much so that he couldn't tan—and he *was* tanned, hardly winter-pale at all, and no paler under the shirt, but the upper thigh where the kilt was disarranged was much lighter.

Outdoor worker and in the habit of doing his job stripped to the waist, and quite recently in a place with strong sun.

He felt the palms. Both were covered from fingertips to the heel of his hands with heavy callus, of the sort you got from handling ropes a good deal. A seaman's hands; the pattern was quite distinctive.

"It's nei more summer up in Scotland than it is here—rather less so, in fact—but this man was exposed to a good deal of sun lately," Rutherston said. "We can't be certain that he's Scottish, but he definitely was a sailor and fresh from the tropics."

"Mmm, but he's certainly *dressed* like a Scot," Arnson pointed out.

Besides the kilt, he was wearing a plaid, a blanketlike swath of tartan fabric across the torso and pinned at one shoulder with a silver brooch; a small knife was tucked into the top of one knee-stocking—a *sgian dhu*, with a hilt of black bone carved in knotwork—and a double-edged dirk with a ten-inch blade at his belt. There was similar curling interleaved work tooled into the leather of the belt and worked on the bronze buckle. The oddest feature was a narrow ring of twisted gold around the man's neck, ending in two knobs over the throat, graved with an interlaced design of elongated gripping beasts.

Two of the uniformed policemen brought a stretcher forward and rolled the body onto it, pressing until he lay straight, then set the ends of the poles on barrels to leave the corpse at just above waist-height.

"He's not really dressed very like a Scotsman," Rutherston said thoughtfully. "Or rather, too much so. Orkneymen and Shetlanders wear trousers, of course, but I've met visiting lairds from the Hebrides and the new mainland settlements dressed very much like this for visits at Court."

"Are they as dour a lot as rumor has it, Inspector?" McTavish asked curiously.

"Ah... let's put it this way; it's not hard to tell the difference between a man from North Uist and a ray of sunshine. But more to the point, while they *do* wear kilts up there as ordinary wear... at least in the Western Isles... they're not always dressed up in the rest of it, not most of the time. When they do, it's for swank and in the best they have. This is a plain man's working clothes—the fabric was never anything fancy, and it's worn; see the fraying here, and how the elbows are shiny."

"And that thing around the neck?" Arnson asked.

"I've never seen anything like *that* except in books and the New British Museum. It's a torc; the ancient Celts wore them. Contemporary Scots most certainly do *not*."

The detective turned the battered face to the light with an impersonal gentleness. "Do you have a mirrored probe?"

"Here it is, Inspector."

It was the kind dentists used. Rutherston put pressure on the jaw with his left hand and slid it into the open mouth with the right.

"Ah-ha! Take a look."

"Good teeth," the doctor said. "Portsmouth people eat too bloody many sweets… wait a bit, that crown looks odd."

"It's not gold; some sort of porcelain, I think. The Scots use the same sort of dentistry as we… only they've a good deal less of it."

Rutherston laid down the probe, drew the little "black knife" from the dead man's sock and balanced it on his palm. "And this isn't a toy for ceremony. It's a working blade."

"It is," Arnson said, taking it from him for a moment. "My family's in the metal trade. This is layer-forged—beautiful work. It would set you back a pound at least."

That was most of a week's wage for a laboring man; two days for an inspector.

"Hmmm. There's a crescent moon tattooed at the base of his throat," Rutherston said.

"Or a strung bow, Inspector," the doctor pointed out.

"Perhaps. But I've never seen this particular mark on a knife before," Rutherston continued. "And it's *definitely* the moon, in three phases."

There was a symbol inlaid in silver on the hilt, a circle flanked by two outward-pointing crescents. There was another on the dirk, and…

He turned over the left hand. The same mark was tattooed on the inside of the wrist.

"Well, well, well," he said softly.

"Why do you say it's definitely the moon?" Arnson said sharply. "It *could* be, but—"

"It's Hecate's Moon," Rutherston said. "Waxing, full and waning. I've run into it before, during an investigation near the New Forest. There are some of them in the villages there. Quite a few, in fact."

At their blank looks, he went on: "It's the witch-mark. The Old Religion."

The blankness turned to wide-eyed surprise. Arnson crossed herself, and the others followed. By law Greater Britain had freedom of religion, but even in a polyglot seaport town like this the Anglican Rite Catholics were overwhelmingly dominant; the minority of Dissenters tended to be Lutheran or Anti-Reunionist Evangelical or Presbyterian. Outright non-Christians were very rare.

"There really *are* witches there?" she said. "I thought that was a fairy-story."

"Most certainly; a quiet and inoffensive lot for the most part. But they don't, to my knowledge, wear kilts!"

Bramble slid down the rope; he had a length of wood in his hand roughly the size and shape of a quarterstaff.

"Odd you should say that, sir," he said.

Then he extended the baulk of wood. It was yew, heavy and hard, roughly triangular and split from a single tree-trunk; about seven and a half feet long and four inches through. *Good* yew, at that, straight and free from knots, and mostly the deep orange-brown of heartwood, with a thinner, paler band of sapwood on one side. And tapped into the wood with a punch near one end was the same triple-moon symbol.

"Most of them had the stamp shaved off—looks like someone overlooked this one," Bramble said with satisfaction.

"And our witches don't usually deal in yew, either," Rutherston said meditatively. "They're mostly farmers or craftsmen or charcoal-burners. Is there much up there, Constable?"

"Four or five tons of it, sir. All about this quality."

Bramble took the baulk and put it across his shoulders, bending it with the orange core in and the paler side out as it would be in a finished weapon and grunting a little with the effort. Yew was a natural laminate, the heartwood strong in compression and the sapwood when it was stretched, which made it the finest of all timber for bows.

"Not 'alf bad," he said. "Well-seasoned. And not from Blighty, either."

Rutherston nodded. Yew flourished in England and you could use it for bows—but the climate was really too mild and wet for the best quality bowyer's wood, and English yew tended to be crooked and knotty as well. Straight, dense slow-growth timber from cold mountains or drier country was much better; the lands around the Mediterranean were the traditional source for high-quality staves. The government of Greater Britain had big yew plantations in Iberia and the Maghreb, planted and guarded at considerable expense.

The problem is that slow growth is ... very slow, Rutherston thought. *It takes at least a century for a good tree to be ready to harvest. Two or three centuries are better. And we only really started the plantations about the time I was born.*

And in the meantime, the Empire needed bowstaves. By law, everyone not blind or crippled started archery training when they turned six and enrolled in school. Adults under sixty had to keep a bow and quiver at home as part of their muster-kit for the militia and practice with it every Sunday. Regular soldiers and the navy and Royal Marines used them far *more* often, of course. A bow in active service didn't last more than a few years at most. The load up in the loft would make at least five or six thousand of the great six-foot mankillers, allowing for wastage when they were trimmed to shape.

"Signor Vadalà?" Rutherston called politely.

The portly Italian merchant came over, fiddling a little with his cravat and followed by his secretary. She looked foreign too, even darker than the Sicilian and subtly different in general appearance, though very pretty in a slim, hawk-featured fashion, with flashing eyes so black the pupils vanished in the iris. The detective judged her age to be somewhere in the mid to late twenties; a small golden crucifix hung from a chain around her neck, vivid against the indigo linen of her high-necked blouse.

"I presume this stack of yew is yours, Signor?" Rutherston said.

"Yes, Detective-Inspector," the man said, in very good English—Portsmouth dialect, to be precise—but with a very un-English bow. "Antonio Vadalà, at your service."

The detective shook hands, then turned to the woman.

"Miss Llesenia Vargas, Inspector," she said, giving him a firm shake.

She pronounced the first name as *Yesenia*, in the Hispanic style; he'd had some contact with the language in his Army days, and he mentally filled in the double-l.

"Gibraltar, Miss Vargas?" he said; he didn't think she was South American.

She smiled, showing very white teeth against a skin as dark as Bramble's, but with a strong olive tint.

"*Sí*. From the Rock itself. So many of you Anglos moving south, I thought there would be plenty of room here if I would come north."

Gibraltarian was what he'd have guessed, anyway. Her English was very fluent, but it had a rapid accent, soft for the most part yet occasionally guttural. Most of the original population of Gibraltar had spoken a Spanish dialect before the Change. In the city itself some still did, though those who'd joined in the resettlement of the empty land to the north and south had mostly been swallowed up in the northern influx.

And she has the look, Rutherston thought. *Might even be*

Rom, or partly, she's so dark.

"You discovered the body?" he said, poising his fountain-pen over his notebook.

"*Sí*. At—" she touched a pocket of her jacket, which had the gold links of a watch-chain "—about eleven-thirty. I was here from the office—"

"That is also my home," Vadalà said. "About ten minutes' walk from here."

Rutherston nodded; living over the shop was common, and most merchants kept as close as they could to the docks without actually setting up among the sailors' dosshouses and slop-shops.

"—to oversee the loading of the Marsala." Vargas nodded towards one of the pyramids of wine-barrels. "The body was there but I did not notice it until after I had done the inventory; it was you see, dark inside. When the laborers came with the cart, I saw the body and called to them. The blood was still flowing. I stayed here with the team, and sent one immediately for Signor Vadalà."

"Thank you, Miss Vargas," he said.

That agreed with the initial report… which was a little odd, since witness statements were usually chaotic and contradictory, particularly under stress, and finding a body was fairly stressful for a civilian. On the other hand, Miss Vargas was apparently a very cool customer and not given to the vapors. That she'd left home and ended up working here argued for wit, nerve and experience beyond the usual.

"Signor?" he said.

Her Italian employer went on: "Fifteen years I have been resident for my firm in Portsmouth, always paying my taxes in full and—"

Rutherston cleared his throat and poised his notebook. "I'm sure you're a most valued resident," he said.

What I'm mainly sure of is that you're smarter than you would like me to believe, he thought. *The gesticulating-fat-man performance is supposed to make me or Englishmen in general take you less seriously, I think.*

"Importing yew is a major part of your business, Signor Vadalà?"

The merchant looked a little surprised; his shrug was far more accented than his command of the spoken language.

"No, but it's very useful, for the customs. You see, the tariffs on other items are reduced if yew staves are included in the shipment. The price of the yew, that does not produce much profit—even in the Kingdom of Sicily, or the Umbrian League, it is not cheap, you see? There is finding the trees, cutting, transport, taxes—all expensive. But the tariff reduction, it makes the difference. Also sometimes I buy a great many yew staves when I have the opportunity, and I trade them to other importers, from the Italies, and from Cyprus. Then *they* can get the reductions. The Crown gets the yew, everyone is happy."

It was policy to encourage yew imports from other countries to give the plantations time to mature. Of course, it was *also* policy to give preference to the wine and brandy and olive oil and fruit and so forth produced in the Empire's continental colonies; they were becoming more important as settlement spread out from the first posts along the Gironde and Loire and Rhone and north and south from Gibraltar. Hence the tariffs on the foreign equivalents… which were partly remitted if a shipment included the valuable bow-wood.

Rutherston showed him the mark at the end of the stave. Vadalà shrugged again, smiled and spread his hands.

"I simply take it on consignment. My dear, what ship did this lot come on?"

The woman put her briefcase on a stack of crates marked *Fichi secchi di Trapani*, riffled through the documents inside and handed Rutherston a bill of lading.

He inclined the paper to catch the lamplight. Part of it was in Italian, but simple enough to follow if you had a smattering of Spanish and some Latin: four-point-five tons (it actually used the eccentric metric measurements) of seasoned yew staves purchased in Trapani, ultimate origin "the Adriatic," then shipped from Sicily to Portsmouth on the ship *Bella Fortuna*. He checked the dates with disgusted foreknowledge. The Sicilian vessel had cleared Portsmouth Water with the morning tide, bound for Trapani with a cargo of British woolens, Irish linens, miscellaneous hardware, weapons and armor, Zanzibari cloves, Tanga sisal, Hinduraj printed cottons, Sri Lankan quinine and South American coffee, a typical mixture of exports and re-exports.

"The *Bella Fortuna* is owned by Vadalà and Sons?" he asked, returning the document.

Vadalà spread his hands apologetically. "Yes, Inspector. Our other two ships, they are for now on the direct run from Sicily to West Africa, mostly the Ashanti ports or Abidjan, sometimes as far south as the Congo mouth."

His voice took on a caressing note, and his hands made unconsciously voluptuous gestures: "For peppers, cocoa, palm oil, rare woods, coffee, ivory…"

"Are you aware of what this stamp means?" the detective said.

Again the apologetic spreading of hands. "I am sorry. Perhaps some tribal mark? Much yew comes from the mountains behind Trieste and the Dalmatian coast, and there they are very savage. They are Croats," he added, as if that was all the explanation needed. "Or still worse, they are Serbs, or Albanians, the worst in the world, as bad as *saraceni*."

"It's the mark of Hecate's Moon," Rutherston said, and dredged a translation out of his memory. "Of *La Vecchia Religione*."

"*Stregheria!*" Vadalà blurted, signing himself and then bringing out his crucifix to kiss. "No, I did not think even the Croats were so fallen away from civilization as *that*."

"Thank you, Signor. I will be in contact with you over the next few days."

"I am always at the service of the King-Emperor of Greater Britain, the Defender of the Faith and right hand of the Holy Father, the Emperor of the West, Detective-Inspector," Vadalà said fervently.

He may even mean it, Rutherston thought, when he and Bramble were preparing to leave. *But then again, he may not.*

"Odd thing, sir," Bramble said. "Maybe it's nothing, but…"

"Yes?"

"When the little dago got all upset about the witches… his secretary didn't cross 'erself. Made a sort of sign with her hand instead."

"I think we should look into both of them," Rutherston said thoughtfully. "In the morning, we'll start by taking statements from everyone who deals with Vadalà and Sons. I want to know where that yew came from. I suspect it wasn't the Adriatic. There's something… I can't remember it but I know that I should."

He looked up. Across the big dimly lit room Vargas was staring at him intently. She nodded and turned away when she felt his gaze.

Bramble shrugged and yawned enormously. "We'll be thinking straighter in the morning, sir."

"We're putting you up at the Anchor," Arnson said. "I eat there myself when I can't get home, which is too damned often. When I do manage a flying visit, my girls say: *Has the strange lady with the truncheon come to arrest you, Daddy?* I'll join you now—no rest for me anyway until the paperwork's finished and the stiff is stowed."

Rutherston and Bramble followed her back towards the railway station; nearby was a three-story, slate-roofed brick building that occupied a wedge-shaped plot between two converging stretches of cobblestones. The Anchor was either quite old or built in the modern style after the fires; here in Portsmouth Old Town all the impractical concrete-and-steel structures from just before the end had been torn down, for the room and the salvage metal and for rubble fill to extend the piers.

A real anchor stood by the entrance, beneath the sign with a painted one; pleasant yellow light showed through the windows, and a blast of noise and warmth and cooking-smells and tobacco-smoke came through when they opened the door. Someone was playing an accordion, and someone else a fiddle; a chorus of voices roared out:

> "*Get a move-on, Johnny Bowline*
> *If you mean to come away—*
> *For the tide is at the flood*
> *And the anchor's off the mud*
> *And they are trampin' round the capstan*
> *In the darkness and the rain—*"

Which was natural enough; if you wanted song, you sang—unless you could afford one of the rare, expensive and rather scratchy and tinny-sounding wind-up gramophones. The crowd within gave the three a cursory glance as they wiped their feet on the mat, then went back to singing, or eating or drinking or the game of darts going on down at the other end of the long irregular rectangle.

Mary Arnson led them through to a booth not far from a cheerful coal fire in the hearth, returning friendly nods and greetings as they threaded their way through the crowd. A few off-duty police waved, but it was obvious from the close-trimmed beards, ruddy weatherbeaten faces, pipes, roll-necked sweaters, and an odor of warming sea-boots and drying wool that this was a sailor's inn. The walls had an appropriate clutter of model ships, crossed harpoons, photographs of distant places and glass net-floats.

The three police officers hung up their dripping outerwear on hooks by the booth, and their sword-belts. All of them had steel infantry bucklers clipped to their scabbards, and Arnson's belt had the handcuffs, metal-cored ashwood truncheon and straight-bladed cutlass with knuckle-duster guard and lead-ball pommel that the local force favored. In Winchester the uniform branch only carried long blades on special occasions, but while Portsmouth wasn't what you'd call a lawless town, it *was* a rough one. That went with being a seaport, even if it was also only thirty-odd miles from Winchester Cathedral, the Houses of Parliament, New New Scotland Yard and the court of King-Emperor Charles IV.

"Here's the preliminaries," Arnson said as they slid into the benches; she took the one across from the two men. "Jock will have the details on the autopsy tomorrow."

The two CID men began reading files and passing them to each other; semaphore telegraph was too expensive to use for more than sending the bare-bones and a summons to Winchester.

The waitress arrived as they did; Rutherston looked up to see a comfortable-looking carrot-haired woman of about forty in sweater and cord trousers. She put a basket with a two-pound loaf and a small crock of butter down on the table between them, unhooked the slate that hung from her belt and poised a stick of chalk to write orders.

"Working at dinner again? Y' look loik the dockside cat dragged you out o' the harbor, luv," she said to Mary Arnson, with an ease that showed the policewoman was a regular. "An' then threw y' back."

"I feel like it, Hofi," she said. "Let's be extravagant today. Hot cocoa. Then the usual."

"Anything stronger than cream in the brew?"

"Nei, not in uniform. And I'll just go to sleep if I do."

"You should; you work too hard. And ye, veinar?" she said to Bramble. "We've a fine mulled cider."

"Ah, m'dear?" Bramble enquired with interest, absently smacking his lips.

"Best on the coast," she replied. "We gets it from this orchard in Devon my cousins has and make it roit, plenty of spice and a red-hot poker. Then there's roast o' pork with spuds, carrots and raudkal, if ye'd loik; Auntie Rose has it just ready now."

"That'll do me fine."

"And fer you, sir?"

"Hot buttered rum, if you would," Rutherston said.

"Roit you are, sir," she said. "And to eat?"

"Something local, I think. Surprise me."

"I will that, sir."

Interesting, he thought, as she turned away.

He prided himself on having a keener ear for accent than most and being a quicker judge of personal detail, but the waitress had placed both the visitors with an effortless ease he could only admire. Bramble as a farmer's son (hence a *lad* and *ye*), and she'd anticipated that a conservative man from an inland shire would prefer honest meat and potatoes. She'd also spotted Rutherston as a younger-son gentry sprig, Winchester College and Sandhurst (hence *sir*, and the more formal *you*), despite him barely opening his mouth.

Her own voice had an interesting tang to it; the inevitable Hampshire—England had been resettled from the Isle of Wight Refuge, after all—but overlain with a crisp treatment of the vowels not at all like the slower Winchester accent or the thick burr of a villager. The superintendent had much the same sound, modified by a bit of old-fashioned middle-class bookishness.

And our little ménage here makes things just a little touchy. Superintendent Arnson is senior in rank, age and local experience, I in social background, which isn't supposed to matter, but does, and Bramble and I are both down from the capital, and are CID to boot—which isn't supposed to give us a leg up either, but rather does. Remember, Ingmar... Manners Makyth Man.

The tray with their drinks came quickly. Arnson warmed her hands on hers before she raised it to her lips, and Rutherston wasn't ashamed to follow her example. Weather like this got into your bones, worse than a hard freeze. When he drank he could feel the warmth and buttery richness all the way down to his mostly empty stomach, and the cloves and nutmeg added an agreeable tang to the smooth burnished taste of the hot Barbados rum. It made him feel much better, which in turn made him realize how ferociously hungry he was.

"Where's Jack?" Arnson asked as Rutherston closed the last folder and leaned back. "He usually handles things like this for us."

"Jack Drummond? He's over in Bristol. Nasty case; a clerk in one of the import-export firms there was informing on ship movements for a gang of pirates, and *someone* slit his throat to shut his mouth when the net was about to close."

She nodded grimly. "Dead men tell nei tales. So Jack's there working with the RN people? Pity the pirates, then; he's a real bulldog when he gets his teeth into a case."

"Just so. And Arnfinnur broke his leg last week on his own front step—sleet that day. So here we are. Detective-Constable Bramble here is new to the force and the Criminal Investigation Department—lateral transfer from the Army."

Which was common enough; first call on vacancies in the police was a perk for veterans who didn't fancy settling on the land. Arnson ran her hands through her damp and rather short ash-blonde hair; the fingernails were chewed short, he noticed, and she had a wedding band.

The food arrived just then, and there was a hiatus in conversation. All three of them crossed themselves and bowed their heads and murmured:

"*Bless us, O Lord, and these Your gifts, which we are about to receive from Your bounty. Through Christ our Saviour.*"

The *Amen* from the two men was enthusiastic and they propped the documents up against the salt-cellar and the bread-basket, their jaws working as steadily as their eyes.

Bramble tucked into his meat and veg; Arnson methodically plowed her way through grilled whiting with a side of fried oysters, and sprouts and chips. Rutherston found that his "surprise" was a dish of baked cod with lemon sauce, fish landed fresh today—the stocks on this coast had come back nicely—with buttered parsnips and potatoes roasted in the skin, cut open and doused with butter and sharp cheese. The firm flaky flesh of the cod went down well, enhanced by the citrus tang, and parsley and thyme added a nice touch to the bland roots. Really fresh seafood was expensive in Winchester; Fridays could be rather a bore, with the eternal smoked salmon or kippers.

"I suspect that our case may be related to Jack's, anyway," Rutherston said when he'd taken the first edge off. "A man killed to stop his mouth."

Arnson sat up straighter. "Pirates *here?*" she said dubiously. "Portsmouth's Royal Navy HQ!"

"It's also our other main trading port," Rutherston said. "Not necessarily the *same* set of pirates as the ones over in Bristol. This is where most of the African and East Asian trade is based; Bristol deals more with the New World. But pirates always need intelligence on shipping movements—it's a big ocean otherwise."

"The Moorish corsairs?" Arnson said sharply. "The Emir getting above himself again?"

The Emirate of Dakar was on the West African coast where Senegal had once been; there had been trouble with them off-and-on for fifty years. The Emir Jawara ruled a considerable power, much smaller in area than Greater Britain but currently boasting at least three times as many people. Africa south of the deserts hadn't been wrecked quite so completely as the lands further north, not being quite so dependent on the high-energy technologies that stopped functioning the night of the Change.

And those numerous people include an appalling bulk of enthusiastic young men with spears and other sharp and pointy objects, Rutherston thought.

He offered Arnson another cigarillo, lit it, and then his own. He'd been stationed in Morocco with the Blues and Royals, and as an officer had had to acquaint himself with the politics.

"It's not quite as simple as that," he said. "Emir Jawara loves us not, of course. And he *would* love to push up into the southern provinces of the Empire; our settlers are still very thin on the ground there. Let them get a foothold and it would be hard work to stop them south of Gibraltar, if there. The Berbers up in the Atlas range would help them."

"Too much desert between the Senegal valley and our base in Marrakech to go overland, though," Bramble said; he'd been in the same area as an NCO, and a very intelligent one.

"And the RN are in the way at sea, and he knows it," Rutherston agreed. "Jawara's no fool. He won't provoke us directly, in my opinion."

"He doesn't do damn-all about the corsairs, though," Arnson said. "And they're provoking enough! Murdering someone next to the RN dockyards… that goes beyond provoking to downright insolence. The ministry we've got now won't stand for it."

"No, he doesn't try to rein them in. They pay him to look the other way."

The swampy inlets of the Saloum delta and the Casamance coast were their nest; they were native Senegalese, mixed with the Moors proper, from the lands along the north bank of the Senegal river. William the Great had driven them there long ago in the First Moorish War. They harried shipping in those latitudes, and then their sleek little galleys vanished into the labyrinthine mangrove swamps to escape the avenging RN frigates, with ugly little scrimmages in the tangled creeks between them and the landing parties.

"But he doesn't rule the corsairs, not really; he finds them to be overmighty subjects, not to mention their influence at his court. The Marabouts, you see; the Mourides. I'd be surprised if *they* didn't have agents here in Portsmouth, and they'd account it a good deal to annoy us to any degree necessary. If it provoked war between Greater Britain and the Emirate… so much the better. They really do not like us."

"Mourides? What's that?" Bramble said curiously; he didn't have Rutherston's education, but he picked up facts with magpie voracity. "I've 'eard the name, sir, but what does it mean?"

"Mouride? *Murîdiyya*, in Arabic. *One who desires*, literally. Supposedly one who desires union with God, and it may have been true once. Religious brotherhoods, rather like a monastic order except that they aren't celibate; they've always been powerful in that part of Africa. In practice, these days, it means one who desires to kill and rob unbelievers; and so you get a lot of them in the crews of the corsairs, often as leaders. Their chiefs are the Marabouts—murabatin—and they've one of the factions at the court in Dakar. One that Jawara is a little fearful of."

Arnson looked baffled. "What's that got to do with our dead Jock?"

"Ah, well, he isn't necessarily a Jock. Something's been teasing at my mind since I saw him, and now I remember. Do you remember an expedition to Nantucket, a generation ago?"

"The Count of Azay's expedition?" Arnson said, looking upward and frowning in concentration. "Well before my time; I was about ten."

"It was hush-hush at the time and hushed up more later," Rutherston said. "My father had something to do with it, back about thirty years ago. To make a long story short, he—they—had contact with some people from… Orey-something."

He snapped his fingers. "Oregon! It's on the west coast of North America. In any case, I do remember two aspects of it; that yew is common as dirt in the mountains there… and that a group of them revived a lot of Scottish… Celtic… customs after the Change. They also practiced the Old Religion, like our witches in the Old Forest."

Arnson sat up; so did Bramble. "Aha!"

"Precisely," the detective said.

"But—" Arnson frowned. "How does that tie in with the corsairs?"

"That I don't know. But I suspect that it does, and I intend to look into it. Perhaps if there's another around besides the dead man, we can flush or tempt him into the open before the pirates kill him too!"

He sighed and stubbed out his cigarillo; another was tempting, but it would turn his tongue to leather. "I *do* wish I had a better feel for the local details," he added.

Arnson nodded. "We need our own bloody CID," she said. "There are what, over a million and a quarter people in England alone now—"

"Million and a half, nearly," Rutherston said. "We'll be back to the *Domesday Book* level soon."

"And having the entire detective branch working out of the Yard in Winchester doesn't make sense anymore. It takes too long to bring an outsider up to speed… nei offense."

"None taken, I assure you. It's quite true."

She made a half-spitting sound of frustration. "I can have a few constables put onto watching Vadalà in their own clothes—"

"Please do, and immediately, if you would."

"I will. But it's not their proper job. We need trained plain-clothesmen. This is *Portsmouth*, not some village in deepest Buggritshire where a black eye or a pregnant ewe is news."

If only I could tell you what happened in Eddsford last summer, Rutherston thought. *But that wouldn't do, not while the Special Branch is still tidying up the tag-ends.*

Aloud he went on: "I quite agree, Superintendent… and just between thee and me, there will be a bill to that effect before Parliament at the next session. In the meantime…"

Bramble grunted; his own home was close enough for

government work to being *exactly* the sort of place Inspector Arnson had meant. The most urban thing in Buckinghamshire was the forest covering the ashes, ruins and bones that had been Milton Keynes. Unless you counted Newport Pagnell, a vibrant metropolis which had all of a thousand people now.

When they'd finished the dessert of plum duff with red currant jelly Arnson groaned her way to her feet.

"And now I've another hour or two of *typing* before I can go home… or at least it's the place I keep my spare underthings. See you in the morning, Inspector, Constable."

"I'll turn in now too, I think," Rutherston said, yawning.

"Think you can sleep, sir, with that lot enjoying themselves?"

The crowd inside was thicker if anything, but the group of merchant-service men were still singing with enthusiasm:

> "*When I was young and in me prime*
> *I'd take those flash girls two at a time*
> *Now I'm old and turning gray*
> *Rum's my sweetheart every day…*"

"Right now, I could sleep through the flash girls themselves, much less a song about them."

Rutherston's room in the Anchor was small, under the eaves, with only a dormer window looking out over the harbor and another over the street to one side. The hissing of the rain on the slates of the roof overhead made a haze of white noise that hid everything but the occasional *clunk* of something heavy being set down by a cargo-sling on the docks a block away. There was a good lantern, though; the bluish alcohol flame fell on the table before him, with his own notebook and a tattered old copy of *Tournaments Illuminated* and a sheaf of writing-paper.

Bramble had stayed behind in the common room when

Rutherston left… but now he'd turned in next door—though from the sounds, not alone.

"Fast work," the detective smiled wryly to himself, dipped his pen in the ink and finished his letter to Janice:

"… and so, my dearest, I am confronted with a Scot who may not be a Scot but is probably a veritable witch and is most certainly a murder victim, a Sicilian who is also not all he seems, and a lady from Gibraltar who may be a Gypsy sorceress or a reincarnated Egyptian princess for all I know. All my love to you, and to our little Beatrice. I hope to see you before this letter arrives, but if I do not, I am thinking of you always and remember me in your prayers as I do the two of you. Yours forever, my dearest, Ingmar.

"Damnation, but that sounds lame," he said to himself. "Well, that's what you get for marrying a poet, Ingmar. Your words will always pale by comparison."

Then he turned back to his notebook, staring at it with his chin propped on thumb and forefinger as if sheer concentration could force a solution out of it. One of the last entries caught his eye: Vadalà and Sons ships on African run?

That was a profitable trade, but also a dangerous one—right past the haunts of the Moorish corsairs.

Could he be bent? Rutherston thought. Intimidated, bought off, an active collaborator? Hmm. He would be a very valuable agent for the pirates—and would stand to make a very large amount of money. But then he wouldn't have called the police right away when his secretary found the body; he'd have worked with her to hide it. There are at least two contending parties here; the man from the west, the corsairs… and possibly others, or divisions within the ranks of the pirates.

Then he yawned. "No point in trying to think with sand in the gears," he said. "I need more data anyway."

He turned down the lamp, and knelt by the bed, clasped his hands around his crucifix and murmured:

"Lord, I beg you to visit my house and banish from it all

the deadly power of the Enemy. May Your holy angels dwell there to keep my family in peace, and may Your blessing be upon us always. I ask this through Christ our Lord. And if you could help me find the murderer or murderers, Lord, I would be truly thankful, because there's at least one villain loose in this town who badly needs catching. Amen."

Then he stripped and slid into the bed; he always felt a little better after giving God His marching-orders when a difficult case was in hand. The hot-water bottle the maid had left had gone lukewarm at best, but it had also taken the curse off the linen, and the quilt above was thick with goose-down. His head hit the pillow, and he was asleep before he had time to breathe three times.

The cold air woke him, and a spray of rain, and the hard wet *twack* of an arrow striking flesh, and then the sharper *tock* of one driving into wood. He blinked his eyes open, just in time to see a dark figure by his bedside—dark save for the long curved knife raised over his head, glinting dully in the faint gaslight from the street below.

Rutherston had been a policeman in a fairly peaceful land for a long time. But that hadn't been his only calling... or this the only time he'd woken to naked steel in darkness.

"*Turn out!*" he shouted, automatically and from the bottom of his lungs. "*Infiltrators! Turn out!*"

And dodged with a wordless yell as the blade came down, struggling with the quilt and sheets even as the dagger plunged into the pillow by his neck and released a blizzard of goose-down. That gave him the instant he needed to punch at the man's veiled face.

Beneath the black cloth a nose squashed with an intensely satisfying crumbling feeling, and the dagger-man stumbled back, flailing his arms to keep his balance. Rutherston jack-knifed out of bed and made a snatch at his swordbelt. The assassin recovered with a cat's reflexes; the only thing the Englishman had time to do was grab the foot-wide buckler from its snap-fastening on the scabbard of his sword.

That saved his life slightly less than a second later, as he whirled and caught a thrust on its surface. The point of blade grated across the buckler's steel with a tooth-hurting squeal, scoring the blue paint. Then they faced each other, circling in the cramped confines of the darkened room, with the knife-blade the only bright thing in it.

When I was twenty, single and stupid, this sort of thing was unpleasant enough. As an intelligent husband and father in my thirties it's worse, some remote corner of Rutherston's mind thought.

Everything else narrowed down to a point of concentration like the diamond at the working-end of a drill-press. There were noises elsewhere in the inn; all he had to do was stay un-punctured for a few moments longer. The other man knew it as well; he feinted twice with blinding speed, spun the weapon from his left hand to his right and struck like a viper, slashing forehand and backhand—the best way to kill quickly and surely with a knife. Rutherston felt a thin line of cold across his stomach, and then the knife-wrist smacked into his hand. The man in black blocked Rutherston's smashing blow with the side of his buckler, hacking at the arm that held it with the edge of his free hand.

The steel circle spun free and clanged off the wall; Rutherston forced his numbed fingers to grab for the other's free wrist. For an instant the two men were face-to-face, straining against each other; the assassin seemed to be made of India-rubber and spring steel, twisting and writhing. His knee came up, but Rutherston caught it on his thigh. At the same instant the detective whipped his head forward; the butt made chill white light flash through his head, but the other man gave a stifled shriek as the Englishman's forehead smacked into the already-damaged fabric of his nose.

Then the door opened, and the dim light of the corridor night-lamps seemed almost blinding-bright. Steel flickered, and the dark eyes above the veil went wide for an instant; Rutherston could feel the impact through the other's wrists even as he heard the wet crack of parting bone. The detective released him, and the man fell to the threadbare carpet.

Bramble stood panting, his sword in his hand. He was also stark naked. A girl wearing not much more scurried by behind him, her golden hair fluttering as she sped downstairs giving little shrieks and holding her dress in front of her face. Then others began crowding in up the narrow stairs.

"You there!" Rutherston snapped.

It was the Anchor's landlord, a grizzled RN veteran with a steel hook in place of his left hand, and a businesslike cutlass in his right; both clashed with the pajamas he was wearing, which were blue and printed with small pink rabbits.

"Get these people out of the way and send immediately for Superintendent Arnson; tell her that there's been an attack by foreign agents! The same to the duke's palace."

"Aye-Aye, sor!" the man said, and began enthusiastically carrying out the order, with the assistance of several younger men who were probably his sons.

Bramble was looking around his superior. Rutherston turned, stepping aside to keep his bare feet out of the pool of blood. There was a second figure in the same nondescript dark clothing lying slumped in an ungainly pile three-quarters through the window, with his feet still up on the sill. And a clothyard arrow buried to the feathers in his back; the pile-shaped head had smashed out through the thickness of his breastbone in a brutal exclamation point.

"Good God," Rutherston said. "*How could I not have* noticed *that?*"

"You were just a little busy, sir," Bramble said, as he stepped up to the window and looked downward.

Rutherston swallowed and joined him. "There!"

A dark figure darted into the little alley across from the Anchor. Rutherston's eyes went a little wider as the shadowed form ran at a brick wall, ran *up* it for four paces with a cloak fluttering behind, turned and bounced to a windowsill on the opposite side, bounced back across, zigzagging its way up the narrow space between buildings until it crouched on a ledge only one brick wide, *leapt* to grab the guttering and swung up onto the roof.

The whole process had taken no more time than running the same distance on level ground, and then the stranger disappeared across the slick dark slates and over the ridgeline.

"I take it back, sir," Bramble said, with a long whistle. "Someone *was* following us to the ware'ouse. And 'e'd be a proper delight to my old gymnastics sergeant-instructor at 'bars and rings,' he would. Maybe it's an ape?"

Rutherston nodded, a little dazed. None of it had been strictly impossible... but he wouldn't have believed it if he hadn't seen it with his own eyes. And it was quite certain that raising an alarm would be entirely futile. Anyone who could do *that* could travel across Portsmouth's rooftops faster than constables could comb the streets. He snorted as he suppressed a burst of semi-hysterical laughter at an image of Superintendent Arson's coppers plunging to the pavement as they tried to follow his benefactor in their hobnailed boots.

"Someone is very determined to cut my investigation short, by cutting *me* short," he said. "Someone else is trying to stop them... and saved my life, without a doubt."

"From that angle... tricky shot, four stories... whoever did it knows how to use a bow, too, and nei mistake," Bramble said. "Ah, and there's another!"

He turned and pointed at a second shaft, with its head buried in a black oak rafter just left of the door.

"That one would have been aimed at your little friend with the curved knife, but it missed." Then he looked at Rutherston: "You're hurt, Inspector!"

The detective turned up the lamp and looked down, seeing with slight surprise that he had a bleeding cut across his stomach, from left hip-bone nearly six inches upward and across.

"Just barely broke the skin," he said, with an inward shudder; that had come about one inch or a tenth of a second from gutting him. "Unpleasantly sharp knife, though. Thank you for interrupting the process of disembowelment."

"You're welcome, sir. Wish I could have kept him alive for a while to talk, but..."

"But that might have left me *dead* for a good long while."

While Bramble dressed, Rutherston applied stinging aloe vera from his traveling kit, bandaged himself and pulled on his own clothes—working in a pair of cotton drawers wasn't really practical, and boots and trousers were an aid to thought. Then he laid out the bodies and pulled down the veils that were also the tails of the turbans both men wore, and turned up the lamp.

"Well, they're not Scottish either, that's for certain," Bramble said, returning to look them over.

The man Rutherston had fought and Bramble killed was coal-black, with parallel rows of ritual scars on his face. The one with the arrow in his back was light-brown but had a broad stain of indigo-blue across the face from his aquiline nose downwards, and a straight dagger with a broad double-edged blade strapped to his left forearm with a leather band. Rutherston pushed back the sleeves of his knitted jersey; there was a silver armlet on one wrist, set with polished stones.

"*He* came a long way from home to die," Rutherston said. "Tuareg—the Veiled Men; they get that stain from the dye in the cloth. And an *imajeghen* at that, aristocrat from a noble clan; they're camel nomads, in the sand-seas of the deep Sahara. *There's* a long story there that won't be told."

Both men had their hair in a medusa's tangle of thin tight braids; the detective flipped one, then held up an arm to show another amulet, this one of thick leather.

"More importantly," he said, "they're both *Baye Fall*. Who

are the Brute Squad for the Mouride Brotherhood. Or, if you believe Emir Jawara, they're just peaceful, spiritual groundnut cultivators who've never set foot on the deck of a River Saloum rover, and there aren't really any pirates there anyway, it's all in our imaginations."

"And I'm the Duke of Portsmouth, if you're in the mood to believe things," Bramble grunted. "Speaking of which, sir, good thing you sent to notify him, eh? Getting definitely political, this is. We don't want Military Intelligence rapping our knuckles."

"Too right," Rutherston said agreeably. "But I want to get to the bottom of it myself, as well. We'll have to arrange a quiet arrest for Signor Vadalà, too, before he does a flit."

"As long as we don't get our own arse in a crack, sir," Bramble said. "Which has 'appened, just now."

He went over to the door, gripped the arrow embedded in the rafter between thumb and forefinger and drew it out with a grunt and a back-and-forth motion, offering the slender piece of wood for Rutherston's examination.

"Hmm," the detective said, as he took out his magnifying glass and looked it over carefully. "The shaft was split from a billet and then turned on a lathe, just the way we do it; the grain is vertical along the long axis. But it's some sort of heavy reddish softwood. Cedar, not ash. And that's a bodkin head. Just like the one in our dead friend, minus the blood of course. Whatever it is, it certainly isn't Senegalese or Moorish."

The arrowhead was the armor-piercing military style, shaped in a narrow pyramid tapering to a point like a metalsmith's punch.

"Not one of ours, though, either," Bramble said thoughtfully. "Machine-made like the Winchester Armoury model, but three-sided, see? And the shank's longer. Thirty-inch shaft and goosefeather fletching. Horn nock—good 'un, but not done quite our style; the feathers are hog-backed, too."

"Bring it over by the lamp, please, Constable. Let's see if

there's a maker's stamp."

Rutherston peered more closely with the glass, turning aside from time to time to sketch what he saw in his notebook.

"Not ours, you're right about that, Bramble. Nor any of our neighbors."

Greater Britain's mark was a Cross of St. George and a crown. Norland used a horizontal cross, the Umbrian League put the Keys of St. Peter on the heads of their crossbow bolts; the Kingdom of Sicily had a three-armed triskelion. This was…

"More witch-marks, sir?"

"Not this time. It's… let's see… I think it's a little tree, or possibly a squid dancing on its head, with seven stars around it."

"Never heard of it."

Rutherston frowned; something was teasing at his memory. Then a thunder of feet on the stairs interrupted them. The door burst open, and Superintendent Arnson shoved through.

"Oh, bloody hell," she said, taking in the scene at a glance. "And I hoped it wasn't as bad as the message said."

Ten minutes later the two bodies were carried out the front entrance of the Anchor on stretchers by the Portsmouth constables. The innkeeper came around with mugs of coffee, brewed snarling-strong in the style the RN used to keep watchstanders alert. Rutherston tamed his with cream and sugar, sipped, then looked at the clock ticking over the main hearth as the caffeine hit his stomach and nerves; five o'clock, and several hours to dawn this time of year. A rhythmic clash of boots and metal sounded outside, and a volley of harsh orders.

Bramble muttered under his breath: "For lo, it was established from the Ages that when-so-ever the bloody 'orse hath gone, even so shall they then and only then locketh the stable door."

His father had been a deacon in the parish church. Bramble had also spent years in the Regulars, and he went on:

"Bet those lads are roit 'appy they've been turned out of their nice warm barracks to stand around doing sod-all in aid to the civil power at five o'clock of a fine January morning."

A company of archers and billmen was deploying in the street, no doubt as overjoyed at being in the wet cold murk as Bramble thought. Two men-at-arms armed cap-a-pied in plate came through the door, looking like living statues of green steel with their visors down and beads of rain and melting sleet trickling down the enameled metal; another man followed them.

He was in uniform as well, a gold-frogged scarlet jacket with an entirely unceremonial sword at his belt, and a rain-cape thrown over his shoulders. Rutherston noted that the trousers were non-regulation too, and might well be pajama bottoms; he'd probably just grabbed whatever was to hand.

"Your Grace," Superintendent Arnson said, bowing.

Everyone else but the soldiers followed suit. Colonel His Grace, Duke of Portsmouth, George Caruthers—and holder of a bundle of other titles military and civil—nodded curtly in reply.

He was a compact muscular man in his mid-forties, with a close-trimmed light-brown mustache shot with gray and cold hazel-green eyes. They hadn't met personally before, but the files in Rutherston's mind filled in the details: Caruthers had been retired from the Active list as a battalion commander, and given a Reserve commission as a colonel. He would have been in line for promotion and the Imperial General Staff if he hadn't inherited the title after the death of his father and elder brother, and been translated to the House of Lords.

He'd been Undersecretary of War for three years now, since the Tories came in after the last general election, on a take-no-nonsense-from-the-damned-foreigners platform. They'd been quite frustrated at the upsurge in corsair attacks, to put it very mildly, and looking for an excuse to thump someone.

"Quite right to roust me out," he said to Arnson, patting his pockets absently. "This is more than a murder investigation now."

Rutherston offered one of his own cigarillos and snapped his lighter. The duke accepted, and puffed with silent ferocity for an instant. Outland suns had baked his complexion a permanent red. It flushed a little more now, and his eyes narrowed. Rutherston would not have cared to be on the receiving end of that glare. The quiet flat deadliness in his voice was even more disturbing, in its way:

"In fact, a preliminary report is on its way to GHQ and the PM in Winchester. It's a good thing that these Moorish chappies were bloody stupid and tipped their hands."

"Only because of our unknown helper, my lord," Rutherston said, shivering a little inwardly at how close it had been even so. "I doubt they intended to use my blood to write: *Death to all pig-eating unbelieving faranj dogs! Signed, Emir Jawara and the Mouride Brotherhood* on the wall. If both of them had gotten into the room intact before I woke, it would just be a mystery when I was found stabbed to death in the morning."

"And dead men tell nei tales," Arnson repeated.

Caruthers snorted a laugh. "How *did* they get in?"

"Up the wall, my lord. It's brick, and easy enough to climb if you're strong and active."

His mind's eye saw the figure of his rescuer bounding from wall to wall, *upward* in that weird display of free-running gymnastics. They hadn't been as active as *that*, probably.

Aloud he went on: "They left a rope and grapnel, probably intended to aid their escape. This is a cosmopolitan town—there are probably several hundred Africans here, from Ashanti and the Cape Republic and other friendly powers, not to mention South Americans of similar appearance; nobody would remark them on the street, once they took off their turbans and veils."

"Good man," the nobleman grunted, and turned back to Arnson. "Now, Superintendent, give me a complete briefing from the beginning. Witchy Scots and foreign arrow-marks…

quite a tangle. But our Moorish friends are another matter; they're all too familiar. Some people are going to learn that our forbearance has limits. Limits far smaller than our supply of warships, arrows, or the available store of shot and incendiary bombs for our catapults."

Bramble and Rutherston looked at each other. Ships would sail because of this; south of the Tropic line men would die and villages would burn. To the senior detective's surprise the former NCO quoted softly under his breath:

> *"They called us out of the barrack-yard*
> *To God-knows-where from Gosport 'ard..."*

Rutherston nodded soberly. The attempt to hush things up had backfired badly on whoever made it...

"God-*dammit* but I'm an idiot!" he burst out suddenly, as pieces suddenly slid into place in his mind. "They won't stop with me!"

The duke and the superintendent stopped and looked at him. He went on, his voice clipped:

"Your Grace, there's no time to explain: I need your men, *now.*"

"You have them. Captain Smythe! On the inspector's orders!"

Smythe was in his twenties, but he was still puffing a bit when the party arrived at the office-cum-dwelling place of *Vadalà And Sons.* Rutherston found that vaguely reassuring—the effects of sitting at a desk were a minor background worry of his life, even if he still had the same belt-size as the year he'd graduated from Sandhurst.

But then, I'm not running while wearing seventy pounds of plate armor, he thought.

Arnson was puffing as they came up, but she had breath enough to swear lividly when she saw the sprawled body of the man she'd had watching the merchant's house, lying staring with a long knife in his side. The building was a solid plain house, four stories of salvage brick and blue-painted windowframes and shutters. The flames behind the upstairs windows became visible just as they arrived, and that only because of the solid dark outside; this was a side-street, and the city didn't have enough methane to light everything. The sleet-rain had turned to wet snow, and it was falling more heavily every instant.

"Saunders, run and fetch the fire department! And… *charge bills!*" the officer shouted.

The points of the weapons came down in a ripple, three deep and bristling, with a barking *hurrah* from the soldiers, sounding loud but muffled by snow that swallowed echoes. The bills pointed inward in a semicircle around the front door, blocking any escape with a wall of edged steel.

"Nock shafts!"

The forty archers behind the billmen reached over their shoulders for arrows, no doubt cursing what the damp would do to their strings and hoping the wax and water-glue would keep them from going slack. It would, at least for a while; a weapon that wouldn't function when it was raining would be of little use in England.

"Oh, this is a friendly-fire incident waiting to 'appen," Bramble said, peering at the growing ruddy flicker from above. "Just what we need, two-score of squaddies behind us shooting in the sodding dark!"

"More constables would be better," Rutherston agreed. "But one works with what one has. You and I will go in first. Captain Smythe, remember that we want living prisoners, if you would—"

The two policemen drew their swords and took their bucklers in their left hands as they walked towards the door; Rutherston knew an instant's sharp nostalgia for the much bigger heater-shaped shield he'd carried as part of a lancer's kit in the Blues. It covered a reassuringly larger part of your body, and so did a full set of plate armor. A scream came from behind the house, and a clash of steel; someone was trying to get out that way, and discovering they had the building surrounded.

Almost at the same instant the big front door burst open and two dark-faced men charged down the steps, shrieking like files on iron. The pair were dressed in unremarkable dark baggy sailor's woolens, but they had long curved swords in their hands, and they attacked without hesitation, leaping like leopards half-seen in the dimness. Rutherston was first in their path, and edged steel flickered at his face.

"*Allllaaahu Akbar!*" the man screamed.

This time the Englishman had his own blade out. *Cring- ting!*

The scimitar crashed against his straight longsword and slid down until the guards locked. The man was taller than Rutherston, and stronger; the hilts bent back towards the Englishman's neck, and he could feel his feet skidding on the slick pavement.

"*Don't—*" Rutherston began.

A billhook thrust at the Moor's face. He ducked, released the detective's sword so quickly that he staggered, and turned to slash at Bramble's back where he fought the other stranger. Rutherston recovered, pivoted and lunged in a savage blur of speed he hadn't been sure was still in him.

"*Don't kill him,* I meant to say," as he jerked the blade free from the man's lower back.

He sank with a bubbling shriek, kicked, and died on the wet slates. Which was a pity; the military had different regulations—Rutherston carefully thought of them as *more robust*—concerning interrogation, at least for foreigners who weren't Imperial subjects. They'd have gotten his story out of him.

Some of the billmen were trying to catch the sword of the

man fighting Bramble on the hooks at the rear of the blades. Others had reversed their weapons and were smashing the blunt butt-caps at the swordsman, to knock him down or disarm him. But it was crowded and dark and the footing was bad as the snow built up on the pavement, and the man was shrieking and slashing in a heedless berserker frenzy that was probably intended to make them kill him. One of the soldiers staggered and sprawled backward, a long dint in the steel of his breastplate where a cut had landed that would have bisected an unarmored man.

This is where we could use more coppers, Rutherston thought as he poised his blade—his service at least got training in subduing without killing. *Now, a thrust to the hamstring…*

Light suddenly blossomed, lantern-light as the door to the house swung open again. Llesenia Vargas was there, staggering, one side of her face covered in blood. She also had a cocked crossbow cradled in her arms, a powerful Italian military model. Men scattered with a yell as she raised it to her shoulder.

The man with the scimitar turned, eyes and teeth white and wild in his dark face, screaming: "*Ana haneji nehawi dine deyemak!*"

Which was Arabic, and *very* rude; he didn't speak the language but he had a working command of its obscenities.

Tunngg!

The steel prod gave a single deep note as she shot. The thick short bolt was invisible in the snowy murk; it disappeared from the weapon and reappeared buried to its vanes in the man's chest. His high-pitched battle scream cut off with startling abruptness; everyone froze as he collapsed, and the steel of his blade rang on the slate of the landing steps. Rutherston darted forward as the woman buckled in turn, caught her before her head struck the stone and passed her on to one of the soldiers.

"Follow me, Bramble!" he shouted, and went in through

the opened door.

He stooped as he did, raising the buckler in his left hand, just in case, but no blow descended. The delay for the scrimmage on the steps had let the fire take firmer hold, and it seemed to draw in a breath and then roar at him with dragon-wind. He coughed as his panting sucked in harsh smoke and charged up the stairs. Vadalà was in the hallway on the second story, a rapier in his hand and the remains of a nightshirt on his slashed body; another dead man with a curved blade and the thin braids of the *Baye Fall* lay dead before him. His wife and children huddled behind him, hacked to pieces. Rutherston made a single attempt to storm up the stairs to the topmost floor, but the heat drove him back. He could just glimpse tumbled office furniture and stacks of papers crisping into black.

"Here, Inspector!" Bramble called.

He had a figure in his arms—a woman dressed in black trousers and jerkin, her long blonde hair trailing. She wore a sword-belt with an empty scabbard, and a quiver over her back; Bramble had a longbow in one hand as well, looking subtly different from the English type. They retreated down the stairs and outside into the snow. The fire-truck had come, its big gray-coated horses snorting as they trotted with a crash of platter-sized hooves on the pavement, and the men jumped down and deployed, dragging their hoses forward and attaching them to the hydrants.

"Any chance of saving the house?" Rutherston asked their chief.

"Nei, it'll burn to ash. We'll be lucky to save the house t' either side, even with the snow. Now get these sojers out of our way!"

Rutherston did. McTavish and two nurses were working on the women. He rose from the stranger's side as the detective approached.

"Miss Vargas will be all right, provided there's no cerebral haematoma," he said. "Blow with the flat of a sword, I'd say."

"Someone trying to put her out?"

"Not intentionally; see how there's a cut along here on the side of the head? A slice, not a pressure-cut. Whoever landed that intended to top her head like a boiled egg but something threw off the stroke. She was very lucky—not really out, even, just very woozy. You can tell the pattern of the blade from the shape of the contusion. A longsword, I'd say."

Rutherston looked down at the stranger's body; the scabbard from her belt was lying nearby, and it was much like his own—intended to house a straight double-edged blade about thirty inches long.

"The other?"

"The stranger? She's a lot worse. Moving her again before we have her stabilized would kill her, with the knife like that. I'm typing her blood and giving her plasma for now; the ambulance should be… ah, there it is. Touch and go, but she has a chance. Murdoch at the General Hospital has a lot of experience with this sort of injury. It rather depends what was pierced inside."

"Knife?" Rutherston said.

"Look."

The detective went to one knee. The gaslights and the flames bursting out of Vadalà's house gave good light; the woman was young and tall and strikingly pretty, with golden hair caught in a fighting braid that leaked strands. He could see the rounded hilt of a stiletto under her ribs. There was still a flutter of breath as her leather jerkin rose and fell, but blood leaked out of the corner of her mouth. The wide unseeing eyes were blue, but with an odd striation, silver rims around the iris and veins of silver running inward.

His eyes fell to the jerkin; it had the same device as he'd found stamped on the arrowhead that saved his life, a stylized tree surrounded by an arch of seven stars, and topped by a crown.

Llesenia groaned and sat up, clutching at her head and

moaning. The light was uncertain, and the noise heavy; he couldn't be sure what she said, something like *sharmuta*. Then she looked over at him, and the woman on the other stretcher.

"Is she alive?" the Gibraltarian woman called sharply, sharply enough to make her wince and put a hand to the bandage McTavish had applied.

"Yes," Rutherston said. Then: "Wait! She's saying something!" He bent and put his ear next to her lips, cupping a hand around it. Then his cold gray eyes flicked to the other woman and he began to rise, implacable purpose in his movements, hand going to the hilt of his sword.

Even half-expecting it, the cobra speed of her response surprised him. She snatched a dagger from the belt of one of the soldiers next to her and threw herself through the air at the other stretcher, leaping with all her body off the ground like a cat. Rutherston spun, grabbing for knife-wrist and body. She cut at him in mid-leap, parting the heavy cloth like paper and slashing the flesh beneath, but he caught her and twisted and threw with trained strength. The slender body pinwheeled through the air and she landed on her back, hard.

"Bramble!" Rutherston barked.

The big man was already moving; he caught the wrist of her knife-hand as she came up with a vicious underarm thrust. Then he tightened his grip. She screamed shrilly as bone broke and hung panting in his grip, shivering uncontrollably when he stopped a movement with a warning twist.

"Emir Jawara must value your services highly, *sayyida*," Rutherston said, flexing the fingers of his left hand.

The cut was long, but it was shallow and ran with the grain of the muscle. The pain was white and hot, and blood dripped freely as he gripped it with his right.

The woman who'd called herself Llesenia Vargas spat at him.

"The *emir!* Jawara, that cowardly apostate son of ten fathers, the dog who licks the privates of the kufr kings! It was not for *him* I lived among infidels and ate the filthy pig. It was for the holy Marabout! But the *At-Tarîqat al-Murîdiyya* would have *forced* him to war in the end—he is like that fat pig Vadalà, who sold his own folk for our cargoes—Jawara could not forsake the share we gave him and in the end it would mean he had to fight—"

She stopped. Rutherston prodded: "If that shipment of yew from the far west hadn't started a train of bad luck. God must hate you, eh?"

"It was the witch, and the sorcerer! Only magic could have kept them hidden in the cargo!" Her eyes grew wilder. "You filth must not have a new source of wood for your accursed bows—you swine who kept us from the Maghreb and al-Andalus—who drove us into the swamps where our children die of fevers and you breed like maggots and fill the empty lands God meant for us—"

Her words trailed off into an incoherent scream of sheer rage, and then she stood silent, nursing the broken wrist and glaring at him like a chained hawk. Bramble kept a heavy hand on her shoulder, until two of the billmen took her arms. They lashed her hands together before her and thrust the shaft of a bill between her back and her elbows, keeping a tight grip on the ashwood.

The pain must have been quite agonizing. *And my sympathy is underwhelming,* he thought.

"Nice piece of work, Inspector," Bramble said. "Now let's get that cut seen to. It's your night to leak, eh?"

McTavish was bandaging Rutherston's wound when the duke and Inspector Arnson arrived; there was nothing else for him to do, with the ambulance on its way to the surgery. The nobleman was fully dressed now, in ordinary field-green uniform and half-armor, breastplate and vambraces and tassets; snow drifted down out of a sky the color of wet cement and clung to the cold steel, sparkling occasionally in the light of the burning building. He stood and listened as Rutherston explained to him:

"—Vadalà was slipping corsairs information on our ships, as well as fencing their loot," he finished. "His family has two ships on the African run; they'd transfer the stolen goods at sea, sell them in Sicily under his own firm's auspices, buy Mediterranean produce and ship it here. Then he'd buy British manufactures the corsairs wanted—weapons made for the African trade, shipbuilding supplies, medicines—and ship them south on his firm's own vessels. They'd meet the rover galleys off the Saloum mouth or the Casamance, and transfer the goods… and continue perfectly legitimate voyages to Ashanti or wherever, folding the profits into their ordinary gains."

The duke nodded. "We need tighter controls," he said. "But what about the yew? And the damned Scotsman, and the lady with the bow?"

"That was where the wheels came off the coach for them, my lord. You remember the Count of Azay, how he married a woman from the Far West, about thirty years ago, before he inherited from his father? That business with Nantucket."

"Vaguely," he said. "Quite a fuss at the time. Official Secrets Act, buried deep."

"That was what prompted my memory," Rutherston said, and explained. "We'll get the details if our mysterious guest recovers, but I suspect from what Vargas—the one calling herself Vargas—said, that the rovers took a ship from there… one with a cargo of yew. It grows like a weed over there in Oregon, far more of it than anywhere in Europe—and someone must have decided a cargo of it would pay the long voyage to Europe. There's not much else that would."

"And didn't kill all the crew?"

"The dead man we found in the warehouse and the mysterious lady with the starry jerkin must have been on that ship and managed to hide from the corsairs and then from Vadalà's men until it was dropped off here. God alone knows how."

"Why didn't they contact the authorities at once?" the duke said indignantly.

"My lord, all they knew was that a plundered cargo sailed in here on a ship that dealt with the pirates who'd attacked theirs, with no apparent objection. They wouldn't know who to trust—but they did know who and what to follow."

"But it wasn't they who killed Vadalà," Superintendent Arnson pointed out.

"No. Vargas was watching Vadalà for the Mourides—they knew better than to trust a traitor even when he was working for, or with, them. There are Moors who can pass for a European of the darker kind, and obviously our Vargas was one. The *Baye Fall* would have been in town disguised as ordinary African sailors—or better still, from Maracaibo or Belize or Bahia, one of the South American countries where men of those looks are common. When she needed them, they'd be on hand to act, but with no obvious connection to her."

"Clever," Bramble said, and the Duke of Portsmouth nodded. "Who'd expect that lot to use a female agent?"

"Just so," Rutherston said. "She killed the man in the kilt as he was looking over the yew in the warehouse, but didn't have time to conceal the body—the laborers were on her heels. Instead she very coolly reported it as a murder… reporting a crime she'd committed herself! If the mysterious lady who saved my life was watching, the way Vargas was friendly with the police would make her more reluctant still to contact us. But I'm afraid I rather slipped up then. I mentioned that the sight of Hecate's mark and the yew together made me remember *something*."

"Not so she could hear it," Bramble said. "You were speaking quietly and she was a good fifteen yards away."

"But she was looking at me very carefully; I can read lips myself… it's a useful skill for an officer and still more so for a detective. That's when she must have decided to have me silenced too."

"And the merchant?" the duke enquired.

"From the timing, she decided to do a clean sweep and kill Vadalà and his household too when the stranger prevented those *Baye Fall* from knifing me just a little while ago. She must have realized at once that Vadalà would turn King's evidence to save his skin. From what she said, the Marabouts are interested in putting us and Emir Jawara at loggerheads, as well as simple piracy."

Bramble nodded. "There must have been a pretty little dust-up in that house when our bouncy-bouncy friend arrived. Funny it's a girl, sir." He shook his head. "I'll never forget the way she went up that wall!"

"Just so," Rutherston repeated. "At a guess Vargas planned to disappear afterwards with her *Baye Fall* hatchetmen. We'd assume she died in the fire, leaving us nothing but some circumstantial evidence that men from the Emirate were responsible. But our blue-eyed lady of mystery back-tracked the assassins sent to kill me, found the massacre underway, and intervened. We owe her a good deal."

"And we'll see that she gets it, if she lives," the nobleman said. "Go on, Inspector."

"Vargas managed to knife *her* too, not before being clouted across the head, and left her for dead upstairs. She staggered out and shot her own man to prevent him from talking if captured. Doubtless she modified her plan on the spot—she'd be one of the innocent victims, a heroine even. A resourcefully wicked lass."

Rutherston spread his hands ruefully. "All that's ex-post-facto, of course, and pure deduction at this point. I didn't really know for sure until Vargas tried to kill the stranger."

Bramble grunted. "Fortunate the lady could tell you enough to put you on to Vargas, hurt as she was, sir," he said.

"Very fortunate indeed," the duke said. "If Vargas hadn't revealed herself she could have covered her tracks and escaped in the next few days and we'd never have figured out what really happened. Or even carried out her plan to remain as the heroine of the piece, if the stranger dies."

The detective smiled thinly. "The lady didn't say a word; she never recovered consciousness. I simply gave Vargas the... ah... hairy eyeball... and *pretended* the stranger had whispered something. I wasn't at all sure—but something made me suspect our putative Gibraltarian wasn't what she seemed."

"What?" Arnson said. "The way she was wounded, it must have looked as if the same people who killed Vadalà went after her?"

"No. The wound on her head came from a straight longsword, not a scimitar; and the mysterious lady from the west carried a straight blade. And there was something that happened in the warehouse; Bramble pointed it out. When I mentioned witchcraft, she didn't cross herself... which someone pious enough to wear a crucifix of that sort would have done. Those two clues were little enough, but if I could spook her into breaking cover, as it were..."

The duke nodded somberly. "Clever, Inspector. Very clever indeed."

He extended a hand, and Rutherston shook it. The detective went on earnestly:

"My lord, I think you'll find that she's not actually an agent for the Emir, only for the Mourides and the corsairs. As I said, it appears the Mourides are *trying* to provoke hostilities. Doubtless Jawára has been taking a cut of the corsairs' profits, indirectly, but... well, he wouldn't be sorry to see the Marabouts of the Brotherhood cut back a bit either, I suspect. He might even help us with a punitive expedition against them, if the alternative was war with the Empire, and then we'd have no reason to attack the Emirate as a whole. It would be a simple punitive expedition writ large, not a proper war."

The duke turned to one of his officers. "Lieutenant, take charge of that woman; we're removing her from civilian jurisdiction under the Defense of the Realm Act. Have her conveyed to the holding cells at the naval station and prepared for interrogation—I'll supervise that myself. If she succeeds in killing herself before she talks, rest assured that you will soon be envying her."

The smile that followed as he turned back to the three police officers was remarkably unpleasant.

"Don't worry, Inspector: we'll get the whole story before she hangs. Oh, yes, every jot and tittle of it."

Bramble and Rutherston and Inspector Arnson nodded, with varying degrees of relief; it was out of their hands now. The nobleman began to draw on his metal-backed gauntlets, cocked an eye at the detective, and went on:

"And if her testimony confirms your... theory... Inspector Rutherston, you've prevented a war as well as solved a murder. Or at least made it considerably smaller, and saved a good many lives."

Rutherston bowed in return; the soldiers formed up and tramped away, and the policemen left the burning house that shed black smoke into the white-gray blur of the snow-ridden sky. It was a relief to escape from the harsh smoke, full of the smell of things that should not burn.

"And now we can go back home," Rutherston sighed, pulling the coat across his chest where the injured arm rested in a sling. "That was a short investigation, if a remarkably... strenuous... one."

"You're not going back to Winchester before you write up the reports!" Arnson said. "I'm not putting this lot on paper all by myself."

"Well, at least you could buy us breakfast, then," Bramble grumbled.

"The Anchor has the best kippers on the coast."

THE MASTER OF FANTASY AND ALTERNATE HISTORY

978-1-59780-131-7
Mass Market / $7.99

Find this book and many other great Science fiction, fantasy and horror titles published by Night Shade Books at your favorite bookstore or online at: www.nightshadebooks.com

1945: Russian troops have entered Berlin, and are engaged in a violent orgy of robbery, rape, and revenge...

Wehrmacht officer Hasso Pemsel, a career soldier on the losing end of the greatest war in history, flees from a sniper's bullet, finding himself hurled into a mysterious, fantastic world of wizards, dragons, and unicorns. There he allies himself with the blond-haired, blue-eyed Lenelli, and Velona, their goddess in human form, offering them his knowledge of warfare and weaponry in their genocidal struggle against a race of diminutive, swarthy barbarians known as Grenye.

But soon, the savagery of the Lenelli begins to eat at Hasso Pemsel's soul, causing him to question everything he has long believed about race and Reich, right and wrong, Ubermenschen and Untermenschen. Hasso Pemsel will learn the difference between following orders... and following his conscience.

From Harry Turtledove, the master of alternate history, comes After the Downfall, a novel of magic, epic warfare, and desperate choices.